ORDINARY
IN A TIARA

BY
JESSICA HART

Jessica Hart was born in West Africa, and has suffered from itchy feet ever since—travelling and working around the world in a wide variety of interesting but very lowly jobs, all of which have provided inspiration on which to draw when it comes to the settings and plots of her stories. Now she lives a rather more settled existence in York, where she has been able to pursue her interest in history, although she still yearns sometimes for wider horizons. If you'd like to know more about Jessica, visit her website: www.jessicahart.co.uk.

CHAPTER ONE

To: caro.cartwright@u2.com
From: charlotte@palaisdemontvivennes.net
Subject: Internet dating
Dear Caro
What a shame about the deli folding. I know you loved that job. You must be really fed up, but your email about the personality test on that internet dating site really made me laugh—good to know you haven't lost your sense of humour in spite of everything that skunk George did to you! All I can say is that compared to Grandmère's matchmaking schemes, internet dating sounds the way to go. Perhaps we should swap lives??!
Lotty
xxxxxxxxxxxxxxxxxx

To: charlotte@palaisdemontvivennes.net
From: caro.cartwright@u2.com
Subject: Swapping places
What a brilliant idea, Lotty! My life is a giddy whirl at the moment, what with temping at a local insurance company and trying to write profile for new dating site (personality test results too depressing on other one) but if you'd like to try it, you're more than welcome! Of course,

living your life would be tough for me—living in a palace, having (admittedly terrifying) grandmother introducing me to suitable princes and so on—but for you, Lotty, anything! Just let me know where and when and I'll have a stab at being a princess for a change...ooh, that's just given me an idea for my new profile. Who says fantasy isn't good for you???

Yours unregally

Caro XXX

PRINCESS SEEKS FROG: Curvaceous, fun-loving brunette, 28, looking for that special guy for good times out and in.

'What do you think?' Caro read out her opening line to Stella, who was lying on the sofa and flicking through a copy of *Glitz*.

Stella looked up from the magazine, her expression dubious. 'It doesn't make sense. Princess seeks frog? What's that supposed to mean?'

'It means I'm looking for an ordinary guy, not a Prince Charming in disguise. I thought it was obvious,' said Caro, disappointed.

'No ordinary guy would ever work that out, I can tell you that much,' said Stella. She went back to flicking. 'You don't want to be cryptic or clever. Men hate that.'

'It's all so difficult.' Caro deleted the offending words on the screen, and chewed her bottom lip. 'What about the curvaceous bit? I'm worried it might make me sound fat, but there's not much point in meeting someone who's looking for a slender goddess, is there? He'd just run away screaming the moment he laid eyes on me. Besides, I want to be honest.'

'If you're going to be honest, you'd better take out "fun-loving",' Stella offered. 'It makes it sound as if you're up for anything.'

'That's the whole point. I'm changing. Being sensible didn't get me anywhere with George, so I'm going to be a good time girl from now on.'

She would be like Melanie, all giggles and low cut tops and flirty looks. Melanie, who had sashayed into George's office and knocked Caro's steady, sensible fiancé off his feet.

'I can't say what I'm really like or no one will want to go out with me,' she added glumly.

'Rubbish,' said Stella. 'Say you're kind and generous and a brilliant cook—*that* would be honest.'

'Guys don't want kind, even if they say they do,' Caro said bitterly, remembering George. 'They want sexy and fun-loving.'

'Hmm, well, if you want to be sexy, you'd better do something about your clothes,' said Stella, lowering *Glitz* so that she could inspect her friend's outfit with a critical eye. 'I know you're into the vintage look, but a *crochet top*?'

'It's an original from the Seventies.'

'And it was vile then, too.'

Caro made a face at her. With the top she was wearing a tartan miniskirt from the nineteen-sixties and bright red pumps. She was the first to admit that she couldn't *always* carry off the vintage look successfully, but she had been pleased with this particular outfit until Stella had started shaking her head.

Still, there was no point in arguing. She went back to her profile. 'OK, what about *Keen cook seeks fellow foodie*?'

'You'll just get some guy who wants to tie you to the stove and expect you to have his dinner ready the moment he comes through the door. You've already done that for George, and look where that got you.' Stella caught the flash of pain on her friend's face and her voice softened. 'I know how miserable you've been, Caro, but honestly, you're well out of it. George wasn't the right man for you.'

'I know.' Caro caught herself sighing and squared her shoulders. 'It's OK, Stella. I'm fine now. I'm moving on, aren't I?'

Pressing the backspace key with one finger, she deleted the last sentence. 'It's just so depressing having to sign up to these online dating sites. I don't remember it being this hard before. It's like in the five years I was with George, all the single men round here have disappeared into some kind of Bermuda Triangle!'

'Yeah, it's called marriage,' said Stella. She picked up *Glitz* again and flicked through in search of the page she wanted. 'I don't know why you're looking in Ellerby, though. Why don't you get your friend Lotty to introduce you to some rich, glamorous men who eat in Michelin starred restaurants all the time?'

Caro laughed, remembering Lotty's email. 'I wish! But poor Lotty never gets within spitting distance of an interesting man either. You'd think, being a princess, she'd have a fantastically glamorous time, but her grandmother totally runs her life. Apparently she's trying to fix Lotty up with someone "suitable" right now.' Caro hooked her fingers in the air to emphasise the inverted commas. 'I mean, who wants a man your grandmother approves of? I think I'd rather stick with internet dating!'

'I wouldn't mind if he was anything like the guy Lotty's going out with at the moment,' said Stella. 'I saw a picture of them just a second ago. If he was her grandmother's choice, I'd say she's got good taste and she can fix me up any time!'

'Lotty's actually going out with someone?' Caro swivelled round from the computer and stared at Stella. 'She didn't say that! Who is he?'

'Give me a sec. I'm trying to find that photo of her.' When

the flicking failed, Stella licked her finger and tried turning the pages one by one. 'I can never get over you being friends with a real princess. I wish I'd been to a posh school like yours.'

'You wouldn't have liked it. It was fine if you had a title and your own pony and lots of blonde hair to toss around, but if you were only there because your mum was a teacher and your dad the handyman, they didn't want to know.'

'Lotty wanted to know you,' Stella pointed out, still searching.

'Lotty was different. We started on the same day and we were both the odd ones out, so we stuck together. We were both fat and spotty and had braces, and poor Lotty had a stammer too.'

'She's not fat and spotty now,' said Stella. 'She looked lovely in that picture…ah, here it is!'

Folding back the page, she read out the caption under one of the photographs on the *Party! Party! Party!* page. 'Here we go: *Princess Charlotte of Montluce arriving at the Nightingale Ball*—fab dress, by the way—*with Prince Philippe.*

'*Philippe, the lost heir to Montluce, has only recently returned to the country,*' she read on. '*The ball was their first public outing as a couple, but behind the scenes friends say they are "inseparable" and royal watchers are expecting them to announce their engagement this summer. Is one of Europe's most eligible bachelors off the market already?*'

'Let me see that!' Caro whipped the magazine out of Stella's hands and frowned down at the shiny page. 'Lotty and *Philippe*? I don't believe it!'

But there was Lotty, looking serene, and there, next to her, was indeed His Serene Highness Prince Philippe Xavier Charles de Montvivennes.

She recognised him instantly. That summer he had been seventeen, just a boy, but with a dark, reckless edge to his glamorous looks that had terrified her at the time. Thirteen years on, he looked taller, broader, but still lean, still dangerous. He had the same coolly arrogant stare for the camera, the same sardonic smile that made Caro feel fifteen again: breathless, awkward, painfully aware that she didn't belong.

Stella sat up excitedly. 'You *know* him?'

'Not really. I spent part of a summer holiday in France with Lotty once, and he was part of a whole crowd that used to hang around the villa. It was just before Dad died and, to be honest, I don't remember much about that time now. I know I felt completely out of place, but I do remember Philippe,' Caro said slowly. 'I was totally intimidated by him.'

She had a picture of Philippe lounging around the spectacular infinity pool, looking utterly cool and faintly disreputable. There had always been some girl wrapped round him, sleek and slender in a minuscule bikini while Caro had skulked in the shade with Lotty, too shy to swim in her dowdy one-piece while they were there.

'He and the others used to go out every night and make trouble,' she told Stella. 'There were always huge rows about it, and one or other of them would be sent home on some private plane in disgrace for a while.'

'God, it sounds so glamorous,' said Stella enviously. 'Did you get to go trouble-making too?'

'Are you kidding?' Caro hooted with laughter. 'Lotty and I would never have had the nerve to go with them. Anyway, I'm quite sure Philippe didn't even realise we were there most of the time. Although, actually, now I think about it, he *was* nice to me when I heard Dad was in hospital,' she remembered. 'He said he was sorry and asked if I wanted to go out with the rest of them that night. I'd forgotten that.'

Caro looked down at the magazine again, trying to fit the angular boy she remembered into the picture of the man. How funny that she should remember that moment of brusque kindness now. She'd been so distressed about her father that she had wiped almost everything else about that time from her mind.

'Did you go?'

'No, I was too worried about Dad and, anyway, I'd have been terrified. They were all wild, that lot. And Philippe was the wildest of them all. He had a terrible reputation then.

'He had this older brother, Etienne, who was supposed to be really nice, and Philippe was the hellraiser everyone shook their heads about. Then Etienne was killed in a freak water-skiing accident, and after that we never heard any more about Philippe. I think Lotty told me he'd cut off all contact with his father and gone off to South America. Nobody knew then that his father would end up as Crown Prince of Montluce, but I'm surprised he hasn't come back before. Probably been too busy hellraising and squandering his trust fund!'

'You've got to admit it sounds more fun than your average blind date in Ellerby,' Stella pointed out. 'You said you wanted to have fun, and he's obviously the kind of guy who knows how to do that. You should get Lotty to fix you up with one of his cool friends.'

Caro rolled her eyes. 'Do you really see me hanging around with the jet set?'

'I see what you mean.' Pursing her lips, Stella studied her friend. 'You'd definitely have to lose the crochet top!'

'Not to mention about six stone,' said Caro.

She tossed the magazine back to Stella. 'Anyway, I can't think of anything worse than going out with someone like Philippe. You'd have to look perfect all the time. And then, when you were doing all those exciting glamorous things, you wouldn't be able to look as if you were enjoying it, because that's not cool. And you'd have to be stick-thin, which would mean you'd never be able to eat. It would be awful!'

'Lotty doesn't look as if she minds,' said Stella with another glance at the photo. 'And I don't blame her!'

'You never know what Lotty's really thinking. She's been trained to always smile, always look as if she's enjoying herself, even if she's bored or sick or fed up. Being a princess doesn't sound any fun to me,' said Caro. 'Lotty's been a good girl all her life, and she's never had the chance to be herself or meet someone who'll bother to get to know her rather than the perfect princess she has to be all the time.'

A faint line between her brows, she turned back to the computer and opened Lotty's last email message. Why hadn't Lotty said anything about Philippe then?

To: charlotte@palaisdemontvivennes.net
From: caro.cartwright@u2.com
Subject: ?????????????
You and Philippe?????????????????????????????????

Lotty's reply came back the next morning.

To: caro.cartwright@u2.com
From: charlotte@palaisdemontvivennes.net
Subject: Re: ?????????????
Grandmère is up to her old tricks again and this time it's serious. I can't tell you what it's like here. I'm getting desperate!

Caro, remember how you said you'd do anything for me when we joked about swapping lives for a while? Well, I've got an idea to put to you, and I'm hoping you weren't joking about the helping bit! I really need to explain in person, but you know how careful I have to be on the phone here, and I can't leave Montluce just yet. Philippe is in London this week, though, so I've given him your number and he's going to get in touch and explain all about it. If my plan works, it could solve our problems for all of us!

Lxxxxxxxxxxxxxxxxx

Deeply puzzled, Caro read Lotty's message again. What plan, and what did Philippe have to do with it? She couldn't imagine Philippe de Montvivennes solving any of *her* problems, that was for sure. What could he do? Make George dump Melanie and come crawling back to her on his knees? Persuade the bank that the delicatessen where she'd been working hadn't gone bankrupt after all?

And what problems could *he* possibly have? Too much money in his trust fund? Too many gorgeous women hanging round him?

Philippe will explain. A real live prince, heir to the throne of Montluce, was going to ring her, Caro Cartwright. Caro nibbled her thumbnail and tried to imagine the conversation. *Oh, hi, yeah*, she would say casually when he called. *Lotty mentioned you would ring.*

She wished she knew what Lotty had told him about her. Not the truth, she hoped. Philippe would only sneer if he knew just how quiet and ordinary her life was.

Not that she cared what he thought, Caro reminded herself hastily. She loved living in Ellerby. Her dreams were ordinary ones: a place to belong, a husband to love, a job she enjoyed. A kitchen of her own, a family to feed. Was that too much to ask?

But Philippe had always lived in a different stratosphere. How could he know that she had no interest in a luxury yacht or a designer wardrobe or hobnobbing with superstars, or whatever else he'd been doing with himself for the past five years? She wouldn't mind eating in the Michelin starred restaurants, Caro allowed, but otherwise, no, she was happy with her lot—or she would be if George hadn't dumped her for Melanie and the deli owner hadn't gone bankrupt.

No, Philippe would never be able to understand that. So perhaps she shouldn't be casual after all. She could sound preoccupied instead, a high-powered businesswoman, juggling million pound contracts and persistent lovers, with barely a second to deal with a playboy prince. *I'm a bit busy at the moment*, she could say. *Could I call you back in five minutes?*

Caro rather liked the idea of startling Philippe with her transformation from gawky fifteen-year-old to assured woman of the world, but abandoned it eventually. For one thing, Philippe would never remember Lotty's friend, plump and plain in her one-piece black swimsuit, so the startle effect was likely to be limited. And, for another, she was content with her own life and didn't need to pretend to be anything other than what she was, right?

Right.

So why did the thought of talking to him make her so jittery?

She wished he would ring and get it over with, but the phone remained obstinately silent. Caro kept checking it to see if the battery had run out, or the signal disappeared for some reason. When it did ring, she would leap out of her skin and fumble frantically with it in her hands before she could even check who was calling. Invariably it was Stella, calling to discover if Philippe had rung yet, and Caro got quite snappy with her.

Then she was even crosser with herself for being so twitchy. It was only Philippe, for heaven's sake. Yes, he was a prince, but what had he ever done other than go to parties and look cool? She wasn't impressed by him, Caro told herself, and was mortified whenever she caught herself inspecting her reflection or putting on lipstick, as if he would be able to see what she looked like when he called.

Or as if he would care.

In any case, all the jitteriness was quite wasted because Philippe didn't ring at all. By Saturday night, Caro had decided that there must have been a mistake. Lotty had misunderstood, or, more likely, Philippe couldn't be bothered to do what Lotty had asked him to do. Fine, thought Caro grouchily. See if she cared. Lotty would call when she could and in meantime she would get on with her life.

Or, rather, her lack of life.

A summer Saturday, and she had no money to go out and no one to go out with. Caro sighed. She couldn't even have a glass of wine as she and Stella were both on a diet and had banned alcohol from the house. It was all right for Stella, who had gone to see a film, but Caro was badly in need of distraction.

For want of anything better to do, she opened up her laptop and logged on to right4u.com. Her carefully worded profile, together with the most flattering photo she could find—taken before George had dumped her and she was two sizes thinner—had gone live the day before. Perhaps someone had left her a message, she thought hopefully. Prince Philippe might not be prepared to get in touch, but Mr Right might have fallen madly in love with her picture and be out there, longing for her to reply.

Or not.

Caro had two messages. The first turned out to be from a fifty-six-year-old who claimed to be 'young at heart' and boasted of having his own teeth and hair although, after one look at his photo, Caro didn't think either were much to be proud of.

Quickly, she moved onto the next message, which was from a man who hadn't provided a picture but who had chosen Mr

Sexy as his code name. Call her cynical, but she had a feeling that might be something of a misnomer. According to the website, the likelihood of a potential match between them was a mere seven per cent. *I want you to be my soulmate*, Mr Sexy had written. *Ring me and let's begin the rest of our lives right now.*

Caro thought not.

Depressed, she got up and went into the kitchen. She was starving. That was the trouble with diets. You were bored and hungry the whole time. How was a girl supposed to move on with her life when she only had salad for lunch?

In no time at all she found the biscuits Stella had hidden in with the cake tins, and she was on her third and wondering whether she should hope Stella wouldn't notice or eat them all and buy a new packet when the doorbell rang. Biscuit in hand, Caro looked at the clock on wall. Nearly eight o'clock. An odd time for someone to call, at least in Ellerby. Still, whoever it was, they surely had to be more interesting than trawling through her potential matches on right4u.com.

Stuffing the rest of the biscuit into her mouth, Caro opened the door.

There, on the doorstep, stood Prince Philippe Xavier Charles de Montvivennes, looking as darkly, dangerously handsome and as coolly arrogant as he had in the pages of *Glitz* and so bizarrely out of place in the quiet Ellerby backstreet that Caro choked, coughed and sprayed biscuit all over his immaculate dark blue shirt.

Philippe didn't bat an eyelid. Perhaps his smile slipped a little, but he put it quickly back in place as he picked a crumb off his shirt. 'Caroline Cartwright?' With those dark good looks, he should have had an accent oozing Mediterranean warmth but, like Lotty, he had been sent to school in England and, when he opened that mouth, the voice that came out was instead cool and impeccably English. As cool as the strange silver eyes that were so disconcerting against the olive skin and black hair.

Still spluttering, Caro patted her throat and blinked at him through watering eyes. 'I'm—' It came out as a croak, and she coughed and tried again. 'I'm Caro,' she managed at last.

Dear God, thought Philippe, keeping his smile in place with an effort. *Caro's lovely*, Lotty had said. *She'll be perfect.*

What had Lotty been thinking? There was no way this Caro could carry off what they had in mind. He'd pictured someone coolly elegant, like Lotty, but there was nothing cool and certainly nothing elegant about this girl. Built on Junoesque lines, she'd opened the door like a slap in the face, and then spat biscuit all over him. He'd had an impression of lushness, of untidy warmth. Of dark blue eyes and fierce brows and a lot of messy brown hair falling out of its clips.

And of a perfectly appalling top made of purple cheesecloth. It might possibly have been fashionable forty years earlier, although it was hard to imagine anyone ever picking it up and thinking it would look nice on. Caro Cartwright must get dressed in the dark.

Philippe was tempted to turn on his heel and get Yan to drive him back to London, but Lotty's face swam into his mind. She had looked so desperate that day she had come to see him. She hadn't cried, but something about the set of her mouth, about the strained look around her eyes had touched the heart Philippe had spent years hardening.

Caro will help, I know she will, she had said. *This is my only chance, Philippe. Please say you'll do it.*

So he'd promised, and now he couldn't go back on his word.

Dammit.

Well, he was here, and now he'd better make the best of it. Philippe forced warmth into his smile, the one that more than one woman had told him was irresistible. 'I'm Lotty's cousin, Ph—' he began, but Caro waved him to silence, still patting her throat.

'I know who you are,' she said squeakily, apparently resisting the smile without any trouble at all. 'What are you doing here?'

Philippe was momentarily nonplussed, which annoyed him. He wasn't used to being taken aback, and he certainly wasn't used to having his presence questioned quite so abruptly. 'Didn't Lotty tell you?'

'She said you would *ring*.'

That was definitely an accusing note in her voice. Philippe looked down his chiselled nose. 'I thought it would be easier to explain face to face,' he said haughtily.

Easier for him, maybe, thought Caro. *He* hadn't been caught unawares with no make-up on and a mouthful of biscuit.

There was something surreal about seeing him standing there, framed against the austere terrace of houses across the road. Ellerby was a quiet northern town on the edge of the moors, while Philippe in his immaculately tailored trousers and the dark blue shirt open at the neck appeared to have stepped straight out of the pages of *Glitz*. He was tall and tanned with that indefinable aura of wealth and glamour, the assurance that took red carpets as its due.

A pampered playboy prince…Caro longed to dismiss him as no more than that, but there was nothing soft about the line of his mouth, or the hard angles of cheek and jaw. Nothing self-indulgent about the lean, hard-muscled body, nothing yielding in those unnervingly light eyes.

Still, no reason for her to go all breathless and silly.

'You should have rung,' she said severely. 'I might have been going out.'

'*Are* you going out?' asked Philippe, and his expression as his gaze swept over her spoke louder than words. Who in

God's name, it seemed to say, would even consider going out in a purple cheesecloth shirt?

Caro lifted her chin. 'As it happens, no.'

'Then perhaps I could come in and tell you what Lotty wants,' he said smoothly. 'Unless you'd like to discuss it on the doorstep?'

Please say you'll help. Caro bit her lip. She had forgotten Lotty for a moment there. 'No, of course not.'

Behind Philippe, a sleek black limousine with tinted windows waited at the kerb, its engine idling. Tinted windows! Curtains would be twitching up and down the street.

No, this wasn't a conversation she wanted to be having in full view of the neighbours. Caro stood back and held the door open, tacitly conceding defeat. 'You'd better come in.'

The hallway was very narrow, and she sucked in her breath to make herself slimmer as Philippe stepped past her. Perhaps that explained why she suddenly felt dizzy and out of breath. It was as if a panther had strolled past her, all sleek, coiled power and dangerous grace. Had Philippe always been that *big*? That solid? That overwhelmingly male?

She gestured him into the sitting room. It was a mess in there, but that was too bad. If he didn't have the courtesy to ring and let her know he was coming, he couldn't expect the red carpet to be rolled out.

Philippe's lips tightened with distaste as he glanced around the room. He couldn't remember ever being anywhere quite so messy before. Tights hung over radiators and there were clothes and shoes and books and God only knew what else in heaps all over the carpet. A laptop stood open on the coffee table, which was equally cluttered with cosmetics, nail polishes, battery chargers, magazines and cups of half drunk coffee.

He should have known as soon as the car drew up outside that Caro wasn't going to be one of Lotty's usual friends, who were all sophisticated and accomplished and perfectly groomed. They lived on family estates or in spacious apartments in the centre of London or Paris or New York, not in poky provincial terraces like this one.

What, in God's name, had Lotty been thinking?

'Would you like some tea?' Caro asked.

Tea? It was eight o'clock in the evening! Who in their right mind drank tea at this hour? Philippe stifled a sigh. He'd need more than tea to get himself through this mess he'd somehow got himself into.

'I don't suppose you've got anything stronger?'

'If I'd known you were coming I would have stocked up on the Krug,' she said sharply. 'As it is, you'll have to make do with herbal tea.'

Philippe liked to think of himself as imperturbable, but he clearly wasn't guarding his expression as well as he normally did, because amusement tugged at the corner of Caroline Cartwright's generous mouth. 'I can offer nettle, gingko, milk thistle…'

The dark blue eyes gleamed. She was making fun of him, Philippe realised.

'Whatever you're having,' he said, irritated by the fact that he sounded stiff and pompous.

He was *never* pompous. He was never stiff either. He was famous for being relaxed, in fact. There was just something about this girl that rubbed him up the wrong way. Philippe felt as if he'd strayed into a different world, where the usual rules didn't apply. He should be at some bar drinking cocktails with a gorgeous woman who knew just how the game should be played, not feeling disgruntled in this tip of a house being offered tea—and herbal tea at that!—by a girl who thought he was *amusing*.

'A mug of dandelion and horny goat weed tea coming up,' she said. 'Sit down, I'll just be a minute.'

Philippe couldn't wait.

With a sigh, he pushed aside the clutter on the sofa and sat down. He'd let Lotty talk him into this, and now he was going to have to go through with it. And it suited him, Philippe remembered. If Caroline Cartwright was half what Lotty said she was, she would be ideal.

She's not pretty, exactly, Lotty had said. *She's more interesting than that.*

Caro certainly wasn't pretty, but she had a mobile face, with a long upper lip and expressive eyes as dark and blue as the ocean. Philippe could see that she might have the potential to be striking if she tidied herself up and put on some decent clothes. Not his type, of course—he liked his women slender and sophisticated, and Caro was neither—but that was all to the good. The whole point was for her to be someone he wouldn't want to get involved with.

And vice versa, of course.

So he was feeling a little more optimistic when Caro came in bearing two mugs of what looked like hot ditchwater.

Philippe eyed his mug dubiously, took a cautious sip and only just refrained from spitting it out.

Caro laughed out loud at his expression. 'Revolting, isn't it?'

'God, how do you drink that stuff?' Philippe grimaced and pushed the mug away. Perhaps he made more of a deal about it than he would normally have done, but he needed the excuse to hide his reaction to her smile. It had caught him unawares, like a step missed in the dark. Her face had lit up, and he'd felt the same dip of the stomach, the same lurch of the heart.

And her laugh...that laugh! Deep and husky and totally unexpected, it was a tangible thing, a seductive caress, the kind that drained all the blood from your head and sent it straight to your groin while it tangled your breathing into knots.

'It's supposed to be good for you,' Caro was saying, examining her own tea without enthusiasm. 'I'm on a diet. No alcohol, no caffeine, no carbohydrates, no dairy products... basically, no anything that I like,' she said glumly.

'It doesn't sound much fun.' Philippe had managed to get his lungs working again, which was a relief. Her laugh had surprised him, that was all, he decided. A momentary aberration. But listen to him now, his voice as steady as a rock. Sort of.

'It isn't.' Caro sighed and blew on her tea.

She had been glad to escape to the kitchen. Philippe's presence seemed to have sucked all the air out of the house. How was it that she had never noticed before how suffocatingly small it was? There was a strange, squeezed feeling inside her, and she fumbled with the mugs, as clumsy and self-conscious as she had been at fifteen.

Philippe's supercilious expression as he looked around the cosy sitting room had stung, Caro admitted, and she had enjoyed his expression when she had offered the tea. Well, they couldn't all spend their lives drinking champagne, and it wouldn't do him any harm to have tea instead for once.

Caro thought about him waiting in the sitting room, looking faintly disgusted and totally out of place. In wealth and looks and glamour, he was so out of her league it was ridiculous. But that was a good thing, she decided, squeezing the teabags with a spoon. It meant there was no point in trying to impress him, even if she had been so inclined. She could just be herself.

'I'm reinventing myself,' she told him now. 'My fiancé left me for someone who's younger and thinner and more fun, and then I lost my job,' she said. 'I had a few months moping around but now I've pulled myself together. At least I'm trying to. No more misery eating. I'm going to get fit, lose weight, change my life, meet a nice man, live happily ever after...you know, realistic, achievable goals like that.'

Philippe raised an eyebrow. 'It's a lot to expect from drinking tea.'

'The tea's a start. I mean, if I can't stick with this, how am I supposed to stick with all the other life-changing stuff?' Caro took a sip to prove her point, but even she couldn't prevent an instinctive wrinkling of the nose. 'But you didn't come here to talk about my diet,' she reminded him. 'You're here about Lotty.'

CHAPTER TWO

'AH, YES,' said Philippe. 'Lotty.'

Caro put down her mug at his tone. 'Is she OK? I had a very cryptic email from her. She said you would explain about some idea she'd had.'

'She's fine,' he said, 'and yes, I am supposed to be explaining, but it's hard to know where to start. Presumably you know something of the situation in Montluce at the moment?'

'Well, I know Lotty's father died last year.'

The sudden death of Crown Prince Amaury had shocked everyone. He had been a gentle man, completely under the thumb of his formidable mother as far as Caro could tell, and Lotty was his only child. She had taken her dead mother's place at his side as soon as she'd left finishing school, and had never put a foot wrong.

Lotty was the perfect princess, always smiling, always beautiful, endlessly shaking hands and sitting through interminable banquets and never, ever looking bored. There were no unguarded comments from Lotty for the press to seize upon, no photos posted on the internet. No wild parties, no unsuitable relationships, not so much as a whiff of scandal.

'Since then,' Philippe said carefully, 'things have been… rather unsettled.'

'Unsettled' was a bit of an understatement, in Caro's opinion. Montluce was one of the last absolute monarchies in Europe, and had been in the iron grip of the Montvivennes family since Charlemagne. Small as it was, the country was rigidly traditional, and the ruling family even more so. Lotty's grandmother, known as the Dowager Blanche, was only the latest in line of those who made the British royal family's attitude to protocol look slapdash.

Since Lotty's father had died, though, the family had been plunged into a soap opera of one dramatic event after another. A car accident and a heart attack had carried off one heir after another, while one of Lotty's cousins, who should have been in line for the crown, had been disinherited and was currently serving time for cocaine smuggling.

Now, what the tabloids loved to refer to as the 'cursed inheritance' had passed against all the odds to Philippe's father, Honoré. In view of the tragic circumstances, his coronation had been a low-key affair, or so Lotty had told Caro. There had been much speculation in the tabloids about Philippe's absence. None of them could have guessed that the current heir to the throne of Montluce would turn up in Ellerby and be sitting in Stella and Caro's sitting room, pointedly not drinking his horny goat weed tea.

'Amaury was always more interested in ancient Greek history than in running the country,' Philippe went on. 'He was happy to leave the day-to-day business of government in his mother's hands. The Dowager Blanche is used to having things her own way, and now all her plans have gone awry. She's not happy,' he added dryly.

'She doesn't approve of your father?' Caro was puzzled. She'd only ever seen photos of Philippe's father, but he looked tailor-made for the part of Crown Prince. She couldn't imagine why Lotty's grandmother would object to him.

'Oh, he's perfect as far as she's concerned. His sense of duty is quite as strong as hers.' There was an edge to Philippe's voice that Caro didn't understand.

'So what's the problem?' she asked. The truth was that she was having trouble focusing. Part of her was taken up with thinking: there's a *prince* on the sofa! Part was trying not to notice that beneath the casual shirt and trousers, his body was taut and lean.

And another part was so hungry that she couldn't concentrate on any of it properly. She could feel her stomach grumbling. Caro wrapped her arms around her waist and willed it to be quiet. How could she follow Philippe's story when she was worried her stomach might let out an embarrassing growl at any minute?

'Can't you guess?' Philippe smiled but the silver eyes were hard.

Caro forced her mind away from her stomach. 'Oh,' she said slowly. '*You're* the problem?'

'Got it in one,' said Philippe. 'The Dowager thinks I'm idle and feckless and irresponsible and has told me so in no uncertain terms.'

The sardonic smile flashed again. 'She's right, of course. Personally, I've never seen the appeal of duty and commitment. The thought that the future of the Montvivennes dynasty rests with me is almost more than my great-aunt can bear,' he added. 'She's decided that the only way to keep me in line and ensure that I'm not a total disaster for the country is to marry me to Lotty.'

'Lotty said that her grandmother was matchmaking,' said Caro, adding, not very tactfully, 'I'm surprised she'd approve of you, though.'

Philippe acknowledged that with a grim smile. 'She doesn't but, from her point of view, it's the only solution,' he said. 'Once shackled to Lotty, I'll settle down, they think. Lotty's bound to be a good influence on me. She's the perfect princess, after all, and there's no doubt it would be popular in the country. Compared to what the people think, what does it matter what Lotty and I feel?' Bitterness crept into his voice. 'We're royal, and we're expected to do our duty and not complain about it.'

'Poor Lotty! It's so unfair the way she never gets to do what she wants to do.'

'Quite,' said Philippe. He was leaning forward, absently turning his unwanted mug of tea on the coffee table. 'With a new Crown Prince in place, she thought that she would have a chance to get away and make a life of her own at last, but of course my father doesn't have a wife, having been careless enough to let his wife run off with another man, and now Lotty's being manoeuvred into being a consort all over again. I'm fond of Lotty, but I don't want to marry her any more than she wants to marry me.'

'But there must be something you can do about it,' Caro protested. 'I know Lotty finds it hard to resist her grandmother, but surely you can just say no?'

'I have.' As if irritated by his own fiddling, Philippe pushed the mug away once more and sat back. 'But the Dowager doesn't give up that easily. She's always pushing Lotty and I together and leaking stories to the press.'

'It said in *Glitz* that you were inseparable,' remembered Caro and he nodded grimly.

'That's the Dowager's handiwork. She adores that magazine because they're so pro-royalty. And you've got to admit, it's not a bad strategy. Start a rumour, let everyone in the country whip themselves up into wedding fever and wait for Lotty to cave under the pressure. Montlucians love Lotty, and she'll hate feeling that she's disappointing everyone by being selfish, as the Dowager puts it.'

Caro's mouth turned down as she thought about it. It did seem unfair. 'Why don't you go back to South America?' she suggested. 'Surely the Dowager Blanche would give up on the idea of you and Lotty eventually.'

'That's the trouble. I can't.' Restlessly, Philippe got to his feet. He looked as if he wanted to pace, but the room wasn't big enough for that, so he picked his way through the clutter to the bay window and stood staring unseeingly out to where the limousine waited at the kerb.

'It hasn't been announced yet, but my father is ill,' he said, his back to Caro. 'It's cancer.'

'Oh, no.' Caro remembered how desperate she had felt when her own father had been dying, and wished that she had the courage to get up and lay a sympathetic hand on Philippe's shoulder, but there was a rigid quality to his back that warned her against it. 'I'm so sorry,' she said instead.

Philippe turned back to face her. 'His prognosis isn't too bad, in fact, but the press are going to have a field day with the curse of the House of Montvivennes when it comes out.' His face was carefully expressionless.

'Montluce doesn't have specialised facilities, so he's going to Paris for treatment, and he's been told to rest completely for at least six months. So I've been summoned back to stand in for him. Only nominally, as he and the Dowager keep saying, but they're big on keeping up appearances. I'm taking over his commitments from the start of the month.

'I thought about refusing at first. My father and I don't have what you'd call a close relationship,' he went on with an ironic look, 'and I don't see why they need me to shake a few hands or pin on the occasional medal. If I could have some influence on decisions that are made, it would be different, but my father has never forgiven me for not being a perfect son like my older brother. When I suggested that I have some authority, he was so angry that he actually collapsed.'

Philippe sighed. 'I could insist, but he's ill, and he's my father...I don't want to make him even sicker than he is already. In the end, I said I would do as they asked for six months, but on the understanding that I can go back to South

America as soon as he's well again. There's no point in me hanging around with nothing to do but disappoint him that I'm not Etienne.'

So even royal families weren't averse to laying on the emotional blackmail, thought Caro.

'Meanwhile, you're being thrown together with Lotty at every opportunity?' she said.

'Exactly.' He rolled his shoulders as if to relieve the tension there. 'Then, the other day, Lotty and I were on one of our carefully staged "dates" and we came up with a plan.'

'I wondered when we were going to get to the plan,' said Caro. She made herself take another sip of tea. Philippe was right. It was disgusting. 'What is this great idea of Lotty's?'

'It's a simple one. The problem has been that we're both there, and both single. Of course Lotty's grandmother is going to get ideas. But if I go back to Montluce with a girlfriend and am clearly madly in love with her, even the Dowager Blanche would have to stop pushing Lotty and I together for a while.'

Caro could see where this was going. 'And then Lotty can pretend that it's too awkward for her to see you with another woman and tells her grandmother she needs to go away for a while?'

'Exactly,' said Philippe again.

'I suppose it could work.' She turned the idea over in her mind. 'Where do I come into this? Does Lotty want to come and stay here?'

'No,' said Philippe. 'She wants you to be my girlfriend.'

Caro's heart skidded to a stop, did a funny little flip and then lurched into gear again at the realisation that he was joking. 'Right.' She laughed.

Philippe said nothing.

Her smile faltered. 'You can't be serious?'

'Why not?'

'Well, because…you must have a girlfriend.'

'If I had a serious girlfriend, I wouldn't be in this mess,' he said crisply. 'I'm allergic to relationships. When I meet a woman, I'm clear about that, right from the start. No emotions, no expectations. It just gets messy otherwise.'

Caro sighed. 'Commitment issues…I might have guessed! What is it with guys and relationships?'

'What is it with *women* and relationships?' Philippe countered. 'Why do you always have to spoil things by talking about whether we have a relationship or not and, if we do, where it's going? Why can't we just have a good time?'

Balked of the prowling he so clearly wanted to do, Philippe stepped over to the mantelpiece, put his hands in his pockets and glowered down at his shoes as if it was their fault. 'Six months is about as long as I can stand being in Montluce,' he said. 'It's a suffocating place. Formal, stuffy, and so small there's never any chance to get away.'

He lifted his eyes to Caro's. They ought to be dark brown, she thought inconsequentially, not that clear, light grey that was so startling against his dark skin that it sent a tiny shock through her every time she looked into them.

'I'll be leaving the moment my father is better, and I don't want to complicate matters by getting involved with a woman if there's the slightest risk that she'll start taking things seriously. On the other hand, if she gets so much as a whiff that I'm not in fact serious, the Dowager Blanche will have Lotty back in a flash. For me, that would be a pain, as I'd have to go back to fighting off all the matchmaking attempts, but it would be far, far worse for Lotty. She'd lose the first chance she's ever had to do something for herself. And that's why you'd be perfect,' he said to Caro.

'You're Lotty's friend,' he said. 'I could pretend to be in love with you without worrying that you'd get the wrong idea, because you'd know the score from the start. I'm not going to fall in love with you and you don't want to get involved with me.'

'Well, *that's* certainly true,' said Caro, ruffled nonetheless by the brutal truth. *I'm not going to fall in love with you.*

'But you could pretend to love me, couldn't you?'

'I'm not sure I'm that good an actress,' said Caro tartly.

'Not even for Lotty?'

Caro chewed her lip, thinking of her friend. Lotty was so sweet-natured, so stoical, so good at pleasing everyone but herself. Trapped in a gilded cage of duty and responsibility. From the outside, it was a life of luxury and privilege, but Caro knew how desperately her friend longed to be like everyone else, to be ordinary. Lotty couldn't pop down to the shops for a pint of milk. She couldn't go out and get giggly over a bottle of wine. She could never look less than perfect, never be grumpy, never act on impulse, never relax.

She could never have fun without wondering if someone was going to take her picture and splash it all over the tabloids.

I'm getting desperate, Lotty had said in her email.

'No one would ever believe you would go out with someone like me!' Caro said eventually.

Philippe studied her with dispassionate eyes. 'Not at the moment, perhaps, but with a haircut, some make-up, some decent clothes…you might brush up all right.'

Caro tilted her head on one side as she pretended to consider his reply. 'OK, that's one answer,' she allowed. 'Another might be: why wouldn't anyone believe that I could be in love with you? Don't change a thing; you're beautiful as you are.' She smiled sweetly. 'Just a suggestion, of course!'

'See?' said Philippe. 'That's what makes you perfect. I can be honest with you if you're not a real girlfriend.'

'Stop, you're making me feel all warm and fuzzy inside!'

He smiled at that, and went back to sit on the sofa. 'Look,

just think about it seriously for a moment, Caro. You don't need to come for the whole six months. Two or three would probably be enough for Lotty to get away. We'd both know where we were. There would no expectations, nobody needs to get hurt and, at the end of two months or whatever, we could say goodbye with no hard feelings. I stop my great-aunt hassling me about marriage, you get two months away living in a palace—' the glance he sent around the sitting room made it clear what a change *that* would be '—and Lotty gets a chance to escape and have a life of her own for a while.'

He paused. 'Lotty…Lotty needs this, Caro. You know what she's like. Always restrained, always dignified. She wasn't going to cry or anything, but I could tell how desperate she feels. She's been good all her life, and just when it looks as if a door is opening for her at last, the Dowager and my father are trying to slam it closed again.'

'I know, it's so unfair, but—'

'And you did say you wanted to reinvent yourself,' Philippe reminded her.

Caro winced. She had said that. She clutched at her hair, careless of the way it tumbled out of its clip. 'I just don't know… There's so much to consider, and I can't think when I'm hungry like this!' Uncurling her legs, she put her feet on the floor. 'I'm going to get a biscuit,' she announced.

'I've got a better idea,' said Philippe, checking the Rolex on his wrist. 'Why don't I take you out to dinner? We can talk about the practicalities then, and I could do with a proper drink, not that disgusting stuff,' he said with a revolted glance at his tea. 'Where's the best place to eat around here?'

'The Star and Garter at Littendon,' said Caro automatically, perking up at the prospect of dinner. There was the diet, of course, but she couldn't be expected to make life-changing decisions on a salad and three biscuits, could she? Besides, it was Saturday. It was dinner with a prince, or stay at home with herbal tea and Mr Sexy online.

The prince in question might not be quite as charming as in the fairy tales, but it still wasn't what you'd call a hard choice.

'But you'll never get in on a Saturday,' she added as Philippe took out a super-slim phone and slid it open. 'They get booked up months in advance.'

Ignoring her, Philippe put the phone to his ear. 'Why don't you go and get changed?' was all he said. 'I'm not taking you out in that purple thing.'

The *purple thing* happened to be one of Caro's favourites, and she was still bristling as she pulled it over her head. She hoped the Star and Garter refused him a table and told His Obnoxious Highness that he'd have to wait three months like everyone else.

On the other *hand*, she reminded herself, the food was reputed to be fabulous. Way out of her price range, but no doubt peanuts to Philippe. It wouldn't be *so* bad if he got a table after all.

Now, what to wear? The Star and Garter—if that was where they were going, and Caro had the feeling that Philippe usually got what he wanted—deserved one of her best dresses. Caro ran her eye over her collection of vintage clothes and picked a pale blue cocktail dress made of flocked chiffon. Perhaps the neckline was a *little* low, but she loved the way the pleated skirt swished around her legs when she sashayed her hips.

Sucking in her breath to do up the side zip, Caro tugged up the neckline as far as she could and sauntered back downstairs with a confidence she was far from feeling. Philippe was still on the sofa, looking utterly incongruous. Unaware of her arrival—she could have spared herself the sauntering—he was leaning forward, reading something on the laptop she had abandoned earlier when she had gone in search of biscuits.

Her laptop! Too late, Caro remembered what she had been doing when depression had sent her to the kitchen. Shooting across the room, she banged the laptop closed, narrowing missing Philippe's fingers.

'What are you *doing*?'

Not at all perturbed, Philippe sat back and looked up at her.

'You know, I'm not sure Mr Sexy is the right guy for you.'

'You shouldn't look at other people's computers.' Caro was mortified that he had witnessed how she had been spending her Saturday night. She glared at him. 'It's very rude.'

'It was open on the table,' Philippe pointed out, unfazed. 'I couldn't help but see what you'd been doing. It was quite an eye-opener, I must say. I've never looked at a dating site before.'

Well, there was a surprise. Young, rich, handsome, a prince, and he'd never had to resort to internet dating. Incredible, thought Caro.

'I don't see you finding Mr Right amongst that lot, though,' he said. 'They're not exactly oozing charisma, are they?'

'They can't all be princes,' snapped Caro, pushing him out of the way so she could shut the computer down. 'That's not what I'm looking for either. I just want an ordinary life with an ordinary guy, which is not something *you'd* be able to understand.'

Philippe shook his head. 'You know, I don't think you've been entirely honest in your profile,' he said, nodding at the computer. 'You didn't say anything about how prickly you are.'

'You read my profile?'

'Of course,' he said. 'It's called research. If we're going

to be spending time together, I need to know what I'm going to be dealing with. I must say, I don't think that picture does you justice,' he went on.

He eyed Caro's dress, unimpressed. 'You might want to warn any prospective matches about your odd taste in clothes before you meet,' he added with unnecessary provocation. 'What are you wearing *now*?'

'I'll have you know this is one of my best dresses,' she said, too cross with him to care what he thought about her clothes. 'It's an original cocktail dress from the Fifties. I had to save up to buy it online.'

'You mean you handed over money for that?' Philippe unfolded himself from the sofa. 'Extraordinary.'

'I love vintage clothes,' said Caro. She held out the skirts and twirled. 'I wonder who bought this dress when it was new. Did she buy it for a special occasion? Was she excited? Did she meet someone when she was wearing it? A dress like this has a history. I like that.'

Philippe blinked at the swirl of chiffon and the tantalising glimpse of a really excellent pair of legs. The dress was an improvement on the purple cheesecloth, there was no doubt about that, but he wished that she had put on something a little less…eccentric. A little less *provoking*. Only Caroline Cartwright would choose to wear a sixty-year-old dress!

Maybe it did suit those luscious curves, but it still looked odd to Philippe, and he scowled as he sat in the back of the limousine next to Caro. He had decided to ignore—loftily—her fashion faux pas, and was annoyed to discover that the wretched dress kept snagging at his attention anyway. He blamed Caro, who kept tugging surreptitiously at the neckline, which only drew his eyes to the deep cleavage. Or she was crossing those legs so that the chiffon skirt slithered over her thighs. Philippe shifted uneasily, adjusting his seat belt. He was sure he could hear the material whispering silkily against her bare skin. She had twisted up the mass of nut-brown hair and fixed it with a clip so obviously casually shoved in that he expected any moment that it would all tumble free.

It was very distracting.

Caro wasn't supposed to be distracting. She was supposed to be convenient. That was all.

'I can't believe you got a table!' Caro looked as if she couldn't decide whether to be delighted or aggrieved when the limousine pulled up outside the Star and Garter.

'I didn't. Yan did.' Philippe nodded at an impassive giant who sat next to the driver in the front seat.

Caro lowered her voice and leant closer, giving Philippe a whiff of a clean fresh scent. 'Is he your bodyguard?'

'He prefers to be known as my personal protection officer,' said Philippe. 'He's a very handy man to have around, especially when it comes to getting tables.'

'Everyone else has to wait months. I suppose he dropped your title?' she said disapprovingly.

'I'm sure he did. What else is it for?'

'We can go somewhere else if you object to Yan pulling rank,' he said, but Caro shook her head quickly, so that more strands escaped from the clip. She smoothed them from her face.

'I've always wanted to eat here,' she confessed. 'It's horrendously expensive and most people only come for special occasions. I wanted to come with George when we got engaged, but he didn't think it was worth the money.' She sighed a little and the generous mouth curved downwards. 'We had pizza instead.'

To Philippe, who had eaten at some of the world's top restaurants, there was nothing special about the Star and Garter. It was pleasant enough, he allowed, simply decorated with subtle lighting and enough tables for the place to feel lively without being so close together you were forced to listen to anyone else's conversation.

He was used to the way the buzz of conversation paused when he walked into a restaurant, used to ignoring it while the manager came to greet him personally, used to exchanging pleasantries on automatic pilot, but all the time he could *feel* Caro beside him as clearly as if she were touching him. He kept his eyes courteously on the manager, but he didn't need to look at Caro to know that she was looking eagerly around her, practically humming with anticipation, careless of the fact that her fashion sense was fifty years out of date. Her eyes would be bright, that wretched, tantalising hair escaping from its clip.

And then, abruptly, he felt her stiffen and inhale sharply, and he broke off in mid-sentence to glance at her. She was rigid, her face white and frozen. Philippe followed her stricken gaze across the restaurant to where a couple were staring incredulously back at her.

It wasn't his problem, Philippe told himself, but somehow his arm went round Caro and he pulled her into his side in a possessive gesture. 'I hope you're hungry, *chérie*?' he said, trying not to notice how the dress slipped over her skin beneath his hand.

Caro looked blindly up at him. 'Wh…What?'

'Do you want to go straight to the table or would you rather have a drink at the bar first?' He kept a firm hold on her until the blankness faded from her eyes and understanding dawned.

'Oh.' She moistened her lips. 'Let's go to the table.'

'Excellent.' Philippe turned to the manager. 'We'll have a bottle of your best champagne.'

'Certainly, Your Highness.'

Caro was tense within the circle of his arm as they followed the waiter to their table. She didn't look again at the couple, but her lips were pressed tightly together in distress or anger, Philippe couldn't tell.

'All right?' he asked, when the waiter had gone.

'Yes, I…yes.' Caro shook out her napkin and smoothed it on her lap with hands that were not quite steady. 'It was just a shock to see them here.'

'That was your ex, I take it?'

'George, yes, and his new fiancée.' Her voice vibrated with suppressed anger. 'I can't *believe* he brought Melanie here. She doesn't even *eat*! That's how she looks like a stick insect.'

Philippe glanced over at the table. As far as he could see, Melanie was slim and pretty and blonde, but she would look muted next to Caro.

'I wonder if they're celebrating their engagement?' Caro went on, but he was glad to see the colour back in her face. Shock, it seemed, had been superseded by fury. 'Clearly, Melanie's too good for *pizza*!' She practically spat out the word.

'Maybe she'll wish that they'd gone for pizza instead now that you've arrived,' said Philippe, picking up the menu. 'It can't be much fun trying to celebrate your engagement when your fiancé's ex is on the other side of the room and he can't take his eyes off her.'

'Oh, he's not looking at *me*,' said Caro bitterly. 'He's looking at *you* and wondering what on earth a guy like you is doing with a boring frump like me!'

Philippe's dark brows shot up. 'Boring? *You?*'

His surprise was some consolation, Caro supposed. She opened the menu and pretended to read it, but the words were a blur and all she saw instead was George's face the day he'd told her it was over. He'd waited until she came back from the supermarket, and told her while she was unpacking the bags. Now Caro couldn't look at a carton of orange juice without feeling queasy.

'George thinks I'm boring.' She pressed her lips together against the jab of memory. 'He always said that he wanted to marry someone like me, but then he fell in love with Melanie because she was sexy and fun and everything I'm not, apparently.'

Turning a page unseeingly, she went on, 'There's a certain irony in that. I spent five years being careful and dressing conventionally, and deliberately *not* being fun or obvious, just so that I would fit into his world. I'd have done anything for him.'

Whenever she thought about how much she had loved George, her voice would crack like that. It was mortifying because she was over him now. Pretty much.

'Lotty said you'd been engaged, but that it was over,' Philippe said in that cool, couldn't-give-a-damn voice. 'It's one of the reasons she thought you might like to come to Montluce. A chance to get away for a while.'

'It *would* be nice.' Caro hadn't thought of that aspect of things before. She'd been too busy thinking what it would be like to spend two months with Philippe, who was sitting opposite her looking remote and gorgeous and totally out of reach in spite of being only a matter of inches away.

'Ellerby's a small town,' she said, 'and I spend a lot of time dreading that I'm going to bump into George, like just now.'

Although this time it hadn't been so bad, after all, she realised. There'd been that horrible moment when she'd seen George there with Melanie, and she'd been gripped by that old mixture of misery and rage and humiliation. They were a cosy twosome and she was left alone...and then, suddenly, she hadn't been on her own. Philippe had put his arm around her and made it look as if they were a couple, and she'd seen the astonishment flash in George's face.

Caro looked at Philippe. The dark brows were drawn together as he studied the menu and, with those piercing eyes shielded for once, she could let her gaze travel down his straight nose to the cool set of his mouth, where it snagged in spite of her efforts to tear her eyes away. Looking at it made her feel quite…funny.

He hadn't hesitated to step in and rescue her, while she had been floundering.

'Thank you for earlier,' she said.

'Earlier?'

'You know, making George think we were a couple.' He'd been so quick, seeing instantly what was needed, before she'd even thought about how to react. 'They always see me looking lonely and miserable and pathetic,' she said, laying down the menu so that he could see how grateful she was. 'I don't look like that when I'm with you.'

CHAPTER THREE

'ARE you still in love with him?' Philippe asked and then looked as if the question had caught him unawares. 'I mean, it would be difficult for you to act as my girlfriend if you were,' he added.

'No.' She didn't sound quite as sure as she should have done, Caro realised. 'No,' she said again. 'I adored George. When he broke off our engagement, it broke my heart. For a long time I told myself that I wanted him back, that I still loved him, but now…now I think maybe I love the idea of him more than the reality.'

She saw Philippe flick a brief, uncomprehending glance at George. No, he wouldn't understand.

'I know he's not particularly good-looking or glamorous, but he was everything I've ever wanted. He belongs.'

Philippe looked mystified.

'I never belonged anywhere,' she tried to explain. 'My dad was a mechanical engineer, and when I was small we moved around from project to project overseas. Then he got ill, and we moved to St Wulfrida's.'

'That was Lotty's school,' he remembered, and Caro nodded.

'That's where we met. My mother got a teaching post there, Dad applied to be the handyman so they could be together, and I got a free education as part of the deal. Except I was never going to belong in a school like that, where all the other girls had titles or triple-barrelled names. I wasn't nearly posh enough for them. Lotty was my only friend, and I wouldn't have got through it without her.'

'Funny,' said Philippe, 'that's what she said about you.'

Caro smiled. 'We got each other through, I think. Neither of us could wait to leave. St Wulfrida's doesn't exactly excel in academic achievement, so after GCSEs Lotty went to finishing school, and I went to the local college to do A levels. I thought that would be better, but of course I didn't fit in there either. I was *too* posh for them!'

'What's the big deal about belonging, anyway?' asked Philippe. 'You're lucky. You can go wherever you like, do what you like. That's what most of us want.'

'I don't,' said Caro. 'Dad died when I was fifteen, and my mother five years later, so I don't have any family left.'

She smiled wistfully. 'I suppose I've been looking for a home ever since. When I came to Ellerby and met George, I really thought I'd found a place to belong at last,' she went on. 'George's family have been here for generations. He's the third generation of solicitors, and he's *part* of Ellerby.' Caro searched her mind for an example. 'He's on the committee at the golf club.'

Philippe raised his brows.

'I know,' she said, even though he hadn't said a word, 'it doesn't sound very exciting. But being with George made me feel safe. He had a house, and it felt like being part of the community. I think that's what I miss more than anything else.'

The wine waiter arrived with the bottle of champagne just then, and they went through the whole palaver of showing Philippe the label, opening the bottle with a flourish, pouring the glasses.

Caro concentrated on the menu while all that was going on, a little embarrassed by how much she'd blurted out to

Philippe. He was surprisingly easy to talk to, she realised. Perhaps it was because he so clearly didn't care. Or maybe it was knowing that he was so far out of her league she didn't even need to try and impress him with her coolness or her success. She wasn't here to be clever or witty or interesting. It didn't matter what he thought of George, or of her.

The realisation was strangely exhilarating.

When they'd ordered, Philippe picked up his glass and chinked it against hers. 'Shall we drink to our plan?'

Anything for you, Lotty, she had said once. Still in the grip of that odd sense of liberation, Caro touched his glass back with the air of one making an irrevocable decision. 'To our plan,' she agreed. 'And to Lotty's escape.'

Philippe sat back in his chair and eyed her thoughtfully across the table. 'You're good friends, aren't you?'

'Lotty was wonderful to me when my father died.' Caro turned the stem of her champagne glass between her thumb and fingers. 'He'd been ill for months, and there was no question of us going on holiday, so Lotty asked me if I wanted to spend part of the summer with her, in her family villa in the south of France.'

She lifted her eyes and met Philippe's cool ones. 'You were there.'

'Lotty said that we'd met once,' he said. 'I vaguely remember that she had a friend who was around and then suddenly gone. Was that you?'

'Yes. I hung around with Lotty until my mother rang to say that Dad had had a relapse and was in hospital again. She said there was nothing I could do, and that I should stay in France and enjoy myself. She said that was what Dad wanted, but I couldn't bear it. I was desperate to see him.'

The glass winked in the candlelight as Caro turned it round, round, round.

'I didn't have any money, and Mum was too worried

about Dad to think of changing my ticket,' she went on after a moment. 'Lotty was only fifteen too, and she was so shy that she still stammered when she was anxious, but she didn't even hesitate. She knew I needed to go home. She talked to people she would normally be too nervous to talk to, and she sorted everything out for me. She made sure I was booked onto a flight the next day. I've no idea how she did it, but she arranged for someone to pick me up at the airport in London and take me straight to the hospital.

'Dad died the next day.' Caro swallowed. Even after all that time, the thought of her beloved father made her throat tight. 'If it hadn't been for Lotty, I'd never have seen him again.' She lifted her eyes to Philippe's again. 'I'll always be grateful to her for that. I've often wished there was something I could do for her in return, and now I can. If spending two months pretending to be in love with you helps her escape, even if just for a little while, then I'll do that.'

'It must have been a hard time for you,' said Philippe after a moment. 'I know how I felt when my brother died. I wanted everything to just…stop. And I wasn't a child, like you.'

He set his glass carefully on the table. 'Lotty was good to me then, too. Everyone understood how tragic it was for my father to lose his perfect son, but Lotty was the only one who thought about what it might be like for me to lose a brother. She's a very special person,' he said. 'She deserves a chance to live life on her own terms for a change. I know this is a mad plan,' he went on, deliberately lightening the tone, 'but it's worth a shot, don't you think?'

'I do.' Caro was happy to follow his lead. 'If nothing else, it will convince George and Melanie that I've moved on to much bigger and better things!'

She shot George a victorious look, but Philippe shook his head. 'Stop that,' he said.

'Stop what?'

'Stop looking at him.' He tutted. 'When I take a girl out to dinner, I don't expect her to spend her whole time thinking about another man!'

'I'm not!'

'You're supposed to be thinking about *me*,' said Philippe, ignoring her protest. 'George is never going to believe we're having a wild and passionate affair if he sees you sneaking glances at him.'

'He's never going to believe we're having a wild and passionate affair anyway,' said Caro, ruffled. 'He thinks I'm too boring for that.'

'Then why don't you show him just how wrong he is?' Philippe leant forward over the table and fixed Caro with his silver gaze. He really had extraordinary eyes, she found herself thinking irrelevantly. Wolf's eyes, their lightness accentuated by the darkness of his features and the fringe of black lashes. It was easier to think about that than about the way her heart was thudding in her throat at his nearness.

'How do you suggest I do that?' she said, struggling to hold on to her composure. 'We can hardly get down and dirty under the table!'

A faint contemptuous smile curled the corners of Philippe's mouth. 'Well, that would certainly make the point, but I was thinking of rather subtle ways of suggesting that we can't keep our hands off each other. For a start, you could keep your attention fixed on me, rather than on him! If we were really sleeping together, we'd be absorbed in each other.'

'It doesn't always have to be about you, you know,' grumbled Caro. 'Anyway, I *am* looking at you.' She fixed her eyes at him. 'There. Satisfied?'

'You could make it look as if you adore me and can't wait for me to drag you back to bed.'

'Oh, that's easy.' Caro summoned a suitably besotted expression and batted her lashes at him.

'What's the matter?' asked Philippe.

'Nothing's the matter! I'm looking adoring!'

'You look constipated,' he said frankly. 'Come on, you must be able to do better than that.'

'You're the expert on seduction,' said Caro, sulking. 'You do it.'

'OK.' Philippe reached across the table for her hand, turned it over and lifted it. 'Watch and learn,' he said, pressing a kiss into her palm.

Caro sucked in a breath as a current of warmth shot up her arm and washed through her. Her scalp was actually tingling with it. Bad sign. Willing the heat to fade, she struggled to keep her voice even.

'Oh, that old chestnut,' she said as lightly as she could. 'I would have done the hand-kissing thing, but I thought it would be too boring.'

'Kissing's never boring,' said Philippe. Now he was playing with her fingers, looking straight into her eyes, brushing his lips across her knuckles until she squirmed in her seat. 'Not the way we do it, anyway. Or that's what we want it to look like. We want everyone to think that we've just fallen out of bed, don't we? They ought to be looking at us and seeing that we can't keep our hands off each other. That we can't wait until we get home and I can undress you, very, very slowly, until you beg me to make love to you again.'

The sound of his voice and the tantalising caress of his fingers were doing alarming things to Caro. Heat was uncoiling in the pit of her belly and her mouth was dry. She had to get herself back under control.

'I never beg,' she said, but not nearly as steadily as she would have liked.

Philippe looked into her eyes and smiled. 'You do when you're with me.'

'I don't think so,' said Caro, but his smile only deepened.

She could see the candlelight flickering in the silver eyes, and her heart was thumping so loudly she was afraid the other diners would turn round and complain about the noise.

'Yes, you do, because I'm the only one who knows that behind closed doors you're a wild, passionate woman.' His voice was a tangible thing, velvet smoothing seductively over her skin. It would be so easy to succumb to it, to the warm, sure hands and the wickedly attractive smile, and Caro had to physically brace herself against it.

'Gosh, do women really fall for this stuff?' she asked.

'It's working, isn't it?'

For one horrible moment, Caro wondered if he could see her toes curling. 'Working?'

'You haven't been looking at what's-his-name at all.' It was true. She had completely forgotten about George for a while there. 'But he's been looking at you,' Philippe went on in the same disturbingly arousing voice, 'and he's very much afraid that you've found yourself a much, much better lover.'

Caro's eyes flickered to George, who was looking as if he'd been stuffed. Maybe there was something in this technique of Philippe's after all.

Philippe sat back smugly. 'And that's how it's done,' he said. 'Now you have a go.'

Her hand was throbbing where his lips had grazed her skin. Flustered by Philippe's abrupt transition from lover to teacher, Caro tucked the stray strands of hair behind her ears and assumed a nonchalance she wasn't feeling.

'Well, I *would*, but the food will be arriving any second and I don't want to spoil your appetite.'

'Coward,' he said softly. 'Besides, it's good practice for you. You're going to have to do better than screwing up your face if you're going to convince the Dowager Blanche that we're mad about each other.'

'Oh, all right.' Caro took a fortifying sip of her champagne and moistened her lips nervously while she thought, and saw Philippe's gaze fix on her mouth. She hadn't even started yet! Surely it couldn't be as easy as that?

Leaning forward, she rested her arms on the table, hugged them together and tried a seductive smile. She felt a fool, but Philippe's eyes dropped to her cleavage, and his eyes darkened unmistakably.

Encouraged, Caro felt around with her foot and managed to hook the toe of her shoe around his ankle. With a little manoeuvring, she could rub her foot tantalisingly up and down his calf. It felt awkward but it seemed to be working.

She waited for Philippe to burst out laughing, but he didn't. There was just the suspicion of a smile around his mouth as the light gaze returned to her face.

'How am I doing?' she asked.

'I think you may be a natural.'

Was he being sarcastic? Caro eyed him suspiciously but it was impossible to tell what he was really thinking.

It was a relief when their starters arrived and she could sit back. Funny, she had forgotten about how hungry she was while Philippe had been kissing her fingers. Now she picked up her fork to dig into her wild mushroom risotto and discovered that for possibly the only time in her life, her appetite had deserted her.

But Caro wasn't going to waste her one and only opportunity to eat at the Star and Garter. She made herself savour the food and refused to let herself think about Philippe sitting opposite her with his warm hands and his warm mouth.

'That was delicious,' she said, putting her fork down at last.

'Yes, it wasn't bad,' said Philippe indifferently. Michelin starred restaurants would be two a penny to him, of course. He held out his hand. 'Come on, back to looking besotted.'

'Must I?' sighed Caro, but she took his hand and, at the feel of his strong fingers curling around hers, a shiver of pleasure snaked through her.

Clearing her throat, she said, 'We ought to talk about practicalities.'

'Practicalities?'

To her consternation, Philippe turned her hand over so that the soft skin of her forearm was exposed. Now he was rubbing his thumb softly over her wrist, where her vein pulsed with awareness.

Caro swallowed hard and soldiered on. 'What's going to happen next?'

He would go back to Montluce in the next couple of days, Philippe told her. He would break the news about their supposed relationship to the Dowager Blanche and give Lotty a chance to make her own plans to leave. Then he would escort his father to Paris for his treatment.

'He won't want me, but he ought to have someone other than servants there for the operation,' he said. 'Once he's through that, I'll come and pick you up, and we'll go back to Montluce together. Will ten days or so be enough time for you to get ready?'

She nodded, desperately trying to ignore that stroking thumb, which was playing havoc with her breathing. 'I'm only temping,' she said unevenly. 'I just need to give a week's notice.'

'Once we're there, you won't have to do much,' Philippe said. 'Hang around with me. Convince my great-aunt that you adore me. Hold my hand like this. The usual stuff.'

'It doesn't sound very interesting,' said Caro austerely to cover the booming of her pulse.

'No, but it shouldn't be hard either.'

'Where—' She stopped, mortified by how high her voice sounded, and coughed. 'Where will I stay?' That was better, huskier, almost normal.

'With me,' said Philippe. 'We're not going to convince anyone that it's a serious relationship if we're not living together. I've got apartments in the palace in Montvivennes. Not where I'd choose to live, but it's comfortable enough.'

Apartments, plural? That sounded big. Caro was reassured. 'Plenty of space for both of us, then?'

'Oh, yes.' His eyes met hers, clearly knowing exactly the way her mind was going. 'Of course, we'll have to sleep together,' he said.

'That won't be necessary, surely?' Caro stiffened and tried to pull her hand away, but he held her tight. 'No one need know where I'm sleeping as long as I'm staying with you.'

'That's what you think.' Philippe's voice was crisp. 'There are servants in and out of the apartments all the time, and it would be a miracle if they didn't talk to each other. They'll wonder just what kind of relationship we have if we're not sleeping together, and word will get back. My great-aunt knows everything that goes on in the palace. She's got a spy network that would put the CIA to shame.'

'Couldn't we tell her you respect me too much to sleep with me before marriage?'

He offered her a sardonic smile in return. 'Yes, she'll believe that!'

Caro managed to tug her hand away at last. It was all very well for Philippe to sound coolly amused about the whole business, but he must have slept with millions of beautiful women. He was probably used to sleeping with strangers. The thought of sleeping with her clearly hadn't left *him* with an unnerving fluttering underneath his skin and in the pit of his stomach. *He* hadn't been misery-eating, so he didn't have to worry about what she would think when he took his clothes off.

Philippe naked…Caro's mind veered off track momentarily to imagine him pulling off his shirt with a grin. She could picture the lean, hard planes of his body with startling ease: the flex of his muscles under his skin, the broad chest, the flat stomach. The power and the grace and the sheer, sinful sexiness of him.

Her cheeks burned at the thought. She *really* didn't want her imagination to start running wild like that, especially not when taking off her own shirt would reveal all those extra pounds she had put on since George dumped her...and it wasn't as if she had been sylphlike to start with. No, there would be no undressing going on, under any circumstances.

'We can put a pillow down the middle, if you like,' said Philippe, apparently reading her mind without difficulty.

Without being aware of what she was doing, Caro cupped the wrist where he had stroked her with her free hand as if to calm the soft skin there, which was quivering still from his touch.

'You don't sound bothered one way or the other,' she said, unable to keep the snippiness from her voice.

He shrugged. 'I'm not. It's entirely up to you, Caro. I'm more than capable of keeping my hands to myself, so there's no need to panic.'

'I'm not panicking,' she said crossly. 'I'm just trying to think how it would work.'

She took her hand from her wrist and sat straighter. It was time to be sensible. 'If you say that we need to share a bed, then that's what we'll do. I'm not going to be silly about it. But I think sex would just confuse the issue,' she said, rather proud of her coolness this time. 'I think it would be easier if we agreed that we would be just friends while we're together.'

'Friends?' he repeated, expressionless.

'Yes, you know, when you have a good time but don't want to sleep together.'

'I've got friends,' he said. 'They're just not usually women.'

'There's nothing usual about our relationship, though, is

there, Philippe? You're a prince, I'm an ordinary girl with no interest in anything other than an ordinary life. You're wealthy by any standard, and I'm temping to pay my rent. You go out with beautiful, glamorous women, and I'm neither,' Caro said. 'We've got absolutely nothing in common apart from Lotty, but just for two months we're going to be together. I'm not interested in you, and I think it's pretty clear you're not going to be interested in me, so it makes sense that we should agree to be friends at least, don't you think?'

Why not? Philippe asked himself. Caro was right. It would be much easier this way. The last thing he wanted was to get involved with someone who would fall in love with him. That would complicate matters and it would all get very messy. There would be tears and scenes and demands for commitment and stormings off. Philippe had been there before, and he couldn't afford anything similar this time if he didn't want to be left at the mercy of the Dowager Blanche's matchmaking plans again.

So it was just as well Caro had made it clear that she wasn't interested in him. There was no need to feel nettled. It wasn't as if she was *his* type either. Caro was right: she wasn't beautiful, she wasn't stylish. She was untidy and distracting, that was all.

It was just that he couldn't shake the feel of her. When he'd put his arm around her to cross the restaurant, he'd rested his hand on the flare of her hip and felt the silky material of her dress shift over her skin with a shock of awareness. He'd held her wrist and felt the blood beating in her veins, and that, too, had been like a current thrilling through him. He looked away from her mouth.

'Fine by me,' he said, as carelessly as he could. 'Friends it is, and we'll get that pillow out as soon as we get there.'

Philippe was used to eating with women who automatically chose the least fattening meal on the menu and it was a revelation to watch Caro oohing and aahing over her choice. Philippe himself was largely indifferent to food—he reserved his passion for the wine list—but it was impossible not to enjoy eating with someone who took so much pleasure in it. Caro would close her eyes blissfully while she savoured every taste and texture. She loaded up forkfuls from her dish and insisted he try it, and reached over to help herself to a taste of his, until he suggested that they simply swap plates.

He was being sarcastic, but Caro was delighted at the suggestion and promptly handed over her plate. 'George always refused to share like this,' she confided. 'He said it was embarrassing to pass plates over the table and that everyone would look at us.'

'And this was a guy who accused *you* of not being any fun?'

'He probably swaps plates with Melanie,' she said with a sigh.

'You should have tried leaning over the table so that he could fall down your cleavage,' Philippe said. 'I'm sure he'd have swapped anything you wanted then.'

'Do you really think so?' The blue eyes rested wistfully on George and Philippe was conscious of a quite irrational stab of jealousy.

He was used to being the centre of attention. His dinner companions were invariably beautiful, just as Caro had said. They flirted and sparkled and charmed and laughed at all his jokes. It was a salutary experience to be with Caro, who was far more interested in her ex-fiancé than in him. She was more interested in the *food* than in him, come to that.

Philippe told himself that he was amused, but the truth was that he was just a little piqued by her indifference. Here was he, a prince famous for his charm and his wit and his sexual prowess, having to work to keep the attention of a woman who wasn't even really pretty, and who didn't feel the least need to keep him entertained. Not that he wanted to be entertained, of course, but still…

It was annoying to find that his leg was tingling where she had rubbed her shoe so tantalisingly, and that his eyes kept snagging on that mouth, or drifting to that luscious cleavage. Philippe suspected that Caro had no idea how she looked, with that provocative mouth and that wickedly lush body, so at odds with the combative glint in her blue eyes and the sharpness of her tongue.

I'm not interested in you, she had said.

Just as well.

For the first time in her life, Caro refused pudding. Finally, she'd made it to the Star and Garter, and she wasn't hungry! Life could be so unfair sometimes.

'Ready to go?' asked Philippe. 'Let's make sure we make an exit.' Very casually, he rested a hand at the nape of her neck as they passed George's table. It was a perfect proprietorial gesture, and it felt disturbingly intimate to Caro. The warmth from his fingers snaked down her spine, making her shiver.

'They'll be leaving any minute themselves,' Philippe murmured as he opened the door for her. 'Do you want to kiss me?'

'What?' Caro stopped dead and stared at him. 'No, of course not!'

'Sure? Because here's an opportunity to convince George that you're having a passionate affair, if you want to,' he said, all reasonableness. 'He *might* have been convinced by all the hand-holding, but it was all a bit tame, wasn't it? Whereas if he sees you enjoying a steamy kiss, there's not going to be much doubt in his mind that you're a passionate, exciting woman having a better time without him, is there?'

Caro hesitated. The idea of making George believe that she was in the throes of a wild affair was deeply appealing, she had to admit. For too long, she'd felt dull and repressed next to bubbly Melanie, and hated that deadly feeling that they both felt sorry for her.

But this was His Serene Highness Prince Philippe of Montluce… Did she really have the nerve to kiss him? On the other hand, they *had* agreed to be friends, hadn't they? 'Are you sure you wouldn't mind?' she asked doubtfully.

In reply, Philippe spread his arms. 'What are friends for? Besides, it'll be good practice for us. We're going to have to kiss in Montluce, so we might as well get used to it.'

True. Good point. Caro took a deep breath. 'Well…okay, then.'

'Come over here.' Philippe took her hand and led her over to the limousine, which waited in the glow of a single street light immediately opposite the door. 'There's no point if George can't see us, is there? They won't be able to miss us here.' He turned and leant back against the limousine. 'Off you go, then.'

'Where's Yan?'

'Don't worry about Yan. He's used to looking the other way.'

'Right.' Above them, the sky was a dark, dark blue, and the cool night air brimmed with the scents of a northern summer. A little current of excitement ran under Caro's skin. Moistening her lips, she stepped towards him, then hesitated.

'I feel silly.'

'That's because you're too far away. You'll find it easier if you get a bit closer.'

Caro took another step. It brought her up against him. She could smell his cologne—subtle, expensive—and, when she rested her palms against his chest, she felt the hard solidity of him through the fine material of his shirt.

The street lamp cast a surreal orange glow over everything, but at the same time Caro could see exactly what she was doing. It was like being on stage, and now she had to perform.

Gripped by shyness, she stared fixedly at Philippe's collar while her hands pressed against his chest and the warmth of his skin seemed to pulse through her, slow and steady like his heartbeat.

'I don't want to hurry you, but they'll be out soon,' said Philippe and his voice reverberated through her hands.

'Right,' she said again, and swallowed. Passionate, exciting…she could do it.

Forcing her eyes up from his collar, she let them drift up the strong column of his throat. She could see the faint prickle of stubble and, without giving herself time to think, she touched her lips to the pulse beating there.

Philippe inhaled slowly. His hands hung loosely by his sides, but she felt the tension in his body, and she smiled. Maybe he wasn't quite as cool as he made out.

Her heart was thudding painfully, *bang, bang, bang* against her ribs. She kissed the pulse again, then drifted soft kisses up to his jaw. It felt deliciously rough beneath her lips and she slid her hands to his shoulders.

'I think you'd better get on with it,' said Philippe, but a smile rippled through the words.

'Stop talking,' she mumbled, making her way along his chin. 'You're putting me off.'

'I'm just saying. George will be out any second.'

Caro pulled away, exasperated. 'I can't do it if you're going to do a running commentary!'

'Then make me stop talking,' he challenged her.

'Fine.' Defiantly, she stepped back up to him and put her hands on his shoulders once more. Then she leant into him, angling her face up and pressing her mouth against his. His lips were warm and firm and relaxed and curved into the faintest of smiles.

Was he laughing at her? Caro kissed him again, nibbling little kisses at the edge of his mouth where his smile dented, teasing his lips open so that their tongues could twine together, and it felt so warm, so right, that she forgot everything else. She forgot George and Melanie. She forgot the plan. She forgot about just being friends. There was only the taste of him and the feel of him and the astonishing sweetness spilling through her.

Then Philippe's arms closed round her at last and he pulled her hard against him, and the sweetness was swept away by a surge of heat. It was wild and dark and fierce, a current that swirled around them, sucking them down, pulling them off their feet. Caro was lost, tumbling in the frantic wash of desire. She linked her arms around his neck to anchor herself, murmuring low in her throat, something inarticulate that might have been protest, or might have been longing.

Somehow Philippe had found the clip in her hair and pulled it free. It fell, unnoticed, to the ground while he slid his fingers through the silky mass, twisting, twining, holding her head still so that he could kiss her back, and he was good, oh, he was good...Caro thrilled at the sureness of his lips, the hard insistence of his hands that slid down her spine to cup her bottom and lift her against him.

She could feel his arousal, and she pulled her mouth from his so that she could gasp for breath.

'Philippe...'

She wasn't even sure what she meant to say, but Philippe, who was kissing her throat and making her shiver with delight at the heat and the hunger of it, stilled as if she had whacked him across the head.

Caro felt him draw a ragged breath, then another. 'Good God,' he said, sounding shaken, and let her go. 'Maybe that's enough practice for now.'

Practice? Desperately, Caro tried to bring her scattered senses back under control. She needed a decompression chamber, somewhere to learn to breathe again, a staging post between heady pleasure and the slap of reality where there was no touch, no taste, no feel, no giddy swing of the senses but only the chill of standing alone on a summer's night remembering that none of it had been real.

CHAPTER FOUR

MONTLUCE was such a tiny country that it didn't even have its own airport, so they were to fly to France and drive the rest of the way. In Caro's experience, flying meant a lot of queuing, a lot of delays, a lot of shuffling onto a crowded plane and shifting impatiently for the inevitable passenger who blocked the aisle for long minutes while he fussed about stashing away his duty-free in the overhead lockers.

Flying with Philippe was very different. The limousine he'd sent to pick her up in Ellerby that morning bypassed the terminal and deposited her right by the plane on the tarmac. Her bags were whisked away while Caro climbed out and stood looking dubiously up at the private jet. It looked very small. The wind was whipping tendrils of hair around her face and plastering them against her lips as fast as she could pull them free.

She was very nervous.

And cross with herself for feeling that way. Everything was going ahead exactly as they'd planned. Lotty was ecstatically grateful and would be gone before Caro and Philippe arrived. Once in Montluce, there would just be the two of them.

Which would be *fine*, Caro told herself. They had agreed to be friends, hadn't they? If it hadn't been for that stupid kiss…

But she wasn't supposed to be thinking about that. It had

been a mistake, they'd agreed afterwards. Both of them had been carried away by the pretence, but pretence was all it had been. It wasn't as if it had been a real kiss.

The trouble was that it had *felt* real. The firm curve of his mouth, his breath against her skin, the insistence of the sure hands cupping her buttocks and pulling her into him…oh, yes, it had felt real, all right. She could still feel the glittery rush, the heat. Philippe had been so hard, so surprisingly solid, so *male*. Every time Caro thought about him, her muscles would clench and a disturbing sensation, half shiver, half shudder, would snake its way down her spine.

Not that she would make the mistake of believing it had meant anything to Philippe. Just because she could admit he was attractive didn't mean that she was going to lose her mind. Caro might be many things, but she wasn't a fool.

After announcing their relationship to a relieved Lotty and a furious Dowager Blanche, Philippe had escorted his equally disappointed father to Paris to start his treatment, but for the last three or four days he'd been in London. Caro knew this because she'd seen his picture in *Glitz*. He'd been snapped coming out of a nightclub with Francesca Allen. Usually referred to as 'Britain's favourite actress', Francesca was famously beautiful, famously intelligent, famously nice— and famously married. The tabloids were having a field day speculating about what they were doing together.

It was a stupid thing to have done, given everything Philippe had had to say about convincing the Dowager Blanche that he was serious about *her*, Caro thought, and told herself that was the only reason she was feeling monumentally miffed. She wasn't silly enough to be jealous. *I'm more than capable of keeping my hands to myself*, Philippe had said, and Caro had no problem believing him, kiss or no kiss. A man like Philippe, used to hanging around with beautiful women the likes of Francesca Allen, was hardly likely to be tempted by an ordinary, overweight, eccentrically dressed Caroline Cartwright, was he?

No, being friends was the only way to get through the next few weeks. As a friend, she wouldn't have to worry about what she looked like, and there would be no need to feel twitchy about other, far more beautiful, women prowling around him. She could relax and enjoy herself with a friend.

Caro had barely reminded herself of that when Philippe appeared, ducking out of the cabin, long and lean and tautly muscled in a pale yellow polo shirt and chinos, and the breath whooshed out of her. He looked the same, and yet different, more *immediate* somehow: the cool mouth, the winged brows, the crisp line of his jaw, the startling contrast between the icy eyes and the darkness of his hair.

It must be something to do with the brightness of the light, the freshness of the breeze. Why else would the sight of him sharpen her senses and make her feel as if every cell in her body was alert and tingling?

At the top of the steps, Philippe looked down at Caro and was startled by how pleased he was to see her.

Of course, it would have been horribly awkward if she'd changed her mind, Philippe told himself. His announcement that he was bringing a girlfriend no one had ever heard of back to Montluce hadn't gone down well, to say the least, and he'd been subjected to endless harangues on the subject from his great-aunt, while his father had retreated into bitter disappointment as usual. Only Lotty, hugging him with a speaking look of gratitude, had stopped him from telling them what they could all do with their duty and responsibility and booking himself on the first plane back to Buenos Aires.

Philippe had been glad to escape to London and enjoy his last few days of freedom for a while. He'd met up with friends, played polo at the Guards Club, been to parties and dinners and renewed his acquaintance with the beautiful Francesca

Allen. He wasn't looking forward to the next six months, and couldn't decide whether this mad pretence with Caro Cartwright was going to make things better or worse. She was so different from the other women he knew. Not beautiful, not glamorous. Just ordinary. And yet Philippe had been surprised at how vividly he remembered her.

How vividly he remembered that kiss.

He'd been prepared for awkwardness, not for sweetness. Not for softness a man could lose himself in if he wasn't careful.

The memory made Philippe uncomfortable. He didn't do losing himself. But he'd been taken unawares by the way the dress slipped over her skin. The heat shooting through him had sucked the air from his brain, and the message to step back and keep his cool hadn't reached his hands.

Or his mouth.

Or the rest of him.

Philippe didn't understand it. Caro Cartwright ought to be the last woman to have that kind of effect on him. She wasn't even pretty, and as for her clothes…! Today she wore jeans and boots, with a plain white T-shirt, which wouldn't have looked too bad if she hadn't spoiled it by wearing an oversize man's dinner jacket over the top, its sleeves rolled up to show a brilliant scarlet lining. At least she was tall enough to carry it off with a certain panache, he allowed grudgingly.

No, Caro wasn't his type at all.

And yet there she stood, blue eyes wary and all that hair blowing around her face, and his heart unmistakably lifted.

Odd.

'There you are,' he said, pushing the discomfited feeling aside. It was too late to change his mind now. He went down the steps to greet her. 'I was beginning to wonder if you'd changed your mind.'

'I did think about it,' Caro confessed. 'But then I heard

from mutual friends that George is worried I might be going off the rails. He's obviously found out who you were, and he thinks you've got a bad reputation,' she said cheerfully. 'Now he's afraid that I'm going to do something stupid and get hurt—and, as we all know, he's the only one allowed to hurt me! So I thought I'd come after all, and send lots of messages home to make sure he knows what a glamorous time I'm having while Melanie is going to the supermarket and making George his tea the way he likes it. Then we'll see who's having the most fun, fun, fun!'

'Excellent,' said Philippe. 'In that case, you'd better come aboard.'

Caro was deeply impressed by the inside of the plane, which was fitted out with six plush leather seats, wall-to-wall carpeting and a lot of polished wood. Yan was already there, sitting in the cockpit.

'Take a seat,' Philippe said. 'Now you're here, we're ready to go.'

Caro looked around. 'Where's the pilot?'

'You're looking at him.'

'You're not a pilot!'

'I'm not? Then we're going to be in trouble because there's no one else to fly the plane.'

'I'm serious,' said Caro uneasily as she sat down in the seat nearest the front. 'Are you sure you know how to fly?'

Philippe settled himself in the cockpit and began flicking switches. 'Sure. I did a five-minute course a few years ago.'

'Really?'

'No, of course not really!' he said, exasperated. 'You don't think they let you in the air unless you're properly qualified, do you?'

'They might if you can stick Prince in front of your name,' said Caro with a dark look, although she was reassured to see Yan beside him. Surely he wouldn't let Philippe fly unless he knew what he was doing? 'The rules don't usually apply to people like you.'

'Well, in this case they do,' said Philippe. 'I've got a licence, I assure you. What do you think I've been doing for the past few years?'

'I don't know. Playing polo?'

'Pah! Who wants to get on a horse when you can fly a plane?'

'What, you mean you just get in your plane and fly around in the sky?' It seemed a bit pointless to Caro.

'No, I fly to places,' he said, his hands busy checking dials and switches. Caro just hoped he knew what he was doing.

'What places?' she asked suspiciously.

'I go wherever a plane is needed. I've got a friend who organises logistics for a number of aid organisations. They might need a development worker transported in a remote village, or tents dropped after an earthquake…if you haven't got the time or the money to get through the bureaucratic red tape, I'm your man.'

Philippe glanced over his shoulder at Caro. 'It gives me something to do when I'm bored,' he said, as if he feared he might have given too much of himself away. 'And it's more fun than polo! Now, fasten your seat belt while we finish the pre-flight check here.'

He turned back to the controls. 'Er, what's this red button again?' he pretended to ask Yan. 'Oh, right, the eject seat. Oops, better avoid that one! So the start button must be…oh, yes, I remember now. All right in the back there?' he called over his shoulder to Caro.

'Ha, ha, ha,' she said in a monotone. 'That's a fake laugh, by the way!'

'Relax,' he said. 'I hardly ever crash. Besides, I thought you'd decided to have fun, fun, fun, and what could be more fun than flying around in a private jet?'

'It won't be much fun when the plane crashes,' she grumbled.

The plane didn't crash, of course, but it felt as if something even more disastrous was happening inside her as she watched Philippe push the throttle remorselessly forwards. His long hands were absolutely steady as they shot along the runway, and Caro's stomach dropped away as the plane lifted into the air.

She was more impressed than she wanted to admit. Why had she assumed that he had been living an idle trust fund existence? She should have realised that a man like Philippe would be bored with nothing to do but party all day. There was that reckless edge to him that she had noticed even as a boy. It was all too easy to imagine him flying planes into war zones, dodging bullets or volcanic ash or pot-holed runways. He would thrive on the danger.

Philippe had been very quick to dismiss what he did, Caro had noticed. *Something to do when I'm bored*, he had said. There must be plenty of other jaded rich people out there, but how many of them would risk their lives for others the way he did? Philippe could get his thrills racing cars or helicopter skiing or doing any of the other extreme sports that catered to the very rich and very bored, but instead he flew his plane where it was needed. No doubt he did enjoy it, but Caro thought it was more than possible that he would go anyway.

She liked that about him, and she liked the fact that he clearly didn't publicise what he was doing. He wasn't like so many other celebrities, using charity work to raise their own profiles. Caro wondered if even Lotty knew.

From where she sat, she could see the hard edge of Philippe's jaw, the flash of his smile as he turned to speak to Yan beside him. Caro could see one powerfully muscled arm. Her eyes drifted from the dark, flat hairs on his forearm to the broad, strong wrist, and on to the firm fingers holding the joystick, and a disquieting ache stirred low in her belly.

She made herself look away, out of the window. The seat was pressing into the small of her back as they climbed up through great blowsy drifts of clouds, up into the blue. There was no going back to real life now. Instead, she would spend the next two months as Philippe's girlfriend. Caro's eyes slid back to his profile, etched now against the bright sky. She could see the creases at the edge of his eye, the corner of his mouth, and remembering how warm and sure it had felt against her own made her stomach tilt anew.

Two months beside him. Two months trying not to notice the cool set of his mouth or remember the feel of his hands.

The squirmy feeling in Caro's belly intensified. Nerves, she decided at first, but when she looked out at the clouds and felt the plane soaring upwards and thought about the weeks ahead she finally recognised the feeling for what it was.

Excitement.

'Oh, what a beautiful car!' Caro gasped when she saw the Aston Martin waiting for them at the quiet airfield where they landed. Philippe watched her practically fall down the steps in her eagerness to get at it.

Unless it was her eagerness to get out of the plane, of course.

'Oh, you beauty!' she said, running a hand lovingly over the bonnet. 'A DB9! I've never seen one before.' She looked up at him, her eyes shining. 'Is it yours?'

'It is.' She was so vivid standing there in the sunlight, her face alight with enthusiasm, that Philippe's breath hitched in a new and disturbing way, and for a moment he couldn't remember how to be.

'This isn't like you.' Ah, yes, that was better. Cool, indifferent. That was him. 'You know the car's not second-hand, don't you? And you can't eat it? I wouldn't have thought it was your kind of thing at all.'

'I make an exception for cars.' Caro let her hand smooth over the bodywork in a way that made Philippe's throat dry ridiculously. He fought for a casual expression, but all he could think, bizarrely, was: *lucky car*.

'Can I drive?' she asked, with a speculative look from under her lashes, trying it on.

'Absolutely not,' he said firmly.

'Oh, please! I'll behave very, very nicely.'

'No.'

'You're supposed to be in love with me,' she pointed out as she straightened.

'I'd have to be besotted before I let you drive my car,' he said, and opened the passenger door for her. 'Most girls would be happy to be driven.'

'I'm not most girls,' said Caro, but she got in anyway and he closed the door after her with a satisfying clunk.

'You can say that again,' said Philippe, walking round to get in behind the wheel. Now she was stroking the seat and the wooden trim, leaning forward to gaze at the dashboard, wriggling back into her seat with a sigh of pleasure. It was practically pornographic! Not enough oxygen was getting to his brain and he had to take a breath, horrified to find that the hands he laid on the steering wheel weren't entirely steady.

The clear glass starter button glowed invitingly red, reminding him that he was in control. Philippe pressed it and the engine purred into life.

'What about Yan and the luggage?' Caro dragged her attention back from the car for a moment.

'He'll follow in the other car,' said Philippe, nodding back to a black SUV with tinted windows.

'Isn't he supposed to be protecting you?'

'He'll be right behind.' Philippe put the car into gear. 'But for now it's just you and me.'

'Oh,' was all Caro said, but a little thrill shivered through her all the same.

Just you and me.

It wouldn't be just the two of them, of course. Lotty had told her about the palace servants, and there would always be Yan or a member of the public wanting their hand shaken. Just as well, Caro told herself firmly. It would be much easier to be friends when there were other people around.

'Where did you learn about cars?' Philippe asked as they turned onto the main road.

'From my father.' The road was clear ahead, and Philippe put his foot down. The car responded instantly, surging forward. Caro felt the pressure in the small of her back and settled into it with a shiver of pleasure. 'He loved cars. He always had some banger up on the blocks and he'd spend hours tinkering with it. When I was little I'd squat beside him and be allowed to hand him a spanner or an oily rag. Even now the smell of oil makes me think of Dad.'

Caro smiled unevenly, remembering. 'Driving an Aston Martin was his dream. He'd be so thrilled if he could see me now!' She stroked the leather on either side of her thighs. 'And envious!'

Distracted by the stroking, Philippe forced his attention back to the road. 'It sounds like you had a good relationship with your father.'

'I adored him.' She touched the lapels of the jacket she wore. 'This is Dad's dinner jacket. He wore it for a school dance once, and no one recognised him. It was as if none of them had ever looked at him when he was wearing his handyman overalls, but put on a smart jacket and suddenly he was a real person, someone they could talk to because he was dressed like them.'

Caro fingered the sleeve where she'd rolled it up to show the scarlet lining. 'I remember Dad saying that some people are like this jacket, conventional on the outside, but with a bright, beautiful lining like this. He said we shouldn't judge what's on the outside, it's what's inside that really matters. I think of him every time I put this jacket on,' she said.

'My father thinks the exact opposite,' said Philippe. 'For him, it's *all* about appearances. No wonder I'm such a disappointment to him.' He was careful to keep his tone light, but Caro looked at him, a crease between her brows.

'He can't be that disappointed if he trusts you to stand in for him while he's sick.'

'Only because it wouldn't look right if he didn't make his only surviving son regent in his absence, would it? What would people *think*?'

In spite of himself, Philippe could hear the bitterness threading his voice, and he summoned a smile instead. 'Besides, it's not a question of trust. It's not as if they're going to let me loose on government. My father thinks it'll be good for me to experience meetings and red boxes and the whole dreary business of governing, but all that's just for show too. There's a council of ministers, but the Dowager Blanche will be keeping a firm hold of the reins. I'm trusted to shake hands and host a few banquets, but that's about it.'

'You could take more responsibility if you wanted, couldn't you?'

'They won't let me.' Caro could hear the frustration in his voice, and she felt for him. It couldn't be easy knowing that any attempt to assert himself would be met by his father's collapse. 'And I daren't risk insisting any more,' Philippe said. 'Not when he's so sick, anyway. My father and I may not get on, but I don't want him to die.'

'Why doesn't he trust you?' Caro asked, swivelling in her seat so that she could look at him. 'I know you were wild when you were younger, but that was years ago.'

'It's hard to change the way your family looks at you.'

Philippe glanced in the mirror and pulled out to overtake a lumbering truck in a flash. 'Etienne was always the dutiful, responsible son, and I was difficult. That's just the way it was.

'Etienne was a golden boy—clever, hard-working, responsible, handsome, charming, kind. I could never live up to him, so I never tried. I was only ever "the spare" in my father's eyes, anyway,' he said. 'I didn't even have the good sense to look like him, the way Etienne did. Instead, I take after my mother. Every time my father looks at me, he's reminded of the way she humiliated him. I sometimes wonder if he suspects I'm not even his son.'

Philippe hoped that he sounded detached and ironic, but suspected it didn't fool Caro, who was watching him with those warm blue eyes. He could feel her gaze on his profile as surely as if she had reached out to lay her palm against his cheek.

'I never heard anything about your mother,' she said. 'What did she do?'

'Oh, the usual. She was far too young and frivolous to have been married to my father. It's a miracle their marriage lasted as long as it did. She ran away from him eventually and went to live with an Italian racing driver.'

He thought he had the tone better there. Careless. Cynical. Just a touch of amusement.

'Do you remember her?'

'Not much,' he said. 'Her perfume when she came to kiss me goodnight. Her laughter. I was only four, and left with a nanny a lot of the time anyway, so I don't suppose it made much difference to me really when she left. It was worse for Etienne. He was eleven, so he must have had more memories of her.'

Philippe paused. 'He would have been devastated, but he

used to come and play with me for hours so that I wouldn't miss her. That was the kind of boy he was.'

'I didn't realise you were so close to him.'

Caro's throat was aching for the little boy Philippe had been. Her father had been right. You could never tell what someone was like from the face they put on to the world. All she'd ever seen of Philippe had been the jacket of cool arrogance. It had never occurred to her to wonder whether he used it to deflect, to stop anyone realising that he had once been a small boy, abandoned by his mother and rejected by his father.

'He was a great brother,' said Philippe. 'A great person. You can't blame my father for being bitter that Etienne was the one who died, and that he was left with me. You can't blame him for wishing that I'd been the one who died.'

'That's…that's a terrible thing to say,' said Caro, shocked.

'It's true.' He glanced at her and then away. 'It was my fault Etienne died.'

'No.' Caro put out an instinctive hand. 'No, it was an accident. Lotty told me.'

'Oh, yes, it was an accident, but if it hadn't been for me, he'd never have been on the lake that day.' The bleak set to Philippe's mouth tore at her heart. 'Lotty's father was Crown Prince, and his brother still alive, with his two sons,' he went on after a moment. 'There was no reason to believe we'd ever inherit. My father had a vineyard, and Etienne was going up to look at the accounts or something equally tedious. He envied me, he said. To him it seemed that I was the one always having a good time. He said he wished he could do the same, but he was afraid that he didn't have the courage.'

He overtook a car, and then another and another, the sleek power of the Aston Martin controlled utterly in his strong hands.

'"Come water skiing with me", I said,' he remembered

bitterly. '"For once in your life, do what *you* want to do instead of what our father wants you to do." So he did, and he died.'

'It wasn't your fault,' said Caro.

'My father thinks it was.'

'It wasn't.' Without thinking, she put her hand on his shoulder. Through the yellow polo shirt, she could feel his muscles corded with tension. 'It was Etienne's choice to go. You didn't make him fall, and you didn't kill him. It was an accident.'

'That was what Lotty said. She was the only one who stood by me then,' said Philippe. 'If it had been up to my father, I wouldn't even have been allowed to go to the funeral. "If it wasn't for you, Etienne would still be alive," he said. The Dowager Blanche persuaded him to let me go in the end, for *appearance's sake*.' His voice was laced with pain.

'As soon as it was over, I left for South America. I didn't care where I went, as long as it was a long way from Montluce, and my father felt exactly the same. If it hadn't been for inheriting the throne, he'd have been happy never to see me again, I think, but when he became Crown Prince, he didn't have much choice but to be in touch. He'll never be able to forgive me, though, for the fact that Etienne didn't have time to get married and secure the succession.'

'There's a certain irony in that,' Philippe said with a sidelong glance at Caro. 'Etienne was gay. He was very, very discreet, and my father never found out.'

'You didn't tell him?'

'How could I? It would have destroyed him all over again. All he's got left is his image of Etienne as his perfect son. I'm not going to spoil that for him. It wouldn't bring Etienne back and, anyway, he *was* perfect and, clearly, I'm not.'

'But why don't you tell him that you've changed?'

'Who says that I have?'

'The old Philippe wouldn't have flown in emergency supplies,' said Caro, and he lifted a shoulder.

'It would take more than a few flights to change my father's view of me,' he said. 'My father isn't a bad man, and if it's easier for him to keep thinking of me as difficult, why should I insist that he changes his mind? He's had enough grief without me demanding his attention and approval. I'm not a child,' said Philippe.

'I think it's unfair,' said Caro stoutly. 'I think if they're going to make you regent, they should give you the responsibility to act too.'

'Lots of people live with unfairness, Caro. I've seen people struggling to get by without food or shelter or a stable government. They haven't got schools or hospitals. There's no running water. *That's* unfair,' he said. 'Compared to that, I think I can bear a few months of not being allowed to make decisions. I'll use the time to familiarise myself with how the government works and then, when I'm in a position to make a difference, I will. Until then, I can live with a few pointless rituals.'

Caro was still looking dubious. 'It's not going to be much fun for you, is it?'

'No,' said Philippe, 'but we're not there yet.' Leaning across, he turned up the volume on the sound system and slanted a smile at her. 'We've got about an hour until we hit the border. Let's make the most of being able to behave badly while we can, shall we?'

Caro never forgot that drive. The poplars on either side of the road barred the way with shadows, so that the sunlight flickered exhilaratingly as the car shot beneath them with a throaty roar, effortlessly gobbling up the miles and sliding around the bends as if it were part of the road.

The sky was a hot, high blue. Cocooned in comfort, enveloped in the smell of new leather and luxury, she leant back in her seat and smiled. The windscreen protected her from the worst of the wind, but a heady breeze stirred her hair and she could feel the sun striping her face while the insistent beat of the music pounded through her and made her feel wild and excited and *alive*.

She was preternaturally aware of Philippe driving, of the flex of his thigh when he pressed the clutch, the line of his jaw, the alertness of his eyes checking between the road and the mirror. He changed gear with an assurance that was almost erotic, and she had to force herself to look away.

Caro could have driven on for ever that morning, her face flushed with wind and sun and Philippe beside her, with that long, lean, powerful body, his smile flashing, his hands rock-steady on the wheel, but all too soon he was slowing and reaching out to turn the music off.

'Time to behave, I'm afraid,' he said. 'This is it.'

Tucked away in the mountains, Montluce was one of Europe's forgotten back waters, cut off from the great traffic routes where borders flashed past in the blink of an eye. Not only was there a real border with a barrier across the road, but there were two guards in braided uniforms. Caro began to dig around in her bag for her passport as Philippe slowed down.

'You won't need that,' said Philippe. 'This is my border, remember?'

The guards came sharply to attention when they recognised Philippe, who stopped long enough to exchange a few words in French with them. Caro watched the men relax. There was some laughter before they saluted smartly and, at a word from the officer, the junior guard leapt to open the barrier.

Philippe acknowledged his salute as he drove through. 'What?' he said, feeling Caro staring at him.

'That's the first time I've realised that you're royal,' she said. 'I mean, I knew you were, of course, but I hadn't *seen* it. Those men were *saluting* you!'

'You'd better get used to it,' Philippe said. 'Montluce is big on formality. A lot of bowing and curtseying and saluting goes on.'

'But you knew what to do.' Caro didn't know how to explain what a revelation it had been to see the assurance with which Philippe had received the salutes, how clearly he had been able to put the guards at their ease without losing his authority. Even casually dressed, there was no mistaking the prince. That was when it had struck her.

He was a prince.

CHAPTER FIVE

PHILIPPE might say Montluce didn't mean much to him, but a subtle change came over him as they drove up into the hills. Caro puzzled over what it was, until she realised that he looked at home. Perhaps it had been hearing him speak French. His English was so flawless that it was easy to forget that he wasn't British, but here he looked more Gallic than usual, his gestures more Continental.

It was a beautiful country, with wooded hills soaring into mountains whose bare tops glared in the sun. The smell of pines filled the drowsy air as they drove through picturesque villages, past rushing rivers and up winding roads dappled with the light through the trees. Caro felt as if she were driving into a magical kingdom, and she was sure of it when they came over the range and saw the valley spread out below them. A large lake gleamed silver between the mountains and the city of Montvivennes on the other. Caro could see the palace, a fairy tale confection with turrets and terraces made of pale elegant stone, and she couldn't prevent a gasp.

From a distance, it could have been made of spun sugar, mirrored serenely in the lake. She wouldn't have been at all surprised to see princesses leaning out of the towers, goblins guarding the gate and princes hacking their way through rose thickets. There would be wicked stepmothers and fairy godmothers, pumpkins that turned into coaches, wolves that climbed into bed and licked their lips when Little Red Riding Hood knocked at the door.

'Please tell me there's a tame dragon,' she said.

'Well, there's my great-aunt,' Philippe said, 'but I wouldn't call her tame.'

Montvivennes was an attractive city with the same timeless air as the palace. It seemed almost drowsy in the sunshine, the only jarring note being a group of protestors with placards clustered beside the main road that led up to the palace.

Caro tried to read the placards as they passed. 'What are they protesting about?'

'There's a proposal to put a gas line through Montluce,' said Philippe. 'They're worried about the environmental impact.'

A few moments later, they drove through the palace gates to more saluting and presenting of arms and came to a halt with a satisfying crunch of gravel in a huge courtyard.

'Wow,' said Caro.

Close to, the palace was less whimsical but much more impressive. The imposing front opened onto a square with plane trees. Behind, long windows opened onto terraces and formal gardens leading down to the lake, beyond which the hills piled up in the distance to the mountains.

Philippe switched off the engine and there was a moment of utter stillness. Caro saw two ornately dressed footmen standing rigidly at the top of the steps. It all felt unreal. Any minute now she was going to wake up. She wasn't really here with a prince, about to walk into his palace.

And then the footmen were coming down the steps, opening the car doors, and somehow Caro found herself standing on the gravel looking up at the elaborate doorway.

'Ready?' Philippe muttered out of the corner of his mouth as he came round to take her arm.

'Oh, my God.' Caro was frozen by a sudden surge of panic. 'Do you think we can really do this?'

Philippe put a smile on his face and urged her towards the steps. 'We're about to find out,' he said.

It wasn't your usual homecoming, that was for sure. No family members hurried out to greet them with a hug. Instead, they passed through serried ranks of servants, all dressed in knee breeches and coats with vast quantities of gold braid. Caro was all for vintage clothes, but that was ridiculous.

Philippe greeted all of them easily, not at all daunted by the formality. Caro's French wasn't up to much, but she caught her name and it was obvious that he was introducing her, so she smiled brightly and tried to look as if she might conceivably be the kind of girl Philippe would fall madly in love with.

She trotted along behind Philippe as they were led ceremonially to his apartments, trying hard not to be intimidated by the palace. It was decorated with the extravagant splendour which, like the footmen's livery, had been all the rage in the eighteenth century. There were sweeping staircases, vast glittering chandeliers, marble floors, massive oil paintings and lot of gilded and uncomfortable-looking Baroque furniture.

There were an awful lot of long corridors, too. 'It's like being in an airport,' Caro whispered to Philippe, 'and having to walk miles to the gate. You should think about having one of those moving walkways put in.'

Of course, airports didn't have footmen placed outside every room, presumably so that no member of the royal family would have to go to the effort of opening a door for themselves. As Philippe appeared, they would get to their feet and stand to attention, only to sink back onto their chairs when he had passed with a nod of acknowledgement. It was like a very slow Mexican wave.

Philippe's apartments were on the second floor of one of the palace wings. They were airy, gracious rooms, most with

views out over the lake to the mountains beyond, but imper-
sonally decorated.

'Home, sweet temporary home,' said Philippe, looking
around him without enthusiasm.

'It's not exactly cosy, is it?' Caro was wandering around the
room, touching things and feeling ridiculously self-conscious.
The rooms were huge, but knowing that there were all those
servants outside the door made it feel as if she and Philippe
had been shut away together.

Just you and me.

They certainly weren't going to be cramped. There was a
large sitting room, a dining room with a beautifully equipped
but untouched kitchen behind a breakfast bar, a study and
three bedrooms, each with a luxurious en suite bathroom.

'And this is our love nest,' said Philippe and opened the
last door with a mock flourish.

'Oh.' Caro made an effort of unconcern but all she could
see was the huge bed. The bed where she was going to sleep
with Philippe tonight. The fluttering started again in the pit
of her stomach.

'Plenty of pillows, as you can see.' Philippe's voice was
Martini dry. 'And the bed is wide enough to put one down
the middle if you're feeling twitchy.'

She was, but no power on earth would have made her admit
it.

I'm more than capable of keeping my hands to myself.

'You said yourself that won't be necessary,' she managed. 'I'm sure you have more experience than I do of these
situations.'

'I don't know about that. The pillow question hasn't come
up very often before, I must admit.'

No, because the women Philippe took to bed would be
sexy, sophisticated and size six at the most. They wouldn't
have to worry about holding in their tummies. Their legs

would always be waxed, their nail polish unchipped, their skin perfect. Caro was prepared to bet they never, ever dribbled into their pillows or woke up with mascara rings under their eyes.

'But then, you don't usually sleep with someone like me, do you?'

'No,' he said slowly. 'That's true.'

It was odd seeing her here, in her father's old jacket. She was completely out of place in all the baroque splendour, but her eyes were a deep blue and the sun through the window cast a halo of gold around the cloud of hair that tumbled to her shoulders. The formal apartments were warmer and more welcoming with Caro in them.

Philippe remembered quite clearly dismissing the idea that he might want to sleep with Caro. But that was before he'd kissed her. It didn't seem nearly so unlikely now.

She had wandered over to the window and stood there looking out, hugging the jacket around her so that he could see the flare of her hips. Her legs were strong and straight in the jeans. There was nothing special about her, not really. Other girls had blue eyes and creamy skin and hair that felt like silk when he slid his fingers through it. Caro was lusher than most, warmer than most, more vibrant than most, but she was still just an ordinary girl, Philippe reminded himself. Not the sort of girl he desired at all.

'I won't lay a finger on you unless you ask me to,' he said. 'So you can relax.'

'Oh, sure,' said Caro, turning from the window. 'Great idea. Relax. After all, I'm in a strange country, living in a palace and I'll be going to bed with a prince tonight. What on earth have I got to be nervous about?'

Philippe rolled his eyes at her sarcasm. 'Nothing,' he said. 'We're friends, remember?'

He could see her remembering that had been her idea. 'Yes,' she conceded reluctantly at last.

'And friends trust each other, don't they?'

'Ye...es.'

'So you're going to have to trust me when I say you've got nothing to worry about.'

Caro stood there, chewing her lip. 'You're right,' she said after a moment. 'I'm sorry.'

'Well, now we've got that sorted, we can get on,' said Philippe briskly. 'We've been summoned to an audience with the Dowager Blanche at four o'clock. Sadly, saying we're busy is not an option. At some time I need to see my father's equerry, too, but what would you like to do until then?'

Caro looked hopeful. 'Have lunch?' she said.

To: charlotte@palaisdemontvivennes.net
From: caro.cartwright@u2.com
Subject: I'm here...where are you?

Dear Lotty

I was going to ask where you are, but then it might be better if you didn't tell me, as I might not be able to withstand your grandmother's interrogation. She's pretty scary, isn't she?

Philippe took me to meet her today—oh, no, that's right, I didn't meet her, I was presented. And I had to learn how to curtsey! Philippe gave me a whole lesson on etiquette before we went. I suppose you take it all for granted, but I was completely bamboozled by everything I had to remember. I was really nervous, and I think Philippe was too. He had that aloof look on his face, the one that doesn't give anything away, but I noticed that on the way there (a five mile trek along the palace corridors, or that's what it felt like) he kept shooting his cuffs and running his finger around his collar as if it was too tight. He'd changed into a suit for the Dowager Blanche, and I must say he looked pretty good, although I didn't give him the satisfaction of saying that, of course. Philippe knows perfectly well how attractive he is, without me puffing him up any more.

Caro lifted her fingers from the keyboard and flexed them as she reread what she had written. Was there too much about Philippe in there? She didn't want Lotty getting the wrong idea. But how could she not mention him? She'd better make it clear that they had a strictly platonic relationship.

We've decided to be friends, which is great because it means we don't have to be polite to each other. He's certainly not polite about me. I put on my best dress in honour of the occasion (you know, the apple-green tea dress I bought last year) and he was beastly about it. I won't repeat what he said, but it was very rude. And I won't repeat what I said to him in return, because that was even ruder!

There, that sounded suitably casual and friendly, didn't it? Caro started typing again.

Anyway, back to the Dowager. She doesn't exactly operate an open door policy, does she? When we finally made it to her apartments, we had to go through endless antechambers, each one bigger than the last, and naturally we never had to do anything demeaning like opening a door ourselves. Instead, there was a whole army of footmen whose sole job seems to be to fling open doors. Weird. (Or maybe it seems perfectly natural to you???)

We eventually found ourselves facing your grandmother across acres of polished parquet. Philippe didn't tell me about that, and I'd worn my pink shoes, the ones with the kitten heels. BIG mistake! The floor was so slippy the best I could manage was a teeter and we'd just about made it when my foot skidded out beneath me. I would have fallen splat on my face if Philippe hadn't grabbed my arm. He's pretty quick when he wants to be, isn't he? I was mortified, but then I looked at Philippe and I saw that he was trying not to laugh, and of course that set me off, and I got the giggles.

Caro felt her lips tugging at the memory, although it hadn't been that funny at the time. There was nothing worse than trying not to laugh when you knew that you absolutely, definitely mustn't. With the Dowager Blanche's glacial eyes on her, she had had to bite down hard on the inside of her cheeks, and at one point she had been convinced that her eyeballs had been about to pop with the pressure of keeping the giggles in.

Still, I managed a curtsey, which I thought was pretty good under the circumstances but Philippe told me afterwards I looked as if I was laying an egg.

I wouldn't say your grandmother gave me the warmest welcome I've ever had. In fact, a midwinter swim in the Antarctic would probably have seemed balmy in comparison, but it was obvious she blamed me for you leaving. Don't worry, I played along and Philippe was brilliant! He lifted my hand to his lips and kissed my knuckles and told your grandmother that he was in love with me and that he would only stay if he had my support, so he expected me to be treated with respect!!!! He almost had me fooled.

She had better not tell Lotty that her hand had tingled all evening from the impression of his fingers, or that she could still feel the graze of his lips against her knuckles.

I could tell your grandmother didn't like it, but at least she didn't seem to realise it was just an act, so that's something. I had to sit through an icy interrogation about my family, friends, utter lack of connections (or job, come to that), but don't worry, I only gave her my name, rank and serial number. Actually, Lotty, I felt a bit sorry for her. I think that beneath all the guff about duty and responsibility and behaving like a princess, she's really worried about you. Can you get a message to her to say that you're all right at least? Don't say where you are, though, as she's ready to send in the entire Montlucian army to bring you back if necessary! But I think she needs to know you're safe—and I do too!

I suspect the grilling Philippe got was even worse, but it was in French so I didn't understand it. But when our audience was finally at an end we were both very relieved to get out of there. I had to hang on to Philippe as we walked backwards (!!!!!!) across that floor, and he kept hold of me when we were allowed to turn our backs at last and escape. We started off walking sedately through the anterooms, but the further down the corridor we got, the faster we walked, and by the time we reached the staircase we were running and laughing. It was such a relief to be able to let all the giggles out, and somehow it didn't seem so bad knowing that Philippe had had to grit his teeth to get through it too.

Caro paused, remembering how the two of them had run down the grand staircase, laughing. The steps were shallow and carpeted in red, and they swept round and down to the magnificent marble hall where an array of footmen watched impassively.

Philippe had let go of her hand by then, but his eyes had been warm and alight with laughter and that dark, sardonic look had disappeared altogether. Caro's heart had stumbled for a moment when they'd reached the bottom of the stairs and she'd looked into his face. It had been like looking at an entirely different man, one whose brother hadn't died, one whose father didn't blame him.

Shaking the memory away, she went back to her email.

So, I've survived my first encounter with the Dowager Blanche. It wasn't a complete disaster. For some reason her little pug—Apollo?—took a shine to me. He sure is one ugly dog! Difficult to know which end of him is less attractive. I was worried he was about to have a heart attack with all that wheezing, but he came to sit on my foot while your grandmother was lecturing Philippe in French about something, and I made the mistake of patting him. After that, he wouldn't leave me alone. I said I'd take him for a walk sometimes, which Philippe thought was heroic of me, but he was quite cute really, I suppose, and besides, what else am I going to do with myself? Philippe seems to be lined up for royal duties, but there isn't a lot for me to do except sit on the balcony and look at that beautiful lake (which isn't such a bad plan, now I come to think of it.)

It's beautiful here, Lotty. I don't think I'll ever find my way round the palace or get to grips with all the formality, but the setting is magical. Like being in a fairy tale kingdom, where nothing feels quite real.

I'd better stop. Philippe had to go to some reception for financiers, so I've had the evening to myself, and I thought it would be a good chance to drop you a line— or quite a few lines, as it's turned out. It's all so new to me, and there's so much I'd love to talk to you about. Can't wait to catch up properly when all this is over and compare notes!

Hope you're having a fab time out there in reality, Lotty. Let me know, OK?
Lots +++++++++ of love
Caro

When Philippe came back later that night, Caro was already in bed. She was sitting up against the pillows, a book in her hands and a pair of glasses on her nose. Her face was scrubbed, the cloud of chestnut hair tucked behind her ears, and she was buttoned up to the throat in a pair of old-fashioned pyjamas, patterned with sprigged rosebuds so faded they were almost invisible.

No sheer negligees for Caro, Philippe realised. No wispy lace or dainty straps designed to slide seductively over a shoulder. He ought to be glad that she had so little interest in attracting him, so why did the sight of her make him feel so grouchy?

'Don't tell me, they're vintage pyjamas?' he said, loosening his tie and trying to roll the irritation from his shoulders.

'As a matter of fact, I bought them when they were new.'

'What, when you were twelve?'

'I've had them a long time,' she admitted with a defiant look over her glasses. 'They're comfortable.'

'There couldn't be any other reason for wearing them,' said Philippe sardonically. She certainly hadn't bought them with seduction in mind!

So it was annoying to realise how appealing she looked, there in bed. The modest pyjamas only drew attention to her lush curves, and the glow from the bedside lamp picked out golden lights in her hair. Seduction was clearly the last thing on Caro's mind, but she looked warm and soft and inexplicably inviting all the same.

Philippe jerked his tie free from his collar with unnecessary force.

'How was your evening?' Caro asked.

'Tedious. I shook hands, smiled, pretended to listen intelligently to someone droning on about financial forecasts. Welcome to the exciting world of royalty.'

Sitting on the edge of the bed, he tugged off first one shoe, then the other and tossed them aside. 'And that was just one evening! I'm not sure I can stand the thought of another six months of this. I'm going to expire of boredom by the end of the week!'

'Lots of people have to put up with boring jobs,' Caro pointed out as his socks followed the shoes.

'Very true. But give me a night flight through a thunderstorm any day!' Philippe swung his legs up onto the bed and made himself comfortable against the pillows, linking his arms behind his head.

Coming home to someone felt strange. Not as uncomfortable as he'd thought it would be. In fact, he'd even found his steps quickening as he said goodnight to Yan and approached the apartments, and he'd been glad to see the light on in the bedroom and to know that Caro was still awake.

He'd been surprised at how pleased he was to have her

with him that afternoon too. Grimly enduring his great aunt's tongue-lashing, he'd watched her tussling with that stupid dog and felt a smile quivering at the corners of his mouth. Once or twice she had met his eyes with a speaking look, or the tiniest roll of her eyes.

Funny how the Dowager's lecture hadn't seemed nearly so bad when there was someone there to sympathise, to be an ally. To escape with and run laughing down the great palace staircases.

Philippe rolled onto his side to face Caro and propped himself up on one elbow. 'What about you? What have you been doing?'

'I emailed Lotty.' Abandoning the pretence of reading, she put her book on the bedside table and took off her glasses. 'I'd feel better if I knew she was OK. Wherever she is, it's going to be very different from here.'

'She'll be all right. Lotty's tougher than she looks.'

Philippe stretched, yawned and rubbed the back of his head. It felt surprisingly comfortable to be lying here, chatting to Caro at the end of a long day. He'd never done this with a woman before. They'd been lovers, or he'd been leaving. They'd never been friends.

'Did you have anything to eat?' he asked her.

Caro laughed, that husky, faintly suggestive laugh that crisped every nerve and sinew in Philippe's body. 'Have you ever heard that expression involving bears and woods?' she said. 'Of course I did! I felt really lazy ringing the kitchen and asking them to send something up the way you told me. I can't get used to not doing everything myself.

'It's weird with all these servants around,' she said, pulling up her knees and shifting a little so that she could look at Philippe. 'You must have half the population of Montluce working here!'

'Hardly that.' Aware of the swing of her breasts, her

scent, Philippe was horrified to hear that his voice sounded hoarse.

'They asked me what I wanted to eat, so I said could they let me try some Montlucian specialities? They sent up these amazing quenelles of trout from the lake, and the most wonderful tart made with apricots.'

Caro chattered on about food, and Philippe kept his gaze firmly fixed on her face so that he wouldn't think about how close she was, or how it might feel to undo the buttons on her pyjama top very, very slowly, to slide his hands beneath the soft material, to roll her beneath him and press his lips to her throat and let them drift lower and lower until she stopped talking about food and what the head chef said and—

'What?' He sat up, tuning in belatedly. 'You went to the *kitchens*?'

'That's what I'm telling you. I took the tray back so that I could ask the chef for the tart recipe and he was *so* nice. Jean-Michel...do you know him?'

'No,' said Philippe, who had never been to the kitchens in his life.

'He wrote it out for me, but it's in French, of course. I might have to get you to translate it. I can get the gist of it, I think, but—'

'Caro,' he interrupted her, clutching his hair, 'what were you doing wandering around in the kitchens? The footman is supposed to take the tray away.'

'Laurent?' she said knowledgeably. 'He did offer, but I said I'd rather go myself. I'm glad I did. I had much more fun down there.'

Philippe pinched the bridge of his nose between thumb and forefinger. 'It didn't occur to you that it might be inappropriate for you to be sloping off to the kitchens and being on first name terms with the staff? Everyone's watching to see if you're going to be a suitable princess, and fraternising with the servants makes it look as if you don't know how to behave.'

'One, there's no question of me being a princess, so it doesn't matter how I behave,' said Caro, 'and two, it's an absurd attitude in any case. This is the twenty-first century.'

'This is also Montluce, which is an absurd place.'

Philippe sat up and began undoing the top buttons of his stiff dress shirt and Caro looked at him sharply.

'What are you doing?'

'What does it look like I'm doing? I'm getting ready for bed.' His voice was muffled as he took hold of his collar and pulled the shirt over his head.

'Aren't you going to use the bathroom?'

Philippe's hands paused at the top of his zip. Caro was sitting straight up, the colour running high in her cheeks. 'You don't need to look,' he said. 'We're stuck with each other for the next few weeks. Don't you think we should at least get used to being comfortable together?'

'There's nothing comfortable about watching you strip off in front of me,' she snapped. 'I bet you don't even have a pair of pyjamas!'

'I can't rival yours for style, I agree, but I've got these.' He waved a pair of dark silk pyjama bottoms at her. 'I've had to get used to wearing them in this damn place. People are wandering in and out the whole time.'

Alarmed, Caro pulled the sheet up to her chin. 'Not in here?'

'Not unless there's a constitutional crisis, but you never know, so don't worry, I'll be decent,' said Philippe. 'But I'll get changed in the bathroom if that makes you feel better.'

When he came out, Caro was lying under the cover, holding it tight under her nose. A pillow was wedged firmly down the middle of the bed.

'I know what you said about having no trouble keeping your hands off me,' she said, seeing his expression. 'It's just to stop me rolling against you in the night by mistake. I think we'll both sleep better having it there.'

Philippe threw back the cover on his side of the bed and got in. 'If you say so,' he said.

To: caro.cartwright@u2.com
From: charlotte@palaisdemontvivennes.net
Subject: Re: I'm here…where are you?

I'm here, and loving it! Thank you so much for being there, Caro. Without you and Philippe, I'm not sure I would ever have had the courage to go. I won't tell you where I am, but it's wild and beautiful, and I've got a job!!! I'm doing all sorts of things I've never done before—peeling potatoes, answering the phone, writing a shopping list, making a pot of tea—and it's fun! I know you'll roll your eyes, but it's exciting for me. By the time I go to bed, though, I'm exhausted, so I'd better be quick. Just so you know that I'm fine, and yes, I've sent a message to Grandmère as well.

I know she can be daunting, but her bark is really worse than her bite. And if Apollo liked you, that will be a big thing. Grandmère might not let on, but she adores that dog. He's her only weakness, so I'm sure she'll be impressed that he's taken to you, as he hates everyone else and is always biting people.

I'm really glad you and Philippe are getting on so well. How well, exactly????? Should I be reading anything between the lines??? Tell me all!

Grosses bises
Lxxxxxxxxxxxxx

Caro was smiling as she read Lotty's message—only Lotty would be excited at peeling potatoes!—but her smile faded when she got to the end. How had Lotty got the idea that there might be anything between her and Philippe? She thought she'd been so careful to make it clear that they were just friends!

Not that there had been much friendliness that morning. Philippe had been crabby from the moment he woke up, and had stomped off to a meeting with the First Minister in a thoroughly bad mood. When Caro had told him she planned to take Apollo for a walk, he'd just grunted at her and told her to stick to the grounds—as if she'd risk taking the Dowager Blanche's dog out into the city. She wasn't *stupid*.

The truth was that Caro was feeling scratchy and out-of-sorts too. She hadn't slept well. How could she be expected to sleep when Philippe was lying next to her half naked?

Yes, he'd had those low-slung pyjama bottoms on, but that had left his chest bare. Solid, brown, tautly muscled, it taunted Caro from the other side of the bed. Her hands had twitched and throbbed with the longing to reach out and touch him, to feel the flex of muscles beneath the smooth skin. She'd tried not to look, but it had been impossible not to notice the power-ful shoulders, the fine dark hairs arrowing downwards.

Heart racing, blood pounding, Caro lay and imagined slid-ing her fingers through those hairs. His body would be hard, solid, *warm*. He was so close, too. It would be so easy to roll over and reach for him.

And that would have been a big mistake.

Thank God for that pillow.

She'd been too hot in her pyjamas, but she didn't want to thrash around in case she woke Philippe. As far as she could tell from her side of the pillow, he was sleeping peacefully, quite unbothered by her presence in the bed with him. She might as well be a *bolster*, Caro decided vengefully.

Eventually irritation had subsided into glumness, swiftly followed by brisk practicality. What did she think? That Philippe would take a look at her in her pyjamas and rip them off her? She *looked* like a bolster, and if she knew what was good for her she would behave like a bolster too.

Otherwise it was going to be a very long two months.

Well, there was no point in sitting around feeling cross. Caro finished the *pain au chocolat* that the palace kitchen had sent up for breakfast along with a perfect cup of coffee—she was going to be the size of a house, if not a palace, by the time she left—and pushed back her chair.

From the kitchen window she could look down at the courtyard at the front of the palace. Outside the railings, tourists milled around, pointing and taking photographs.

She belonged down there with the ordinary people, Caro thought, not up here in a palace, like a Cinderella in reverse, having her breakfast brought up by soft-footed servants. She belonged with an ordinary man, not a prince.

It wouldn't do to forget that.

The *pain au chocolat* had been delicious, but she wanted to make her own breakfast. Philippe was in meetings most of the day, so she could amuse herself. She would go back to the real world where she belonged, Caro decided, washing up her breakfast dishes without thinking in the kitchen. Grabbing her bag, she thrust her feet into comfortable walking sandals and set off for the great sweeping staircase that led down to the palace entrance.

She would go and explore.

CHAPTER SIX

INSTINCT led Caro away from the smart part of town and into the old quarter, with its crooked lanes and balconies strung with washing. Even at that hour of the morning it was warm, but the tall buildings cast the narrow streets into shadow and Caro was content to wander in the shade until she found herself on the edge of the market square, dazzled and blinking at the sudden flood of sunlight.

Settling her sunglasses on her nose, Caro took one look at the stalls selling a spectacular range of local produce and drew a long breath of appreciation. There were glossy aubergines, and artichokes and great piles of onions, stalls selling great hams and salamis or piled high with bread, or enormous wheels of cheese. Her bad mood quite forgotten, Caro drifted along, sniffing peaches, squeezing avocados, tasting tiny bits of cheese and hams that the stallholders passed over for her to try.

Her French was rusty, to say the least, but when it came to food Caro had never had any problems communicating. She pantomimed swooning with pleasure, which seemed so much more appropriate than the only words she knew: *c'est très bon*, which didn't seem at all adequate. It went down well with the stallholder, anyway, who laughed and offered her a different cheese to try.

Before she knew what had happened, she was being plied

with different cheeses and urged to try every one. Everyone was so friendly, Caro thought, delighted. They were all having a very jolly time. She learnt what all the fruit and vegetables were called, and the stallholders or her fellow shoppers corrected her pronunciation with much laughter and nods of encouragement. This was much more fun than sitting in the palace feeling cross about Philippe.

She would get some cheese and bread for lunch, Caro decided, and some of those tomatoes that looked so much more delicious than the perfectly uniform, perfectly red, perfectly tasteless ones they sold in the supermarkets in Ellerby. It was only then that she remembered that she hadn't had an opportunity to change any money yet. All she had was some sterling, which was no help at all when you wanted to buy a few tomatoes.

Caro was in the middle of another pantomime to explain her predicament when the stallholder stopped laughing and stared over her shoulder. At the same time she became aware of a stir in the market behind her and she turned, curious to see what everyone was so interested in.

There, striding towards her between the stalls, was Philippe, and at the sight of him her heart slammed into her throat, blocking off her air and leaving her breathless and light-headed.

Philippe was smiling, but Caro could tell from the tightness of his jaw that he was furious. Behind those designer shades, the silver eyes would be icy. Yan was at his shoulder, expressionless as ever.

The market fell silent, watching Philippe. It was difficult to tell quite what the mood was. Wariness and surprise, Caro thought, as she disentangled her breathing and forced her heart back into place. She could relate to that. It was what she felt too. Not that she had any intention of letting Philippe know that.

'Oh, hello,' she said, determinedly casual. 'What are you doing here?'

'No, that's my question,' snapped Philippe, who was gripped with a quite irrational rage at finding Caro safe.

Lefebvre, the First Minister, had spent the morning droning on about the increased threat from environmental activists who were protesting about some pipeline, although why he was telling him Philippe couldn't imagine. The Dowager Blanche had no doubt already decided what would be done.

He'd found his mind drifting to Caro. He'd been short with her that morning, but it wasn't actually her fault that he hadn't been able to sleep. Philippe couldn't get the image of her in those shabby pyjamas out of his mind. He'd imagined unbuttoning the pyjama top very slowly, slipping his hands beneath it to smooth over silky skin. Imagined hooking his thumbs over the waistband to slide the bottoms down over the warm curve of her hips and down those legs she insisted on hiding away.

This was ridiculous, Philippe had told himself, shifting restlessly. He liked women in silk and sheer, slithery lingerie, nightclothes that were feminine and flirty and fun. He was in a bad way when he was getting turned on by a pair of frumpy pyjamas.

The fact that he needed that damned pillow stuffed between them had left Philippe feeling edgy and irritable and he'd woken in a thoroughly bad mood.

When Lefebvre had finally left, Philippe had gone back to apologise to Caro, only to find the apartments empty. Mademoiselle Cartwright had gone out, the dolt of a butler had informed him when Philippe had established that she wasn't in the gardens either.

'She said that she wanted to explore the city. Mademoiselle Cartwright was charming,' he had added.

Mademoiselle Cartwright was a damned nuisance, Philippe

had corrected him, Lefebvre's warnings running cold through his veins. What if someone had seen Caro strolling out from the palace? She would be an easy target.

Yan had made him stop and work out where Caro was most likely to be. Anywhere there was food, Philippe realised, and they had headed straight for the market. It was that or trawling through every café and restaurant in town.

And now here she was, quite safe and obviously having a wonderful time, and Philippe was perversely furious, with her and with himself, for having, for those few minutes, been so ridiculously worried.

'I thought I told you to stay in the palace grounds?' he said, smiling through clenched teeth. Even though they were talking in English, he couldn't have the row he really wanted in front of all these people, which made him even crosser.

Caro looked taken aback. 'I thought you just meant if I was taking Apollo out.'

'What do I care about the dog? It's you I'm worried about! I told you that there's been unrest recently. I *told* you that's why Yan goes everywhere with me, but you, you toddle off on your own without a thought for security!'

'You also told me the situation wasn't likely to affect me.' Caro actually had the nerve to roll her eyes at him. 'So let me get this right…I'm not allowed to go to the kitchens, and I'm not allowed to go outside the palace either?'

'Welcome to my world,' gritted Philippe, still smiling ferociously. 'Anyone could have got to you without protection.'

'Oh, rubbish,' said Caro. 'Nobody's the slightest bit interested in me. Or at least they weren't until you appeared. If you hadn't come rushing down here, nobody would have had a clue I had anything to do with you at all.'

This was so patently true that Philippe could only grind his teeth and glare at her.

'Anyway, I'm glad you've come, actually,' she went on

breezily. 'I wanted to buy some of this cheese, and I was trying to explain that I didn't have any money.' Completely ignoring Philippe, who was still trying to make her understand the reality of the security situation, she smiled at the stallholder and mimed trying the cheese. He nodded, delighted, and cut off a generous piece, which she handed to Philippe, who was trying to talk about security threats.

'Now, try this,' she said. 'Tell me if that's not the best cheese you've ever tasted!'

Philippe felt the flavour burst on his tongue and he was gripped by a strange heightened awareness, as if all his senses were on full alert. He could smell the bread on a nearby stall, hear the murmurs of the people watching. And then there was Caro, her face bright, head tilted slightly to one side, blue eyes fixed on his face to see what he thought of the cheese.

Cheese! That was all she cared about! *She* wasn't knotted up about the night before. And he shouldn't be either, Philippe reminded himself, irritated. How could he be knotted up about a woman who dressed the way Caro did?

Today's outfit was evidently based on a Fifties theme. Some kind of red top and a turquoise circle skirt with appliquéd tropical fruits. Ye Gods! Only Caro could stand there covered in bananas and pineapples and look so right in them. She ought to look ridiculous, but actually she looked bright and vivid and fresh, and pretty in a quirky way that was just her own.

'Well?' she demanded.

Philippe swallowed the last of the cheese. If she could be relaxed, so could he.

'Very good,' he said, and repeated it in French for the stallholder, who puffed out his substantial chest and beamed.

'Can we buy some? I haven't got any cash.'

'I haven't either,' he had to admit.

They turned as one to look at Yan, who didn't miss a beat,

producing a wallet and handing it over to Philippe without expression while his eyes checked the crowd continuously.

'Thanks,' said Philippe as he flipped it open in search of cash. 'I'll sort it out with you later.'

Caro craned her neck to see inside the wallet. 'Fantastic,' she said. 'How much have we got to spend?'

She was very close, close enough for her hair to tickle his chin, and Philippe could smell her shampoo, something fresh and tangy. Verbena, perhaps, or mint.

They bought the cheese, and then Caro insisted on dragging him onto the next stall, and then the next. She made him taste hams and olives and tarts and grapes, made him translate for her and talk to people, while Yan followed, his eyes ever vigilant.

For Philippe, it all was new. Nobody had ever told him how to behave on a walkabout—the Dowager Blanche and his father were great believers in preserving the mystique of royalty by keeping their distance—but, with Caro by his side, chatting away and laughing as they all corrected her French and made her practice saying the words correctly, it wasn't hard to relax. People seemed surprised but genuinely delighted to see their prince among them, and he found himself warmed by their welcome as he shook hands and promised to pass on their good wishes to his father in hospital.

Montluce had always felt oppressive to Philippe before. He associated the country with rigid protocol and fusty traditions perpetuated for their own sake and not because they meant anything. The country itself was an anomaly, a tiny wedge of hills and lakes that survived largely because of its powerful banking system and the tax haven it offered to the seriously rich. Until now, the people had only ever seemed to Philippe bit part actors in the elaborate costume drama that was Montluce. For the first time, he found himself thinking about them as individuals with everyday concerns, people who shopped and cooked and looked after their families, and looked to *his* family to keep their country secure.

He'd never been to the market before, had never needed to, and suddenly he was in the heart of its noise and chatter, surrounded by colour and scents and tastes. And always there, in the middle of it all, Caro. Caro, alight with enthusiasm, that husky, faintly dirty laugh infecting everyone around her with the need to smile and laugh too.

'What are you planning to do with all this stuff?' he asked, peering into the bag of tomatoes and peppers and red onions and God only knew what else that she handed him.

'I thought I'd make a salad for lunch.'

'The kitchens will send up a salad if that's what you want,' he pointed out, exasperated, but Caro only set her chin stubbornly in the way he was coming to recognise.

'I want to make it myself.'

By the time Philippe finally managed to drag her away from all her new friends at the market, both he and Yan were laden with bags. He hoped the Dowager Blanche didn't get wind of the fact that he'd been seen walking through the streets with handfuls of carrier bags or he would never hear the end of it.

'You know, it would be quicker and easier to order lunch from the kitchens,' he said to Caro as she unloaded the bags in the kitchen.

'That's not the point.' She ran the tomatoes under the tap and rummaged around for a colander. 'I like cooking. Ah, here it is!' She straightened triumphantly, colander in hand. 'I worked in a delicatessen before it went bust, and I loved doing that.

'That's my dream, to have a deli and coffee shop of my own one day,' she confided, her hands busy setting out anchovies and bread and peppers and garlic, while Philippe watched, half fascinated, half frustrated.

'I thought your dream was to belong in Ellerby with the pillar of the community?'

'George.' Caro paused, a head of celery in her hand. 'Funny, I haven't thought about him at all since I've been here...' She shook her head as if to clear George's image from her mind. 'No, not with George,' she said, upending the last bag, 'but with someone else, maybe. The deli would be part of that. I'd know everyone. I'd know how they took their coffee, what cheeses they liked.'

She stopped, evidently reading Philippe's expression. 'At least I've *got* a dream,' she said. 'All *you* want is to avoid getting sucked into a relationship in case some woman asks you to do more than stay five minutes!'

'We don't all have your burning desire for a rut,' said Philippe. 'I've got plenty of dreams. Freedom. Independence. Getting into a plane and flying wherever I want. Seeing you wear clothes bought in this millennium.'

Caro stuck out her tongue at him. 'You can give up on that one,' she said, peering at the high-tech oven. 'I suppose there's no use asking you how this works?'

'I've never been in here before,' he said, but he eased her out of the way and studied the dials. If he could fly a plane, he could turn on an oven, surely?

'Brilliant!' Caro bestowed a grateful smile on him as the grill sprang to life, and Philippe felt that strange light-headed sensation again, as if there wasn't quite enough oxygen in the air. She was very close, and his eyes rested on the sweet curve of her cheek, the intentness of her expression as she adjusted the temperature.

Caro had her sights fixed firmly on her return to England, that was clear. Well, that was fine, Philippe told himself. He had his own plans. As soon as Caro had gone, he would invite Francesca Allen to stay, he decided. Her divorce should have been finalised by then, and they could embark on a discreet affair to see him through the last stultifying months of boredom here in Montluce. Francesca was always elegantly dressed, and she knew the rules. She had a successful career and the last thing she'd want right now would be to settle down. If Philippe had read the signs right, she was looking to enjoy being single again. She'd be perfect.

The trouble was that he couldn't quite remember what Francesca looked like. Beautiful, yes, he remembered that, but nothing specific. He didn't know the exact curve of her mouth, the way he knew Caro's, for instance, or the precise tilt of her lashes. He didn't remember her scent, or the warmth of her skin, or the tiny laughter lines fanning her eyes.

'If you're going to stand around, you might as well help,' said Caro, shoving a couple of ripe tomatoes into his hands. 'Even you can manage to chop up those!'

So Philippe found himself cutting up tomatoes, and then onions and celery, while Caro moved purposefully around the kitchen.

'How did your meeting this morning go?' she asked him as she watched the skins of red and yellow peppers blister under the grill.

'Pointless. Lefebvre is clearly under instruction to tell me everything but stop me from interfering in anything. Apparently, I'm to go out and "meet the people". It's clearly a ruse to get me out of the way so that he and the Dowager Blanche can get on with running things,' said Philippe, pushing the chopped celery into a neat pile with his knife. 'I'm supposed to be getting the country on the government's side about this new gas pipeline they're trying to put in but that's just my token little job.'

Caro turned from the grill. 'What pipeline?'

'It's taking gas from Russia down to southern Europe.' He pulled an onion towards him and turned it in his hand, trying to work out the best way to peel it. 'The easiest and most

convenient route is through Montluce, and the government
here has been in discussions with the major energy companies across Europe. We—as in my father and the Dowager
Blanche—are keen for it to go ahead as it will allegedly bring
in money and jobs.'

'So what's the problem?'

'That's what I asked Lefebvre but he was evasive and, when
I pressed him, he said that my father had made the decision
and did I feel it was important enough to challenge him when
he was so sick. So I don't know. People need jobs, and they
need energy. On the face of it, the gas line makes sense to
me.'

When the salad was ready, Caro tossed it with her hands
in a bowl and carried it out to the balcony overlooking the
lake. They ate at the table in the shade, and Philippe poured
a glass of wine, surprised at how comfortable it felt.

'I forgot to tell you,' he said, leaning over to top up Caro's
glass, 'we're dining with the First Minister and his wife
tonight.'

Caro sat up in consternation. 'But I thought I wasn't going
to any official events!'

'It's not a state occasion.' Philippe didn't think that he
would tell her that he had made it clear to Lefebvre that he
would like her invited. Even now, Madame Lefebvre would
be tearing up her seating plans. He wouldn't be popular.

Caro was looking dubious. 'Will it be very smart?'

'Very,' said Philippe firmly. 'Is it too much to ask you to
wear a dress made this century?'

'I can't afford to buy new clothes.'

'*I'll* buy them,' he said, exasperated. 'I don't care what it
costs.'

'Absolutely not, said Caro stubbornly. 'I'm not going to do
some kind of Cinderella makeover for you! That wasn't part

of our deal and, anyway, I don't want any new clothes. I've got a perfectly adequate wardrobe.'

Although that might not be *strictly* true, Caro conceded later as she contemplated the meagre collection of clothes spread out on the bed. She had two evening dresses, one midnight-blue and the other a pale moss colour subtly patterned with a darker green. She was fairly sure Philippe would hate both of them, but Caro thought they were quite elegant.

After a brief eeny-meeny-miny-mo, Caro picked up the moss-green and wriggled into it. It was cut on the bias so that the slippery silk hung beautifully and flattered those pesky curves. She smoothed it over her hips, eyeing her reflection critically. She didn't think she looked too bad.

The dress had a long zip at the back, and she couldn't quite reach the fiddly fastening at the top. Clicking her tongue in exasperation, she braced herself for his reaction and went to find Philippe.

He was waiting on the balcony, watching the lake, with his hands thrust in his pockets. He'd changed earlier into a dinner jacket and black tie, and he looked so devastating that Caro's mouth dried and her nerve failed abruptly. She stopped, overwhelmed by shyness. How could she ever walk into a room and expect anyone to think that she could attract a man like this?

Then he turned and the familiar exasperation swept across his face. 'Good God,' he said. 'Where do you *find* these clothes?'

Perversely, that made Caro feel much better and she stepped out onto the balcony. 'Online, mostly,' she said, 'although there are some wonderful vintage shops around. Do you like it?' she added provocatively.

'I'm not going to say anything.'

Caro laughed. She could cope with Philippe when he was being rude or cross. She could deal with him as a friend. It was only when she let herself think about that lean, hard body that she ran into strife. When she let herself notice the easy way he moved or those startling silver eyes.

The heart-clenching line of his jaw.

His mouth. Oh, God, his *mouth*.

No, she couldn't afford to notice any of it.

Friends, Caro reminded herself. That was what they were.

'Can you do me up?' she asked, glad of the excuse to turn her back to him. She had left her hair loose, and now she piled it on top of her head with her hand so that he could pull the zip up the last half inch and fasten the hook and eye at the nape of her neck.

Philippe didn't move for a moment, but then he took his hands out of his pockets and stepped towards her. His first impression had been exasperation that Caro was wearing yet another frumpy dress, but the closer he got, the less dowdy it seemed. She was standing, quite unconsciously, in a shaft of evening sunlight that made her look as if she had been dipped in gold. It warmed the creamy skin and burnished her hair, turning it to the colour of aged brandy.

He set one hand to the small of her back to hold the base of the zip still, and took hold of the zip with fingers that felt suddenly clumsy. Her neck was arched gracefully forward and he could see the fine, soft hairs at the nape of her neck. She smelt wonderful, with that elusive fragrance that was part spice, part citrus, part something that was just Caro.

Very slowly, *very* slowly, Philippe drew the zip upwards. He saw those tiny hairs on her neck stiffen as his fingers brushed her skin, and he smiled. Caro wasn't quite as indifferent as she pretended. That was good.

On an impulse, he bent and pressed his lips to the curve of her throat where it swept up from her shoulder, and she inhaled sharply.

No, definitely not indifferent.

'Th…thank you,' she managed and would have stepped away, but he put his hands lightly on her hips. Beneath his fingers, the silk shifted and slithered over her skin and every cell in his body seemed to tighten. So small a detail and yet so erotic, he marvelled. It was only an old green dress, it was only Caro, and yet…

And yet…

Philippe wasn't looking forward to the evening ahead. Lefebvre and the other members of the government would go through the motions with him, but their contempt for the Crown Prince's feckless son was thinly veiled. You had to earn respect. Philippe was OK with that, but it would be nice to be given a chance.

But he could forget all that with Caro between his hands. As he turned her, she let her hair fall and put out her own hands to capture his wrists. Her eyes were wide, the deep, dark blue that made him think of the ocean surging out beyond the reef.

'I don't think this is a good idea,' she said.

'What isn't?'

'Whatever you've got in mind.' A flash of the old Caro there, and Philippe smiled.

'I'm tense,' he said. 'I need to relax, and what could be more relaxing than kissing a beautiful woman?'

Faint colour flushed her cheekbones. 'It's just me. You don't need to bother bringing out all the old lines.'

'Maybe it's not a line,' he said. 'Maybe I mean it. Maybe you are beautiful.'

'I'm a friend,' Caro said with difficulty, but her eyes were snared in his and they were darkening with desire, Philippe could tell.

'A beautiful friend,' he agreed.

Dipping his head, he put his mouth to hers, softly at first, but when she parted her lips on a soft sigh, he deepened the kiss, startled by the jolt of lust. His fingers tightened at her hips, but the material just slipped over her skin and he couldn't get a good grip of her.

Almost reluctantly, Caro's hands were sliding up his sleeves to his shoulders, and with something like a groan he gathered her closer. There was a kind of desperation to his kiss as he fisted the dress over her bottom, then let it go in frustration when he realised he was holding silk and not her.

Caro was mumbling 'I'm not…I don't…oh…' but she was kissing him back, warm, generous kisses, and his head reeled with the rightness of it and the sweetness and the hunger.

The ordeal of the dinner ahead forgotten, he eased the zip back down and was backing through the doors and towards the bedroom when a throat was cleared somewhere in the room.

'The car is waiting, *Altesse*.'

Philippe sucked in an unsteady breath as he lifted his head. That was the trouble with having servants. They were always there, ready to remind you that you had somewhere to go, someone to see, something to do. They could never just *leave you alone*…

Squeezing his eyes shut, he fought for control. 'We'll be there in a minute,' he grated.

'*Altesse*.' The door closed softly behind the footman.

Philippe dragged a hand through his hair and looked ruefully down at Caro, who was flushed and trembling, mouth soft and swollen. 'I'm sorry,' he sighed. 'We're going to have to go.'

Somehow she managed a smile. 'Perhaps it's just as well. I told you it wasn't a good idea,' she added, which sounded more like her.

'I thought it was a very good idea. Didn't you enjoy it?'

Her eyes slid from his and she stepped back, away from him. 'That's not the point. We agreed to be friends.'

'Friends can kiss, can't they?'

'Not like that,' said Caro. 'I don't think we should do it again.'

They were going to have an argument about that, thought Philippe, and it was an argument he was determined to win.

'We'll talk about it later,' he said, taking her arm. 'Right now, we've got to go.'

Dinner was preceded by a drinks reception to which the great and good of Montluce had been invited to meet Philippe. Caro stood beside him, smiling and shaking hands. If she was feeling intimidated by the ferociously smart women whose gazes flickered over her dress, she didn't show it. Amongst all those elegant little black dresses, Caro looked gloriously different.

Philippe was proud of her. She *wasn't* beautiful, but he was having trouble keeping his eyes off her all the same. How was he supposed to concentrate on being a prince when his body was still humming with that kiss? When all he could think about was the creaminess of her skin, her warmth, the delicious softness shot through with excitement? When every time her mouth curled in a smile the blood drained from his head?

And when she was murmuring comments out of the side of her mouth that made him want to laugh and strangle her and carry her off to bed all at the same time?

The Foreign Affairs Minister came up to be presented. 'Look, Apollo's here,' Caro whispered in his ear, and Philippe found himself looking at bulbous brown eyes, a stubby nose and mournful jowls that gave Marc Autan an expression so exactly like his great-aunt's pug that it was all Philippe could do not to burst out laughing. Out of the corner of his eye, he could see Caro biting down hard on the inside of her cheeks. Shaking Monsieur Autan's hand and making small talk with a straight face was one of the hardest things Philippe had ever done.

'Behave yourself,' he said out of the side of his mouth when Monsieur Autan had at last moved on. 'You're going to get me cut out of the succession.'

Still, he missed her at the dinner, which was just as pompous and tedious as he had expected. They sat at a long table so laden with candelabras and silverware that he could only converse with the person on either side of him.

Caro had been put at the other end of the table, no doubt on Dowager Blanche's instructions. Her lack of French didn't seem to be stopping her having a good time. He kept hearing that laugh, the laugh that whispered over his skin and made his blood throb.

Philippe gripped his glass and glared down the table at the men on either side of Caro, who were so clearly enjoying her company. This wasn't the way it was supposed to be at all. He was the jaded one, the one who was always in control. The one who left before things got out of hand. He wasn't the one who sat there and longed desperately for her to notice him.

And then Caro did look up and their eyes met. She didn't smile, and nothing was said, but Philippe looked back at her and the awful pressure in his chest eased at last.

They were silent in the back of the limousine that took them back to the palace. Still silent, not touching, they walked along the quiet corridors and up the double staircase. Only when the last footman had bowed and closed the last door did Caro break the silence.

'I don't think we should do this,' she said as if they were in the middle of a conversation, which perhaps they were. Her voice trembled with nerves. 'I think we should stick to what we agreed.'

'You want to leave the pillow in the middle of the bed?'

'Yes.' She swallowed, knowing that she was doing the right thing but unable to remember why. 'You said you'd wait until I asked,' she reminded him. It was hard to keep her words steady when her throat was tight with desire and the air struggled to reach her lungs. 'You said you wouldn't sleep with me if I didn't want to.'

Philippe reached out and twisted a lock of her hair around his finger almost casually. '*Are* you sure you don't want to?'

'No…yes…I don't know,' she said with a kind of desperation, and he dropped his hand and stood back.

'All right.'

Her heart cracked to see the guarded look back on his face. 'Philippe—'

'It's OK.' He smiled, but it didn't reach his eyes. 'You go and put that pillow in place. I'll be out on the balcony.'

Caro sat on the edge of the bed and looked down at her shaking hands. Who was she trying to kid? Of course she wanted him.

And she could have him, she knew that.

She should be sensible. Philippe was never going to want to settle down and if he did, it wouldn't be with her. There was no point in dreaming about a future with him, but tonight Caro didn't care about the future. She only cared about now, and right then she wasn't sure she could bear to lie there in her pyjamas and know that he was on the other side of that pillow.

The boom and thump of her pulse reminded her of the pounding music as they drove through France towards the border with Montluce. *Let's make the most of being able to behave badly while we can*, Philippe had said as he'd turned up the volume.

Caro's head knew that she ought to behave sensibly, but

her body wanted to behave very badly indeed and, in the end, her body won.

And she couldn't undo the zip on her own.

Philippe was sitting on the balcony, beyond the block of lamplight from the open French windows. His feet were up on the railings, his face in shadow. He had taken off his jacket and tie and the white shirt gleamed against his throat. In silence he watched Caro as she paused in the doorway.

'I can't reach the zip,' she said.

He got slowly to his feet. 'Come here, then.'

Deliberately, Caro stepped out of the rectangle of light into the shadows.

'Turn around.'

She turned and lifted her hair as she had done earlier. Philippe took the zip and eased it slowly downwards.

The night air was cool against her skin. Caro drew an unsteady breath and let her hair fall without turning.

There was a long pause, and then Philippe gently brushed her hair aside to blow softly on the hollow of her neck. Caro shivered, so snarled in longing that she couldn't have moved if she had tried. She was taut, desperate for his touch, and when his arms slid round her to pull her back against him, she nearly wept with relief.

'You know no one's going to interrupt this time, don't you?' he said as he pressed kisses down the side of her throat.

Caro tipped her head to one side and closed her eyes with pleasure. 'Yes.' Her voice was barely a thread.

He cupped her breasts, his long fingers warm through the silk, then slid them lower, burning her bones to liquid, her blood to fire. His mouth was so wickedly exciting, his hands so insistent. Caro leant back into him, helpless against the hungry thud of desire.

'Shall I stop?' Philippe murmured against her ear.

'No,' she whispered. 'Don't stop.'

'I have to wait until you ask me,' he reminded her wickedly, and she could feel his mouth curving on her skin.

An answering smile curled the corners of Caro's mouth. 'Please,' she said. 'Please don't stop. Please make love to me.'

Philippe eased the dress from her shoulders. It fell in a puddle of silk and Caro turned to face him, her skin luminous in the dim light. Putting his hands to her waist, her drew her back against him. 'It will be my pleasure,' he said.

CHAPTER SEVEN

SHE had known it would be a mistake. Her head had known, anyway. Her body still thought it had been a great decision.

Caro lay on her side and looked at Philippe, who was sprawled next to her, his face buried in a pillow. She could hear him breathing, deep and slow. She wanted to lay her hand on his warm flank and feel it rise and fall, wanted to press her lips to the nape of his neck and kiss her way down his spine, vertebra by vertebra, wanted to wrap her arms around him and press into him, to lose herself in his sleek strength.

But then she would wake him, and she couldn't think clearly with those silver eyes on her. Caro tucked her hands under the pillow, out of temptation's way.

She needed to think, to get a grip on herself.

She hadn't known it could be like *that*.

Caro had liked making love with George. She'd liked the intimacy of it, liked the cosiness and the familiarity, liked lying next to him and feeling reassured that he wanted her.

There had been nothing cosy last night with Philippe. It had been harder, fiercer, more urgent. It had been hot and wild, and once slow and sweet. It had been terrifying and thrilling and extraordinary. Every cell in Caro's body was still reeling, drunken with amazed delight.

For her, the night had been a revelation. Philippe had made

her feel sexy exciting, *powerful*. Caro knew that she would never be the same again.

But she was no different from all the other women Philippe had made love to. Caro knew that too. She would be a fool if she thought that she could be. If all those sophisticated beauties hadn't been able to hold Philippe's interest, it was hardly likely that ordinary Caroline Cartwright would be able to, was it?

Her eyes roamed over him, lingering on the curve of his shoulder, the sheen of muscles in his back, the lean lines of hip and thigh. He was all sleekness and leashed power, like a big cat at rest.

How could a girl like her ever hold on to a man like Philippe?

She couldn't.

The pale light of early morning was sneaking through a crack in the curtains. It was time to start being sensible. Caro would have liked to have been the kind of woman who could enjoy a passionate affair without getting emotionally involved, but she had a feeling that it would be a lot harder in practice than in theory.

She was more than half in love with Philippe already, she acknowledged to herself in the half light, with her body humming with satisfaction from his touch. It wasn't surprising. She was only human, after all, and he was gorgeous and intelligent and funny and an incredible lover and a friend. What was not to love?

The fact that he would leave. The fact that he wouldn't, and maybe couldn't, love her in return. And even if Philippe were to think himself in love, it would only ever be on a temporary basis. Nothing in his experience had led him to accept that love could last. Abandoned by his mother, dismissed by his father...it wasn't surprising Philippe didn't believe in happy-ever-afters.

But that was what *she* wanted. Glow fading, Caro rolled onto her back and looked at the ceiling. She did want that happy-ever-after. She wanted to be with a man she could love unreservedly, who would love her back and let her stay and who would always be there for her. A man she could build a life with. A man she could be happy with.

That man would never be Philippe.

If she had any sense, she would tell Philippe it mustn't happen again. She would say that she wanted to go back to being just friends. She would put her pyjamas back on tonight and shove that pillow back down the middle of the bed.

Caro's body rebelled at the thought. How stupid for two single, healthy adults to lie side by side for two months without touching, without exploring the dark, delicious pleasure of making love, without giving into the passion that could burn so high between them. It would be a sinful waste.

Why *not* make the most of these next few weeks? Time enough to be sensible after that, Caro told herself. Here in Montluce, she was living a fairy tale. Living in a palace, with a prince, with a man like Philippe…how could it be real? One of these days, she was going to wake up and discover that she was a frog again, but it wasn't time to go back to the real world just yet.

She would have the next two months, Caro decided. Two months with Philippe, two months to learn about loving and living in the moment. She could allow herself that, surely?

As long as she never forgot that it would only be for those two months. The dream would end and she would go back to the real world, and that meant that she had to be careful. Somehow she would have to find a way of not getting any more involved than she already was. It would be easier for Philippe if she didn't spoil things by getting clingy and needy, and it would be better for her, too, to put up some defences before it was too late.

Beside her, Philippe stirred and rolled over, throwing an arm over her in his sleep and pulling her back into the hard curve of his body. Caro felt the weight of his arm and allowed herself to stroke it up from the wrist, loving its strength and solidity and the silkiness of the fine, flat hairs.

She just hoped it wasn't too late already.

By the time Philippe woke, Caro had showered, was dressed and had herself well under control. She hoped.

Yawning and rubbing his hair, he wandered out onto the balcony where Caro was sitting with her feet up on the railings. For once she looked positively normal, in capri pants and a sleeveless shirt.

In fact, Philippe realised, she looked more than normal. She looked fresh and pretty and glowing, and he smiled, liking the feeling that he was the one who had made her glow like that. He had a feeling that he was glowing himself. Last night had been unexpected. Incredible. Who would have thought it?

'There you are! Good morning...' He put a hand on top of Caro's head and tipped it back so that he could kiss her mouth but, although she smiled, she turned her head at the last moment and his lips touched her cheek instead.

Taken aback by her reaction, Philippe looked down into her face with raised brows. 'What?' he said. 'You didn't mind kissing me last night!'

Caro flushed. 'That was last night. It's morning now.'

'Yes, and it's early morning too. Let's go back to bed.' His hand slid down her hair moved slid beneath it to caress her neck. 'I missed you when I woke up,' he told her, his voice deep and caressing. 'What are you doing out here?'

'Thinking,' said Caro.

'It's too early to think,' said Philippe, but he pulled out a chair to sit down and put his feet up on the railings beside hers. 'What are you thinking about?' he asked after a moment. 'Last night?'

'Yes,' she said. 'And you.'

He slanted a look at her face, hoping to coax a smile. 'I hope you're thinking good things?'

'I'm thinking sensible things,' said Caro firmly. 'I'm not going to pretend last night wasn't fantastic, because it was. You know that. And I hope...well, I'd like to do it again—if you wanted to, of course,' she added quickly.

More relieved than he wanted to admit, Philippe grinned and reached for her hand. 'I think I could bear it. In fact, let's do it again right now!'

'I haven't got to the sensible bit yet.' Caro tugged her hand free with some difficulty. 'In the bedroom, at night, we can do whatever we want, but during the day, I think we should go back to being just friends.'

'What, so I can't kiss you or hold your hand?' Philippe tried for sarcastic but only succeeded in sounding put out. 'What, in God's name, is the point of that?'

'It would help us keep things separate.'

'Separate? What for?' He scowled. 'What are you talking about?'

Caro got up, hugging her arms together the way she did when she was uncertain. 'Philippe, I'm going home in a few weeks,' she said. 'I want to meet someone else then and have a real relationship. I don't want to be hung up on you. Can't you see that if we kiss each other like you wanted to do just now, it'll be so much harder to remember that we're only pretending?'

Philippe's expression hardened. 'I wasn't pretending last night. Were you?'

'We're pretending that we're in love, and we both know that's not going to happen.' Caro turned to look at the lake, picking her words with care. 'I don't want to fall in love with you, Philippe.'

'There's no danger of that, is there? You're always telling me I'm not your type,' he said.

'You're not, but who's to say what madness I'll take into my head if there are more nights like last one and if the nights turn into days? If you're…affectionate…I might forget myself and do something silly.' She mustered a smile as she glanced over her shoulder at him. 'You know how women get ideas in their heads!'

That was true, Philippe thought. Spend two consecutive nights with a woman and suddenly it was all about a 'relationship' and what he wasn't doing right. It was the reason he avoided intimate situations. So why was he getting all grouchy because Caro was suggesting exactly what he wanted?

'I've had my heart broken,' Caro was saying. 'I don't want to go through that again. I'd rather keep things in separate compartments.'

She drew a breath. 'Sometimes…with George…I was trying too hard to be what he wanted. With you, I didn't need to worry about being right for you because I know I'm not, and you're not right for me. I know I'm never going to have a proper relationship with you and it's…liberating, I suppose.'

Unable to meet his eyes, she stared fixedly at his collar-bone. 'But one day I'd like to find someone who *is* right for me and, when I do, I want it to be really special. I don't want to be so hung up on you I can't give myself completely to him.'

Philippe scowled. 'What are you trying to say here, Caro? I'm just a fling before you settle down with Mr Perfect?'

'No…well, sort of, I suppose.' Caro stepped back out of his grasp. 'I just want to enjoy myself,' she said. 'I want to have fun and not feel inhibited, but at the same time I don't want to get so involved that I lose sight of the fact that I'll be going back to Ellerby in a couple of months and then it will all be over.

'No strings, no commitment,' she said, her blue eyes direct. 'Strictly temporary. I'd have thought it would be your dream scenario,' she added with a touch of her old asperity.

It was. Philippe knew that he ought to be delighted.

'We're not going to convince many people of our supposed love affair if I'm not allowed to touch you,' he found himself grumbling.

Caro had thought of that, too. 'Obviously, I'll do whatever's needed to give the right impression, but when we're on our own, well, I'd prefer to keep any intimacy for the bedroom.'

Philippe eyed her almost resentfully. For someone so warm, she could be a very cool customer.

'So I'm to keep my hands to myself until the bedroom door is closed, is that right?'

'I think it would be easier for both of us,' she said. 'You don't want me complicating matters by falling in love with you, do you?'

Of course he didn't. Why would he want that? He'd spent his whole life running away from precisely that situation.

Philippe glared out at the lake.

'You do see that it makes sense, don't you?' said Caro after a moment.

'Oh, yes, yes, I suppose so,' he said irritably.

But it wasn't how he had planned to start the morning.

'Have you seen the papers today?'

The Dowager Blanche picked up a sheaf of newspapers and dropped them back on the table as if she couldn't bear to touch them.

'I haven't had a chance yet,' said Philippe, wishing he were down in the gardens with Caro, who had taken Apollo the pug for a walk.

'Your father gets up at five o'clock every morning to familiarise himself with the news before breakfast.'

Philippe set his teeth. He towered over his great-aunt, but she always made him feel like a grubby schoolboy. 'What are the papers saying?'

For answer, the Dowager Blanche picked up the paper on top of the pile and tossed it across to him. Philippe caught it and turned it round. The front page was dominated by a huge headline: *THE NEXT PRINCESS?* Below was a photo of the market, filling half the page. The camera had caught Caro popping a piece of cheese in his mouth. Her sunglasses were perched on her head and they were both smiling.

It was a good picture of Caro. Her expressive face was alight with laughter and fortunately the head and shoulders shot cut off most of her eccentric outfit. Philippe thought she looked vivid and engaging, and he…he looked *happy*, he realised with something of a shock.

'I could hardly believe my ears when I heard that you had been wandering around the *market*.' The Dowager Blanche's voice was like a lash.

Once she had been a great beauty. You could still see it in her bone structure and her famous elegance, but her expression was one of icy hauteur. She could hardly have been more different from Caro.

'What were you thinking?' she went on. 'We are not one of those populist monarchies, thank God. Your father keeps his distance, and the people are respectful. If you start behaving like the people, you will be treated like one of the people, and you will lose your throne before you have even sat on it!

'This…this *Caroline* is totally unsuitable.' She cast a glance of dislike at the newspapers. 'They're saying you're besotted with her.'

'Perhaps I am,' said Philippe, dropping the paper back onto the table and clasping his hands behind his back once more.

'How can you want her and not Charlotte?' The Dowager's

expression was uncomprehending. 'She's clumsy and badly groomed and she has no idea how to behave.'

'She's warm and friendly,' said Philippe. 'What better way is there to behave? And she may not be classically elegant, but she has her own style. She's…unusual.'

'She looks like a scarecrow,' said the Dowager, unimpressed. 'She's not even beautiful!'

'She is to me,' he found himself saying.

'Then you must be in love! How vulgar.'

Contempt dripped through her voice. Philippe inclined his head in courteous agreement, but inside he felt jarred, as if he had walked smack into a wall.

Love? He didn't do love. Lust, yes, he did that. And that was *all* he felt. He might want to smile at the thought of Caro. He might want to touch her and already be thinking about how he would tell her about this interview. Sometimes meeting her eyes might make him want to laugh, but that wasn't being *in love*.

His great-aunt was watching his expression and her eyes narrowed. 'You can't marry her,' she said.

Philippe turned abruptly and went over to stand by one of the long windows that looked out over the gardens. Below, he could see Caro, who was trying to teach Apollo to run after a stick.

She waggled the stick in front of the pug's nose, and then threw it onto the lawn. Apollo sat on his rump and looked at her blankly. Caro pointed at the stick, then demonstrated by galloping onto the grass to fetch it. She brought it back and dropped it in front of Apollo, who regarded it without interest.

Watching her, Philippe felt some of his frustration ease and the corner of his mouth twitched.

'Why can't I marry her?' he asked.

'I'd have thought it was obvious! You will be Crown Prince

one day,' the Dowager said. 'You owe it to your father to find a suitable bride. We don't want Montluce to become the laughing stock of Europe.'

'Several heirs to thrones around Europe have married commoners,' Philippe pointed out. 'It hasn't done those countries any harm.'

'Those brides at least look the part.' The Dowager joined him at the window. 'Can you say the same of Caroline Cartwright?'

She gestured down at Caro, who had repeated her demonstration with the stick and had stopped to catch her breath. Her face was pink, her shirt creased and her hair tumbled messily to her shoulders.

No, she didn't look like a princess.

Unaware of their gaze, Caro pulled a clip from her pocket and put her hair up in an untidy twist before fixing it into place and smoothing the stray hairs from her face. The shirt strained across her breasts as she lifted her arms, and Philippe felt the sharp stir of desire.

'Everyone likes her,' he told his great-aunt.

'The staff.' She waved a dismissive hand. 'I heard she's been hobnobbing with the footmen and distracting the kitchen staff. Tell her to stop it.'

'It's not just the staff.' Philippe crossed back to pick up the paper she'd shown him earlier. 'The people like her too.' He tapped the article. 'It says so here.'

A lesser woman would have snatched. As it was, there was a definite crispness in the way his great-aunt took the paper from him and reread the enthusiastic piece with an expression of distaste.

'*Everyone was charmed,*' she read, not sounding in the least charmed. 'Hmm.' Her expression grew thoughtful. Philippe could see her clever mind calculating.

'This English girl isn't for you, Philippe,' she said at last.

'You know that yourself. Perhaps you're jaded and she's a fresh taste for a while, but I don't expect it to last and, if you were honest, you'd know that too. As it is, you'll be bored in a month or so and then you'll be ready for someone more sophisticated again.'

And then I'll find Charlotte and bring her home, Philippe could practically hear her thinking.

'In the meantime, if you insist on keeping Mademoiselle Cartwright with you, we might as well capitalise on her popularity. She's new and different, so of course the people are enthused.' She shrugged elegantly. 'Take her with you when you go out on official visits. Perhaps she'll draw some attention away from all these pipeline protests.'

'It might be a better idea to talk to the protestors and settle the issue,' Philippe suggested and his great-aunt stiffened.

'Your father has already made a decision about the pipeline. These people have no business making a fuss about things they know nothing about. Camping on the streets!' She snorted. 'Ridiculous!'

'Perhaps they have legitimate concerns.'

But the Dowager Blanche was having none of it. 'That's not how things are done in Montluce. It is not for you to interfere.'

'One day it *will* be for me to interfere,' he pointed out.

'Fortunately, that day has not yet come,' she flashed back. 'I suggest you stick to what you agreed to do, unless you are hoping to drive your father to his death. He has already suffered enough from your recklessness and irresponsibility.'

She launched into a scathing lecture about his attitude, behaviour and prospects while Philippe gritted his teeth and reminded himself that she was an old lady who had lost both her sons.

'Leave the government to Lefebvre,' she said, winding down at last. 'If you want to make yourself useful, encourage your more famous—and sober—friends to come to my annual ball. It's in aid of an international medical charity, so it's a good cause, and some celebrity guests might lend a certain cachet to the proceedings. That's something you *can* do.'

Philippe thought about the flights he had funded, the planes he had flown into disaster areas, the boxes of tools and tents and water purification tablets that had helped people survive.

'Certainly, *Altesse.*'

When at last the Dowager let him go, Philippe went straight down to the garden to find Caro. She was sitting on the steps from the terrace with Apollo, both of them puffing, in spite of the fact that Caro had had about ten times as much exercise as the pug.

Philippe was aware of his tension loosening at the sight of her. 'It's like a soundtrack to a porn film out here with all this heavy breathing.'

Caro swung round, her heart lurching unmistakably at the sight of him, tall and dark and devastating in the suit he had to wear to meet his great-aunt every day. Every fibre of her sang and cheered in recognition. This was the man who had loved her last night, the man whose hands had taken her to mindless delight. Whose body she had explored, inch by inch. Whose mouth…

Stop it! Caro told herself fiercely.

It was too early to be thinking like that, but once that bed-room door closed tonight… She shivered in anticipation.

'I'm exhausted,' she said. 'Apollo doesn't seem to have the least idea of how to be a dog. He doesn't do walking or running after sticks or anything.' She fondled the dog's ears all the same. 'Do you, dog?'

Philippe's face was set in grim lines as he sat down on the steps beside her, hooking two fingers inside his collar to loosen it. He was looking forbidding, and Caro leaned against his shoulder, bumping it in greeting.

'How did today's ticking off go?' she asked, wanting to see him smile, wanting to see the tension leak from his shoulders.

'Oh, you know. I'm a disappointment to everyone. No sense of duty. Why couldn't I just marry Lotty, blah, blah, blah. The usual.' Philippe spoke lightly, but she sensed it was with an effort.

'Oh, dear, she's not warming to me, is she? After I walked Apollo, too!'

'She's hoping my passion for you will burn out before your wardrobe brings the entire state of Montluce into disrepute. Our little trip to the market didn't go down well,' he told her. 'You're on the front of all the papers.'

Caro sat bolt upright. '*I* am?'

'You're a celebrity now,' said Philippe, 'and now the Dowager Blanche is going to use you. You're to accompany me on the various visits I've got to do. The idea is that everyone will be so excited about what you're wearing that they won't be interested in the gas line protests. She's counting on a media frenzy.'

'A media frenzy? About *me*?' Caro stared at him in disbelief.

'Hard to believe, I know,' he said. 'Especially given your propensity for jumble sale cast-offs. You can start tomorrow. I'm opening a new wing at the hospital in the afternoon, so you can come to that.'

'But won't it look a bit official?' Caro pulled a face. 'Everyone will think we're about to announce our engagement if I start tagging along like that. I wouldn't have thought the Dowager Blanche would have wanted to encourage that idea.'

'She doesn't, but I managed to convince her that I am utterly besotted by you.'

Caro leant so that their shoulders were touching once more. It was amazingly comforting. 'She's still worried about Lotty, and she's fretting about us,' she said. 'Maybe we should tell her that you've no intention of marrying me. That would make it easier for her. You could say you're just obsessed with my body.'

'I could, but I'm not going to. Let her fret,' said Philippe. 'In fact,' he went on, smoothing her hair behind her ear and fixing his eyes on her mouth, 'let her fret right now.'

It was pathetic. The merest graze of his fingers and she went to pieces. Caro swallowed. 'I thought we agreed no touching when we're alone?'

'But we're not alone,' he said. 'My great-aunt is certainly glaring down at us from the window up there, and who knows who else is watching? There'll be some footman who might like to earn a little more by leaking how in love we are to the press. I don't think we should deny him his perk, do you?'

His hand slid underneath her hair and he tugged her gently towards him and, as he put his mouth to hers, Caro closed her eyes at the jolt of wicked pleasure. She ought to push him away, she thought hazily. This was a mistake.

But it didn't feel like a mistake with the sunlight spilling around them on the steps. It felt right, it felt perfect. Parting her lips with a little sigh, she abandoned herself to the sweetness that surged through her, and the current that ran like wildfire under her skin.

One hand rested on the stone step, the other crept up to Philippe's arm and she sank into him, giving back kiss for kiss until Apollo decided that he needed her attention. He started to bark and scrabble at Philippe until they broke reluctantly apart.

'Get out of here, dog,' said Philippe, telling himself to keep it light, not wanting Caro to guess how shaken he was.

'He's defending me,' said Caro, giving Apollo a pat with a hand that was still trembling. 'He thinks you're hurting me.'

'I'm not hurting her, mutt.' Philippe pretended to glare at Apollo and reached for her again, but Caro evaded him and got to her feet, brushing herself down.

'Not yet,' she said under her breath.

To: charlotte@palaisdemontvivennes.net
From: caroline.cartwright@u2.com
Subject: Waving and shaking
Isn't it amazing how quickly you can get used to things? I feel as if I've been living in a palace and hanging out with royalty for ever! It's only been a month, but already I'm an old hand at waving and shaking hands, and my curtsey is coming on a treat.

I'm not sure why, but your grandmother decreed that I should accompany Philippe on official visits—maybe she thinks I'll embarrass him so much he'll dump me in favour of someone more suitable, i.e. you? But you're safe for now. Philippe still can't accept that vintage is a style choice and is invariably rude about what I'm wearing, but otherwise we're getting on fine.

Caro stopped typing. *Getting on fine.* It sounded so bland, but she couldn't tell Lotty the truth. She couldn't tell her how Philippe closed the bedroom door every night and looked at her with that smile that made her blood zing. How they made love with an abandon that made Caro burn just to think about it. How the touch of Philippe's lips or Philippe's hands quivered over her body all day. Sometimes she would look at him and the knowledge of how the muscles in his back flexed at

her touch would thrill through her, and she would long for
night to come so that she could hold him again.

No, that was between her and Philippe. It was their secret,
their other life, the one she struggled to keep separate the
moment they stepped through the bedroom door.

Philippe has a punishing schedule, arranged by Lefebvre
and your grandmother to keep him out of mischief, he
thinks. Over the past month we've visited hospitals, in-
spected factories, attended receptions, sat through endless concerts and admired some really impressive charity
projects. I guess you're used to all of this, but it's all new
for Philippe as well as for me. I think he's really good at it,
actually. He always rolls his eyes when he sees what's on
the schedule for the day, but I've noticed that he's got a
real knack for seeming charming and interested without
losing that glamour that makes people feel special for
having the opportunity to meet him in the first place. It's
charisma, I suppose.

I tag along in the background. Philippe always tells me
I'm going to be bored, and sometimes when I hear what's
in store, my heart sinks a bit, but you know what? I always
end up enjoying myself. I've been overwhelmed by the
welcome we get. I know it's for Philippe, but sometimes
people call out to me and want to shake my hand too!
Little girls are always thrusting posies at me, and by the
time I get home—

Caro broke off. She shouldn't think of the palace as home.
It was a place she was staying for a couple of months and she
had better not forget it. Ellerby was *home*. She deleted 'home'.
She typed instead:

By the time I get back to the palace I'm laden with flowers. My French is improving by leaps and bounds, but I still need Philippe to interpret most of the time. I'm not sure he always translates correctly, because there always seems to be a lot of laughter, and I have a funny feeling it's all at my expense! But he swears blind he's not taking liberties.

So basically, Lotty, I'm having a great time! Even on the most tedious of visits, I can always catch Philippe's eye, which makes it easier to sit through some symphony of squeaky chairs or an earnest explanation of the difference between pre-stressed and reinforced concrete (bet you're sorry you missed that one!) It's hard not to enjoy yourself when everyone is so kind and friendly and nice to you all the time! Maybe I would get sick of it after a while, and I don't need to tell you how sore your hand is at the end of the day after it's been shaken a million times, but for now it's good fun. I've got the rest of my life to be just one in a crowd, after all!

Caro

xx

Not every day was taken up with visits. Sometimes Philippe had meetings with ministers or senior officials and, of course, he had to check in daily with the Dowager. Every morning a red box of government papers would arrive, which he would have to read and discuss with his great-aunt. Caro knew how much he loathed those meetings, and how torn he was between wanting to make some real changes and a reluctance to distress his father.

In spite of the difficult relationship between Philippe and the Dowager Blanche, Caro suspected that he didn't want to hurt her either, so he swallowed his frustration and talked about going back to South America, where he could fly and do something more useful than shake hands. Caro thought it was a shame. He had the potential to be a thoughtful and progressive ruler, if only his family would accept him for how he was.

It was hard now to remember how dismissive she had been about Philippe at first. She had seen him as a two-dimensional figure, a cardboard cut-out of a playboy prince, and he played up to that, as if he didn't want anyone to guess that beneath the glamour and the good looks, beneath that dazzling surface gloss, was a man of integrity and intelligence, who chafed at the restrictions of royal life, while yearning—Caro was sure—for his father's approval?

She fell into the habit of walking Apollo in the gardens whenever Philippe met with the Dowager Blanche so that she could be there for him when he came out. He was always rigid with frustration, and it took a little while to coax him back into good humour, but Caro made him stroll with her by the lake and, between the tranquil water and the mountains and Philippe gradually unwinding beside her, that soon became one of her favourite parts of the day.

By and large, they were sticking to their agreement, although Philippe cheated whenever they were in public. It gave him the perfect excuse to touch Caro: a hand in the small of her back to move her along, an arm around her waist, fingers tucking stray tendrils of hair behind her ears, a knuckle grazing her cheek in a brief caress.

'Just annoying the Dowager Blanche,' said Philippe, holding up his hands innocently whenever Caro tried to protest.

'Stop it,' she would mutter, but she didn't mean it. Ignoring the strict instructions of her brain, her body clamoured for his touch, however brief. She only had to watch him turn his head and smile at the crowd, or bend down to shake an old lady's hand, and Caro's treacherous body would clench with longing for the night to come.

She didn't tell Lotty that either.

CHAPTER EIGHT

To: caro.cartwright@u2.com
From: charlotte@palaisdemontvivennes.net
Subject: Style icon
Caro, you're in Glitz!!!! There was a whole piece about how you've revolutionized fashion in Montluce. I understand a vintage dinner jacket is now the must-have item in every Montlucian woman's wardrobe! I was drinking a cup of tea (I LOVE tea!) when I opened the magazine and nearly spat it everywhere when I saw your picture. Then I couldn't explain what was so funny to Corran and had to make up some lame excuse about thinking that I recognised you. I hardly did! You look like you'd be a fabulous princess. Why didn't we swap places before? Why don't you and Philippe think about making it permanent? It says in Glitz that he adores you…is there anything I need to know?????
Xxx Lotty

To: charlotte@palaisdemontvivennes.net
From: caro.cartwright@u2.com
Subject: Re: Style icon
Who's Corran?????
Cxxxxxxxx

Caro didn't want to lie to Lotty, and it was too complicated to explain the arrangement she and Philippe had made, so she left it at that.

In her inbox at the same time was a message from Stella, who had also seen the *Glitz* article and had made a point of showing it to George and Melanie. George looked sick as a pig, she reported gleefully, and Melanie wasn't looking nearly as perky now.

Caro closed Stella's email without replying immediately. George and Ellerby seemed so distant now. It was hard now to remember how desperately she had loved George, how hurt she had been when he had left her for Melanie.

She was glad that Stella had emailed. It would be too easy to start thinking that this life with Philippe could last for ever, too easy to forget that it was all nothing but an elaborate pretence.

It was time to get a grip on reality again, Caro decided. Already a month had passed. Only another four weeks, and she would be back in Ellerby. Back to where she could find the life she had always wanted: settled, secure, in the heart of a community.

A life without Philippe

She was going to miss him. Caro made herself realise it every day, so that she never forgot that it was going to happen. Because what alternative was there? Philippe wasn't in love with her and, even if he were, she didn't have what it took to be a princess. Her face wasn't right, her clothes weren't right and, however friendly the welcome she'd had at Philippe's side, *she* wasn't right either.

Anyway, she didn't want to be a royal, Caro reminded herself. She would go wild, hanging around with nothing to do but cook the occasional meal. No, she needed to go home and get on with her life. She had been thinking a lot about her deli, and how she could borrow enough money to set it up.

She wanted to stock some of Montluce's specialities. She had learned to make quenelles and the famous *tarte aux abricots* from Jean-Michel, the palace chef, who had given her his secret recipe when he recognised a kindred obsession with flavour. So she concentrated on that, and not on how much would miss laughing in bed with Philippe.

Philippe lay stretched out on one of the sofas and reached down to pull a sheaf of documents from the red box on the floor beside him. 'You wouldn't believe a country this small would generate quite so much paperwork, would you?' he grumbled, flicking through them. 'Report and accounts from the potato growers of Montluce… Waste management solutions for the city of Montvivennes… Forests have been felled to print these reports and who's interested in them? Nobody!'

'The potato farmers might be,' Caro suggested.

'Show me a farmer who wants to read a report!' Philippe looked up at Caro, who was sitting at the table, laptop open in front of her. Her lips were pursed, the fierce brows drawn together. 'What are you doing?'

'Checking my account at right4u.com… Can you believe it? I've only had *one* message in a month, and that's from Mr Sexy so it doesn't count.'

Philippe sat up. 'What are you checking dating sites for?' he demanded, outraged. 'You're with me.'

'Only temporarily,' Caro pointed out, cucumber-cool. 'I wouldn't want to miss out on someone perfect. The good guys get snapped up straight away.'

'You couldn't do any snapping up, anyway,' said Philippe crossly. 'You may only be a temporary girlfriend, but you've still got a good month to go.'

To his annoyance, Caro clicked on a link, and he got up to see what interested her so much. 'I wouldn't arrange to meet him or anything,' she said. 'I could just make contact and see if we've got anything in common. A sort of cyber flirtation. You don't want me to miss out on Mr Right, do you?'

Philippe was standing at her shoulder, glaring at the profiles on the screen. 'Which one is Mr Right?'

'I was wondering about this one.' She pointed at a photograph of someone who had called himself Homebody. He was a serious-looking man who described himself as loyal, trustworthy and affectionate.

Her hair was tumbling down from its clip as usual. He wanted to tidy it up, clip it neatly so that it wasn't so...distracting. Or did he want to pull the clip out completely to let the silky mass tumble to her shoulders? Did he want to push his fingers through it and tilt her face up to his?

Philippe scowled. That wouldn't be *allowed*, or at least not according to Caro's rules. He couldn't believe he had agreed to them. She was supposed to be his girlfriend. He ought to be able to put his hands on her shoulders, or kiss the side of her throat. He ought to be able to cajole her away from that stupid site and over to the sofa so that he could kiss her properly.

But they were outside the bedroom and there was nobody else around, which meant that he wasn't allowed to touch her at all. And he had given his word.

'Affectionate?' he jeered, taking out his bad temper on Homebody instead. 'You might as well get yourself a dog!'

'I think he sounds nice,' said Caro defiantly. She scrolled through Homebody's profile. 'Look, he's a teacher.'

'Why's that a good thing?'

'He'll be sensible, and reliable, and good with kids.'

'Not if he's anything like any of the teachers I ever had!'

She ignored that, and read on. 'He likes eating out and staying in—just like me.'

'Everybody likes eating out sometimes and staying in

sometimes,' said Philippe, determined to dismiss Homebody. 'That doesn't tell you anything.'

'You don't,' said Caro. 'When do you ever have a cosy night in?'

'We've stayed in a couple of evenings.' Philippe had been surprised how much he'd enjoyed both of them, in fact. He'd never done the whole lying-on-a-sofa-watching-a-DVD thing before. With a glass of wine and Caro commenting all the way through it, he had been able to see the appeal, definitely.

'Only because you're here in Montluce. You wouldn't do that normally, would you?'

Philippe couldn't remember what normal was any more. There was only this life, with Caro. Coming home from some tedious meeting and finding her humming in the kitchen. Enduring his great aunt's lectures, knowing that she would be able to make him laugh afterwards. Watching her engage with everyone she met, watching her smile, taking every opportunity to touch her.

Lying in bed with her, talking, laughing, making love.

Waking up with her in the morning.

That was normal now.

Sometimes he would sit on the stool at the counter and watch her moving around the kitchen while he told her about his meetings, and she listened to what he said, unlike the First Minister or the Dowager Blanche. She'd listen and ask questions and challenge him, and Philippe had a horrible feeling he was going to miss all that when she went.

Because she would go. She was always talking about her plans for the delicatessen she wanted to open when she got back to Ellerby. Philippe wanted to tell her to stop it, but how could he? It wasn't as if he wanted her to stay for ever. There was no question of that. He was only here until his father came home, and then he would go back to South America. He could fly when he wanted, party when he wanted. He could date sophisticated women who wouldn't know where the kitchen was. There would be risk and challenge and uncomplicated relationships. That would be much more fun than red boxes and watching Caro cook.

Wouldn't it?

'This Homebody guy sounds catastrophically dull,' he decided. 'You'd be bored witless at the end of one of those cosy nights in.'

'You don't know that,' said Caro, obviously perversely determined to see Homebody as the perfect man for her. 'Look, he says he's got a good sense of humour.'

Philippe was unimpressed. 'Everyone's going to say *that*,' he said. 'He's hardly going to admit that he's dullness personified, is he?'

'We've got lots in common,' Caro insisted. 'He ticks all my boxes: steady, decent, ordinary. A guy like that isn't looking for a glamourpuss or a sex kitten. He wants someone steady and decent and ordinary—like me.'

'I don't know why you persist in thinking of yourself as ordinary,' said Philippe, throwing himself back down onto the sofa.

He felt edgy and restless at the idea of Caro with another man. What if Homebody *was* the one for her? He would be the one coming home to find Caro pottering around in the kitchen. *He* would be able to reach for her in bed and have all that warmth and passion to himself.

Was everything he was showing Caro really going to benefit a man who could describe himself as Homebody?

'Ordinary girls don't dress out of a jumble sale catalogue, for a start,' he said, forgetting that he'd come to appreciate her quirky style. No matter how eccentric the clothes, Caro wore them with flair. Not that he was going to tell her that. It would be no fun if he couldn't give her a hard time about her wardrobe, would it? 'They don't spend their whole time in the kitchen or hobnobbing with the staff.'

As far as Philippe could tell, Caro was on first name terms with every footman and maid in the palace. She knew everyone in the kitchen, and had met all the gardeners on her walks with Apollo. She was always telling him about Yvette's worry about her elderly mother, or the fact that Michel rode a motorbike on his days off, that Gaston grew wonderful tomatoes or that Marie-Madeleine had a crush on the head butler, which no one, including Philippe, could understand.

'Ordinary girls don't have servants to hobnob *with*,' Caro pointed out dryly. 'I'm just being myself.'

'I still don't think you should waste your time on Homebody,' said Philippe, disgruntled. 'He looks shifty to me. What if he's a serial killer?' he asked, raising another objection. 'He's not going to put that in his profile, is he? It could all be a ruse to lure someone ridiculously trusting like you back to his lair.'

Caro rolled her eyes. 'I'd meet him somewhere public at first and, anyway, I've got to do *something* if I want to find someone to have a serious relationship with.'

'I don't know why you're bothering. I wouldn't waste my time on online dating sites.'

'You don't have to. I'm sure the women will all be queuing up to console you the moment I've gone!'

She could at least sound upset at the prospect, thought Philippe darkly. Scowling, he went back to the red box. 'Don't be ridiculous!'

'Is Francesca Allen coming to the Dowager's ball?'

Philippe looked up, eyes narrowing at the apparent non sequitur. 'She's invited, yes. Why?'

'I remember reading in *Glitz* that you and she had a bit of a thing going,' said Caro casually.

'Oh, well, if you read it in a magazine, it must be true!'

'Is it?'

Philippe opened the first file. 'More exploring the possibilities of a thing,' he found himself admitting. 'She's a beautiful woman,' he said, to punish Caro for talking about going home. 'I hope she will come to the ball. It's only a week or so before you leave, so it would be a good time to catch up with her again.'

He remembered being bowled over by Francesca's beauty when he'd met her. Maybe he would be again. Someone like Francesca Allen would be just what he needed once Caro had gone. They could amuse each other until he could go back to South America. Francesca wouldn't be interested for longer than that, anyway. Yes, she would suit him fine.

'She'd make a good princess,' Caro said in a neutral voice.

'If I ever think about marrying, I'll bear her in mind,' he said with a sarcastic look that successfully disguised, he hoped, the way the thought of her going pressed on his chest like a small but leaden weight.

Silence fell. Philippe forced his attention back to the contents of the red box. He skimmed through the first two files, dropping them onto the carpet when he'd finished.

'Now what?' he sighed as he pulled out yet another sheaf of papers. 'Good grief, a report on integrated weed management! Who writes this stuff?'

He took the first page and made it into a paper plane, which he sent sailing over to land on Caro's keyboard.

She threw it back. 'That could have a state secret on it. You should be careful.'

'Yes, I'm sure that intelligence agencies around the world are in competition to see who can find out how Montluce manages its weeds!' Philippe flicked through it. 'I don't know why they think I need to read this stuff, anyway. It's not as if anyone is interested in my opinion. That weasel Lefebvre just sneaks round to see the Dowager Blanche and does what she tells him to do.'

The weed management report tossed aside, he picked up the next file and pulled out a piece of paper to make another paper plane.

'Stop that,' said Caro, as it came sailing her way. She batted it aside. 'You won't be able to throw paper planes at Francesca Allen.'

'I'm bored. I hope you're not sending a message to Dullbody—' Philippe broke off in the middle of folding another plane. 'Hang on…'

'What is it?'

Frowning, he smoothed out the page once more. 'This is about the pipeline,' he said slowly.

'The one all the protests are about?'

He nodded as he read on. 'It's an estimate of costs. It looks as if the construction company are lobbying to build the pipeline overground, which would obviously be much cheaper for them. That's a little detail they haven't mentioned to anyone yet!

'What's the betting Lefebvre slipped this in amongst all these boring documents in the hope that I wouldn't notice?' His jaw tightened. 'They've spent a few weeks making sure I'm not expecting anything remotely interesting and now they're banking on the fact that I'll just scrawl my signature without reading this properly. Here, let me have that plane back, will you, Caro?' he said. 'I think I'd better see what that says too.'

Caro retrieved the page from the floor and sent it back to Philippe, who unfolded it carefully and put the report back together. Sitting up, his brows drawn together in concentration, he read it from beginning to end, so absorbed that he barely noticed when Caro got up to make some coffee.

There were footmen waiting outside, but she couldn't get

used to the idea of asking someone to go along to the servants' galley and boil water for her when she had access to a perfectly adequate kitchen to use herself. The Dowager Blanche, she had heard, insisted on a tray of coffee at exactly the same time every day. Everything had to be set out precisely, and woe betide the maid or footman who put the sugar in the wrong place, or piled the biscuits haphazardly on the plate instead of setting them out in a neat circle. Caro had heard that there was a plan of the tray pinned up in the servants' galley but she thought this was probably a myth.

Philippe was looking very grim by the time he had finished reading He gathered the papers together neatly and put them back in the file. 'I think it's time I had a little chat with the Dowager Blanche,' he said.

Philippe was preoccupied as he made his way back to his apartments. The footman—Guillaume?—leapt to open the door, and he nodded absently in thanks.

As the door closed behind him, he looked around, struck by how homely the apartments felt now. It was hard to put a finger on just why they were more welcoming. It could have been something to do with the recipe book face down on the coffee table, the cardigan tossed over the arm of the sofa.

Or maybe it was the smells drifting out from the kitchen. He usually found Caro there, her face intent as she chopped and stirred. For someone so messy, she was extraordinarily calm and organised when she was cooking and she produced mouth-watering delicacies, pâtés and little tarts and savoury pastries which she brought out for him to taste. He would need to start taking some exercise or he'd put on weight, Philippe thought.

She appeared now, wooden spoon in one hand. 'How did you get on with the Dowager?'

'Pretty much as you'd expect.' Philippe yanked at his tie

to loosen it and unbuttoned his collar. There was no question of popping in on his great-aunt. He'd had to wait until the next day, and put on a suit before he could see her. 'I'm not to interfere. Montluce has a delicate relationship with its powerful neighbours, and we can't jeopardise the little influence we have. My father made his wishes known, and I'm to sign the agreement on his behalf and stop asking questions. Et cetera, et cetera, et cetera.'

'What are you going to do now?' asked Caro.

'I don't know.' Philippe paced restlessly, rolling his shoulders in frustration. 'Let's get out of here, for a start,' he decided abruptly.

They drove up into the mountains, Yan shadowing as always in the black SUV. Philippe drove in silence and Caro let him think without interruption. The sun flickered through the trees and the air was heady with the scent of the pines that lined the winding road.

Away from Montvivennes, the roads were quiet and when they dropped at last into a valley and stopped beside a broad, shallow river it was hard to believe that they were only an hour from the bustling city.

'Let's walk for a bit,' said Philippe.

Yan waited with the cars and they followed the riverbank until the water split around a cluster of boulders deposited by a long-vanished glacier, forming deep green pools. It was very quiet, just the sound of the river and an insect droning somewhere. Caro sat on the smooth rock and took off her sandals so that she could dangle her feet in the water.

'It's so peaceful here.' Leaning back on her hands, she drew a deep breath of pine-scented air. Beside her in the dappled sunlight, Philippe had rolled up his trousers and his feet hung next to hers in the clear, clear water. 'I'm glad we came out.'

She glanced at Philippe. 'You've been here before?'

'This was Etienne's favourite place,' he said slowly, looking around as if comparing it to his memories. 'Our father would bring us up here sometimes, until Etienne grew out of splashing around in rock pools.'

He didn't need to add that his father hadn't thought to bring his younger son on his own.

Deep in thought, Philippe looked down at their feet dangling together in the water, and Caro let her gaze rest hungrily on the uncompromising planes and angles of his face. She knew him so well now. She knew exactly how his hair grew at his temples, how the laughter lines fanned his eyes. She knew the texture of his skin and the precise line of his jaw and his mouth…that mouth that made her heart turn over every time she looked at it.

'This is where the pipeline will go.' Philippe lifted his head and looked around at the peaceful scene. 'It's going to rip through this valley, with no effort made to disguise it, and then they'll blast through those hills there, and push it through into the valley beyond. This river will never be the same.'

Caro was dismayed. 'How can they even think about it?'

'There are only a few villages in this valley. Yes, it's beautiful, but what is one valley compared to the energy needs of millions of people? It's not as if Europe is short of beautiful valleys either, they'll say. And who cares about Montluce, anyway?'

'You do,' said Caro, and he turned his head to meet her eyes for a long moment.

'I can refuse to sign the agreement,' he said. 'I can say that the plan is unacceptable as it stands at the moment, and that construction and energy companies are exploiting our need for international support. I can say that the environmental cost is too high. But, if I do, my father will take it as a direct rejection of his authority. He's over his operation, so that's something, but what if the stress affects him the way they say it might? I don't want to be responsible for my father's death as well as my brother's,' he finished bitterly.

'He won't die,' said Caro. 'He's just using his illness to manipulate you, and it's not fair. You can't threaten to collapse every time your will is crossed!'

'You're probably right,' he said after a moment. 'The best case scenario is that he loses his temper with no side effects. I can live with that, but he won't forgive me.'

Behind the matter-of-factness, Caro could sense what a difficult decision it was for Philippe and her heart ached for him. He might say that he was resigned to his family's contempt, but deep down she knew that he yearned for his father to accept him, to approve of him, to forgive him for living when his brother died. It wasn't too much to ask, surely?

Philippe was watching the mountains. 'But it's not just about me and my father, I know that,' he said after a moment. 'I've been thinking about all the people I've met over last few weeks. Decent, ordinary people, who have trusted my family for centuries to do the right thing for the country. Montluce is theirs. They don't want it ripped up and exploited unnecessarily, and if I'm in a position to make sure that doesn't happen, I can't let them down. I can do what's right for them, or for my father, but not both.'

Caro didn't answer immediately. She was trying to find an answer that would make the decision easy for Philippe, but she couldn't do it. 'Your father trusts you to do the right thing, or he'd never have made you regent,' she said gently, but Philippe shook his head.

'He'll never trust me.'

The bleakness in his face made Caro put out a hand without thinking. 'Give him a reason to trust you now,' she said, twining her fingers with his. '*I* trust you.'

Philippe looked down at their linked hands. 'You're touching me,' he said.

'I know.'

'There's no one around to see us.'

A smile trembled on her lips. 'I know.'

He smiled too, then, and leant towards her, and Caro met him halfway for a kiss that made her senses reel with its sweetness. Disentangling their hands, she slid her arms around his neck and pressed into him, and when Philippe kissed her again something unlocked inside her and she abandoned herself to the rush of pleasure. The sunlight poured around them, in them, spilling through Caro, and there was nothing but Philippe, the taste of him and the feel of him and the rightness of being in his arms.

'We'd better go back,' Philippe sighed against her hair a long time later, and Caro didn't resist when he took her hand as they walked back to the car.

Fishing the car key out of his pocket, he held it out to Caro. 'Do you want to drive?'

Caro's mouth dropped open. 'You'd let me drive?'

'If you want to.'

She took the key slowly. 'I thought you'd have to be besotted to let a woman drive your car?'

'Maybe I am,' said Philippe.

There was uproar when Philippe announced that he was refusing permission for the pipeline to go ahead under the existing agreement. The Dowager Blanche was incandescent, and there were worried reports about the Crown Prince's condition from the doctors in Paris. Lefebvre and the Montlucian government quailed before the might of the great energy companies and all those invested in them.

But the people cheered. On the way back from the river, Caro had dropped Philippe at the protestors' camp and he'd walked calmly into the middle of the angry mob. 'I'll listen,' he had said. 'Let's see if we can work something out.'

Dismissing Lefebvre's spluttering objections, Philippe re-negotiated the pipeline deal over the course of a long and bruising session, at the end of which it was agreed that the pipeline would be laid underground, not just in Montluce but along the entire route. Jobs would still be created, energy still supplied, but Philippe had won a package of concessions on the environment that the protestors had put forward.

The public response was astonishing. Philippe's stand made headlines across Europe. *Plucky little Montluce takes on energy giants* trumpeted the headlines. Suddenly everybody wanted to know about the country and visitors poured in, to the delight of the fledgling tourist trade.

Philippe himself missed most of the excitement. He went to Paris to tell his father in person about the agreement he had made on his behalf. 'He may refuse to see me,' he told Caro, 'but I have to try. Will you be all right here on your own for a couple of days?'

'Of course,' she said. 'Don't worry about me. I hope your father's proud of you, Philippe,' she added. 'I am.'

Barely had Philippe left the palace before Caro was summoned to see the Dowager Blanche.

It was soon clear who the Dowager blamed for Philippe's rebellion. Caro had never been subject to the full force of the Dowager's anger before, and she was more daunted than she wanted to admit, but she thought of how often Philippe had endured tongue-lashings from his great-aunt and gritted her teeth. Arguing would only make things worse, she knew, but when the Dowager started on Philippe, she could hold her tongue no longer.

'He is *not* spoilt!' she said furiously. 'How could he be spoilt when nobody in his family apart from his brother has ever given him any attention or credit for anything he does? And he's not selfish, either! A selfish man would have left the father who had ignored him for years to deal with his cancer by himself. Philippe didn't do that. He gave up his life and came back, and he's had nothing but contempt from you and everyone else as a result.'

The Dowager was outraged. 'How dare you speak to me like that?'

'I dare because no one else will speak up for Philippe, and the truth is that he cares for you too much to tell you this himself. But you should look around you, *Altesse*. The people outside the gates don't despise him. They think he's going to be a bold, innovative prince who will take this country into the twenty-first century a decade after the rest of the world. They like him. He's not stuffy or aloof. He's warm and accessible and he listens. He is a good man who's just discovering what he can do with his position.'

'He's gone directly against his father's wishes and my wishes and the wishes of the government in the matter of this pipeline,' said the Dowager, her voice icy with fury.

'He hasn't done it lightly, but he knows it's the right thing to do. Philippe isn't thinking about what's easy for himself, or even what's easy for you. He's thinking about what's right for Montluce.'

'*We* will decide what's right for this country!'

'No,' said Caro. 'The people will decide.'

Philippe returned two days later to a rapturous welcome that moved him more than he wanted to admit. People lined the streets, cheering as the cavalcade from the border swept past and outside the palace, they thronged around the roundabout.

He wished Caro was with him to share it.

She was waiting for him in the apartments, and Philippe's heart contracted at the sight of her smile. The footman closed the door behind him and she threw herself at him with a squeal of excitement. 'You're a hero!' she said as he swung her round. 'Have you seen the papers?'

'Some of them.' Philippe grinned, pleased by her reaction. 'But I wouldn't have been able to do it without you, Caro.'

'Me? I didn't do anything!'

'I wouldn't have had the courage to stick to my guns without you,' he said seriously. 'I'm not sure I would have cared enough.'

'But you care now.' Belatedly, Caro realised that she was still clinging to him and disentangled herself. 'This is your place, Philippe. You can make a difference here.'

'Perhaps.'

He told her about his father, who had been on the point of disinheriting him before it became clear just how popular Philippe's stand had been. 'He bawled me out for not following orders, of course, but in the end he acknowledged that it hadn't been a bad decision. Coming from him, that's high praise!'

'That's good,' said Caro, pleased. Personally, she thought the Crown Prince should have gone down on his knees and thanked Philippe for single-handedly transforming Montluce's standing in the world, but 'not a bad decision' was progress of sorts.

Philippe picked up a book Caro had been reading and made a show of looking at it. 'He asked if I would stay on after he gets back,' he said abruptly, dropping the book back on the table. 'He thinks he'll find it more tiring now, and I could take on some of his duties.'

'What did you say?'

'I said I would as long as I could continue to take some decisions.'

'Well…' Caro's smile seemed forced. 'That's great.'

CHAPTER NINE

THERE was a long pause. Philippe could practically see the excitement draining out of the air.

Caro hugged her arms together. 'This changes things, doesn't it?' she said at last.

'In what way?'

'Well, now you're ready to be here permanently, you really need the right kind of woman by your side,' she said with difficulty. 'Maybe the Dowager was right about that, at least. You should be looking for a princess.'

Philippe stiffened, instinctively resisting the suggestion. 'I don't have to think about that yet.'

'Why wait? There's no point in us pretending much longer if you're going to stay anyway. I'm just a distraction, Philippe,' said Caro. 'It's been fun, but I think it's time I went home.'

A cold feeling settled in the pit of Philippe's belly. 'You said you'd stay two months.'

'That's only a week or so away. I'm ready to go back,' she said. 'I want to be ordinary again.' She smiled brightly at him. 'All of this...it's been amazing, and I'll never forget this time we've spent together, but none of it's been real, has it?'

It had felt real to Philippe. Smoothing his hands over her skin, listening to her breathe, watching her sleep. The taste of her, the smell of her. That had all been real.

Caro moistened her lips as if unnerved by his silence. 'I've had enough of the fairy tale. I'm not what you need, Philippe, and you can't give me what I really want. I need to go home and meet someone I can build a real relationship with. A real life.'

You can't give me what I really want.

Philippe's face was shuttered. It was true. Caro deserved to be loved in a way he never could. She deserved commitment and security and a belief in happy-ever-afters that he just couldn't give her.

'Very well,' he said, his voice tight.

Caro had done exactly what she had promised to do. She had enjoyed herself, but she had never forgotten that it was all a pretence, and now she had had enough of pretending. It had just been *fun* for her.

The cold feeling solidified into a stone lodged deep inside him. He wasn't going to show her how hurt he was. He *wasn't*.

'If that's how you feel,' he said, 'I'll make arrangements for you to fly home tomorrow.'

The Dowager Blanche, however, had other ideas. Before Philippe had a chance to arrange anything, they were both summoned to see her.

'I think she's going to have my head chopped off for insubordination,' said Caro nervously. 'We had a bit of a row last time.'

'You *argued* with the Dowager? You're a brave woman!'

The Dowager looked coldly at Caro when she curtsied before her but, instead of whipping out the blindfold, she gestured them both to the sofa opposite. This was possibly the most uncomfortable piece of furniture Caro had ever sat on. Designed for elaborate hooped skirts, there were no cushions so you had to sit bolt upright, and its gilt legs were so spindly that Caro was afraid the whole thing would collapse when Philippe sat beside her.

There was a frigid silence, broken by Apollo's wheezing as he recognised Caro. He waddled over to wag his bottom at her, and she patted his head.

'Good boy,' she said. He was never going to be the most beautiful dog in the world, and he had steadfastly refused to compromise his dignity by running after a stick, but she was quite fond of him now.

The Dowager was sitting very erect on the facing sofa. 'Well, I see you have been putting Montluce on the map,' she said to Philippe with a true aristocrat's disdain for popularity. 'I was disappointed that you directly disobeyed your father, I admit, but it seems that the decision is not *quite* the disaster we feared it would be. Indeed, your father tells me that you will be staying on to share his duties with him. I am pleased to hear it. You have learnt responsibility, it seems.'

Philippe manufactured a smile and kept his reflections to himself. 'I hope so.'

'I am getting old,' she said, not looking in the least old with her gimlet eyes and rigidly elegant posture. 'Hosting the ball this year will be too much for me. It is time to hand on responsibility to the next generation, so I would like you two to host it on my behalf.'

She ignored the aghast look that Philippe and Caro exchanged. 'Mademoiselle Cartwright tells me that you are much more competent than I give you credit for,' she added to Philippe in her crisp tones. 'I trust that, between you, you can manage a ball without creating the kind of furore we've seen over the last few days?'

'You can't go now,' Philippe muttered to Caro when the Dowager finally let them go. 'I'm not hosting that ball on my own!'

'I've never even *been* to a ball,' objected Caro. 'I haven't got a clue what to do.'

'You just have to stand there and greet people when they

come in. Look as if you're enjoying yourself, and I know you can do that.' He stopped halfway down the great sweeping staircase. 'I know you want to go, Caro,' he said, 'but please stay until after that.'

Caro bit her lip. The ball would be the first time the Dowager had trusted Philippe with anything, and it was an important test. She couldn't leave him to do it on his own, apparently abandoned by his girlfriend only days before.

'All right,' she said. 'I'll stay for the ball, but then I'll go.'

This was one last thing she could do for Philippe. She would stand by his side and help him show the Dowager Blanche what a great prince he could be if given the chance.

And that meant looking the part for once, Caro decided. This was one occasion her vintage clothes just wouldn't do.

There was an extra buzz of excitement about the preparations for the ball that year. Montluce wasn't used to being in the news, and it suddenly found itself at the top of the cool destinations list. Two days before the ball, Philippe's A-list friends began to arrive, exclaiming at the quaintness of the country. The jet set were enchanted to discover that this was one place they couldn't jet to, and that made it all the more charming.

Philippe was torn between pride in his country and a sense of dislocation. These were his friends. He had partied with them, danced with them, skied with them, dined with them… they shouldn't feel like strangers, but they did. Only Jack, fellow black sheep and hellraising companion for many years was the same.

'I like Caro,' he said to Philippe. 'She's not your usual type.'

'No,' said Philippe shortly. He was trying not to think about Caro.

They were having dinner, about twenty of them, and in one

of her mad vintage outfits, Caro was outshone by everyone. She was wearing the same dress she had worn to that dinner with the First Minister, the one she had worn the night they'd first made love, and Philippe's body clenched at the thought of easing that zip down once more.

Beside him, Francesca Allen had an incandescent beauty. She was witty and intelligent and charming, and everything he could want in a princess. He should have been dazzled by her.

But it was Caro who kept catching at the edge of his vision: her smile, the way she waved her hands around, the hair falling out of its clip as usual. She'd said she would be intimidated by his friends, by their confidence and glamour, but Philippe thought she was the most confident of all. She was just herself. Caro didn't have to put on a front because she didn't care. She was going back to Ellerby.

'She's been a refreshing change,' he said to Jack, deliberately careless. 'But she's going home soon. It's been fun,' he said, using Caro's line, 'but it's run its course.'

He shrugged. If Caro was desperate to leave, he wasn't going to beg her to stay. He was a Montvivennes prince, after all, and he had his pride. 'And, let's face it, she's not exactly princess material. I was wondering if Francesca might need consoling after her recent divorce…' Philippe let his voice trail away suggestively.

'Good idea,' said Jack. 'Francesca would put Montluce on the map. She's got that whole Grace Kelly thing going on.' He eyed Francesca critically. 'High maintenance, but worth it if you're in the market for a princess. She'd be perfect, in fact.' His eyes strayed down the table to where Caro was laughing. 'And you won't mind if I chat Caro up then, will you?'

Yes, Philippe *did* mind, but he couldn't say so. He had to watch jealously as Jack manoeuvred himself into a seat next to Caro and set about entertaining her. Jack was all wrong for her, Philippe thought vengefully. He just hoped Caro had the wit to see through him. Jack could be charm itself when he chose.

From the other end of the table, Caro tried not to notice how beautiful Francesca was, or how Philippe rested his arm on the back of her chair, how he smiled at her and leant close to murmur in her ear. There was no point in being jealous. She was the one who'd insisted he'd be good with Francesca, after all.

But it hurt all the same.

Get through the dinner, Caro told herself. Get through the ball. Then she could go home to Ellerby and remember what was really important.

Philippe and his friends were going sailing on the lake the next day. Caro had excused herself, saying vaguely that she had things to do.

It was all very well deciding to ditch her vintage look for something more elegant, but it was so long since she'd bought anything new that Caro didn't know where to start. In the end, she had enlisted the help of Agnès, the most stylish of the maids, who made even the uniform they had to wear look chic. 'I need a dress,' she told Agnès, whose eyes lit up at the challenge of transforming Caro.

Off the peg wouldn't do, Caro gathered. She needed a *real* dress, and Agnès had a cousin whose sister-in-law—or perhaps it was the other way round, Caro got a bit lost in the rapid French—was a Paris-trained designer just striking out on her own.

Ziggi turned out to have bright blue hair, and for a while Caro wondered if she'd made a terrible mistake in putting herself in her hands, but Ziggi made the dress in record time, and when Caro saw herself she was astounded.

'You like?'

'I don't know what to say…' Caro gaped at her reflection.

Somehow those extra pounds had gone, and she looked svelte and stylish.

Agnès beamed. 'You are like a *princesse*!'

'Oh, no,' said Caro involuntarily, backing away from her reflection. She wasn't supposed to be looking like a princess. She was supposed to be looking smart enough not to embarrass Philippe, that was all.

But it was too late now. Ziggi had made the dress for her, and was confidently awaiting a flood of commissions after Caro wore it to the ball.

'It just needs the hair,' said Agnès firmly.

'I'm ready.'

At the sound of Caro's voice, Philippe turned sharply from the window. He'd been pacing around the apartments while she was closeted with one of the maids, getting dressed for the ball. The two of them were starting the evening with a glass of champagne in the Dowager Blanche's apartments, and there would be hell to pay if they were late.

But that wasn't why he was on edge.

It should have been a perfect day. He'd left the red boxes behind and been sailing with his friends. For those few hours, he'd been Philippe again, not a prince. The sun had shone, the company was good. Everyone had had fun. Only he had spent the entire time wondering where Caro was and what she was doing. She'd been evasive when he'd asked her what her plans were. He pictured her at her laptop, planning her return to Ellerby, maybe even arranging to meet Homebody, and he was seized by an irrational fear that she would be gone by the time he got back.

He'd made some excuse to turn the boat back to the palace earlier than planned, only to find the apartment empty. All the wooden-faced footman at the door could tell him was that Caro had gone out with one of the maids and a protection officer. It sounded safe enough, but Philippe couldn't relax until she came back.

Then she'd come in and all the breath had leaked out of him. She'd had her hair cut, and it bounced chic and shiny around her face. The new look flattered the shape of her jaw, Philippe could see that, emphasising her cheekbones and making the navy-blue eyes look huge. She looked slimmer, sexier, infinitely more stylish.

She looked wonderful.

He hated it. He wanted the old Caro back, Caro with the messy hair that irritated him. He wanted to be able to pull the clip from her hair himself and twist his hands in the silky mass. He didn't want this stunning stranger with Caro's eyes and Caro's voice.

'What do you think?' she asked nervously.

Somehow Philippe found his voice. 'I thought you didn't believe in makeovers?'

'The Dowager Blanche is always going on about my hair,' said Caro. 'I thought I'd save myself another lecture.'

She had done it for him, Philippe knew. Now he turned, braced for another new look, and was astounded to find himself hoping against hope that she would be wearing one of her crazy vintage outfits so that he could go back to being exasperated.

He was out of luck. And out of breath.

The last scrap of air in his lungs evaporated at the sight of Caro standing in the doorway. Her dress, cunningly ruched at the bodice to flatter her figure, was red, a rich ruby colour that fell in elegant folds to the floor. Above the striking neckline, her shoulders rose, lush and glowing. She looked stunning.

Philippe cleared his throat. 'You didn't get that at a jumble sale.'

'No.' She moistened her lips. 'I've never worn a dress like this before. Agnès has done my make-up for me, too. I feel…odd.'

'You don't look odd—for once,' Philippe couldn't resist adding.

That sounded more like him. Caro had been feeling stiff and awkward, like a little girl in her mother's shoes. She couldn't interpret the look in Philippe's eyes, but her pulse was thudding and thumping. She was glad to hear the acerbic note in his voice. It made her feel more herself, too, and she relaxed into a smile until Philippe spoiled it by stepping close to her and tilting her chin with one hand.

'You look beautiful,' he said, stroking his thumb along her jaw line, and Caro's smile faded at his expression.

'So do you,' she said unevenly. It was true. He was magnificent in a formal uniform of a dress coat, with gold epaulettes and a sash.

'We're a pair, then,' said Philippe and held out his arm before Caro could reply. 'Shall we go?'

The Dowager's sharp eyes swept over Caro critically as she negotiated a curtsey in her long dress. 'I see you're wearing a decent dress for once,' she said. 'Simple but very effective. Hmm.' Lifting a hand, she summoned her lady-in-waiting. 'Hélène, can you bring me the Hapsburg set?'

Caro glanced at Philippe, who had gone very still. 'What's a set?' she mouthed, but Hélène was already back from the next room and handing the Dowager a flat leather box.

'Ah, yes…' The Dowager Blanche gave a hiss of satisfaction as she lifted out a diamond necklace that made Caro gasp. 'I wore this at my engagement ball. I think it would be appropriate.'

'Oh, no,' stammered Caro. 'I couldn't…'

'Nonsense,' snapped the Dowager, with a return to her old form. 'You'll look naked in a dress like that without any jewellery, and clearly Philippe hasn't bought you anything appropriate. An oversight,' she said, and Caro saw Philippe wince.

'It's far too valuable,' she tried to protest, but the Dowager stopped her with a disdainful look.

'It's just for tonight.' She held out the necklace to Philippe. 'My fingers are stiff. You put it on her.'

'Avec plaisir.'

The diamonds flashed as he draped the necklace around Caro's neck and fastened it with deft fingers. His hands were warm as they lingered on her shoulders.

'Now the earrings.'

Caro put those in herself. She was trembling. It felt all wrong to be wearing these incredible jewels. She wasn't a princess. But the loan of the necklace was a symbol of the Dowager Blanche's approval, another step towards accepting Philippe. How could she possibly say no?

'There.' The Dowager stood back at last. 'You both look most acceptable for once.'

A select group of guests were invited to a formal dinner before the ball. It was served in the state dining room, at a huge table laden with glittering dishes. Caro was relieved to be sitting next to Philippe's friend, Jack, who had twinkling eyes and a merry smile. He oozed charm and flirted as naturally as breathing, but somehow it was impossible to take him seriously.

But then, that was how she had used to think of Philippe, Caro realised.

'Philippe's changed,' said Jack as if reading her mind. 'He's not as restless. Before he'd take off at a moment's notice and the more dangerous the situation, the more he liked it. Just hearing about some of those aid flights made my hair stand on end, I can tell you. It was like he was driven to risk himself as much and as often as he could, and then he'd come back and party, cool as you please.'

He paused at Caro's expression. 'You *do* know about the flights?'

'Yes,' said Caro, 'I know.'

'Thank God for that,' said Jack, relieved. 'He gets very haughty if I mention it sometimes, and just brushes it aside. A lot of celebrities use charity work to raise their own profiles, but Philippe just gets out of his plane and slips away before anyone can thank him.

'I've never spoken to him about it, but a field director for one of the agencies he helps told me once that he finances a lot of the operations he flies too,' Jack confided. 'Of course, the rest of the time he spends amusing himself—skiing, sailing, partying. People think that's all there is to him.'

They both looked up the long table to where Philippe sat, charming Francesca on one side and a haughty countess on the other, and looking every inch the idle aristocrat, as if a thought beyond amusing himself and others had never crossed his mind.

'It's easy to underestimate Philippe,' said Jack.

Caro's eyes rested on Philippe's face, searching for the man she knew was there behind the playboy mask. The man who was teasing and tender, the man who had risked his relationship with his father to do what he thought was right. The man whose smile as he closed the bedroom door made her bones dissolve.

'Yes,' she agreed, 'it is.'

Philippe watched Caro with her head close to Jack's and made himself unclench his fingers from the stem of his glass before he snapped it. They were getting on well.

Too well.

He couldn't blame Jack. Caro was like a flame in that red dress. Warm, vibrant, mesmerising. Philippe was still reeling from the sight of her. Fastening the necklace around her neck, it had been all he could do to stop himself dragging her back to his apartments and kissing her senseless.

You can't give me what I really want.

It hasn't been real.

I want to go home and have a real life.

Philippe repeated Caro's words to himself like a mantra. She was right. He couldn't ask her to live like this all the time. She would hate it. Tonight she might look the part, but this wasn't what Caro really wanted. An ordinary life, she'd said. An ordinary man who would love her and stay with her and be able to give himself completely.

He couldn't be that man. He couldn't let down his father and give up his inheritance to live in Ellerby with Caro. What would he do there? He didn't know how to be ordinary.

And Caro didn't want to be here, although you would never guess it to watch her chatting to the starry guests in the same way that she talked to the staff and the stallholders in the market.

Philippe saw her smile at one of the footmen and hold up a thumb and finger in a message of approval to the chef, Jean-Michel. She had spent much of the previous week in the kitchens, discussing the menu with him. Philippe suspected that, given the choice, Caro would rather be down there in an apron than up here in the state dining room dripping diamonds.

But she knew instinctively how to circulate amongst the guests when the ball opened. Between them, they tried to talk to everybody and make them all feel welcome. The muscles in Philippe's cheeks ached with smiling as he danced with as many women as possible.

Just once did he succumb to temptation and dance with Caro. Holding her close, he thought about how right she felt in his arms. She fitted him perfectly. Her hair was soft against his cheek, and he could breathe in her scent.

When had she become so familiar to him? Her face was

hidden against his throat, but he didn't need to see her to picture the precise bold sweep of her brows, the exact curve of her mouth, the stubborn set of her chin.

How was he going to manage without her? In one blinding moment, Philippe knew that he couldn't.

'Don't go back to Ellerby, Caro.' The words came out in a rush, unbidden. 'Stay here with me. Please.'

Caro pulled back slightly to look up into his face. 'Philippe, I can't,' she said, her eyes anguished. 'I don't belong here.'

'You do! Look at you! There isn't a person here who wouldn't believe you were born a princess.'

She smiled shakily at that. 'This is make-believe. Perhaps I can look the part in this dress and your great-aunt's diamonds, but what about tomorrow when I hand back the necklace and am wearing my vintage clothes again? Nobody would be fooled then.'

'The truth is you don't want to belong.' Philippe couldn't keep the bitterness from his voice.

'I *do*.' Caro's throat was tight. 'I want to belong more than anything, but not here.'

The ball was a huge success, everyone said so, but it felt like a nightmare to Caro. Her face felt rigid with smiling as she moved through a blur of colour and chatter and music. She could feel the weight of the necklace around her neck and she touched it constantly, alarmed by the dazzling glitter of it that kept catching at the corner of her eye. It felt all wrong to be wearing something so magnificent. Caro smiled and smiled and felt wretched. Every now and then she would get a glimpse of Philippe through the crowds, tall and strong, effortlessly the centre of attention, and every time her heart would flip over and land with a sickening thud.

There was a prince who had finally found his place.

There was a man who flew through gunfire and tropical storms if help was needed.

There was Philippe, who held her every night and whose body she knew almost as well as her own.

She loved all of them, but none could give her the home and family she craved.

'I'm never going to belong in a royal palace, Philippe, and you know that as well as I do.' Caro could hear her voice beginning to crack, and she swallowed. 'Please don't say any more. It'll only make it harder than it already is.' She drew a steadying breath. 'I'm leaving tomorrow.'

All around them, people danced and laughed. The chandeliers sparkled and the band swung into a new number to cheers.

'So tonight is our last night?' said Philippe.

Caro's throat was so constricted she could barely speak. 'Yes,' she managed. 'This will be the last time.'

Caro woke first the next morning. She lay with her arm over Philippe, feeling it rise and fall in time with his steady breathing. Her face was pressed into the back of his neck, and she could smell the clean, male scent of his skin. She loved him, and her heart was breaking because she knew she had to leave him. It would be better for him and better for her, she knew that. But it hurt so much, she couldn't breathe.

It had been nearly three in the morning before they were able to leave the ball. Together they had walked in silence, not touching, up the sweeping staircase and along the corridor to Philippe's apartments. Even at that time of the night, there was a footman on duty outside to open the door.

Philippe had barely waited until they were inside before he reached for Caro, and she had gone willingly, fiercely. Late as it was, they had made love in a desperate silence. There were no more words to say.

Philippe stirred and rolled over to face Caro. He smiled at her, and her heart contracted. This was the man she would remember always, the man with blurry eyes and rumpled hair and early morning stubble, not the magnificent prince of the night before.

'We need to talk,' she said, and his smile faded as memory returned.

With a sigh, he rolled back to stare up at the ceiling. 'Now?'

'We ought to decide what we're going to tell everyone.' Caro pulled herself up against the pillows, taking the sheet with her. She had to be matter-of-fact about this. It wouldn't help Philippe if she started howling the way she wanted to.

'We can say that you met Francesca at the ball and we've had a big row because I'm jealous,' she suggested. 'You can tell everyone I've stomped off in a huff, if you like.'

Philippe scowled. 'I don't like. No one would believe it, anyway. You're not the stomping type.'

'All right, if anyone asks, we'll just say that we've decided we're incompatible,' said Caro. 'At least it has the advantage of being true, in a way.'

Philippe fixed his eyes on the ceiling. He had woken to find Caro beside him and, for one wonderful moment, everything had felt right. And then she had reminded him that she was leaving and the rawness was back. This was why he had never let a woman close before. He had known that she would just abandon him in the end, the way his mother had done.

Intellectually, Philippe knew that wasn't fair. Intellectually, he knew that if it ever came to choosing a wife, he needed one who was prepared to let him keep his distance. He knew that Caro would be happy in Ellerby. Oh, yes, intellectually, he knew quite well that she was right about everything.

But it still felt all wrong.

'How are you going to get home?' he asked later, when they were up and dressed and sharing an awkward breakfast.

'I booked a flight from Paris yesterday,' Caro told him. 'I'll get a taxi to take me across the border, and then I can get a train.'

'Don't be ridiculous,' Philippe said irritably. 'Yan will take you to Paris. When do you want to go?'

'When I've said my goodbyes,' she said. She got up to wash her coffee mug and plate, a habit she had never been able to shake. 'I'd better take the necklace and earrings back to the Dowager, too,' she said, determinedly bright. 'At least I can make her happy. That's one person who'll be glad to see me go!'

But her audience with the Dowager Blanche didn't go at all as expected. When Caro explained that she would be going home that day, the Dowager stared at her unnervingly.

'For good?'

Caro stretched her mouth into a wide smile. 'Yes.'

'Why?'

'I thought you'd be pleased,' she said involuntarily.

'I asked you why,' said the Dowager in freezing accents and Caro jumped in spite of herself.

'Philippe and I have decided that our relationship isn't going to work.'

'Nonsense!'

'It's not nonsense!' said Caro, forgetting that she wasn't allowed to argue back.

The Dowager actually harrumphed. Caro had never heard anyone do that before in real life. 'I was under the impression that you loved my great-nephew?'

'I do,' said Caro in a low voice, her momentary amusement fading. 'I love him very much but, as you keep reminding me, he's a prince and I'm just a very ordinary girl. It's been fun, but it's time for him to get serious now and find a serious woman who'll be a worthy princess for Montluce. But that won't be Lotty,' she thought she had better add, just in case the Dowager got her hopes up.

'No,' said the Dowager, to Caro's surprise. 'I see that now. Not that Charlotte appears to be in any hurry to come home from wherever she is,' she added querulously, suddenly no different from any other confused and irritable elderly lady.

'She'll be back,' Caro said, trying to comfort her.

She bent to fondle Apollo's ears, feeling ridiculously choked up at the thought of never seeing him again. 'Be a good dog,' she said. 'Work on the stick chasing.'

Straightening, she faced the Dowager, who was looking haughtier than ever, her lips were pressed together in a very thin, very straight line. But her eyes were suspiciously bright and, on an impulse, Caro leant forward and kissed her cheek. 'Goodbye, *Altesse*,' she said.

There were other goodbyes to say. Down in the kitchens, there was a gloomy atmosphere and every maid and footman wanted to shake her hand and say how sorry they were that she was leaving. Agnès cried a little, and Jean-Michel presented her with a collection of his recipes.

And then came the last, and hardest, goodbye.

CHAPTER TEN

'So, you're really going?' said Philippe. Caro's bag was waiting by the door, and she was shrugging on her father's jacket and trying not to cry.

'Yes.' She summoned a smile and squared her shoulders, determined to make it a good farewell. 'This has been one of the best times of my life, Philippe. Thank you for everything, and I…I hope we'll always be friends.'

'I'm going to miss you,' he said as if the words had been wrung out of him.

'I'll miss you too,' said Caro, her voice cracking, and when Philippe opened his arms she went straight into them. He held her very tightly, not speaking, for a long, long moment and Caro's throat was painfully tight. She couldn't have spoken if she had tried.

Eventually, Philippe let out a long breath and let her go. 'Goodbye, Caro,' he said.

'Goodbye.' Eyes blurring with tears, Caro turned for the door, lifted her chin and from somewhere found a smile so that she could leave with her head high.

For the last time, she walked down the sweeping staircase and out past the palace servants who had gathered to wave farewell, keeping her smile in place all the way. Yan was waiting with the black SUV, and he held open the door so that Caro could get into the back. Only then, hidden behind the tinted windows, could she let herself cry at last.

It felt as if she were being torn away like a snail from its shell as Yan drove her back over the hills to the border, and then on the fast road to Paris. When they got to the airport, he drove her right up to the entrance, opened the door and got out her bag for her. She was going to have to get used to opening her own doors from now on, Caro reflected.

She turned to hold out her hand to Yan and thank him. Expecting his usually impassive nod, she was astounded when he shook her hand warmly. 'If there is ever anything I can do for you, *mademoiselle*, you have only to ask,' he said.

It was the first time she had heard him speak.

Caro smiled shakily. 'Just make sure Philippe is safe,' she said.

'I will,' said Yan, and then he got into the car and drove away, back to Montluce, leaving Caro alone outside the terminal building with her tatty bag at her feet, just an ordinary girl once more.

To: caro.cartwright@u2.com
From: charlotte@palaisdemontvivennes.net
Subject: What happened???
Caro, I'm worried. What happened?? I've just rung Grandmère, and she said you'd gone. She's cross with you and cross with Philippe. Then I rang Philippe, and he shut me out. He was talking, but it was like after Etienne died. He was very cool and very polite and somehow not there at all. He just said everything was 'fine', which it obviously isn't. I thought everything was going so well? I thought you and Philippe were friends, but he sounds so distant now, and you're not there. Tell me you're OK, at least.
Lotty xxxxxxxxxxxxxxxxxxxxxx

To: charlotte@palaisdemontvivennes.net
From: caro.cartwright@u2.com
Subject: Re: What happened???
Hi, Lotty
Yes, I'm OK. I've been home a couple of weeks, and I'm
starting to remember what real life is like. I'm sorry you've
been worried, but Philippe is right, things are fine. I suppose you've guessed by now that we were more than
friends. I can tell you that now, but we ended it by mutual agreement. Right from the start, we always knew it
couldn't last.

Caro stared at the screen. Her eyes were tight with unshed
tears and her throat felt as if a great stone had been lodged
in it since that awful day she had said goodbye to Philippe.
It had been so easy to tell herself that she understood it was
temporary and that she was just making the most of their time
together. She *had* known it couldn't last, but how did you stop
yourself falling in love?

She had tried so hard to keep those nights separate from
the time when she and Philippe were just friends, but it hadn't
made any difference. Of course she had fallen in love with
him. How could she not?

She missed him. She missed her friend. She missed her
lover. She missed the way he smiled at her and the way he
rolled his eyes whenever he saw what she was wearing. She
missed moving around the kitchen, listening to him talk. She
missed lying next to him in the early morning, curled into the
hard curve of his body.

Caro went back to her email. She owed Lotty the truth
now.

When things aren't so painful, I hope Philippe and I can
be friends again, but I don't know. I don't know if I could

bear to see him with someone else. He's such a special person, he deserves someone perfect. The thing is, I can't talk about him to anyone except you. To everyone else, he's just a prince from some tiny country nobody had ever heard of until the fuss about the pipeline. They can't see beyond the fairy tale to the man he is, and I can't explain. I guess that goes with the territory when you're royal.

I miss Montluce, Lotty. I miss the people and the lake and the mountains. I even miss your grandmother and Apollo! I miss Philippe most of all. Things may be difficult for him at the moment, but he's found his place in Montluce, and that means more to him than he realises right now. When his father comes home, I think Philippe will be able to build a relationship with him at last, and that's what he needs most of all. I don't fit in with Philippe's life now, and he wouldn't fit in with mine, that's for sure, so I know I've made the right decision, even if it hurts right now.

Caro's mouth trembled. Funny how knowing that you'd made the right decision was no comfort at all. Why did everyone pretend that it helped? It didn't. Nothing helped.

Please don't worry about me, Lotty. I'll be fine. I'm thinking of setting up my own deli and café at last, specialising in produce from Montluce, and have even been to the bank to talk about a business loan. That will be exciting when I can get it up and running. Right now I'm temping again, and there's too much time to think, and to remember. Fortunately my 'celebrity status' was very short-lived and limited to those who read Glitz (not that many in Ellerby, thank goodness!) so I haven't had too many people recognise me. My life in Montluce seems so far away now, anyway. It's taken me a little while to adjust to normal life, but I'm nearly there. I know I need to start meeting men, so I've been looking on right4u.com again. To be honest, I can't imagine falling in love with anyone else right now, but I know I have to get back into it. I'm not expecting to meet someone right away, but I can at least show willing.

Caro stopped typing again. It was hard to explain to Lotty the depression that gripped her every time she looked at her potential matches on the site. They were all perfectly decent men, but none of them were Philippe.

I'm glad you've been in contact with the Dowager Blanche, I think she misses you more than she can say.

The way she missed Philippe. But she wasn't supposed to be thinking about Philippe, Caro reminded herself. Hadn't she decided enough was enough? She was tired of this constant ache for him, the constant looking for him and remembering that he wasn't there.

He wasn't there when someone said something ridiculous, or when she turned to catch his eye, knowing that he would share the joke.

He wasn't there to roll his eyes at her clothes or be rude about her cooking.

He wasn't there when she lay wretched at night, longing and longing to be able to turn and reach for him.

Two weeks passed, then three, and it didn't get any easier, whatever Caro told Lotty. She tortured herself imagining Philippe with Francesca Allen. Was Francesca sitting on the balcony with her feet up on the railings beside Philippe's? Was she waving and accepting posies? Did she spend long, sweet nights in Philippe's bed?

The thought of it was a knife twisting inside Caro, and she flinched at the pain of it. The temptation to email Philippe or to look up events in Montluce on the internet was huge, but she wouldn't let herself give in. She couldn't bear to see pictures of Francesca beside him. Knowing would be worse than imagining, Caro decided.

No, she had to get on with her own life. One evening when Stella was out with a new boyfriend, Caro took a deep breath and logged onto right4u.com. Just to look, she told herself. She would never find the perfect man sitting at home. Her mind veered to Philippe, but she yanked it back. She needed Mr Right, not Prince Right.

She hadn't logged on for a while, so she wasn't expecting any messages, but there were two. Mr Sexy was still hopeful, and there was a new message from Ordinary Guy. Well, that sounded promising.

Ignoring the ache in her heart, Caro clicked on his profile. No photo, but that wasn't unusual. He certainly sounded like a perfect match—over ninety per cent. So she ought to be excited, right? This guy was everything she'd ever wanted: steady job, own house, interested in the same things as her. He'd spent a lot of time overseas, he said, but now he wanted to settle down with the right woman. After years of resisting the idea, he was ready for marriage and a family.

He could even punctuate. His message was brief. *You sound like someone I'd like to get to know. What about meeting up for a drink some time?*

So he didn't sound that romantic or glamorous or exciting, but that was fine by Caro. She had done romance and glamour. This time she needed sensible and ordinary.

Stella frowned when she heard that Caro had agreed to meet him. 'Are you sure you're ready for this?'

'No,' said Caro. 'I'm not sure, but I've got to start some time, Stella. I'm not expecting this guy to be the one, but he sounds nice enough. I'm thinking of this as a practice run.'

But it felt as if there was a great weight on her heart as she got ready to go out that night. On the screen, Ordinary Guy was perfect. She should be more excited at the idea of meeting him, Caro knew, but how could she be excited when he wasn't Philippe, when he wouldn't have Philippe's hands and Philippe's mouth and Philippe's body? When he wouldn't click his tongue against his teeth in exasperation, or draw her to him with a smile that promised deliciously sinful pleasure?

How could he do that, when he was just an ordinary man?

Perhaps it was unfair to waste his time, Caro thought guiltily, but she couldn't spend the rest of her life pining for something that could never be. No, she decided. She would go, she would smile and she would be pleasant. She could always come home after one drink.

It was difficult to care what she looked like. Caro rifled through her wardrobe without interest and finally put on the dress she had worn that first night with Philippe when he had taken her to the Star and Garter. She had been wearing this dress the first time he'd kissed her, Caro remembered. How desperate she had been about George then. Perhaps one day she would be able to look back and marvel that she had felt this wretched about Philippe too.

The steps outside the Town Hall were empty when Caro arrived. She looked at her watch. Seven o'clock, as promised. She would wait ten minutes, she decided, and then she would go.

Hugging the light cardigan around her shoulders, Caro sat

on the top step in the last of the evening sun and let herself miss Philippe. Only for five minutes, she promised herself. Five minutes of remembering the taste of him, the feel of his body, the wicked pleasure of his hands. The laughter in his eyes. How easy it was to be with him, how comfortable to lean against his shoulder and feel that everything was all right as long as he was there.

There was a tight prickling behind Caro's eyes and she squeezed them shut, willing the tears away. Just what she needed on a first date: to be caught crying for another man. She shouldn't do this, shouldn't let the bittersweet memories in. It only made things worse.

Oh, God, someone was coming… Caro heard the footsteps and hastily knuckled the tears from under her eyes. Please, please, please don't let this be Ordinary Guy, she prayed.

'Waiting for someone?'

Caro's eyes flew open at the familiar voice. 'Philippe!'

Her heart was hammering high in her throat as she stared at him, longing to believe that he was real, but hardly daring to. He *looked* real. The saturnine features, the lean, powerfully muscled body, his mouth, his hands…yes, they were all as she remembered. Only the anxiety in the silver eyes was unfamiliar.

'What are you doing here?' she asked rudely, too startled to remember her manners or the fact that he was a prince.

'I've got a date,' said Philippe, sitting down beside her on the step.

'A *date*? In *Ellerby*?' Caro couldn't take it in. It was too incredible to have him there, close enough to touch. She wanted to pat him all over to check that he was real. She wanted to burrow into him and press her face into his throat and hold on to him for ever and ever.

'I'm meeting a princess,' he said. 'Who's expecting a frog.'

Understanding dawned through Caro's haze. 'It was *you*?'

'Meet Ordinary Guy,' said His Serene Highness Prince Philippe Xavier Charles de Montvivennes.

Caro couldn't decide whether to laugh or cry. 'You're not ordinary,' she said. 'You're a prince. That whole profile you wrote was one big fib!'

'It said we were a ninety per cent match for each other,' Philippe reminded her. 'And it wasn't a fib. Every word of that profile was true.'

'The steady job?'

'Well, no job's secure for life nowadays,' he conceded, 'but, barring revolution, being prince in Montluce should be safe enough. My father is back in his own apartments, but he's still resting. We've agreed that I'll take over more of his duties on a permanent basis, so I'd call that a job. And I've got somewhere to live, just like I said on the profile.'

'A palace!'

'Hey, it's a roof over my head.' Philippe's smile faded. 'But that's all it is without you, Caro. It isn't a home. It hasn't been since you left that day. That damn palace, stuffed with paintings and antiques and footmen and it's just been…empty. I hate it without you, Caro,' he said. 'Please come back.'

Caro had begun to tremble. 'Philippe…'

'I know what you're going to say,' he interrupted her before she could go on. 'You want an ordinary life, an ordinary man to share it with. I know that. That's why I let you go.'

He still hadn't made any move to touch her, but sat, like her, with his feet drawn up on the step below and his arms resting on his knees. 'I told myself that you were right, that you would only be happy if you came back here, and that I should look around for someone else, who was comfortable with life in a palace.

'I did try, Caro.' Philippe turned his head to look at her and his silver eyes were so warm Caro marvelled that she could ever have thought of them as cold. 'I took Francesca out to dinner, and tried to imagine her as a princess. And I could do it, no problem. She'd make a great princess...but I couldn't imagine her with *me*.

'That's when I realised that under all the trappings, I *am* just an ordinary guy. I'm like everyone else: muddled, insecure, blaming my parents for my own failures. I'm going to stop doing that now, Caro. I'm grown up, and I can make my own choices and live with the consequences.'

He looked away, across the square, squinting a little in the slanting evening sun.

'I've spent so many years afraid to commit myself to anyone in case they left and I had to *feel* something, and then you did leave, and it did hurt, but I survived. If I hadn't known you, hadn't loved you, I wouldn't have been hurting, sure, but I wouldn't have given up that time for anything, Caro.'

Caro found her voice at last. 'You *love* me?'

'Of course I love you.' Philippe sounded almost impatient as he looked back into her eyes. 'I just didn't dare admit it to myself, or to you.' He took Caro's hand at last. 'You must have known.'

'I thought it was just lust.' Caro's pulse was pounding so hard she was sure the steps must be shaking with it.

'There was a lot of lust,' he agreed.

'Or friendship.'

'That too,' said Philippe, lifting her hand to brush a kiss on her knuckles. 'I missed that, Caro. I've never had a friend like you before. I've never had anyone I could just be myself with. I don't think I knew who "myself" was until you kissed me and turned me into a frog.'

He smiled at her. 'You made me realise that I'd been a frog all along. I didn't lie in that profile. Maybe I do live in a palace and maybe I am a prince, but those are just trappings. Underneath, I want the same things all ordinary guys do. I want someone to come home to at the end of the day. Someone I can talk to, laugh with. Someone I can hold and who'll hold me through bad times and the good. That's ordinary, isn't it?'

Caro's heart was so full it was pressing painfully against her ribs and swelling up to block her throat. 'It's…amazing,' she managed while her fingers twined around his as if they had a mind of their own.

'I want *you*, Caro,' said Philippe, his voice deep and urgent. 'Not just someone. You. I need you there, with me.'

'But what about your father? He'll be so angry. And the Dowager Blanche…they won't let you be ordinary, Philippe.' Caro was struggling to be sensible. In her head, she had been through this so many times. 'It's incredible that you love me,' she made herself say, 'but it doesn't change who I am, and it doesn't change who you are. You're still a prince and I'm never going to make a princess.'

Tenderly, Philippe pushed a curl back from her face. 'You're the only one who thinks so.'

'The Dowager Blanche certainly doesn't think so!'

'Oh, yes, she does. She might not show it, but she likes you. She liked the way you stood up to her. Apollo might have put in a good word too, because she told me that I was a great dolt for letting you go.'

Caro's jaw dropped. *'Really?'*

'Really,' said Philippe with a smile. 'The Montlucians think you'd make a great princess, too. There's an entire country waiting for you to come back, Caro! As for my father, he's just pleased that I'm ready to settle down. Even Yan opened his mouth and wished me luck.'

Caro shook her head to clear her spinning mind, but Philippe misinterpreted the gesture. 'Don't say no!' he said, grabbing her other hand and pulling her round to face him. 'I know how you've always dreamed of an ordinary life, Caro, but why settle for ordinary when what we've got could be *extraordinary*?

'And I don't mean where and how we live,' he went on with an edge of desperation. 'I mean being together, being friends, loving each other and trusting each other and being there for each other. We're so lucky to have found someone we can have that with. *That's* what's extraordinary.'

Caro stared at him. Philippe was right. Was she holding onto one dream because she was scared to reach for a bigger and better one?

'Ordinary Guy sounded so perfect,' she said slowly. 'Exactly the man I'd always wanted.'

'He is perfect,' said Philippe. 'I made damn sure he would be when I wrote that profile. I didn't want to risk you not agreeing to meet me.'

'I still don't understand why you didn't just ring. It would have been much easier.'

'But then you'd have just come out with all that you're-a-prince-I'm-unsuitable stuff and refused to meet me,' he pointed out. 'It was the only way I could think of to talk to you and make you see me not as a prince, but as the ordinary guy you've wanted all along.'

Caro pulled her hand from his to lay her palm against his cheek. 'You did it very well,' she told him. 'I was convinced that I would never find anyone more suitable for me, and yet when I walked down here I was more depressed than I've ever been in my life.'

'*Depressed?*'

A smile trembled on her lips. 'Because I knew that however perfect Ordinary Guy was on paper, I'd already met the perfect man for me, and he wasn't ordinary at all.'

Philippe let out a long breath. 'He wouldn't happen to be a prince, would he?' he asked hopefully, turning his face so that he could press a kiss into her palm.

'He would,' said Caro. 'When you came just now, I was crying. I'd just realised that even though he was nothing like the kind of man I thought I wanted, only he would do.' The blue eyes filled with tears. 'And now you're here, and I'm so happy, I can't believe it…' Her voice broke.

'Caro.' Philippe reached for her then, pushing his hands into her hair and pulling her into him for a long, long, sweet kiss. 'Caro, say you love me,' he mumbled against her temple when he lifted his head at last.

'I love you…I love you…I do,' she stammered, incoherent with happiness.

'Say you'll marry me and be my princess.'

She stilled at that, knowing that this was her last chance to grasp at being sensible. Placing the flat of her hands against his chest, she held herself away from him. 'Are you sure, Philippe?' she said doubtfully. 'I do love you, but we're so different. It won't be easy.'

'No, it won't be,' said Philippe. 'But who wants easy when they can have incredible? Yes, we'll have to work through some tough bits, but won't that be worth it when we see what an amazing life we can build together?'

He drew her back against him. 'Come on, Caro, stop looking for difficulties. Just kiss me again and tell me you'll marry me.'

Caro's eyes were starry with happiness as she wound her arms around his neck. 'All right,' she said obediently. 'I will.'

'Ready?' Lotty smiled as she twitched Caro's train into place. 'How do you feel?'

'I can't believe this is really happening,' Caro confessed. Outside, she could hear the church bells ringing across the wintry city in great, joyous peals. 'I keep thinking I must be dreaming.'

'Then I'm in the same dream,' said Stella, peeking out of the window. 'Have you *seen* how many people there are out there? The entire population of Montluce has come to see you married, Caro!'

'No pressure, then!'

'You'll be fine,' Lotty soothed. 'And you look incredible.'

'Thanks to your grandmother.' Caro smoothed down her dress with unsteady hands. Soon after she'd returned to Montluce, the Dowager had taken her aside and stiffly offered her the dress that she had worn for her own wedding fifty-five years earlier.

'I've observed that you don't wear new clothes,' she had said. 'But of course, if you would prefer a new designer dress, that is entirely up to you.'

But Caro had been thrilled with the dress. It was a dress fit for a princess, with full skirts, a fitted bodice and a spectacular train. Lace covered her arms and the ivory satin was sewn with seed pearls that gleamed and shimmered as she moved. It had had to be let out in places, that was true, but it felt very special to be getting married in the Dowager's dress. Lotty's grandmother had lent her diamond drop earrings, too, and the antique corsage tiara that held the gossamer fine veil in place.

Now it was time to go. Caro was shaking with nerves as she lifted her skirts to walk carefully down the great staircase. Philippe's father was waiting for her at the bottom. He was an austere man, still thin from his treatment, but growing stronger every day. Caro had been pleased to see the wary relationship that was growing between father and son. As she had no father and no close male relatives, the Crown Prince had offered to give her away himself, and now he smiled at the sight of her.

'My son is a lucky man,' he said. 'Come, let us go.'

A big, low limousine with wide windows waited in the courtyard, where what seemed like the entire palace staff had turned out to wish her well for her wedding. They cheered as Caro was helped into the car by a footman, and the train was piled in after her. Then Philippe's father got in beside her.

As the car came out of the gates, another huge cheer went up from the waiting crowds. The flag at the front of the car fluttered as they drove along streets lined with smiling, waving people and the frosty air rang with bells. Caro's throat thickened with nervousness and emotion and she gripped the bouquet of white roses so tightly her knuckles showed white.

A feeling of unreality had her in its grip, and her smile felt as if it had been fixed on her face. This couldn't be real. This couldn't be her, Caro Cartwright, being driven through cheering crowds to marry a prince. Any minute now, she would wake up and find that she had been dreaming.

Then they were at the cathedral, and Lotty and Stella were there to help her out of the car and pull out the train onto the red carpet. The cheers were even louder there. Caro's smile felt more wooden than ever. She wasn't nervous, she realised. She was terrified.

The Crown Prince offered his arm. As they entered the cathedral, the big wooden doors swung shut behind them and the trumpeters in the clerestory struck up.

Caro had an impression of a mass of people, all smiling, all staring at her. She could feel the train dragging behind her, the weight of the tiara on her head, the heavy satin skirts. The aisle seemed to go on for ever, while the music swelled. It had to be a dream.

And then she saw Philippe waiting at the altar. He was dressed in full regalia, with golden epaulettes, medals and a sash across his chest and a sword at his side, but Caro didn't see the uniform. She saw the smile that was just for her and, all at once, the dreamlike feeling vanished, and she forgot the television cameras and the watching congregation. There was just Philippe, waiting for her, and it was real after all.

Theirs might be an extraordinary wedding, but the vows they were making were the same that every couple made, and they were real too.

When it was over, Philippe kissed her there in front of everybody, and they made their way back down the aisle. The bells were pealing and the sun glittered on the snowy rooftops as they emerged from the cathedral to cheers and whistles.

A carriage drawn by six white horses with nodding plumes waited at the bottom of the steps. Philippe and Caro smiled and waved, and then the train had to be negotiated into another vehicle, but at last they were in and they set off through the city streets lined with crowds. Caro's arm was already aching from all the waving.

'You've still got the balcony to go,' murmured Philippe, 'but let's give them something else to cheer about.' And he kissed her thoroughly, to the delight of the cheering, flag-waving crowd.

Caro was flushed and laughing when they got back to the palace. They paused for a moment to wave to the crowds once more before stepping into the cool of the marbled hall out of sight of the cameras. Even then there was no opportunity to be alone. The hall was lined with palace servants, and Caro had her first taste of how her life had changed when she was greeted with smiling bows and curtseys. Laughing, she hooked her train over her arm, and together she and Philippe climbed the staircase she had descended so nervously earlier.

The reception was to be held in the state ballroom. 'Quick,' said Philippe, opening a door to one of the side rooms. 'Before the others get here!' And he pulled Caro inside and kissed her against the door until they heard the unmistakable sounds of everyone else arriving.

'I suppose we can't skip out on our own wedding,' he said regretfully, letting her go at last.

'Careful of the Dowager's dress!' Blushing, Caro patted her hair and wondered if it was going to be obvious to everyone what they'd been doing. She hadn't put up much of a protest. 'Now I need to redo my make-up. Agnès will kill me!'

'She can't be cross with you now. You're a princess,' said Philippe. 'Besides, you look beautiful.' He studied her critically for a moment before straightening her tiara. 'There, you're ready to go again.'

He stayed by her side as they moved through the throng of guests. Caro smiled and kissed endless cheeks, but all the time she was acutely aware of Philippe, of his touch on her back, his hand on hers, his arm at her waist.

Outside, she was vaguely aware of chanting, but it was only when the doors were thrown open and she and Philippe stepped out onto the balcony to a roar of approval that Caro realised how many people were gathered outside waiting to see them. The sheer number and noise of the crowd made her gasp.

The view down over the mass of fluttering Montluce flags was dizzying.

'Philippe,' she said, turning to him with her heart in her eyes. 'I've just had a revelation.'

'I hope that it's how much you love me?' said Philippe, waving at the crowds.

Caro slid her hand into his. 'All those years I longed for a place to belong, and I never dreamt I would feel that I did on a palace balcony! But it isn't about a place,' she realised wonderingly. 'It's about being with you.'

'Quite right.' Philippe grinned and pulled her into him for a kiss while the crowd roared and cheered and whistled and waved flags below. '*This* is where you belong, Caro. Right here in my arms.'

'I've found my frog at last,' she sighed happily.

Philippe watched her turn to wave and smile at her new subjects, and he held her hand tight in his. 'And I've found my princess,' he said.

KISS THE BRIDESMAID

BY
CARA COLTER

With thanks to Shirley Jump for all her great ideas,
and for sharing her Cape Cod summers.

CHAPTER ONE

"LADIES, if you would gather by the chocolate fountain, Mrs. Charles Weston is about to throw her bouquet." Colton St. John had been best man at the wedding of two of his oldest friends, and now he was acting as the master of ceremonies.

The town had been founded by his forefathers, and leadership came easily to him. At twenty-eight, the dark-haired, blue-eyed Colton would have been a more likely movie star than a law school graduate and the youngest mayor St. John's Cove had ever elected.

Not that Samantha Hall, bridesmaid, was admiring the confidence and finesse of her dear friend, Colton, at the moment.

It's nearly over, she told herself as she slid toward the exit of the St. John's Cove Yacht Club. It was hard to be unobtrusive in the bridesmaid's gown that Amanda—make that *Mrs.* Charles Weston—had chosen. Amanda had glowingly described the color as fuchsia, but it wasn't. The dress was the exact shade of pink Sam's current stray rescued dog, Waldo, had thrown up after eating the Jell-O salad Sam had made for Amanda's bridal shower earlier in the week.

As if the color wasn't hideous enough, Sam considered the dress just a little too *everything* for a wedding. Between hitching up the hem so she wouldn't trip over it, pulling the tiny spaghetti straps back on her shoulders every time they slipped down, and tugging at the plunging V-line of the bodice, the dress had felt like a full-time job since she had first put it on nearly twelve hours ago.

Even her three older brothers, who usually teased unmercifully when she put on "girl" clothes, had gone silent when she had come out to the car and they'd seen the dress for the first time.

"I thought you said it looked like dog puke," her oldest brother, Mitch, had said, holding open the door of his ancient station wagon for her. She was driving with her brothers to the wedding because she couldn't manage the clutch of her Land Rover in the three-inch heels, plus was afraid of splitting the hind end out of the dress getting in and out of her higher vehicle.

And then Mitch had done the oddest thing. He'd kissed her cheek and said, almost sadly, "When did you go and grow up, Sam?"

Since she'd been living in her own apartment above the business she had founded here in St.

John's Cove after graduating from high school seven years ago, his comment had been insulting rather than endearing.

Trust a man! Show a little too much cleavage, pile your hair on top of your head and put on a bit of makeup, and you were all grown-up.

Her brothers' reaction had foreshadowed an uncomfortable evening. Guys she had spent her whole life in this small Cape Cod hamlet with—boating and swimming and fishing—had been sending her sidelong looks as if she'd gone and grown a second head.

Thankfully most of them were too scared of her brothers to do anything about it except gawk.

Though there was one man—he'd been introduced in the reception line on the steps of St. Michael's Church as Amanda's cousin, Ethan Ballard—who hadn't been able to take his eyes off of her through the whole evening.

He was gorgeous, too. Tall, lean, broad-shouldered. Dark. Dark eyes, dark hair.

Sam killed the intrigue he made her feel.

He'd asked her to dance four times, but she'd said no. Even his voice gave her the shivers, deep and measured.

The truth was she didn't know how to dance, and wasn't going to make a fool of herself by trying for the first time in the heels. The truth was, Ethan was asking the illusion to dance. If he'd seen her in her normal duds—rolled-up jeans, sneakers, a faded shirt that advertised her pet store and supply business, Groom to Grow, he would have never looked that interested.

Of course, there was always the possibility one of the local guys had dared him to show interest in her, or offered him twenty bucks to dance with her.

Knowing that any man in St. John's Cove who went near Samantha Hall was going to have to run the gauntlet of her brothers.

Sam glanced over to where Ethan was standing, one shoulder braced against the wall, his tie undone, his crisp white shirt open against the end-of-June early-summer heat in the reception room. He was nursing a drink and *still* looking at her.

And he didn't look like a fool, either. Ethan Ballard radiated the confidence, wealth and poise one would expect from a businessman from Boston.

He raised his glass to her, took a long, slow sip without taking his eyes from her. Now how could that possibly seem suggestive, make her insides melt into hot liquid?

How about because she hadn't had a date in over a year? And that date had been with a *sumpie*—she and her friends' pet name for summer people— because the locals were afraid to ask her out. And with good reason. After one drink, her brother Mitch had shown up at the Clam Digger, glowering and flexing muscles earned from plying his strength and guts against the waters of the Atlantic to make his living as a lobsterman.

To the local male population, she was Sam, not Samantha. She could outrun, outsail and outswim most of them—it was a well-known fact no one had beaten her in a race to the buoys since she was sixteen. But even if the local young men weren't totally intimidated by that, nobody wanted to deal with the Hall brothers, Mitch, Jake and Bryce, when it came to their little sister.

Which was okay with her. Fairy tales had finished for her family when her mom and dad had been killed in a boating accident when she was twelve. Mitch, newly married, had stepped up to the plate and taken in his siblings, but his wife, Karina, had not bargained for a ready-made family of two rowdy teenage brothers, and a twelve-year-old girl swimming in pain. Karina, Sam's one chance for a bit of feminine influence, had jumped ship.

Her brothers had raised her so she could fight but not put on makeup, handle a fishing rod but not wear heels, arm wrestle but not dance. They'd given her an earful about what men *really* wanted.

Plus, all three of her brothers had taken Karina's abandonment personally and were commitment phobic, and so was she.

Most of the time. Occasionally Sam felt this odd little tug of wistfulness. She felt it when she watched couples walk hand in hand along the beach at sunset, she felt it when old Mr. and Mrs. Nelson came into her shop, their teasing affection for one another reminding Sam of her mom and dad.

And Sam had felt it with surprising strength when Charlie and Amanda had exchanged their vows earlier at St. Michael's, Amanda glowing, and Charlie choking up on emotion.

Sam's own eyes had teared up, and she was so unaccustomed to that, she didn't have a tissue, and so unaccustomed to mascara that she didn't know crying in it would have unfortunate consequences.

And she had reacted like that even though she personally felt that if there were ever two people who should not have gotten married, it was Charlie and Amanda!

The pair were part of a tight-knit group of six friends, Colton St. John, Vivian Reilly and Sam's brother Bryce, who had been hanging out together since grade school. Sam was the youngest of the group—she had started as a tagalong with Bryce. Amanda and Charlie had been dating on and off since they were fourteen, their relationship punctuated with frequent drama, constant squabbling, and hundreds of breakups and makeups.

Ah. Sam's hand connected with the steel bar of the exit door of the reception hall. She pushed, caught a whiff of the fresh June breeze coming in off the bay. *Freedom.* On an impulse, she turned and wagged her fingers at Ethan Ballard, *goodbye.*

"Oh, no, you don't," Vivian Reilly said. Vivian, also a charter member of the Group of Six, was the other bridesmaid, and she caught Sam's arm just as she was halfway out the door.

"How come the dress doesn't look like dog puke on you?" Sam asked, wishing she could take back that impulsive wag of the fingers.

The color of the dress should have clashed with Vivian's incredible red hair, but, of course, it didn't. Vivian looked leggy and beautiful, but then Vivian could wear a grain sack and make it look sexy. If anything, the dress was slightly more demure than Vivian's usual style.

"It mustn't look all that bad on you, either," Vivian said with a laugh. "Check out that man staring at you. I'm getting heat stroke from it. He's glorious. Ethan something? Amanda's cousin?"

Ethan Ballard. Sam remembered his name perfectly, not to mention the touch of his hand in that reception line. Lingering. Sam slid Amanda's cousin another look, and looked away, though not before her heart tumbled in her chest, and she felt the tug of something a lot stronger than the wistfulness she felt when she looked at old Mr. And Mrs. Nelson picking out a new collar for their badly spoiled Pom, Duffy.

Ethan Ballard *was* glorious. And no doubt just as superficial as every other guy in the world, including her brothers. She did not kid herself that the good-looking cousin would have given her a second look if her hair was pulled back into its usual no-nonsense ponytail, her eyes were not smudged with the plum shadow that Vivian and Amanda insisted made them look greener, and her chest wasn't falling out of the embarrassingly low-cut dress.

The door clicked shut again, and Sam, resigned, tugged at the dress. She glanced up to see Ethan Ballard watching, an amused smile playing at the handsome, firm line of his wide mouth.

There was that hot rush again, so she stuck her nose in the air so he wouldn't ever guess.

"Come on," Vivian said, steering Sam back toward the gaggle of giggling single girls and women waiting for the traditional throwing of the bouquet. "Be a sport."

Amanda was standing at the front of the room now, still glowing, a queen looking benevolently at her subjects. No doubt she was kidding herself that this was the best day of her life, Sam thought cynically.

As soon as Vivian let go of her arm, Sam moved way up to the front of the gathering of hopefuls. She'd played ball with the bride, and Amanda had a strong throwing arm. As long as she didn't do the I'm-cute-and-helpless routine, that bouquet should sail right over Sam's head and hit old Mable Saunders in the back row.

Sixty and never married.

Which will probably be me someday, Sam thought, and given that she was cynical about the institution of marriage she was not sure why the thought made her feel more wistful—and gloomy—than before.

The truth was the whole day had made her feel gloomy, not just because she didn't hold out much hope for Amanda and Charlie—why would they be the one out of two couples who succeeded when they hadn't ever managed to go more than three days in their whole relationship without a squabble—but because Sam didn't like change.

Her five friends were the unchangeable anchor in her life. Vivian, Amanda, Charles, Colton and Sam's brother Bryce had all hung out together for as long as she could remember. Oh, some of them moved, went to college, came back, but the ties remained unbreakable. The constancy of family and friendships were what made life in the small Cape Cod community idyllic for its three thousand permanent residents.

This was the biggest change they had experienced. A wedding. Sam didn't like it. She didn't like it one bit.

Though she had to admit Amanda did look beautiful in her wedding dress, beaming at them all from the front of the room.

The dress, considering the sudden haste to get married, was like something out of a fairy tale, a princess design of a tight-fitting beaded bodice and full floor-length skirt with about sixty-two crinolines underneath it.

Amanda's eyes met hers, full of mischief, so Sam was relieved when someone suggested Amanda turn around with her back to them all, so she couldn't choose who to toss the bouquet to. As soon as Amanda did turn around, Sam shuffled positions, moving closer to the burbling chocolate fountain, still close to the front, gambling on Amanda's good arm.

What she couldn't have gambled on was this: Amanda threw the bouquet over her shoulder with all her might. It arched up and up and up toward the ceiling.

Those who really were eager to catch the thing moved back in anticipation of where it would fall back to earth.

But the bouquet hit an exposed beam, and instead of completing its arc, it fell straight down like a duck shot out of the sky.

It was going to land right in the middle of the chocolate fountain.

Unless someone intervened.

For an uncharitable moment, Sam swore it was not going to be her.

But she caught a glimpse of the horrified look on Amanda's face and wondered in that split second if it wasn't some kind of bad luck for the bouquet not to be caught, to land smack dab in the middle of a pool of burbling chocolate.

Amanda and Charlie were going to need all the luck they could get.

Reluctantly Sam reached out an arm, and the bouquet fell into her hand as if it had been destined to find her.

A cheer went up, though she could hear the lusty challenge of Mitch.

"Anyone who thinks they're going to marry my sister is going to have to arm wrestle me first."

Sam smiled, with so many teeth she felt like a dog snarling, waved the bouquet and headed for the exit.

So that's my future wife, Ethan Ballard thought, watching the bridesmaid head out the exit onto the stone veranda that faced the sea. He bet she was going to hurl that bouquet right off of there, too. He hadn't missed her thwarted attempt at escape earlier, or the way she had looked during the dinner and the toasts. Cynical. Uncomfortable. Bored.

The least romantic woman in the room. Perfect.

He'd been pretty sure she was the one from the moment he'd laid eyes on her. Despite the sexy outfit, and the abundance of rich chocolate upswept hair, he could tell by the sunburn and freckles that she was the wholesome, outdoorsy type that she imagined the Finkles would love.

She'd be perfect for the task he had in mind. When he'd held her hand a little too long in the reception line she'd yanked it away and given him a dirty look with those sea-mist eyes of hers.

Ditto for his offers to dance with her. Though

Ethan felt faintly stung—who didn't want to dance with *him*—it boded well for his plan.

Samantha Hall was the girl least likely to appreciate his offer of marriage. Least likely to want anything else once the assignment was over.

And he only needed a wife for one day.

Tomorrow. Combining his cousin Amanda's wedding with business, Ethan was in Cape Cod looking at real estate. He'd seen a promising property on the Main Street of St. John's Cove this morning, but what he really wanted was an old family cottage up the coast, between St. John's and Stone Harbor. He'd been drooling over the Internet pictures of Annie's Retreat for over a week, and had an appointment to see it tomorrow.

Then his lawyer had called. He'd done his homework, as always. The current owners, the Finkles, had turned down a lot of offers on the place. They knew exactly what they wanted, and it wasn't to sell to a businessman who would see their property as an investment, who would see the development potential in that rare amount of oceanfront.

The Finkles would be more amenable to an offer made by Mr. and Mrs. Ballard, who wanted to raise a dozen children on the place.

Trying not to whistle at his good fortune in finding the perfect Mrs. Ballard so quickly, Ethan headed out the door after her. Job one was to find out if she knew the Finkles. If she did, he wouldn't proceed.

Samantha Hall was in the shadows, on the wide deck behind the exit door, standing so still that for a moment he didn't see her. And when he did he was struck by her loveliness, her slender figure silhouetted by moonlight, her face lifted to the breeze.

She was looking out at the sailboats and yachts bobbing in their moorings, something faintly wistful in her expression.

Very romantic.

She turned, startled when she heard him come out, turned away instantly. He almost laughed out loud when she pulled at the front of her dress, *again*. The dress fit her graceful lines perfectly and showed off her slender curves to mouthwatering advantage.

But for some reason he found her discomfort with it far more delightful than the dress itself.

"Gorgeous night," he said conversationally.

"Hmm." Noncommittal. *Suspicious.*

"Lucky catch on the bouquet."

"I guess that depends what you think lucky is."

"Isn't the one who catches it the next one to get married?" he asked.

"There's a disclaimer clause if you're just saving the bouquet from a disastrous dip in chocolate."

Ethan laughed, and not just because it was the perfect answer for a man with a mission like his.

"What did you do with the bouquet?" he asked.

Her eyes slid guiltily to the left and he saw the

bridal bouquet had been shoved in a planter, the elegant lilies bright white against red geraniums.

"I'm Ethan Ballard," he said, extending his hand.

"We met in the reception line," she said, pretending she didn't see it.

The music started inside. He wondered if he should ask her to dance, *again,* and was surprised that he wanted to dance with her. But on the other hand, there was no sense romancing her. His marriage proposal wasn't about romance, and he didn't want her to think it was.

Job one, he reminded himself, surprised at how hard it was to get down to business with her scent tickling at his nostrils.

"Do you know a family named the Finkles, over Stone Harbor way?" he asked.

Her brow scrunched in momentary concentration. "No," she said. "I can't say I do." Then, with a touch of defensiveness, "My world is pretty small. You're looking at it." And she nodded her chin toward the sea and then the barely visible lights of town.

"I'm looking for a wife," he said, always the businessman, cutting to the chase, even while he kept his tone light, and even while he was aware of being not completely professional. A renegade part of him was looking forward to getting to know her a tiny bit better.

She shot him a look. "Goodie for you."

Despite the fact this was all a business venture for

him, he was a little taken aback at her lack of interest in him. That was not the reaction he got from women at all. Obviously she had no idea who he was, and he found that in itself refreshing.

What would it be like to get to know another human being who didn't know you were heir to a fortune, a millionaire businessman in your own right and a retired major league baseball player?

"You caught the bouquet, it seemed fortuitous. I have a proposition for you," he said carefully.

"Propose away," she said, but he realized when she tucked a wayward strand of her glossy dark hair behind her ear that she was not as cavalier about his attention as she wanted him to believe.

For the first time, he felt a moment's hesitation. Maybe she wasn't right for this job, after all; there was something sweetly vulnerable under all that not very veiled cynicism.

At that moment the side door exploded open. His cousin, Amanda, came bursting out, the skirt of her bridal confection caught in her hands, tears streaming down her face. She raced down the stairs with amazing swiftness given that her outfit was not exactly designed for a one-hundred-yard dash. She was at the bottom of the stairs before the door exploded open again, and Charlie came out it.

"Mandy, honey, come on. Don't be like this."

"Don't you Mandy, honey, me!" she yelled, rounding on him. "How could you?"

Ethan was pretty sure that neither of them had even noticed that he and Samantha were in the shadows behind the door. Samantha had gone still as a statue, and he did the same.

And then the bride turned around, tore past the pier, up a set of stairs on the other side of it and into the parking lot. Charlie gained on her and caught her; a furious discussion ensued that Ethan felt grateful he could not hear.

The discussion resulted in Amanda climbing behind the wheel of her bright yellow sports car convertible, revving the engine and leaving Charlie in a splatter of gravel.

Ethan turned to see how his bridesmaid reacted to the drama. She was leaning on the railing, her small chin on her hands, a knowing little smile playing sadly on her lips as she gave her head a cynical shake.

His doubt of a moment earlier was erased. *She was perfect.*

"Will you marry me?" he asked.

"Why not?" she answered, then smirked at his startled expression. "We have at least as good a chance as them."

And then she looped her arm through his and dragged him back through the door, he suspected so that Charlie, who was coming back up the steps, shoulders drooping, would remain unaware that the horrible little wedding-night drama had had witnesses.

Ethan was struck by how the sensitivity of the gesture, the loyalty to her friends, did not match the cynicism she was trying to display.

She could have saved herself the effort, though. Back inside it was evident the bride and groom had had many witnesses to their first argument as a married couple.

"About my proposal," Ethan told her, taking her elbow and looking down at her, "I'll make it worth your while."

She smiled sweetly at him. "Believe me, it already is."

And that's when he saw a mountain of a man moving toward him, a scowl on his face that could mean nothing but trouble.

CHAPTER TWO

"YOUR boyfriend?" Ethan asked Samantha.

"Worse," she told him, still smiling sweetly at him. "My brother." She reached up and brushed her lips on his, he presumed to make sure he was really in trouble.

But the kiss took them both by surprise. He could tell by the way her eyes widened, and he felt a thrilled shock at the delicacy of those lips touching his, too.

But she backed away rapidly, wiped her mouth with the back of her hand. "And that will teach you to take twenty bucks to pretend you're interested in me. Oh, hi, Mitch, this is Ethan. He just asked me to marry him."

Then she wagged her fingers at him and disappeared into the throng of people milling about discussing the tiff between the bride and groom.

Her lips, Ethan thought, faintly dazed, had tasted of strawberries and sea air.

He watched her go, troubled not so much by the impending arrival of her brother, as by the fact she thought someone would have to pay him to show interest in her, and that she thought, even on the shortness of their acquaintance, that he would be such a person.

Of course, he was trying to buy a bride, not exactly a character reference.

The man stopped in front of him and folded ham-sized hands over a chest so wide it was stretching the buttons on his dress shirt.

"I've got a question for you," Mitch said menacingly.

In a split second an amazing number of possibilities raced through Ethan's mind. *What were you doing outside with my sister? What are your intentions? Why are you kissing someone you just met? You asked my sister to marry you?* None of the answers Ethan came up with boded well for him.

He braced himself. Ethan did not consider himself a fighter, but he wasn't one to back down, either.

"You really are Ethan Ballard, aren't you?"

The question was so different than what he was bracing himself for that Ethan just nodded warily.

"I gotta know why you left the Sox. One season. No injury. Great rookie year. I gotta know."

Despite the menace, Ethan felt himself relax. He could tell Samantha's brother was one of those hard-working, honest men that these communities, once all fishing villages, were famous for producing.

Ethan had his stock answer to the question he had

just been asked, but he surprised himself by not giving it. In a low voice he said, "I wanted to be liked and respected for who I was, not for what I did."

A memory, painful, squeezed behind his eyes, of Bethany saying, her voice shrill with disbelief, *You did what?* And that had been the end of their engagement, just as his father had predicted.

Samantha's brother regarded him thoughtfully for a moment, made up his mind, clapped him, hard, on the shoulder. "Come on. I'll get you a beer and you can meet my brothers."

"About that marriage proposal—"

The big man's eyes sought his sister and found her. He watched her for a moment and then sighed.

"Don't worry. I know she was just kiddin' around, probably kissed you to get me mad, as if I could get mad at Ethan Ballard. Nobody's gonna marry my little sister."

"Why's that?" Ethan asked, and he felt troubled again. Samantha Hall was beautiful. And had plenty of personality and spunk. Why would it seem so impossible that someone—obviously not a complete stranger who had just met her, but someone—would want to marry her?

"They'd have to come through me first," Mitch said, and then, "And even if they didn't, she'd have to find someone who is more a man than she is. My fault. I raised her. Don't be fooled by present appearances. That girl is as tough as nails."

But it seemed to Ethan what Samantha Hall needed was not someone who was more a man than her at all. It was someone who saw the woman in her. And who could clearly see she was not tough as nails. He thought of the softness of her lips on his and the vulnerability he had glimpsed in her eyes when he had joined her outside. And he wondered just what he was getting himself into, and why he felt so committed to it.

Sam couldn't believe it. A complete stranger had asked her to marry him. She knew Ethan Ballard was kidding—or up to something—but her heart had still gone crazy when he had said the words! Having been raised by brothers, Sam knew better than to let her surprise or intrigue show. There was nothing a man liked better than catching a woman off guard to get the upper hand!

She was annoyed to see her brothers *liked* him. She watched from across the room as they gathered around him, as if he was a long-lost Hall, clapping him on the shoulder and offering him a beer. Ethan Ballard had wormed his way into their fold effortlessly.

Well, she thought, *that's a perfect end to a perfect day.* Her feet hurt, she was tired of the dress and she felt sick for Charlie and Amanda. Fighting on a wedding night had to be at least as bad for luck as the bouquet not getting caught. Sam had just postponed the inevitable by making her heroic save.

Still, her work here was done. Much as she would have liked to know what that proposal was really about, she didn't want Ethan Ballard to think she cared! No, better to leave him thinking she shrugged off marriage proposals from strangers as if they were a daily occurrence!

Sam made her way to the front door and finally managed to get away. Outside, she kicked off her heels and went around the parking lot toward the yacht club private beach that bordered it, the shortest route back to the small hamlet of St. John's Cove.

"Hey!"

Samantha turned and saw Ethan Ballard coming toward her, even his immense confidence no match for the sand. If she ran, he'd never catch her. But then he might guess he made her feel afraid in some way she didn't quite understand.

Not afraid of him. But afraid of herself.

She thought of the way his lips had felt when she had playfully brushed them with hers, and she turned and kept walking.

He caught up to her anyway.

"I see you survived my brothers."

"You sound disappointed."

"They usually run a better defense," she said. She could feel her heart pounding in her chest, and she was pretty sure it wasn't from the exertion of walking through the sand.

"Where are you going?" he asked.

A different girl might have said, *Midnight swim, skinny-dipping,* but she couldn't. She didn't quite know what to make of his attention. She was enjoying it, and *hating* the fact she was enjoying it. "Home."

"I'll walk you."

No one *ever* walked her anywhere. She was not seen as the fragile type; in fact her bravery was legend. She was the first one to swim in the ocean every year, she had been the first one out of the plane when the guys had talked her into skydiving. When they were fourteen and had played chicken with lit cigarettes, she had always won. She was known to be a daredevil in her little sailboat, an old Cape Dory Typhoon named the *Hall Way*.

Sam was a little taken aback that she *liked* his chivalry. So she said, with a touch of churlishness, "I can look after myself."

"I'll walk you home, anyway."

There was nothing argumentative in his tone. Or bossy. He was just stating a fact. He was walking her home, whether she liked it or not.

And she certainly didn't want him to know that she did like that feeling of being treated as fragile and feminine.

"Suit yourself."

He stopped after a moment, slid off his shoes and socks. Since she was stuck with him anyway, she waited, admiring the way he looked in the moonlight, silver beams tangling in the darkness of his hair, his now bare feet curling into the sensuousness of the sand.

He straightened, shoes in hand, and she saw the moonlight made his dark eyes glint with silver shadows, too.

She started walking again, and he walked beside her.

"Do you want to talk about the proposal?"

A renegade thought blasted through her of what it would be like to actually be married to a man like him. To taste those lips whenever you wanted, to feel his easy strength as part of your life.

Maybe that's why Amanda and Charlie had rushed to get married even when the odds were against them, pulled toward that soft feeling of not being alone anymore.

"I already said I'd marry you," she said, her careless tone hiding both her curiosity and the vulnerability those thoughts made her feel. "My brothers, strangely enough, liked you. What's to discuss?"

He laughed, and she didn't feel like he was laughing at her, but truly enjoying her. It would be easy to come to love that sensation. Of being *seen*. And appreciated.

"Setting a date?" he kidded.

"Oh. I guess there's that. How about tomorrow?" She reminded herself most of his appreciation was thanks to the costume: the dress and the hair and the makeup.

"I'm free, and by happy coincidence that's when I need a wife. Just for the day. Want to play with me?"

The awful thing was she *did* want to play with him, desperately. But what she considered playing—a day of sailing or swimming—was probably not what he considered playing. At all. His next words confirmed that.

"I'm a real estate investor. I buy higher end properties that have gone to seed, fix them up and flip them."

Oh, he *played* with money.

"I thought the market was gone," she said. She thought of the real estate sign hanging in front of her own rented premises, and thanked the wedding for its one small blessing.

She hadn't thought of *that* all day.

Because ever since the sign had gone up, she'd been getting stomachaches. Her business relied on its prime Main Street, St. John's, location, the summer people coming in and buying grooming supplies, the cute little doggy outfits she stocked, the good-grade dog foods, the amazing and unusual pet accessories that she spent her spare time seeking out. But she knew she'd been getting an incredible deal on the rent, which included her storefront and the apartment above it. A new owner meant one of two things, neither of them good. She would be paying higher rent, or she would get evicted.

"I'm in a position where I can buy and hold if I have to," he said with easy self-assurance, "though the market is never really gone for the kind of clients who buy my properties."

"Oh," she said. He dealt with the old rich, like the St. John family who had founded this town.

"One of my scouts called in a property down the coastline from here a few miles, a little closer to Stone Harbor than here. It's ideal—beachfront, a couple of acres, an old house that needs to be torn down or extensively remodeled, I'm not sure which yet."

The private beach they were walking down intersected with a boardwalk. Sam leaned over to put on her shoes to protect her feet from splinters on the weathered old boardwalk. When she raised up one foot, she took an awkward step sideways in the sand.

She felt a thrilled shock when Ethan reached out quickly to steady her, his one hand red-hot on her naked shoulder, his other caressing as he took her remaining shoe from where she was dangling it from its strap in her hand. He slid it onto her foot, his palm cupping the arch for a suspended second before sliding away.

He stepped away from her, acted as if nothing had happened as he sat down and put on his own socks and shoes.

How could he possibly not have felt that current that leaped in the air between them when he touched her foot? His touch had been astoundingly sexy, more so than when she had touched his lips earlier. She felt scorched; he appeared cool and composed.

Which meant even considering his proposal would be engaging in a form of lunacy she couldn't afford!

She didn't wait for him to finish with his shoes, but went up the rickety stairs in front of him, though she soon realized putting back on her own shoes had been a mistake, the heels finding every crack between the boards to slide down between. She was with one of the most elegant, composed, handsome men she had ever met, and she felt like she was in the starring role of *March of the Penguins.*

On the seaside of the boardwalk she was passing a scattering of small shingle-sided beachfront homes and cottages. Ethan caught up to her.

She slipped up the first side street of St. John's Cove, where it met the boardwalk, and now less wobbly on the paved walkway, marched up the hill past the old saltbox fishing cottages, one of which she had grown up in and where her brother Mitch still lived. The lobster traps in the front yard were real, not for decoration. He must have brought them home to repair them.

The side street emptied onto the town square, and she crossed the deserted park at the center of the square and went past the statue of Colton's great-grandfather. His great-grandfather looked amazingly like Colton—tall, handsome, powerful—but he had a stuffy look on his face that she had never seen on Colton's. The walkway that bisected the park led straight to Main Street, St. John's Cove.

The colorful awnings over the buildings had been all rolled up, the tables and umbrellas in front of the Clam Digger put away for the night. The street-lights, modeled after old gaslights, threw golden light over the wonderful old buildings, Colonial salt-boxes, shingle-sided, some weathered gray, some stained rich brown.

All the window, door, corner and roof trim was painted white, and old hinged store signs hung from wrought-iron arms above the doors. Each store had bright flower planters in front, spilling over with abundant colorful waves of cascading petunias.

St. John's Cove Main Street was picturesque and delightful—bookstores, antique shops, art galleries and cafés, the bank anchoring one end of the street, the post office the other.

And right in the middle of that was her store, Groom to Grow.

With the Building for Sale sign, that she had managed not to think about for nearly twelve whole hours, swinging gently in front of it. And if that wasn't bad enough, she could see the nose of Amanda's yellow convertible parked at a bad angle beside the staircase that ran up the side of her building to her apartment above the storefront.

Well, where else was Amanda going to go? She had given up her own apartment in anticipation of spending the rest of her life with Charlie, starting tonight.

"Well, this is home."

"This is *your* business?"

She turned at the surprised note in his voice. "Yes. I live in the apartment above it."

He put his hands in his pockets, rocked back on his heels. "That's a strange coincidence. I looked at it today."

"To buy it?" she asked, not succeeding at keeping the waver of fear out of her voice. So far, because of the economy, there had been very little interest in the building.

He shrugged, watching her closely. "I'd only pick it up if I bought the other property, as well. The price is reasonable, probably because the building needs a lot of work. Cape Cod is always a good investment."

"Oh." She tried to sound unconcerned, but knew she failed miserably. "What would you do with it, if you bought it?"

"Probably do some much needed maintenance on it, and then rent it out. Just think," he teased, "I could be your landlord."

"I doubt that. The rent is a song right now. Once the roof didn't leak and the hot water tap actually dispensed hot water, it would probably be a different story. I can't pay any higher. Once the building sells, I'll probably be looking for a new home. I was counting my lucky stars that there hasn't been much interest in it since it went on the market."

She wished she hadn't admitted that. The Hall

family was notorious for keeping their business to themselves, but she knew Ethan had registered the slight waver in her voice. She pointed her chin proudly to make up for it.

She wished she could afford to buy the building, but she couldn't. Her brothers would probably help her if she asked them, but she knew the lobster business was a tough one. The Hall brothers had invested in a new vessel recently, and she hated to think of putting more stress on their finances.

Her future, and the future of Groom to Grow, were clearly up in the air.

"Hmm," Ethan said easily, teasingly, "maybe I've found just the lure to get you to agree to be my wife."

As if he wasn't lure enough, damn him!

She wasn't in the mood to kid about Groom to Grow and her future. She had parlayed her love of animals into this business and if it wasn't *exactly* what she had planned for her life, at least it allowed her to live in the town she loved, surrounded by the people she cared about.

"Tell me the details of your *proposal*," she said reluctantly.

"When my lawyer made some initial inquiries about the property for sale up the coast, the couple informed him they were *interviewing* potential buyers. They're old people. They have a sentimental attachment to the place. They want to see another family in there. They've been *interviewing* buyers and turning them down for two years."

"That's kind of sweet, isn't it?"

He groaned. "Sweet? It's sentimental hogwash. What does that have to do with business?

"They could sell it to what they think is the perfect family, and that family could turn around and sell it in a year or two, disillusioned with life at Cape Cod."

He was being very convincing, and she knew that happened all the time. The *sumpies* were fickle in their love of Cape Cod.

They came and bought cottages and properties here during those perfect months of summer. Then they discovered they hated the commute. Or that outfitting and running two households was not very relaxing. That there were really only two or three true months of summer to enjoy their expensive real estate. Spring and fall were generally cold and blustery; winter in St. John's Cove was not for the faint of heart.

"So," Sam said uneasily, "you want me to pretend to be your wife for one day. To go dupe those old people out of their property."

He didn't just play with money—he played with people.

"I don't see it like that," he said evenly. "It's business. It's unrealistic of them to think they're going to control what happens to the property after they sell it."

He was right in a pragmatic way. If she could be

as businesslike as he was maybe the future of
Groom to Grow wouldn't be so uncertain. She made
a decent living at what she did, she loved it and it
allowed her to stay in St. John's Cove. But it had
never taken off to the point where she could sock
away enough money to buy her own property.

"I said I'd make it worth your while."

So, here was the truth about him. She should have
known it the first time she had looked into those
devil-dark eyes. Ethan Ballard was Lucifer, about to
hold out the one temptation she couldn't refuse, the
future of Groom to Grow. Though her eyes slid to
his lips when she thought that, and she realized he
might have two temptations she would have trouble
walking away from.

"If the deal goes the way I want it to, I'll buy this
building, and you can rent the space from me. I'll
guarantee you the same terms you have now for at
least a year, since you'd be putting up with some
noisy and inconvenient repairs."

Sam, of all people, knew life didn't have guaran-
tees, but a reprieve from that For Sale sign almost
made her weak in the knees.

"You want that place badly," she said, trying not
to act as shocked as she felt.

"Maybe. The initial assessments look very
promising."

"Enough for you to throw in a *building?*" she
asked cynically.

He shrugged. "So, I end up with the beachfront house *and* some of St. John's Cove Main Street. The price on this building was very fair. Sounds win-win to me."

"And if the deal doesn't go the way you want?"

"How could it not?" he said smoothly. "With you as my wife?"

In other words, if she played the role well, things would go exactly as he wanted them to. She had a feeling things in Ethan Ballard's life went his way.

"If, despite my best efforts to play your devoted wife, they don't sell you their property?" she pressed. "What then?"

"The deal is off. I'd be heading up a development team to work on the other property—carpenters, plumbers, electricians, roofers—so it would be no big deal to send them over to do some work on this building while we're here. But it wouldn't make good business sense to send them in for this building alone. I'm hands-on. If I can't be here to supervise, I'm not doing it."

"Oh."

"Take a chance," he said in his best charm-of-the-devil voice. "You won't be any further behind if things don't work out. Besides, it might be fun."

Oh, sure. Of course it was fun to dance with the devil, but there was always a price to be paid.

"I have to think about it," she said, deducing he was a man far too accustomed to getting his own way.

She certainly didn't want him to see how easily she was swayed by his charm, or how much she wanted what he was offering. He didn't have to know she was already ninety percent at yes.

Though in truth more than fifty percent of that *yes* was that she was reluctantly intrigued by him, even if she was uneasy about the deal.

A light turned on in her apartment.

They both turned and looked up at the lighted window. Amanda, still in her bridal gown, was pacing in front of the window.

I'm getting a stomachache, Sam noted to herself. Out loud, she said coolly, "It was nice meeting you. Thanks for walking me home."

"I'll drop by in the morning, around nine. I'll pick you up right here, outside, so it's not awkward if you decide against it. If you're here, great, and if you're not, I'll assume you didn't want to come. No problem." He looked at her for a long moment, and she could feel herself holding her breath. He was debating kissing her! She knew it. And she didn't know if she was relieved or regretful when he walked away!

By nine the next morning, the other ten percent had swung over to Ethan Ballard's side. The truth was, Sam would have thrown in with Genghis Khan to get away from the intensity of emotion that had swept into her life with the runaway bride. Sam had spent most of the night trying to console her friend, who was inconsolable, but who wouldn't tell her what horrible crime Charlie had committed this time.

Despite her cynicism about love and marriage, Sam would have done anything to make Charlie and Amanda's relationship work, to see her friends happy. Her sense of powerlessness in the face of Amanda's distress made her eager to escape.

Still, even though she was waiting at the curb for Ethan Ballard, Sam was determined he wasn't going to have it all his way.

No, the girl Ethan had proposed to last night was banished. Gone was the makeup and the hair, gone was the suggestive dress.

Sam's face was scrubbed clean, her hair loose but covered with her favorite ball cap. She was wearing an old pair of faded khakis, and a T-shirt that belonged to her brother Bryce. She had an uglier one that belonged to Mitch, but Amanda was shuffling around the apartment in it this morning since everything Amanda owned was at Charlie's house.

Still, Sam was satisfied that she certainly would not be what anyone would picture as the wife of Mr. Ethan Ballard.

And she had the new dog, Waldo, with her, too. People dropped off strays with her, counting on her to work her magic with them and then to find them good homes. Sam had never said no to a dog who needed a place to go.

This dog was particularly sensitive to emotion,

and when Amanda had become so overwrought that she was puking, he had started sympathy-puking right along with her.

Sam and the dog were actually sitting on the curb when Ethan drove up the street slowly in a gorgeous newer-model luxury car. Waldo, half Chinese pug and half mystery, was dressed in an army camo hoodie since the morning fog had not quite lifted, and the breeze coming off the ocean was sharp. Sam could not stop herself from spoiling the dogs and cats that had temporary refuge with her.

Sam saw the look on Ethan Ballard's face when he saw her sitting by the curb with her mutt. She thought about the mission they were about to embark on and had the uncharitable hope that the dog would puke in his luxurious car.

If Ethan even stopped to pick them up! Maybe he would take one look at the real Samantha Hall and drive right on by!

CHAPTER THREE

ETHAN BALLARD drove down Main Street of St. John's Cove, enjoying the Sunday morning quiet of it, but aware that despite his words last night—*If you're here, great, and if you're not, I'll assume you didn't want to come*—he hadn't meant the *no problem* follow-up. For some reason, he *wanted* her to come with him.

And not necessarily because of the Finkles, either. Last night, after he had left Samantha Hall and walked back down the beach alone, he had thought of her comment about *duping those old people out of their property,* and not liked that very much.

Usually Ethan regarded business as a large chess game. He liked *winning.* He had turned his competitive nature to that and found it far more fulfilling and less full of pitfalls than relationships. But when had he become so focused on the win that he was willing to *dupe* people?

Maybe it would be just as well if Samantha didn't

show up this morning. He'd drive up the coast, present the Finkles with a very good offer, take it or leave it, no games, no *duping*.

So, if it would be just as well if she didn't show up, and if he was a man who avoided the pitfalls of relationships and had made business, pragmatic and predictable, a safe harbor from *emotion,* then it was probably not a good thing that he felt dismayed that Samantha was not waiting for him.

A little boy in a ball cap and a scruffy dog sat on the curb. Ethan slowed, looked past them, to see if Samantha was coming down her staircase. She wasn't, and aware of a sharp pang of disappointment, he debated going and knocking on her door.

But that hadn't been the agreement, and if the yellow convertible was any indication, his cousin, Amanda, was still there. His brow furrowed as he thought of his young, lovely cousin starting the day yesterday so full of hope, and now being so distressed. Should he go say something to her? Or would his own discomfort with all things emotional just make everything worse?

While he mulled over his options, the little boy stood up, and the dog yapped its dislike. Ethan glanced at the pair again.

And slammed on the brakes. His eyes widened.

That was Samantha Hall? Oh, it was her all right, those wide-set gray-green eyes in the shadow of the ball cap, the delicate features, the sensuous curve of her mouth. But all those delectable curves that dress had shown off last night were disguised this morning.

Ethan leaned over and opened the door for her, surprised by how he felt. Intrigued. And he had the same feeling he'd had last night after talking to her brother. That what Samantha needed more than anything else was for someone to see right past the ball cap, and the men's T-shirt, to the woman in her.

The woman he had tasted when his lips had brushed hers so briefly.

The woman he had touched when she had stumbled putting on her shoe, felt the pure and feminine sensuous energy of her.

"Good morning," he said as she slid into the seat beside him. "I nearly drove by. I didn't recognize you."

"This is the *real* me," she said defensively, settling the dog on her lap.

Is it? he wondered. Her dog glared at him and growled. She appeared to have taken more time dressing the dog than herself.

"I thought maybe that was how you felt Mrs. Ethan Ballard would look," he said mildly, and glancing up at the apartment window asked, "Do you think I should go say something to Amanda?"

"She's finally sleeping."

He heard the concern in Samantha's voice, and felt, ridiculously, as if he was the white knight riding in, not to rescue his cousin, but Samantha.

"You look a little the worse for wear this

morning," he said, checking over his shoulder as he pulled away from the curb.

"I don't have the wardrobe to look like Mrs. Ethan Ballard," she said proudly. "Unless I wore the dress from last night and it didn't seem appropriate for daywear."

"I wasn't referring to your clothes," he said dryly. "You just look tired."

"Oh."

"What do you think Mrs. Ethan Ballard's wardrobe would look like?"

She slid him a sideways look. "I guess that depends what kind of woman you go for. I wonder. Trashy? Or classy. I'm going to guess classy."

"Thanks," he said dryly. "I think."

Classy. He thought of Bethany, with her pedigree and her designer wardrobe, her tasteful jewelry, her exotic, expensive scents. Classy, but when he'd scraped the surface, challenged her, she'd been superficial as hell.

The woman beside him in her baseball cap and khakis, with her innate honesty and decency, seemed a lot more classy than Bethany. If classy meant *genuine*. Real. And somehow at this moment that is what it meant to him.

"Classy it is," he said. The next town, Stone Harbor, was past the turnoff to the Finkles, but since it was just a few minutes away on the winding coast road, and it was bigger than St. John's Cove, a few of its Main Street stores would be open on Sunday. He pulled over in front of a boutique, Sunsational, that looked upscale and *classy*.

Luckily the fog was persisting so it wasn't yet hot enough to worry about leaving the dog in the car, though he rolled all the windows partly down.

He opened the door for Samantha, aware he was enjoying this, aware that his rendezvous with the Finkles was shimmering like an oasis he might never arrive at but he didn't mind because the journey there was proving just as interesting. Make that more interesting.

"What are we doing?" Samantha asked, eyeing the boutique.

"Making you into Mrs. Ballard. The classy version." He grinned. "Though trashy would be more fun."

He saw she looked wounded, and that he had insulted her by insinuating she wouldn't make a great Mrs. Ballard just the way she was.

But he felt he saw a truth about her that she might have been missing herself: that what she was wearing now was a disguise of sorts intended to hide who she really was.

"Look," he said, hastily, "you look fine the way you are. But if I don't end up buying your building, you've given me your time for nothing. Let me do something for you. Consider it a thank-you in advance."

Pride played across her face, but he saw the

faintest wistfulness in the quick glance she cast at the door. He knew it! She had every woman's delight in shopping!

Still, when he held open the door of the store for her and she marched by him, she was scowling.

He touched the place where her brow was knit. "Have fun!" he instructed her.

She looked at him, glanced around the store. He could clearly see she was struggling with a decision, and he was relieved when something in her relaxed.

"Okay," she said, and gave him a small, careful smile. It occurred to him that that smile changed everything, changed far more than a dress ever could. He saw the radiance in her, and realized the sighting was precious, the part of herself, along with her femininity, that she kept hidden.

It was a treasure he felt drawn to find.

Still, her idea of *fun* turned out to be a menace, because she gave him the *trashy* version of Mrs. Ballard. She flounced out of the dressing room in a too short white leather skirt and a hot-pink halter top, flipped a dark wave of luscious hair over her naked shoulder and watched his reaction solemnly.

The truth was he was flummoxed. She looked *awful*. And yet his mouth went absolutely dry at the slender temptation of her perfect curves, her toned and tanned legs, the glimpse of her belly button where the top didn't quite meet the skirt.

When he struggled for words, and all that came

out was an uncertain *Ah,* the solemn look faded from her face and she laughed. She was kidding him, paying him back.

But when she laughed her whole face lit up and her eyes danced with mischief, and he knew he'd glimpsed the treasure he'd been looking for. The real Samantha Hall, despite the costume she had put on.

A half hour later and a half dozen more sedate outfits later, she emerged from the dressing room and twirled in front of him. The defensiveness had left her, and he was delighted at how thoroughly she was enjoying herself. From the sassiness of her pose, she knew it was the perfect outfit, and so did he.

She wore a summer skirt, of light silk, an amazing blend of seaside colors, the turquoise of the sea and the pale blue of the sky. She had paired it with casual sandals that showed the delicate lines of her feet, and he remembered the white-hot feeling of holding that tiny foot in the palm of his hand last night.

When she twirled, her loose, glossy hair fanned out and the skirt flew around her, revealing, again, those amazing legs, and hinting at her gypsy spirit.

She had on a cream linen jacket, that she hadn't done up, and under it was a camisole so simple there should be no reason that it made his mouth go as dry as the more flamboyant pink halter top she had tried on first.

"What do you think?" she asked.

He thought she was the perfect Mrs. Ballard. He

thought he had dragged her in here to show her something of herself, and had seen something of himself instead. That he was vulnerable to her.

"You look perfect," he said gruffly, and then tried to short-circuit his own vulnerability, to make her stop looking at him like *that*, in a way that made his heart feel like it would swoop out of his chest and land in the palms of her hands. "Let's go dupe the Finkles."

The happy look faded from her face, and he was sorry even though he knew it was better for both of them if they didn't forget what this was all about.

"This is the one," she said, suddenly cool. "Let's go."

He mourned the loss of the magic of the moments they had just shared, even as he knew they made things way too complicated.

At the front desk, Samantha went outside while he paid. The clerk offered to package up the old clothes for him, but he just shook his head. Even if she was mad at him, he never wanted to see her in those clothes—that particular lie—again.

She didn't ask about her clothes when he joined her. Her eyes were challenging him to back down, to say the subterfuge had gone far enough.

But the look of disdain in her eyes was so much safer for him than the look in her eyes when she had been twirling in front of him, filled with glorious certainty of herself, that he felt more committed than ever to his plan. They'd visit the Finkles, he'd take her home. Leave her with the outfit to assuage some faint guilt he was feeling. If he did end up buying her building, he would keep it strictly business.

Though he wasn't sure how, since he had utterly failed to keep things strictly business so far.

What if it could be real?

He didn't even know her, he scoffed at himself. But when he looked at her, her eyes distant, her chin pointed upward with stubbornness and pride, he felt like he did know her. Or wanted to.

"What's the plan now?" she said.

"We'll go to the Finkles. Let's just say we're engaged instead of married," he told her.

The stiff look of pride left her face and something crumpled in her eyes. "Even dressed up, I'm not good enough, am I?"

"No!" he said, stunned at her conclusion. "That's not it at all. The problem is you are way too good for me. Duper of old people, remember?"

And then he hurriedly opened the car door and held it for her, before he gave into the temptation to take her in his arms and erase any thought she'd ever had about not being good enough, before he gave in to the temptation to kiss her until she had not a doubt left about who she really was, a *woman,* who deserved more than she had ever asked of the world.

He knew if he was smart, he would just pass the turnoff he was looking for and take her straight back to St. John's Cove, cut his losses.

But now he felt he had to *prove* to her it was him that was unworthy, not her.

It was probably the stupidest thing he'd ever done, to continue this charade.

But looking back over the events of the last day, since he had first seen Samantha Hall standing at the altar beside his cousin, it seemed to Ethan Ballard he had not made one smart decision. Not one.

He glanced at the woman sitting with her dog slobbering all over her new silk skirt, trying to read her expression.

"Look," he said awkwardly, "any man would be lucky to call you his wife. And that was before we went shopping." He was a little shocked by how much he meant that, but he had failed to convince her.

He wanted to just call this whole thing off, forget the Finkles and go home to the mess-free life he took such pride in.

"Humph," she said skeptically.

If he did call it off now, was Samantha really going to think she had failed to measure up to his standard for a wife? He sighed at how complicated this innocent little deceit had become.

Here he was smack-dab in the middle of a mess of his own making.

Samantha Hall looked straight ahead, refusing to meet his eyes, but the dog slid him a contemptuous look and growled low in its throat.

Ethan Ballard thought he had heard somewhere that dogs were excellent judges of character.

"I used to play baseball," he said. It was a measure of his desperation that he was trying to *win* her respect back this way, when he hated it when people liked him for his former career. But the truth was, right about now, Ethan would take her liking any way he could get it.

He *wanted* that look back in her eyes, he wanted the radiance back, even though it was a very dangerous game he played.

"Didn't we all?" she said.

"I meant professionally. I played first base for the Red Sox for a season."

"And you are telling me this why?" Not the tiniest bit of awe in her voice.

"I'm trying to impress you," he admitted sadly, "since I've managed to make such a hash of it so far."

"Humph."

"I'll take that as a fail."

"I grew up with three brothers," she told him, and he could hear the sharp annoyance in her voice. "Every single special occasion of my entire life has been spoiled by their obsession with sports. You know where my brothers were the night I graduated from high school?"

"I'm afraid to ask."

"In Boston."

"Oh, boy," he muttered. "Red Sox?"

She nodded curtly and went back to looking out the window.

It occurred to him he really had stumbled onto the perfect woman for him, a woman capable of not being impressed with what he'd done, who could look straight through that to who he really was.

Not that he'd exactly done a great job of showing her that. Maybe he'd even lost who he really was somewhere along the way, in the pursuit of ambition and success.

And maybe she was the kind of woman who could lead him back to it. If he was crazy enough to tangle with her any longer than he absolutely had to.

With relief he saw the sign he'd been looking for—Annie's Retreat—and he pulled off the main road onto a rutted track.

The first thing that would need work, and a lot of it, was the road, he thought, and it was such a blessed relief to be able to think of that rather than the stillness of the woman beside him.

Life was just plain mean, Sam thought, getting out of the car after the long, jolting ride down a rough road. Waldo bounced out with her. He had snagged her skirt, so she had managed to look upscale for all of fifteen minutes.

Ethan, of course, looked like he was modeling for the summer issue of *GQ*, in dun-colored safari shorts that looked like he had taken a few minutes to press them before he left his hotel this morning. Ditto for the shirt, a short-sleeved mossy-green cotton, with a subtle Ballard Holdings embroidered in a deeper shade of green over the one buttoned pocket.

No wonder she had been downgraded to fiancée! No matter what he said, she was pretty sure it was because she didn't fit in his world.

"Maybe we should leave him in the car," Ethan suggested carefully, as if she was made of glass.

But she was all done being what Ethan wanted her to be, and Waldo came with her, *especially* if he didn't fit into Ethan's world and Ethan's plans.

"The dog comes," she said, "and if you don't like it, or they don't like it, *tough.*"

There. That was more like the real Samantha Hall, not like that woman who had stared back at her from the mirror in Sunsational, sensual, grown-up, mature, *feminine.*

Despite her attempts to harden her emotions, Samantha could not deny Annie's Retreat was a place out of a dream she had, a dream that she had been able to keep a secret even from herself until she saw this place. These large properties were almost impossible to come by anymore on this coastline.

It made her remember that once upon a time she had dreamed of turning her love of all things animal into an animal refuge, where she could rescue and rehabilitate animals. Given her nonexistent budget, Groom to Grow had been more realistic, and she still ended up caring for the odd stray, like Waldo, that people brought in. But looking at this property she felt that old longing swell up in her.

The road ended in a yard surrounded by a picket fence, the white paint long since given way to the assaults of the salt air. Early-season roses were going crazy over an arbor; beyond it she could see the cottage: saltbox, weathered gray shake siding, white trim in about the same shape as the paint on the fence.

An attempt at a garden had long since gone wild, and yet it charmed anyway: daises, phlox, hollyhock, sewn among scraggly lawn, beach grass and sand.

A path of broken stones wound a crooked course to the house, where red geraniums bloomed in peeling window boxes. The path ended at an old screen door; the red storm door to the cottage was open through it. Sam could look in the door: a dark hallway burst open into a living room where a wall of salt-stained windows faced an unparalleled view of a restless, gray-capped sea.

She was here to look at a cottage out of a dream, a cottage she would never own. She was here with a man out of a dream, a man who was as unattainable for her as the cottage. *No matter what he said about her being good enough and trying to impress her.*

Ha-ha.

Waldo jumped up on the door, put his paws on the screen, sniffed and let out a joyous howl. A small dog came roaring down the hall, skittered on a rug, righted itself and rammed the door. She was out and after a brief sniff, the two dogs raced around the yard, obviously in the throes of love.

If only it was that easy for people, Sam thought. Though she could fall in love with the man beside her in about half a blink if she allowed herself to.

Not that she would ever be that foolish!

A tiny gnome of a woman came to the door, smiled at them from under a thick fringe of snow-white hair. She opened the door to them, glancing at the dogs with tolerance.

Then she looked at them with disconcerting directness, her smile widened and she stuck out her hand. "Annie Finkle."

Ethan took it, introduced himself, then hesitated before he said, "And this is my, er, fiancée, Samantha Hall."

Samantha glanced at him. He was either a terrible liar, or after downgrading her from the wife position, didn't even want her to be his fiancée!

She decided, evil or not, to make him pay for that. She looped her arm around his waist, ran her hand casually and possessively along his back, just as she had seen in-love couples do. The way her life was going this might be as close as she would ever get, so she was going to enjoy every minute of it.

And enjoy it even more because it made him so uncomfortable.

"Darling," she breathed, following Annie into the

living room, not letting go of her hold on him, "isn't this the most adorable house you've ever seen?"

"Adorable," he croaked, and she looked at him and enjoyed the strain she saw in his face. He tried to lift her arm away from him, but she clamped down tighter.

It was a delightful room, completely without pretension. It had dark plank flooring that had never been refinished, and a huge fireplace, the face of it soot-darkened from use. Worn, much used couches faced each other between the huge window and the fireplace. The entire room cried *home*.

"I love the floor coverings," Sam said. "They're unbelievable."

Annie beamed at her. "I hand-paint historic patterns on oilskins. I make more of them than I can use, unfortunately. Artie would like me to open a shop, but I'm probably too old." But even as she said it, she looked wistful. She brought herself back to the moment. "This is my favorite room in the house."

"I love it, too," Sam breathed. "I can just see myself sitting in that rocking chair in the winter, a fire in the hearth, watching a storm-tossed sea." Then she realized it didn't feel like a game, so she upped the ante to remind herself this was fantasy. "Maybe," she cooed, "there would be a baby at my breast."

Something darkened in his already too dark eyes. The set of his mouth looked downright grim as he looked at her. She knew she was playing way out of her league, and she didn't mean baseball, but she stroked his back again, even though it made her stomach drop and her fingers tingle.

She should have known not to even try to get the best of him, because he leaned close to her, inhaled the scent of her hair and then blew his breath into her ear.

"Stop it," he growled in a low tone, and then he gently nipped her ear, just to let her know if she wanted to play hardball he had plenty of experience.

The tingle Sam had been experiencing in her fingers moved to her toes. And back up again.

"Oh," Annie said. "Babies! And you'd come in the winter?"

"If I owned this place," Sam said, "I doubt I'd ever leave it." No, she could see herself here as if it would be the perfect next stage of her life, not the place of change that she had feared, at all.

She could see all her friends gathering here, the Group of Six not disappearing, but expanding as they acquired mates and children, the circle growing in love and warmth. She could sense those unborn children, see them screeching and running on the beach, toasting marshmallows on bonfires at night, falling asleep in parents' arms.

This house cast a spell on Sam that made it so easy to see her brothers, settling down at last, coming here with their wives and children, raising another generation who loved Cape Cod year-round.

This was the kind of place where friends and

family gathered around the fire on deepest winter nights. Where they played rowdy card games and hysterical rounds of charades, enjoying sanctuary in the love and laughter of friends from the bitter winter storms.

Why was it, it was so easy to imagine Ethan, an outsider to that circle, as being at the very center of it? Why is it she knew that he would slide into the circle without creating a ripple, as if he had belonged there always?

Was it the place that created this sensation of belonging? A longing for things that weren't yet, but that she could sense on the horizon?

She realized she was imagining a life that had been once, already. She was believing in something that had died for her when her parents had died.

"I would never leave," she whispered, and then closed her eyes, remembering what that sense of family and community had been like, and feeling deeply grateful that the love of the Group of Six had kept hope alive inside of her even while she denied it.

She opened her eyes when she realized the room was too quiet, and she feared she had inadvertently revealed too much of herself to Ethan Ballard. She scanned the handsome lines of his face and did not like the quizzical expression as he looked at her, as if he knew she had momentarily forgotten it was a game. She forced herself to explore the curve of his lower back with her fingertips again, to distract him, and herself, from what had just happened.

This time, instead of trying to move away from her, Ethan looked at her hard, and saw way too much. Instead of moving away from her touch, he pulled her closer into his side, so that she could feel the steely length of him…and the strong, steady beat of his heart.

It was a terrible sensation, because it felt to Sam as if he was a man you could rely on when you were tired of being alone and afraid of being lonely, a man you could rely on when you decided, finally, you just wanted to go home.

Annie led them through the dining area to the kitchen. It was small, cramped and dated, but Sam thought it was the coziest kitchen she had ever seen, with its bright yellow paint, white curtains blowing in the breeze from an open window.

She tried to get back into the spirit of pretense by saying, "Oh, I can just imagine baking cookies for you here, darling," but in her own ears her voice sounded forced and faraway.

Because she could imagine using this kitchen, even though she had never baked a cookie in her life. It still could become the cheerful hub for all the activity she had imagined moments ago.

"I can hardly wait," he growled, and then kissed her on the tip of her nose, a playful gesture that seemed all too tender and all too real. It should have been a warning to stop before she had embedded herself further in the quicksand of the heart. But instead, it only egged her on, even though she wanted to quit doing this. Not to him, but to herself.

Down the narrow hall they went, the narrowness forcing her to let go of him.

But she made up for it.

The back bedroom was tiny and dark.

"This is the room I want for the nursery," she declared, but unfortunately, as she said it, she could see it, just as she had so clearly seen the future in those other rooms.

And shockingly, so could he.

"I'd knock out this wall," he said, pensively, "and put in a bigger window, a bay one, with a window seat. We could sit here with the baby, together, in the evenings."

The picture that conjured up for her stole her breath. She could so easily imagine him in that tender scene. And that picture stole her drive to make him uncomfortable, to make him pay for this farce. She was done pretending. What it was doing to her heart was far too dangerous.

She did not renew her possessive encircling of his waist, and made no comment about how romantic the master bedroom was, though it had another fireplace in it, and a window that faced the sea.

He also became more and more silent, and Sam wondered if he was looking at the house through a developer's eyes. If he was, she deduced, a bit sadly, there was probably nothing to be saved.

After a tour of the interior of the house they moved outside. Annie's husband, Artie, was in the garden, and they met him, and then Annie laid tea out for all of them on a worn outdoor table that faced the sea.

The dogs had worn themselves out and flopped down, panting under the table. Waldo nuzzled Annie's hand.

"What an adorable dog," the old woman said gently.

"He's looking for a home!" Sam said, never missing an opportunity to place one of her charges.

"I can barely keep up with the one I have," Annie confessed ruefully. "I do love his outfit. Where did you get that?"

"Groom to Grow in St. John's Cove," Sam said. "I—"

Ethan nudged her gently in the ribs, reminding her she was beginning to complicate things by mixing up her fiction with her facts. So instead of saying she owned it, she said, hearing the slight sullenness in her own voice, "I love shopping there."

"I'm going to get a jacket just like that one for Josie!" Annie declared, and Sam thought what a perfect home this would be for Waldo, even as she remembered what she hated about lies. They never stopped. Now this woman was going to show up at her shop in St. John's. What if she inquired about her fiancé? What if people were listening?

Annie's eyes met hers over the tea. "I can see you here," she said quietly to Sam. "I'm so delighted. Finally I can see someone here."

Artie looked at his wife and smiled, and something passed between them that was so sweet and so genuine that it nearly broke Sam's heart in two. No wonder she could feel love in this house, no wonder the place conjured visions of domestic bliss.

"We don't want to sell to just anybody," Artie said. "Annie's a bit fey. She said she'd know when the right people came along. People who would love this ramshackle old wreck of a place as much as we have."

Sam wanted to sink under the table she felt so dreadful. If Ethan got his hands on this old cottage what would he do with it? Tear it down? She saw Ethan leaning forward. Clearly this was the moment he lived for, closing the deal. He probably had papers they could sign in the car.

And suddenly, she just couldn't do it, not even if her whole future and the future of Groom to Grow was at stake.

"Oh," she said, forcing brightness, "we aren't rushing into anything, are we, darling? I'm just not sure if this is the right place for us. There's only three bedrooms, and we are planning a large family. Ethan wants at least six children."

"Six," Annie said with surprise, though it was approving surprise.

"Of course, we could put on an addition," Ethan

said, the smile belying what she interpreted as a warning look in his eyes as he gazed at her.

She ignored the warning. "Darling! You know I have to be sure. You know what they say, don't you?"

"No, I don't," he said tightly.

"If Mama ain't happy, ain't nobody happy," she sang to him, wagging a stern finger below his nose.

He glared at her while the Finkles laughed with delight.

"I think you're right not to rush into anything," Annie said. "Even though the place is getting to be too much for us—look at the flower beds and the paint, disgraceful—we're in no hurry to sell. I'd feel better if I found exactly the right place for us to move on to first."

"Very wise," Sam murmured, not daring to look at the man beside her.

"We're thinking a condo, but I haven't seen one I like yet. They're all so—"

"Generic," Sam provided. She, too, had looked at condos before finding her own charming apartment, with the storefront beneath it, so suited to her needs.

The one she was about to throw away. Because she couldn't do this. Not if Ethan promised to buy the whole of Main Street, St. John's Cove. She *liked* these people and hated herself for being a part of this pretense. Samantha's business meant a lot to her, the world to her, in fact, but she realized she wasn't prepared to sell her soul for it!

"Exactly," Annie said. "Plus, so many of them seem to be prisons for old people. I don't want to retreat from the world. That's part of what bothers me here. Since we retired and spend so much time here, it seems too isolated. I want to be *part* of the community. Maybe have a little rug shop, where I could meet people every day."

"Well, I guess we all need to think about it for a bit," Sam said, nearly choking on her cheer. She finished her tea in a gulp that was very un-Mrs. Ballard-like and got up from the table. "It was so nice meeting you, Annie. Artie. Darling."

But it was Waldo, getting used to being called *darling* who fell in beside her as she went up the crooked walk beside the cottage to the car. She didn't even glance back over her shoulder at the house of her dreams.

Or to see if Ethan Ballard, pretend fiancé, had followed her.

CHAPTER FOUR

"SORRY," Samantha murmured.

"Don't give it a thought."

He was surprised that he meant it. Ethan Ballard should have been furious. The Finkles had been ready to do some preliminary talking about the property, which was everything he'd hoped for and more. Even the cottage, which he had thought from the Internet pictures would be only worth knocking down, had lots of potential.

He told himself people loved the old saltboxes, and he could knock down interior walls to create a more open space, add windows, expand the house toward the rear. But even as he tried to convince himself that, he wondered if part of how charmed Samantha had been with the old place had rubbed off on him. There was no way she was a good enough actress to have pulled off the enraptured look on her face, the light in her eyes, as she had moved from room to room.

But it was probably all a moot point now. He might never get a chance because the little minx sitting beside him, stroking her dog furiously, had done her best to nix the deal.

But he was aware he did not feel furious with Samantha.

More like *cautious* of her. He had felt something stir in him when she had touched him so possessively, and felt it stir again at an even more powerful and primal level when she had talked about sitting in that living room with a baby at her breast.

Even though she'd clearly been trying to get his goat, the picture had taken on a life of its own inside his mind, and somehow the baby she held had been his.

That, even though he was a man who had never given one single thought to having kids, or to domestic bliss. When he'd been engaged to Bethany he'd been too young to think that far ahead. Bethany had never said a single word about children. He'd been her ticket to *Lifestyles of the Rich and Famous,* not a ruined figure and responsibility.

But there was something about Samantha Hall that made a man not just think of those things, but yearn after them.

Plus, at tea with the Finkles, when Samantha had stunned him by declaring they needed time to think about it, Ethan felt as if he had discovered something more valuable than the property.

The woman beside him appeared to be a person incapable of subterfuge, incapable of deceit. How many people were there in the world who would be so true to themselves? He could tell how badly Sam wanted to stay in her store, but she had been unwilling to lie to do it.

But, he reminded himself, there was an irony here. She did lie to herself, the clothes he had disposed of this morning being a perfect example.

Now as they pulled away from Annie's Retreat, he could tell she was relieved the playacting was over.

"I hated that," she said.

"I should never have asked you to do that," he replied. "It was an impulse. I regret it. " But even as he said it, he knew his regret was not one hundred percent. He thought of her fingers on his back, as she teased him, played with him; he thought of nipping the delicate lobe of her ear.

And was aware he wouldn't have missed that for the world.

She misunderstood him. "I know. You could have asked a thousand girls who could have pulled that off better than me. But Annie and Artie were just such nice people. I hated that they wanted us to have that property when it was all a lie."

He said nothing, digesting what she was telling him about herself.

"So, are you done?" she asked. "You aren't going to try to buy it?"

"I'll back off for the time being. What did you think of the property?"

She was silent, as if she did not want to give anything of herself away to him. Not that he could blame her. But he had already seen things, and she seemed to know it was too late to hide them.

"I loved it," she admitted reluctantly.

"So did I."

"But I loved it just the way it was. I mean a few things needed work, the paint, the flower beds, but it would be a shame to change it. A crime."

"Unless you were going to raise six kids there," he teased her.

She delighted him by blushing. "Just trying to play the part."

"Don't give up your day job."

"Don't worry, I won't. Unless I get evicted from my building. Then I'll put out my new sign, Wife for Hire."

He chuckled, and her stance toward him softened a bit.

"I did like your idea about the one wall in the, er, back bedroom," she admitted.

For a reason he wasn't about to investigate, he was sorry she hadn't called it the nursery. Which is probably why he changed the subject, tried to get it back to the nice, safe area of business instead of the very gray area of nurseries.

"I'm glad you're not going to buy my building,"

she said thoughtfully, somber. "It sounded great, but it made me uneasy, too. I don't want to feel indebted to you, but it's more. Ethan, being the youngest in a family, the only girl, I think I'm used to the boys bailing me out. I don't want to rely on other people to fix my problems."

He was struck by her simple bravery.

"I didn't keep my end of our bargain," she continued. "You can have the outfit back, too."

"You know," he said quietly and carefully, "there's a fine balance between being independent and being alone. Sometimes it's good to rely on others, to share your burdens."

He remembered the joy that had lit her eyes when she had first twirled in that outfit, and cursed himself for stealing that happiness from her.

"And sometimes it's okay," he continued, "to accept a gift. It's no threat to your independence. I want you to have the outfit."

She shrugged and he suspected the outfit was going to enjoy approximately the same fate as the flowers she had caught just last night.

Suddenly he wanted out of this mess he had created for himself. Even if he didn't buy Annie's Retreat, he would never be able to shake the vision of this girl twirling in front of the mirror and him, her hair and her skirt giving her a gypsy air, never be able to quite escape the memory of her hand resting on the small of his back, or her quick intake of air when he'd nipped her ear.

In fact, the sooner he put this whole unfortunate lapse in judgment behind him the better. He'd drop her off and wave goodbye. A kiss, even a casual little goodbye peck, was out of the question; the dog would probably bite him if he got that close to her. Besides, it would be one more memory that he had to outrun.

But when he turned onto Main Street, and slowed in front of her store, he could see Charlie Weston was on the sidewalk in front of it. The poor fool, still in his suit from last night, though he'd lost the bow tie, was seated on a stool, with a guitar across his knee, gazing up at the open window of Sam's apartment, oblivious to the astounded, curious looks of passersby.

"Thank goodness it's Sunday. Look what he's done to my sign," Sam said, annoyance and obvious affection mixed in her voice.

Ethan looked at where a ladder was propped against her store sign. The placement of the spindly ladder looked downright dangerous. A clumsy, hand-drawn *S* and *L* had been taped over her sign, turning "Groom to Grow" to "Groom so Low."

"The English language constantly amazes me in its versatility," Ethan said. "Do you think he meant groom so low, as in depressed, or groom solo, as in single?"

"Charlie is not exactly an academic," Sam said affectionately.

"A romantic," Ethan concluded dryly. "Which

would you rather have?" He realized he was truly interested in her answer, but Samantha ignored him, put her window down halfway, looked as if she planned to intervene.

With the car window open it was painfully apparent Charlie was serenading his runaway bride, wailing an old Don Williams song. Charlie's voice was particularly horrible, part whine, part twang, mostly heartbreak and pathos.

Amanda, light of my life—

Ethan glanced at Samantha. She looked like she was going to get out of the car and try to fix this. Her love for her friends showed in the utter distress on her face. But her hand froze on the door handle when something flew out the open window of Samantha's apartment and hit Charlie square in the chest.

"What was that?" Ethan asked, craning his neck to see better. "A rock?"

"One of the little squares of wedding cake that it took Vivian and me four hours to wrap and tie with fuchsia ribbon."

Charlie set down the guitar. "Mandy, come on—"

The window above Charlie snapped shut.

"Now, that's *reality*," Sam said sadly, as if for a while she had believed something else. Ethan thought of the look on her face when she had looked at the cottage.

"Maannndddyy!" It was like the bellow of a wounded bull.

The window shot up, and Amanda leaned out. "Go away!"

"I think I better try to talk to them," Samantha said.

Not even for his own self-preservation was Ethan dropping Samantha off in the middle of that. He stepped on the gas.

"What are you doing?" Samantha demanded.

"Rescuing you from *that*. Haven't you heard the expression about not going where angels fear to tread? Lovers' quarrels fall solidly in that category."

"I told you before, I can look after myself." But he didn't miss the fact she looked relieved.

"Well, pretend you can't. Pretend I'm a knight in shining armor and you are a damsel in distress."

"Even if my imagination was that good, I think I've done enough pretending for today."

"Me, too," he said quietly, and was startled by how pleased he was that she looked faintly intrigued. "I'll take you for lunch. Charlie and Amanda should have resolved things by the time we get back."

"I hate to break it to you since you look like the kind of guy who believes in happily-ever-after—" that said sarcastically "—but Amanda and Charlie have been trying to resolve things since they were fourteen."

"A long lunch, then," he said, and was rewarded with her smile, which she quickly doused when he smiled back.

"They are both such good people," she said

softly. "I don't know why it's always so volatile between them."

"Passion," he said. "It's hard stuff to tame." As if he was any kind of expert on passion—or wanted to be thinking about the subject when he was in such close proximity to her!

"I can't leave Waldo in the car. It's getting too hot." To prove her point, she slipped the hoodie off her dog.

He hoped that meant the imminent removal of her own jacket, even as he thought Samantha was showing a remarkable lack of gratitude for his chivalry. He should just turn around and dump her on that sidewalk, but he thought of Charlie wailing, and Amanda throwing things, and her thinking she could do something to fix it, and he just couldn't.

"Okay, we'll buy some sandwiches and eat at the beach."

"I guess I could change into my other clothes."

And deprive him of the camisole? At least he'd made one good decision today, and he admitted it to her now, trying to appear contrite. "Um, I forgot to pick them up after I paid for the new things."

She stared at him, her gaze going right through him. He was never going to be able to tell her a lie. Ever. But what did it mean that he was thinking like that? As if there was an *ever* in their future.

They were having lunch. He was sticking around for another day or two to finish looking at properties in Cape Cod and then he was leaving St. John's

Cove far behind him. And that meant this woman, her dog and his crazy cousin and her heartbroken husband were going to be in his past, not his future.

"You didn't forget," she said, those gray-green eyes narrowing. "You left my clothes on purpose! I'm trying to tell you that's who I really am, jeans and T-shirts, baseball caps."

"And I'm trying to tell you it's not," he said softly but every bit as stubbornly as her.

For a moment she looked ready to fight, but then she just sighed.

"Eating on the beach will probably wreck the skirt," she said. She plucked at something on it.

The material already had a run in it, probably from the dog. She looked up at him suddenly, daring him to draw a conclusion about that.

"Who cares about the damned skirt?" he said, and meant it.

"Now you sound like the *real* me," she said, and when he hooted with laughter, she rewarded him with that smile again, and he was aware of being glad their day together had not ended, and that they had been given a chance to start again.

Ethan Ballard was *rescuing* her, Samantha reminded herself, watching as he stood in line to get hot dogs from Ernie's. And before that, the shopping trip, the visit to Annie's Retreat had all been part of a game. That was how he *played,* pathetic as that was.

None of it was about him liking her.

And why should she like him? He was a bigwig investment shark from Boston who didn't care anything about little people like Annie and Artie and her. He didn't even know how to have a good time.

But she did like him, even knowing how damned foolish that was. She liked him and she was glad in some horrible, fickle part of herself that wasn't sensible that he had asked her to play his bride for a day, even if he had downgraded it to fiancée in the last moment. She was glad she'd gone shopping with him, she was glad to have seen Annie's Retreat and she was glad that he had rescued her from that horrifying scene unfolding outside her store.

Look, she told herself sternly, *you're twenty-five years old. It's hardly a news bulletin that you like a man.*

Well, okay, in this town it probably was, which meant they should go eat their hot dogs somewhere else.

In fact, it was more like *It's about time* than a news flash. What if, for once, she just relaxed into what life offered her instead of trying to fight it?

So, she liked him. How big a deal was it? Why not enjoy that? For one afternoon? Why didn't she teach him what playing really meant, show him a little hint of her world, just as he had shown her a little hint of his?

It didn't mean she had to bring him home to meet

her brothers. It didn't mean they were going to get married and have babies at Annie's Retreat, sweetly intoxicating as those thoughts were.

It just meant she could enjoy the moment, and bring him along for the ride. She didn't have to look at the future, and more important she didn't have to look at the past, and measure everything against the scale of potential loss.

And with that in mind, feeling strangely light, Samantha went down the street from where he was buying hot dogs at Ernie's and bought two kites—the satin fabric kind with the wonderful colors and long, long tails—to fly on the beach after they'd eaten lunch.

As she climbed back into the car, she shucked off the jacket, even though the camisole was probably a little too revealing to wear by itself.

Live dangerously, she ordered herself.

And she was so glad she had obeyed when she saw the heat flash through Ethan's eyes when he got back in the car.

"Nice kites," he said, his voice hoarse.

She should have slugged him. That would have made her brothers proud. But for some reason, tired of living her brothers' vision for her instead of her own, she just laughed.

She took the hot dogs and drinks from his hands, but when she noticed he had gotten water for the dog the unwanted stab of tenderness she felt for him made her wonder if it was going to be possible to keep this simple.

But she told herself it was too late to change her mind, and that there was no such thing as a Hall who was a chicken, and she directed him to a beach that was dog friendly and just far enough from St. John's Cove that she hoped they weren't going to see any locals who would be reporting her impulsive outing to Mitch.

CHAPTER FIVE

THIS is what you got when you made the decision to live dangerously, Sam thought. This is what you got when you decided to show six feet of pure, muscled man how to play.

Ethan had shrugged off his shirt fifteen minutes ago, and now he was running on the hardened pack of the surf, the dog at his heels, unraveling the spool of kite string behind him. His laughter rang out, clear and true, like church bells.

"Run faster," she called to him, holding the kite at the other end of the string, waiting for exactly the right moment to toss it into the waiting breeze.

"I'm running as fast as I can," he protested.

"My granny Hall can run faster than that!"

He rewarded her with a burst of speed, and she admired the clean, powerful lines of his legs for a moment—the purely masculine energy of him—before she took mercy on him and tossed the kite in the air.

"Launch attempt forty-two," she called.

"Ninety-two," he shot back, getting the hang of this playing stuff. The truth was neither of them were really counting the number of times they had tried to get the thing in the sky. This time, the kite caught the wind and wiggled upward, a bright yellow sun with thirty feet of rainbow silk unraveling behind it.

But she couldn't watch the kite for long, gorgeous as it was against a sky that had proved flawless once the fog had lifted. The sea, restless during their visit with the Finkles, had become quiet. Instead she watched the play of his muscles under sun-gold skin, admiring the broadness of shoulders and the tautness of belly, the white flash of his teeth as he tilted his head back to watch the kite.

The smile disappeared as the kite tilted crazily one way, then the other, and then nosedived straight down toward the ocean!

"No!" she cried. "Don't let it get wet."

He managed, at the last moment, to maneuver it away from the water, so it planted itself deeply into the sand.

A lesser man might have groaned in frustration, but he laughed, and began rolling up the string, ready to try again. "Get ready for launch attempt one hundred and six," he instructed her.

"My brothers would like that," she said, picking the kite out of the sand and inspecting the frame for damage, while he rolled string. "You're no quitter."

And then she realized she had spoken the thought out loud, as if he was a candidate to squire their sister, but she realized she was taking herself too seriously when Ethan appeared not to notice the comment at all.

She reminded herself again to just play, to just enjoy the gift of this day. They tried to launch the kite again, and then again.

Ethan tried to bring his fine business mind to the activity: he licked his finger and tried to calculate the strength of the wind, he made adjustments to the frame, he fiddled with the tail. But finally, by magic rather than science, his kite lifted on the wind, took string, pulled upward and stayed.

Then, with one hand holding his kite spool, he had to try to help her get hers in the air. It was his turn to hold the kite, while she ran.

The skirt, thankfully, didn't hinder her running ability. In fact, she liked the way it felt skimming along her legs, flying up around her as she raced down the sand.

"Faster," he yelled at her. "Run faster, gypsy woman."

So, he had noticed the flying skirt, too.

The camisole wasn't built for athletic activity; the straps were as annoying as the ones on the bridesmaid's dress had been last night. She nearly lost the kite every time she had to push a strap back up.

Finally, with her gasping like a fish, her kite

joined his in the sky. The kite zinged upward, taking string like a fish on a run.

"Hey," she yelled at him. "Keep your kite away from me!" If she really meant that, she wouldn't keep moving back down the sand toward him, but she did, until they stood almost shoulder to shoulder, heads craned back as they maneuvered the kites.

Naturally he took her command to stay away from her kite as a challenge, and he kept bringing his kite recklessly close to hers so that they nearly touched, so that they looked like they were dancing with each other, swaying, dipping, falling, soaring.

It was like watching a mating ritual. And the result was about the same, too.

The kites finally collided, the strings tangled and they fell to the sand like a parachute that had not opened properly.

"You call yours Charlie, and I'll call mine Amanda," he said, flopping down on his back in the sand.

Waldo, exhausted from chasing the kites, took up a post beside him, eyeing Ethan with the suspicion of a spinster chaperone, but not growling at him anymore.

Sam flung herself on her back on the sand beside Ethan. The camisole was stuck to her, and her hair was glued to her forehead. The skirt was limp and crushed.

Which was probably how she would feel tomorrow when it sunk in that it was over. But for now, she enjoyed the feeling of his eyes on her, warm with appreciation. She wanted to touch his back again.

It probably felt different naked than it had felt with the shirt on it.

She shoved her renegade hands under her back.

"I'm hot," he said. "I've got to get in the water."

She looked wistfully at the calm sea. "No swimsuit."

"So what? Don't worry about it. We're engaged. Practically. Besides, nobody's watching us."

And then, as if it was taking her too long to make up her mind, he stood and stretched. He was going to go in without her!

Except he wasn't. He took one step toward the water, and then ducked back on her, flipped her over, put one arm behind her back and one behind her knees and heaved her up, the motion seeming effortless on his part.

She was cradled against his chest, so shocked by sensation of his naked, sun-heated skin, that for a whole three seconds she didn't even fight him.

But then, grinning wickedly, he moved toward the water.

Whose dumb idea had it been to teach him how to play? Not letting on—she hoped—how much she was enjoying all this, she struggled, and gave a token scream.

"Don't! The camisole will be see-through if it gets wet! Ethan!"

"I won't look." But he winked to let her know he was just a guy, after all, and he probably would.

Her struggles were no match for his strength, a fact that pleased her way too much considering she had always taken such pride in thinking she could look after herself.

He waded out into the surf, carrying her easily over the first few rollers. Waldo barked frantically on shore, afraid to get his feet wet.

"My hair," she told him, one last attempt to save herself from the embarrassment of the camisole that was going to turn transparent. She blinked at him with every ounce of feminine wiles she possessed.

He wasn't fooled. He laughed. "You don't give a rat's whiskers about your hair."

And then he slipped his arms out from under her. She fell into the water with an ungraceful crash, drank a bit of salt and got water in her eyes. Still, despite those discomforts, the water was cold on her hot skin, invigorating, as sensual as a touch.

She was glad he had taken the decision to get wet out of her hands, not that she intended to let him know that!

She stood up, sputtering, to see him already running away, crashing through the incoming rollers, sending gleeful looks back over his shoulder at her.

She yanked off the skirt, sorry to have it meet such an untimely end, and dove into the breakers after him. In water, she could swim faster than she could run! All Halls were part dolphin, and Sam loved water. She moved into a strong crawl, watched him glance back once more before diving, cleanly slicing a wave with the strength of his body.

He moved out past the breakers, then cut a course parallel to the shore. She was amazed that he swam as well as she did, or any of her brothers. She wasn't even sure she could beat him in a race to the buoys.

The initial cold shock of the water had faded; it felt perfect now, like an embrace, like soft silk against her skin.

"What are you going to do with me when you catch me?" he called, flipping over, treading for a moment, *letting* her close some of the gap between them.

"I'm going to drown you."

"That's what I was afraid of." He let her get to where she could almost touch him, and then with an easy grin he took off again, heading back toward the shore, letting the waves carry him.

He paused again, near shore, finally getting breathless. "Wouldn't it just be easier to admit you're glad you're in the water?"

"Easier for you!"

"You love it out here. Woman, you are part fish! Mermaid."

"Don't try to charm me."

He swam close, treaded water, tried to peer beneath the surface at the camisole she was pretty sure was now transparent. She flattened her palm against the water and splashed him hard in the face.

She should have remembered he was not a

quitter, because instead of dissuading him, he took it as a challenge, swam toward her, ignoring her shouts to stay back, her laughter, her increasingly aggressive splashing.

One final duck, and she was in the circle of his arms, his flesh warm through the veil of the sea. Instead of trying to pull away she surrendered to his easy strength and to the sensation of her wet camisole pressed into the slippery surface of his chest.

His feet found the sandy bottom, and he held her and went still. The playfulness died on his face.

"You're beautiful," he said softly.

"I told you not to try to charm me."

He kissed her.

And she was charmed. Completely.

It wasn't like that brushing of lips she had instigated last night. His lips claimed her, possessed her, asked more of her than she had ever thought she had to give. They stripped her to her soul, and built her back up, showed her, finally, that he had been right all along.

He knew who she really was. Not a girl any longer, content to play a child's games.

She was a woman, and it was a wonderful thing to be.

He tasted of salt. And strength. And promises.

She kissed him back, hungry for him, starving for this thing that was happening between them.

Waldo moaned from shore, a plaintive howl, and it pulled her, ever so slightly, from the place she was.

Enough that she remembered all her brothers' warnings about what men *really* wanted. It was what she really wanted, too, wasn't it?

But somehow it wasn't. Some instinct for survival told her it was way too soon, told her that there would be nothing but regret at the end of this road if she followed it too far.

Regretfully Samantha took advantage of the fact he was distracted—very distracted—placed both her hands on his shoulders, pushed hard enough that he lost his footing and went under the water.

He came up laughing, shaking droplets of water from his face and hair, and then he came after her, and they played it all out again, the kisses never quite as deep, never quite as hungry as that first one.

Finally exhausted and exhilarated they moved out of the water. She managed to snag her skirt, now as attractive as a lump of soggy tissue paper, from the surf. Ethan had left his shirt at the water's edge, and he pulled it quickly around her, but not before his gaze burned her.

They had no towels, so they lay down in the white, fine sand, the sun kissing them back to warmth.

His shoulder touched hers, his eyes stayed on her face, a small appreciative smile on his lips.

"Do you think things have blown over at your place? I could drop you off, you could change clothes. I'll go back to my hotel and change, too. Then we could go grab a bite to eat together."

Together. A small word, used every day, thousands of times a day.

How could it sparkle with new meaning? How could she feel like she didn't want to leave him, not even for as long as it took to change clothes?

It was weak to feel this way. So why did she feel as if she had waited all her life to feel it?

"Dinner," he said. "Somebody told me the Clam Digger is spectacular."

She remembered her last date at the Clam Digger. She wasn't quite ready to expose all the rawness of these new feelings to her watching community—or her overly protective brothers. Not that they had acted very protective last night.

But brothers could be unpredictable, especially Mitch.

"I could grab my little barbecue and we could pick up some steaks and shrimp, barbecue down here on the beach." That felt private. And easier than looking at him over a dinner plate, with strangers all around them.

Or worse, in St. John's Cove, not strangers at all! "Perfect."

He didn't seem to care about the effects of the sand and the salt water on his car any more than he had cared about the skirt. He helped her in, and they drove back to her apartment.

She was happy to see that the street in front of her place was quiet. The ladder had been moved and the letters taken down, only straggly pieces of tape left where they had been. Unfortunately she could still see the nose of Amanda's yellow convertible.

He saw it, too. "You want me to come in with you? Maybe I could say something helpful."

She was touched that he didn't want to leave her alone to deal with Amanda's heartbreak, but she wasn't sure if Amanda would appreciate his concern or be embarrassed that her very successful cousin was witnessing the breakdown of her life.

"No, it would be better if you didn't."

"Okay. How about if I come back for you in about an hour?"

"Fine."

Not the least self-conscious—this was a resort town after all—Sam took the stairs two at a time, loving the feel of his too large shirt brushing her naked thighs.

She opened the door to her apartment and felt that wonderful sensation of homecoming that she felt every single time she walked through the door.

Her apartment was a treasure. This building was nearly as old as the town, and Sam's apartment had many of the original features, gorgeous hardwood floors, wainscoting, copper roof panels, leaded glass windows, luxurious oak crown moldings and trim.

It had character, she had always thought with pleasure.

Right now it had one extra character.

Amanda was there still in the too large shirt Sam had left her in this morning.

Her friend was a huddle of misery on the couch, bare legs tucked inside the shirt, patting at her tears, her face swollen and blotchy. She was glued to a DVD. *Wedding Crashers.* Beside it were a number of other DVD cases, *The Wedding Singer, My Best Friend's Wedding, Four Weddings and a Funeral.*

Sam picked up the control and turned off the TV, before putting her arms around her friend. "You've seen some of these a dozen times," she said gently.

"I want to see what real love looks like!"

"These are fantasies, not the greatest source for a reality check. You threw a piece of cake at real love this afternoon."

"I don't think Charlie married me because he loves me," Amanda whispered, forlorn.

"What?" Sam sank down on the couch beside her, but Amanda leaped up and dashed to the washroom. She didn't even get the door shut before she started throwing up.

Waldo, thankfully, was so tired from his big day that he stayed curled up in his bed by the door.

Amanda wandered back in, looking like death.

"Amanda, this has got to stop. You are making yourself sick. Charlie loves you madly. At least talk to him."

"You think I'm sick because I'm upset?" Amanda

asked shrilly, and then bitterly, "I guess he hasn't managed to tell everyone in town yet."

Samantha felt herself go very still. Suddenly she saw Amanda getting sick and the firestorm of emotions in a different light.

"I'm pregnant," Amanda announced joylessly, though Sam had already figured it out. "That's why we rushed everything, why we decided to get married so fast. And then he had to go and tell his mother at the wedding, when he had promised he wouldn't. You know her. She'll tell everybody."

It seemed to Sam everyone would know in fairly short order anyway. "Why the big secret?" she asked carefully.

"Because I don't want everyone in town thinking I got married because I *had* to," Amanda said shakily.

"Amanda, honey, in this day and age no one gets married because they *have* to."

"No, I guess not," she said doubtfully, and laid her head companionably on Sam's shoulder. "He makes me madder than anyone on earth, Sam. Is that love?"

"You're asking me what love is?"

But for some reason she thought of how she had felt at Annie's Retreat earlier today, had that moment of *belief.* She could picture, again, her group of friends there, their young families with them.

And leading the charge would be the oldest of this coming generation, a little boy or girl who would probably look like some delightful combination of Amanda and Charlie.

"I could probably get an annulment," Amanda said, and started crying again.

Sam was no lawyer, but it seemed to her the relationship had been consummated, just not on the wedding night, and that made her uncertain how the whole annulment thing worked. Not that she thought it would be a very good idea to share that with Amanda right now.

Instead she felt again that *sense* she had had in the cottage. Of one stage of life ending, and another beginning, all unfolding seamlessly according to a plan that she might not be able to predict, but that she could trust.

"Everything is going to be all right," Sam said, and she heard the strength and the confidence in her own voice.

"It is?" Amanda asked.

"Yes," she said firmly, "it is."

Amanda lifted her head off her shoulder, regarded her thoughtfully. "There's something different about you."

"Oh," Sam said carelessly, "I've been out in the sun all day. New freckles, salt in my hair. You know."

Apparently Amanda didn't know. "That's not it," she said before asking, her head tilted to one side, smiling, the first smile since she'd run out of the reception, "Whose shirt is that, anyway?" And then she squinted at the fine print that Sam had forgotten was above the pocket.

"Ethan," she whispered, and then she smiled as if the sun had come out.

For a woman disillusioned by the course of true love, Amanda was a hopeless romantic.

Or maybe she wanted to focus on a love story other than her own, her choices in movies being a case in point.

"You and Ethan would be perfect together," she breathed.

"You're being silly," Sam said. "We barely know each other."

But Amanda insisted on acting like they had posted banns at St. Michael's. She hugged Sam hard to her.

"I always knew there would be a perfect guy for you," she whispered. "And I'm so glad it's Ethan."

And then she burst into tears—presumably at her own lack of a perfect guy—all over again.

Or maybe because she was pregnant.

"Look, I don't have to go out tonight," Sam said. "Maybe it would be better if I stayed with you."

"Oh, no," Amanda said. "My mom's coming over in a bit. Before she does, I'll help you get ready."

Unfortunately Amanda, who *had* picked the pink fuchsia, insisted on helping her pick out an outfit for the evening.

And didn't seem to hear her when she said they were barbecuing on the beach.

Looking at herself in the mirror a while later, Sam wasn't quite sure how Amanda had made this outfit materialize from her wardrobe. Her friend had turned a sow's ear into a silk purse. Sam might have tried to stop Amanda's enthusiastic makeover, but Amanda had been so animated, and seemed to be forgetting her own troubles, so she had gone along.

Now what Sam saw made a light go on in her eyes. She looked stunning: shorts ending mid-thigh, underneath a casual short-sleeved beach top that Amanda had totally recreated with the simple addition of a tight belt. Lastly, Amanda had dug up the silk scarf that she had given Sam herself last Christmas, and knotted it casually at her throat.

Then she'd dug into the makeup they had used for the wedding, and again because it was making Amanda so happy, Sam had gone along.

But maybe it wasn't the outfit or the makeup that had put this new light in her eyes, the light that made her look—and feel—as if she was not a little girl, not anyone's little sister anymore.

In the mirror, what looked back at her was one-hundred-percent pure woman. And Sam felt, not a sense of betraying her *real* self, but rather a sense of welcoming a disowned part of herself home.

CHAPTER SIX

ETHAN watched the flames of their fire leap against the black star-studded sky, pulled Samantha deeper into the V of his legs, felt her settle back against his chest. They had just cooked clams in a bucket over the open fire, and now the night was growing a bit chilly.

She was already wearing his shirt over her own. Today, she had been wearing another camisole-style top, misty gray, a delicate concoction that had showed off the fineness of her figure and skin. But what he had noticed most of all was that it made her eyes look more gray than green.

He suspected it was new, and he loved how Sam was, day after day, embracing the feminine side of herself. There was no doubt she liked the reaction an outfit like that got from him, but he saw that she was genuinely enjoying allowing herself to be pretty.

Somehow his business kept getting delayed—he'd now been on Cape Cod for nearly a week. It was the third night they had finished the day like this:

bringing the barbecue down onto the beach, talking, teasing, tormenting each other late into the night.

Last night, on the Fourth of July, instead of joining the crowds in town they had come here, to the place he was beginning to think of as *their* beach.

And as the sky had lit up with the fireworks from town they had floated in calm waters beneath the exploding rockets, staring up at a dazzling sky, the symphony of fire reflecting in the water all around them. It had easily been the most magical experience of his life, more magical than the first big-league game, more magical than the first huge renovation and successful sale.

Ethan, a man who could afford many pleasures, was being constantly awakened to the joy in the simplest of things: a freshening breeze stirring beach grass and her hair, watching her play tag with the dog.

Ethan knew it was getting late and he should take her home, but he had the feeling he'd had every day since he had met her, of not wanting to let go.

Sunday and Monday her business had been closed, but after that he had talked her into playing hooky. Amanda had moved home with her parents and was still holding out against Charlie. Despite her own romantic disaster, Amanda was taking absolute delight in he and Samantha's deepening relationship, and had volunteered to look after Groom to Grow for a couple of days. It was good for his cousin. She obviously needed something to do other than think about Charlie, and she had given them the gift of allowing them to have these wonderful first days of July together.

Today had been the most perfect day he could remember in a long time. Samantha had taken him for his first sailing lesson this morning on her beautiful little boat, the *Hall Way*. He'd been in awe of her expertise and agility, but mostly in awe of the look on her face as the wind caught in the sails: joy, freedom, connection with this world she lived in.

They'd had a long lunch, driven down the coast, explored parts of the Cape Cod National Seashore. She had taken him to a beach after, where they had dug clams for their supper. The day had been playful, honest, intense.

Just like this woman he was with, that he was coming to know, even as he felt a thirst to know her better.

He kissed her hair, ran his fingers through it. "I love your hair," he whispered, but he heard a deeper whisper, and didn't speak it.

Her hand covered his where he touched her hair, and he marveled at this comfort they had in each other.

"My hair is what reminded me I was a girl all those years growing up with my brothers. It would have been so much easier to cut it, and I remember coming close so many times, but in a way, it was what I had left of my mom."

Her voice went very soft as she continued, and he

knew he was being given another gift, maybe more spectacular than all the others.

She was giving him her trust.

"I could remember Mom brushing my hair, our bedtime routine. She would sit behind me and brush my hair until it crackled around my head, and she would tell me what a beautiful girl I was and how glad she was that I was hers, and how glad she was we had each other in our household full of men."

He touched her cheek, and found a tear had strayed down it. And he felt an enormous sense of gratitude for this gift of Sam's trust. After all these days of playing, she was going to show him her more vulnerable side, and he felt honored by her moving effortlessly into the next step between them.

"What happened to your parents?" he asked softly, stroking her hair.

"This is a beautiful place," she said quietly, nodding toward the sea, "and a hard place, too. It's unforgiving out there. And the more time you spend on the sea, the greater your chances of making the one mistake that it won't forgive.

"They loved to sail. They never lost that, even with all the hectic activity of raising four kids, they always carved out time for each other. It was almost as if that time alone with each other was sacred to them. They were very experienced, and they knew these waters, but a sudden storm blew in."

"I'm so sorry, Samantha."

"Thank you. Sometimes, now, all these years later, I feel moments of gratitude that they went together, because I really cannot imagine one of them being able to survive without the other, or one having to watch the other getting sick and dying a slow, painful death."

He realized, then, that Sam had seen real love, deep and abiding, and that was a part of who she really was as much as anything else. He had known her only a short, short while. How was it possible that he was wondering, already, if he could be worthy of that?

But he had known Bethany for eight months before he had popped the question. Time had not made him any more certain of what he was doing. He had confessed his doubt to his father, who had suggested he test her. Quit playing ball. See how long it lasted then. She had failed that test with flying colors!

He had known this woman for a week and felt a deeper sense of connection, of certainty.

Maybe love, of all things, was what most resisted man's efforts to put it in a box, to tame it with time, to place rules and restrictions around it. Maybe it just happened, even when it was inconvenient, even when it made no sense, especially when you were least expecting it.

Love. He had not said those words to her. But that is what his mind had whispered to him when he had stroked her hair. Ethan was shocked that they came to him so easily when he thought of Samantha.

"Still, it couldn't have been easy for you." He slid his hand along the delicate line of her shoulder, let it rest on her upper arm. Such a small gesture. And yet it filled him with a sense of possessiveness, tenderness, warmth.

"No, being a little girl in a totally male household was not easy. Mitch was newly married when we first arrived on his doorstep, me, Jake and Bryce. His wife couldn't handle the sudden death of the honeymoon. She left after a month."

Ethan remembered Sam's deeply cynical expression at the wedding and understood it.

Slowly she told him all of it. The trying to kill her own longing for things feminine because her brothers teased her so much about attempts to dress up, to look pretty, to put on makeup. She was embarrassed instead of overjoyed when she needed her first bra. Her brothers approved of toughness and disapproved of "sissy" things, and since that was her only safe harbor in the world, she became what they wanted her to be.

"I'm sorry," she said finally. "I shouldn't be telling you all of this."

"Why not? It seems to me maybe you've needed someone to tell for a very long time."

"I'm not condemning my brothers," she said hastily.

"I know that. I could see at the wedding their love

for you was very genuine. They just didn't know what you needed. Or not all of what you needed."

"Okay, I've spilled," she said, taking refuge in what he was coming to recognize as her sassy defense, what her brother had told him was tough-as-nails, and wasn't. Not even close. "Your turn."

And so he told her about growing up in a very wealthy family, and about how they hadn't approved when he had been drafted out of college to play major league ball.

"I had the college sweetheart. She was just what my big ego needed. I could do no wrong when I was a college star, and then when I was drafted to the Sox she went into love overdrive. Naturally I was swept off my feet, bought her the biggest diamond you can imagine and asked her to marry me.

"But you know, something in me thought something wasn't right. It was as if we were both playing roles instead of being real. Even though I didn't always get along with my father, especially back then, I went and talked to him. He suggested I tell her I was going to quit baseball and see what happened.

"She jumped ship as quickly as your sister-in-law, and it left me pretty disillusioned. I didn't want to lead a life anymore where people liked me because of what I did or what I had. So, I really did quit baseball and I signed off on the family fortune, too, which wasn't exactly what my dad had been expecting. I set out to make it on my own.

"I had the baseball money, and I had something to prove. Pretty soon, I was finding my relationship with business so much less fickle than my relationship with people. I turned all my substantial competitive nature on that.

"And you know what? It was enough for me. Until now."

And then he turned his face to her and kissed her. And realized once you had tasted someone like her, nothing else was ever going to be enough again.

And he knew it was time for something else.

She had brought him into her world. Now it was time to bring her to his.

"Come to Boston with me," he said softly. "Just for a few days."

She hesitated, but she was full of yearning when she said, "My brothers would kill me. Or you. It hasn't exactly been an accident that all our activities have not taken place in St. John's Cove."

Now that she mentioned that he recalled, even this morning, that her expression had been furtive until they had gotten that sailboat safely out of the harbor.

"The truth is," he told her softly, "that I appreciate the fact your brothers are so protective of you."

"Only because you haven't seen them in action. Last time I was on a date, Mitch showed up, and ever-so-casually mentioned his shotgun collection."

Ethan laughed, but she didn't see the humor. "I'll speak to your brothers," he reassured her. "If you come, it will all be aboveboard. I'll get you a hotel room."

"No," she said softly. "I guess it's time for me to speak to my brothers myself."

But all he heard was that she was coming, and he felt his heart soar upward like the kites they had flown the first day they had been together.

When Samantha got in that night, Amanda was just leaving the store, though it was very late.

"How are things between you and Charlie?" she asked hopefully.

Amanda shrugged, which Samantha took to mean an unfortunate *No progress,* especially when Amanda launched into a detailed blow-by-blow on what had sold at the store, and who had been in that day, deliberately avoiding the topic of her marriage.

"Oh, and the real estate agent brought somebody through. They asked if they could see the apartment, and I didn't know what to do, so I let her take them through. Is that okay?"

In truth, Sam hated the idea of someone touring her personal space. The real estate agent was supposed to give her forty-eight hours notice before showing it. But it was done, and really, there was probably no sense putting obstacles in the way of the sale.

She could *feel* change on the wind, ever since Amanda's wedding she could feel it. Only she didn't feel quite as frightened of it as she had a few short days ago.

In fact, she was aware her stomach didn't knot up at the news somebody had looked at the building, for the first time since it had been put up for sale.

"Amanda, Ethan asked me to spend a few days in Boston with him."

Amanda's delight was as short-lived as her own had been. "Don't tell your brothers," she said with a shudder. "Mitch will kill him."

"Thanks," Sam said dryly. And as tempting as it was not to tell Mitch, she had never lived her life like that and she wasn't starting now.

She picked up the phone. Despite her attempt at bravery, reminding herself that she was the one who made the first plunge into the ocean every year, Sam felt her stomach turn sideways when he answered.

"Mitch, I have to talk to you."

"Talk away, little sister."

But her stomach swooped again, making what she had felt about people looking at the building feel like a small upset.

"In person would be better."

"Is everything okay?" he asked, his voice rough with concern.

"Yes. I'll come over for coffee in the morning. See you then." Her hand was shaking when she hung up the phone.

And she still felt like she was shaking when he opened the door in the morning, pulled her into a crushing bear hug. Then he set her back at arm's length and frowned.

"You're all dressed up. Are you wearing makeup? What's going on? Are you going on a job interview? Did your building sell? I heard there were people looking at it."

That was a small town for you. It was only by the grace of God he hadn't heard about her taking Ethan sailing.

"Mitch, you can wear makeup for things other than going on a job interview!"

"It's a little early in the day for a wedding." And then his scowl deepened. "Uh-oh. A man."

She shoved by him and went into his messy kitchen, back to a typical bachelor pad now that she no longer lived there. She kept her back to him and poured a cup of coffee.

She took a sip, took a deep breath and turned back to him. "I'm nearly twenty-five years old, Mitch. Would a man be such a bad thing?"

"You're not going out with any guy I haven't vetted first, little girl!" His face was like thunder. He was unconsciously flexing and unflexing his huge arm muscle.

"Mitch," she said, "I'm not a little girl anymore."

And just by saying those words, she felt the power and the truth in them and suddenly she felt courageous and not afraid. It allowed her to see the fear in his protectiveness, and she felt tender for him, even though she knew it was time for her to move out of the shadow of his protection.

"I've met a really nice guy," she said, "and I'm going to go to Boston with him for a few days."

"Over my dead body!" he thundered.

"Mitch," she said softly. "I'm lonely. I want what Mom and Dad had. It's time for all of us to move past the pain of them dying, of Karina leaving us when we needed her most. It's time to start living again."

"I don't want you to get hurt," he said, more quietly. "That's all."

"I know that, Mitch. But you know what? I feel alive, fully alive for the first time in a long, long time. I feel as if I'm coming into myself, becoming the person I was always meant to be. I want to feel this way, even if it means taking a chance. And I want you to know this is the last time I'm coming to you about my personal life. I don't need your permission to live it as I see fit. My life is mine, not yours."

"You're firing me as your brother," Mitch said, astounded.

"No. I'm firing you as my parent, and asking you to be my brother."

He was silent for a long time, and then he gave his head a mighty shake and opened his arms. "Come here, little girl. I knew when I saw you all dolled up for the wedding it was only going to be a matter of time. I just wasn't expecting it to be quite this fast."

And she went into his arms, and let him hold her, and then she pulled away.

"Are you going to tell me who the guy is?" he asked as she headed for the door, feeling lighter than air.

"No."

"Ah, hell, do you think I'm just a dumb lobster-man? You tell Ethan Ballard if he hurts you, I'm gonna break both his legs. He doesn't need them since he gave up baseball, anyway."

And then, just when she wondered if he had heard a word she said, he softened the threat by winking at her.

Boston was exhilarating. They took the ferry, that ran only from June until September, from Provincetown Harbor to Boston. Once there, Ethan put her up in a harbor view room at the Boston Harbor Hotel. Located at the super-posh Rowes Wharf, the exquisite five-star accommodations overlooked the magnificent waterfront.

Then they became tourists in his town. Sam had been to Boston many times before, but had never enjoyed it so much as seeing it through his eyes. They went to antique stores and quaint little bistros. They strolled in parks and explored galleries and museums.

They even went on the famous ride-the-duck tour, part sightseeing excursion, part carnival ride. Old World War II DUKW amphibious vehicles charged into waterways and lumbered down streets to some of Boston's favorite must-sees. The "conducktors" had wonderful names like Major Tom Foolery and Commander Swampscott. Each vehicle had a name—theirs was Beantown Betty—and Sam couldn't remember when she had last found an experience so fun and refreshing.

Then there were quieter activities: a sublime dining experience at No. 9 Park, and a romantic one at Mistral.

She took advantage of the wonderful shopping available in Boston, not to scout out items for Groom to Grow as she normally would have done, but to upgrade her wardrobe yet again. She was delighting in the kind of clothes that appealed to her, subtly sexy and feminine, and she was delighting in feeling free to buy whatever she liked, not once imagining Mitch or Jake or Bryce rolling their eyes at her choices.

But Sam did have a moment when she wondered if she was getting in over her head. Ethan brought her to his place for a quick drink and change of clothes before he took her out for dinner. He owned a Back Bay house. It had started as one of his renovation projects, he explained to her, but the old house and the gas-lit neighborhood, located on a reclaimed seabed, had won his heart.

The house was incredible, the exterior and neighborhood reminiscent of nineteenth-century London, the interior modern, masculine and sleek.

For a few minutes, alone while he changed, she

felt acutely their social differences: she was a lobsterman's daughter. But as soon as he came back in the room, and grinned that now familiar grin at her, she felt the difference evaporate. He was just Ethan, not a multimillion dollar businessman.

On her last night there, he sprung it on her that they were having dinner with his parents at their Beacon Hill residence.

"That's why I didn't tell you sooner," Ethan said when she started fretting about what to wear and how to act. "Don't worry. You're going to be fine. I've got your back."

It turned out he was right. Once she got past being intimidated by the enormous wealth of John Ballard and his heiress wife she found his parents were engaging and good-humored. She'd expected stuffy and found them the furthest thing from it. She was particularly taken with his father, who came across as crusty at first, but whose love and concern for his son reminded her so much of the love and concern of her brothers.

On the surface maybe it would be hard to imagine two worlds further apart, the world of merchant banking and the world of lobster fishing, but Sam could see the common denominator of all people.

Love of family. Wanting a place to belong. Wanting to be liked and respected for who you were and not what you had or did.

When she said good-night to the Ballards, Ethan's

father took her hands in both of his, looked her deep in the eye and smiled before kissing her on her cheek.

He dropped her hands and looked at his son. "I like her," he said loudly. "She's a keeper."

And that was the other thing you could count on family for: they were always around to embarrass you with their love!

That night, after Ethan had gone home, she hugged herself and looked out her hotel room over the sparkling lights reflecting in Boston Harbor. There was no doubt in her that she was falling in love, and she could easily see why it was called *falling*. It was exhilarating, like swan-diving off a high cliff, blasting downhill on a roller coaster, launching into the water in Beantown Betty.

Samantha felt as if she had *finally* become a privileged member of a secret club. The club that *knew* why so many songs and stories, paintings and poems were inspired by *this* feeling. Alive, on fire, joy-filled.

She said out loud, "My life is perfect. More perfect than I could have ever imagined it. Even in my wildest dreams."

And she really should have known better. Saying something like that, even thinking it, was like tossing down a challenge to the gods.

CHAPTER SEVEN

AT THE last minute, Ethan had business to deal with and couldn't drive her home. He asked her to stay an extra few days, but Sam said no. She knew people had to continue functioning, difficult as that was when you were floating, when your life had become a love song, when you couldn't stop thinking of that other person's eyes. And mouth. The curve of his smile. The hard line of his muscled arm. The sound of his voice, like a gentle touch on the hairs on the back of your neck.

Still this was the longest she had ever been away from St. John's Cove and her business.

Not to mention her brothers and her friends. How were Amanda and Charlie doing? She suddenly felt guilty that she had escaped so completely that she hadn't even thought to call Amanda, that she had not once looked for stock for her store.

She wanted to take the bus back, but Ethan didn't like it, and insisted on renting her a car. After a drive home that seemed so boring *alone,* she turned in the car at St. John's Cove, and was given a ride home by Matthew Bellinger, the town's oldest bachelor. He told her, shyly, that he was taking Mable Saunders for tea the following day.

Love is in the air, Sam thought happily.

Ethan had insisted she call as soon as she got home so he knew she'd arrived safely, and Sam was so intent on that—and on hearing his voice again, how could she already miss him so completely— that at first she walked right by the sign that swung in front of her store, eager to share her happiness with Amanda who was just closing up inside.

But the bright red sticker grabbed her peripheral vision and she backtracked and stared with disbelief.

The happiness escaped from her with a nearly audible hiss, like air from a pricked balloon.

Sold.

How could that be? How could her life have changed so completely when she had just glanced away for a moment? But isn't that what happened when you let go of control? It was taken from you.

A boat due that never came home. If she had only noticed they were overdue sooner, taken control...

A familiar stomachache, a sensation Sam had not felt for days, twisted in her gut. She approached the door of Groom to Grow, the lightness gone from her step, feeling like a prisoner going to the gallows.

She opened the door and looked around at her

beautiful space as if she was already saying goodbye. This was her business. More, it was *home*.

And she, of all people, knew how quickly you could lose that place called home.

"Oh, Sam, I'm so sorry," Amanda said when she went in the door. Sam knew she had not succeeded at hiding her stricken expression. "They just came by and put up the Sold sticker minutes ago! I was going to try to get the sign down before you got here so I could break it to you gently. Are you okay?"

Actually Sam felt like she was holding it together by a thread, but she smiled bravely and made her escape out the front door and up to her apartment. If she let Amanda hug her, she would break into a million pieces.

She called Ethan and was relieved when she got his voice mail. She left a quick message saying she was home safely and hung up.

She dialed the Realtor, who wouldn't give her any more information than she had given Amanda, even though they were second cousins by marriage.

"You're the *tenant,* Sam. I can't divulge the details of the deal to you. It's between the owner and the purchaser."

"What about my business? What about Groom to Grow?"

"The possession date is only thirty days away."

"Thirty days?" she breathed. "Isn't that awfully fast?"

"To the owner's delight," the Realtor said dryly. "You'll be contacted soon, Sam. Don't worry."

Don't worry. She had spent the last wonderful week not worrying. And look what had happened. Logically she knew *worrying* would not have changed anything, but she had an awful feeling.

As if she had let down her vigilance and her whole life was being shot to smithereens because of it. While she was gallivanting around Cape Cod and Boston, she should have really been scouting a new location for her store! She should have been planning for this contingency, instead of letting herself be swept away.

The phone rang. She hoped it was the Realtor showing proper loyalty to family members, but it wasn't.

It was Ethan. Why did she feel mad at him?

Because he had made her *believe* for a short time that life held only good things.

"How was your trip back?"

For some reason, Sam steeled herself against the way his voice made her feel: as if she just wanted to blurt out every fear she'd ever had, lay them on his broad shoulders, let him help her carry them. It scared her that she didn't want to be *brave* anymore.

"Uneventful," she said. She couldn't trust herself to tell him about the store without crying, and the last thing she wanted to feel right now was more vulnerable.

"Hey, guess who called me this afternoon?"

"Who?"

"The Finkles. They want to meet with us again. What do you think of that?"

She felt as if her heart was doing a free fall, as if it was shooting down that hill in a roller coaster, only it wasn't going to make the turn. It was going to fly right off the track.

She'd always known she wasn't good enough. She'd always known better than to trust life. She thought of the Sold sign swinging gently in front of her store. And of him inviting her to go the Finkles, her blowing the deal the first time.

He'd said he didn't care. But he'd warned her he was competitive. Had everything since then been geared to this moment? How easy it would be for a man like him, worldly and successful, to make a little bumpkin like her believe.

He hadn't ever said he'd given up on Annie's Retreat. He'd said he was backing off "for the time being."

She thought of his eyes and his lips, the way his hand felt in hers, the way she tingled when any part of him came in contact with any part of her.

She thought of his father saying, She's a keeper.

No one could have gone to such lengths to keep a pretense going. No one. But even knowing that, knowing she was being unreasonable, suddenly she could not see any way they could have a happy ending.

This would end in heartbreak, one way or another.
A boat pulling away from a dock and never coming back. She could not survive it again. She had pretended, ever since it had happened, that she was strong. Tough as nails. Brave.

But she wasn't. The truth was she wasn't even brave enough to keep a dog; they passed through her life on the way to somewhere else, because she was afraid to keep them. Afraid to love totally.

And suddenly she didn't want anyone to know how afraid she was of change, good change or bad change, least of all not him. She did not want to be made weak and needy by love, she did not want to be powerless before it.

So, she thought, I will make him despise me.

"You planned it all, didn't you?" she demanded. "From the very beginning, this is what you wanted. For me to go back to the Finkles with you, and be convincing this time. Woman in love."

"What are you talking about?" he asked, genuinely baffled. And then, softly, "Are you a woman in love?"

"No!" Yes. "Would it have made you happy if I was? We could go back out to Annie's Retreat and get what you missed out on the first time. Of course, buying my store, the bride price, was putting the cart before the horse, but why not? You're used to getting what you want, aren't you?"

Stop it, she told herself, but she couldn't. This was safer, this was easier. She had kept her life as unchangeable as she could since her parents had died. She lived in the same place. She saw the same people. She had not even allowed herself to grow up. She was not ready for the kind of change Ethan Ballard represented.

"Buying your store?"

"Don't play the innocent with me! You're just like my brothers! You had to look after me. You couldn't believe I could make it on my own! You could get Annie's Retreat and bail me out at the same time!

"Get this straight, Ethan Ballard. I don't need your help and I don't need you!"

His long silence told her she was succeeding at driving him away, at keeping her world narrow and safe.

"How can you believe such a thing of me?" he asked quietly.

"You're the one who thought you could buy a bride," she reminded him, something in her voice so cold. So cold she was shivering, but he didn't have to know that, and he couldn't see her.

She could hear the thinly veiled fury in his voice when he said, "If that's how you feel, Samantha, goodbye."

She saw Amanda had come up the stairs behind her, not wanting her to be alone. She was staring at her wide-eyed as she set down the phone. A picture of composure, Sam plucked Waldo out from under Amanda's arm, tilted her chin and went to her room, shut the door with a quiet click behind her.

Still lugging Waldo she went over to the stereo in her room and turned it on. Loud. A love song, naturally. And only then did she allow herself to cry at what she had just done.

And over all the ridiculous things, because he had always called her Samantha and never Sam and she was going to miss the way he *saw* her so badly it felt as if she might die.

She hugged the dog she was not keeping to her, let him lick away her tears and thought, Tomorrow I will find Waldo a new place to go, too.

Ethan hung up his phone, and stared at it with disbelief. He was aware he was shaking with fury, and glad he was not anywhere near the delectable Miss Hall at the moment. He might strangle her!

How could Samantha, after these intense days together, not know who he was? How could she not trust him? He thought he loved her, and she could believe the absolute worst of him on so little evidence?

It was the most insulting thing that had ever happened to him. He was astounded by the depth of his hurt. He wanted to smash things. He wanted to stand out on his balcony and yell obscenities at the top of his lungs. He wanted to convince her she was wrong, and in the next breath, he wanted to convince her he was indifferent to her.

He did go stand on his balcony for a moment, and something in him quieted as the sea breeze touched his skin, reminded him of racing across the sand with her, kites behind them. He remembered bonfires, and laughter, digging for clams, swimming under a sky that was exploding.

And he remembered her face when she had looked at Annie's Retreat.

The wistfulness so naked in it, even though she had been trying to hide it.

And suddenly the truth came to him, as quiet as that breeze and just as comforting. She wanted to love him, and she was scared to death at the same time.

This wasn't about *him*. Love was asking him not to make it about him, to rise above his bruised ego and *see*.

And when he looked hard, what he saw was a little girl who had lost her parents at a young and impressionable age.

She had probably been scared to death to trust one single thing about life ever since then. What about her life would have made her believe, not just that good things happened, but that they stayed? Look at what had just happened to her business, the building sold out from under her, reinforcing her belief that nothing good could last, nothing good could stay.

No wonder she was afraid of what he had seen so clearly in her eyes.

She was falling in love with him.

That was going to be his job. To show her. That good things happened. And that they stayed. It was going to be his job to show her that she didn't have to sacrifice her independence to accept love, to not be lonely anymore.

He picked up the phone and called Annie and Artie Finkle. Artie was away but the next day Ethan sat with Annie in the little cottage Sam had loved. He told Annie the truth. All of it. That he had planned to trick them into thinking he was the ideal purchaser for their property. And that he had talked Samantha into going along with it by holding out a carrot he thought she couldn't resist, Groom to Grow. But she hadn't been able to compromise herself, and in that moment, when he had seen the uncompromising strength of her character, he had started to become what he had pretended to be, a man in love.

"Asking her to pretend to be my bride was my worst idea ever," he confessed. "Now she thinks," he said softly, "that I bought the store to win her over more completely, and that I just pretended to love her to get what I wanted from you. And it's not true."

"Of course it's not true," Annie said, and placed her wrinkled, age-spotted hand over his, comforting, *forgiving*. "You couldn't have bought her building. Artie and I did. I didn't realize Groom to Grow was Samantha's business, of course."

"You bought her building?" Ethan asked, stunned.

"I went there shortly after you and Sam had been here. I wanted a cute little hoodie for Josie like the one that Samantha had for her dog. When I saw the For Sale sign on the business, I arranged for Artie and I to see the apartment above it. I just fell in love with it—looking out over the park, over the store, all the wonderful original details giving it so much character.

"I just felt if we lived there we would still be so much a part of the community, not locked up in some gated community where you can't even hear children laugh! I'm going to open my shop there." She lowered her voice. "Artie needs something to do. Retirement is boring him to death. We saw some older gentlemen playing chess in the square the day we were there. I can't wait to be there, right in the heart of things."

"You bought it?" he asked again, and then had a flash of inspiration. "Can I buy it from you, then? I'll give it back to her, and this whole mess will be fixed."

"No," Annie said, smiling. "You can't and it won't. You see, son, you said that getting Samantha to pretend to be your fiancée was your worst idea ever, but in a way wasn't it the best thing that ever happened to you?"

He thought of those days with Sam, so filled with laughter and sunshine and discovery. It was true. His worst idea ever had given him the best days of his life.

"I call that a spirit-shot," Annie said softly, "when

our worst experiences, our mistakes, our lead, are spun into gold. When you get to be my age, you take comfort in knowing something greater than you is running the show."

Ethan thought of that: the string of coincidences that had led him to Sam, the impulses that had driven him, though he was the world's least impulsive man, the "mistake" that had made him deepen his relationship with her.

"I don't think what Samantha needs is her store back," Annie said. "I think maybe she's made that business fill all the spaces in her life that love is meant to fill. I think you are meant to marry that girl and give her the place we all long for."

"And what place is that?"

Annie looked around the coziness of her living room, her eyes brimming with love. "Home," she said softly. "Bring that girl home, young man."

CHAPTER EIGHT

ETHAN knocked on the door of the little fisherman's cottage. It seemed to him the place was badly in need of a feminine hand.

Mitch threw open the door, recognized him, and his whole face tightened. "You," he spat out. "Which leg do you want broken first?"

"Excuse me?"

"My little sister is a mess. Her eyes are nearly swollen shut from crying. She lost about ten pounds—that she can't afford to lose. She's letting Amanda run her business instead of going back to her husband where she belongs. Sam hasn't even been inside the door of Groom to Grow in four days. I may just seem like a dumb lobsterman to you, but I know what a broken heart looks like."

"You don't look like a dumb lobsterman to me," Ethan said evenly. "You look like a guy who would go to the ends of the earth to make sure his sister was happy. That's why I'm here."

Mitch looked at him suspiciously.

"I love her," Ethan said.

"Oh, sure, that's why she's bawling her eyes out as we speak."

"She's afraid to love me back, Mitch. You got any ideas where that would come from?"

Mitch took a sudden interest in his sock, which, in true bachelor style, had a large hole in it that his toe was protruding through.

"It was tough enough that she lost her folks," Ethan said quietly. "But then her brothers wouldn't get back in the game. So, she fell in love with her business, thinking that was safe. And now it looks like that isn't any safer than anything else she's ever loved in her life."

"It was safe for her to love me," Mitch said. "And Jake. And Bryce."

"That's why I'm here. I need your help. I need you to show her exactly how much you love her back."

"Why should I believe you know what's best for her? Why should I help you?" Mitch said, not quite convinced.

"Because, Mitch, I'm about to become your brother-in-law, and that means we're going to be putting up with each other and helping each other out for a long, long time."

Mitch's mouth fell open. He stared hard at Ethan. And then he gathered him up in a bear of a hug that nearly crushed his ribs.

* * *

The banging was at the door again.

"Amanda," Sam said over the soundtrack for *Shrek,* the movie she personally believed to be the most romantic of all time, "you have to talk to Charlie."

"That's not Charlie. He doesn't know I'm here watching a movie tonight."

"He drives around town looking for your car! It's heartbreaking. Give the guy a break." And more softly. "Please?"

"I'm talking to Charlie," Amanda said stubbornly, ignoring the knocking on the door, "when you talk to Ethan."

Well, that was a stalemate. Sam passed Amanda the bucket of Fudge Ripple and got up and answered the door.

It wasn't Charlie who stood there.

It was Mitch. And Jake. And Bryce. Despite Waldo growling ferociously at them, having decided to hate all things male, they were grinning like gorillas who had just hijacked the banana train. They were filthy. Covered in sawdust and sweat streaks, clothes dirty. She could tell they were exhausted and exhilarated at the same time.

"What are you doing here?" she demanded.

"Kidnapping," Bryce announced.

"Kidnapping?" Amanda said from the doorway. "How exciting!"

"You're going to be next if you don't smarten up

about Charlie," Bryce informed her darkly. "You're killing that guy."

"Mind your own business," Amanda told him snippily.

Samantha tried to take advantage of the interchange to slide toward the bathroom where she could lock the door, but Mitch caught her, picked her up, tossed her over his shoulder and headed down the steep stairs with her. The dog bit him.

He handed her easily to Jake and scooped up Waldo and placed him back inside the door. "I thought you were getting rid of that dog?"

"Nobody wants him," she said. It was true. She had interviewed about a dozen prospective owners for Waldo. Twice he'd even gone home with them. But he'd been back the next day, wagging his tail joyously when he saw her.

A moment later she was pinned between Bryce and Jake in the back seat of Mitch's station wagon.

"You stink," she told her brothers.

"That's what happens when you work around the clock," Bryce said.

"What's going on?" she asked him. "I was in the middle of a good movie. And a good bucket of ice cream."

"Oh, well," Bryce said. "You know where to find sympathy. In between—" he paused at Mitch's glare in the mirror, and came up with a version altered from the usual ribald ones the boys used "—sympathize and sympathetic in the dictionary."

Her brothers had mollycoddled her for about twenty-four hours after she had announced to them that she was never speaking to Ethan Ballard again. Her brothers' idea of mollycoddling was Mitch delivering fresh fish off the dock, Jake buying her a new fishing spool for her rod and Bryce cleaning the salt off her sailboat for her.

And then, obviously figuring that was enough tenderness, not wanting to turn her into a *wimp,* they'd stopped. Stopped calling, stopped dropping by, suddenly frantically busy. She'd assumed they were uncomfortable with the intensity of her emotion. Now she saw it differently.

Up to something. She really should have guessed sooner.

Suddenly, even though it was dark, she recognized the road they had turned onto. Or was it? The sign Annie's Retreat seemed to be missing.

"What are we doing here?" she whispered.

"We've been gettin' ready for a wedding," Jake announced.

Mitch turned around and reached over the seat, clubbed his brother on the ear—affectionately, but still making his point. "Shut up," he said. "Next thing you know, you'll be proposing for him."

"For who?" she demanded, but her brothers had

gone very silent. "Let me out," she said. "Let me out right now. I'll walk home!"

Mitch surprised her by complying; he slammed on the brakes. Jake bailed out and held the door for her.

And that's when she noticed the torches burning bright on both sides of the pathway.

"You just follow the light," Mitch said softly out his open window. "It will lead you home."

And then he backed the vehicle out of there, and left her standing alone. It seemed to her she had a choice to make.

She could stand there in the dark.

Or she could go toward the light.

And wasn't that a choice all people had to make, sooner or later? Wasn't that a choice she had made when she had spoken so cruelly to Ethan the night she had found out her store had sold?

She had decided to walk in darkness.

How often were people allowed to make that choice again?

Slowly, and then more and more rapidly, until she was running, she followed the path lit by the torches.

At the end of it was the cottage. A single light glowed within, the light of home, the light that every heart that had wandered until it was weary dreamed of seeing.

She was no longer making a choice. She was being guided by something bigger than herself as she put one foot in front of the other and walked to the door that Ethan held open for her.

He closed it behind her, and she looked at him, and seeing him so close made her realize she had missed him even more than she had thought, and she had thought she had missed him to the point of dying.

He looked as bad as her brothers, though at least he had showered. But the handsome plains of his face were whisker-roughened, and he looked utterly exhausted. And yet a light shone in his eyes that took her breath from her.

He said nothing. Just wrapped his arms around her, pulled her tight into himself, rested his chin on top of her head and sighed.

After a long time, she stepped back from him, drank in his face once more and then, finally, not liking that she was responsible for the torment she saw there, looked around.

The interior of the cottage had been completely gutted. All that remained were the original hardwood floors and the fireplace.

"You bought it," she whispered.

"I did. The bride price."

She could not believe the changes he had made. When she had first looked at this place, she had said it would be a crime to change it.

But then, she'd had a known allergy to change.

And looking at what he had done: at how the space had opened, how the light would pour into every corner in the daytime, at how it would *feel* in here, airy, bright, clean, she realized to not change would have been the crime.

And that was the crime she had been committing against herself. And against him.

She looked at him again and allowed herself to call him, in her mind, what he was to her. *Beloved.*

"I'm so sorry, Ethan. I'm so sorry for the accusations I made. It was never, ever about you. I've been terrified of change. I'm so mixed up...and so afraid."

She thought maybe it was the first time since her parents had died and she'd had brothers to live up to that she had admitted being afraid.

It didn't feel like a weakness to do it. It felt brave to let another person see, finally, who you really were.

"I know you're afraid," he said, "and I have some bad news for you. I didn't buy the store. Artie and Annie did. She wants to open her hand-painted-rug shop there. That's why they were suddenly so eager to sell, and why they called me back. I told them the truth about our first visit here."

Sam felt, looking at him, he was showing her what real bravery was. It was making a mistake, admitting it and then going on.

All this time, she had been so worried about losing Groom to Grow. How could it be possible that it felt so right that that lovely old couple had bought it?

Maybe it felt right because Sam had decided to be truly *brave* and that meant relying on your heart for your strength, not your house. Certainly not your business.

"It's time for you to come home, Sam. To me. And this place. So you don't have to be afraid anymore. I love you, Samantha Hall. I have loved you from the moment I saw you save that bouquet from the chocolate fountain when it was so apparent that was the last thing you wanted to do. I suppose I could live without you, but it seems like it would be a joyless existence, and I don't want it."

He went down on one knee, fished a box from his pocket, opened it.

Inside was a perfect, beautiful ring. The diamonds winked with captured light.

"I can't promise you a life where nothing bad ever happens," he said quietly. "I can't promise you a life with no more heartbreaks, much as I want to. But I can promise you days lived fully, that will fill us up with the strength to deal with life's blows when they come. I cannot imagine my life without you in it. I want you to marry me, for real this time."

"Oh, Ethan, I don't deserve—"

But he silenced her with a look. "It's kind of a yes or no thing."

"Yes," she said, and he slipped the ring onto her finger, picked her up and waltzed her around the enormous expanse of the room he had been working on, and even though the space was altered from what it had been when she first saw it, she *felt* it again.

The future shimmered in the room, danced with them. She could hear the laughter of friends, and the crying of babes, the squeals of children, the cheers of men watching baseball games, the quiet companionship of women.

She could feel the love of her parents, finally victorious, finally going on. Through her.

"Soon," he said breathlessly, not letting her go, burying his face in her neck, kissing it. "I have to marry you soon. Because I can't keep my hands off you much longer, and your brother Mitch will kill me if I don't do this the honorable way."

For a moment, she thought she might have to talk to Mitch again, remind him she was an adult woman. But then she realized she just had to surrender and let her brother love her the way he loved her. In time, he would see she was an adult, her actions speaking louder than her words, and then he would treat her like one.

"We're getting married the second we can get everything in order," she agreed, feeling the delicious, familiar heat of being with him.

"I figured the beach out front would be perfect for a wedding," Ethan said quietly. "And that this room would be big enough for a reception the way it is right now. Your brothers have been helping me. I didn't want to start putting it back together until I'd gone over the plan with you. I moved the nursery. And I wasn't sure how many bedrooms we needed for six kids. Do you put two, or three in each room?"

He was teasing her.

"Maybe we should just think about one to begin with."

"Maybe, though, this might be a good time to let you know my father was a twin."

They were teasing each other. And she had missed it the way a swimmer who went under missed breath.

"Don't forget to make room for Waldo," she said.

"I can't imagine it being home without him," he answered and she thought she would melt at the way he said *home* and at his sincerity.

He *wanted* Waldo. And so, she realized, did she. Waldo, and every other stray that came their way, and six kids. And nieces and nephews, and neighbors and friends and family.

"Welcome home, Samantha," he said softly.

"Welcome home, Ethan," she said and felt the truth of it as her heart opened completely to him.

Home was not her apartment above Groom to Grow, and it was not the home she had grown up in and shared with her brothers. It was not this house, either, even though she could sense the future here. She knew this place could be transient. It was just sticks and stones.

But there was a place that was not transient—it was the place their hearts found refuge and strength. And that place was with each other. *Together.* That was home. Nothing could put it asunder. Nothing. Not even death. Once it had been, that place existed forever.

That place was a universal place that all of the human family longed for and recognized when they found it. Sometimes it was called Love, and she called it that now, touching his face with wondrous fingers, and with welcome.

She chose what she saw as his dark eyes drank her in, as his lips tenderly caressed her fingertips.

Her heart, like a sailor who had been lost at sea, raced toward him, toward the Light of Home.

A BRAVO HOMECOMING

BY
CHRISTINE RIMMER

For good men and true-hearted women everywhere.
May your holidays be filled with good cheer,
family togetherness and much love!

Chapter One

"Honey, are you seeing anyone special?" Travis Bravo's mother asked.

Travis stifled a groan. He should have put off calling her back.

But he'd already done that. Twice. In a row. Aleta Bravo was a patient and understanding mom, and she got that he wasn't real big on keeping in touch. But she did have limits. After the third unreturned call, she would have started to worry. He loved his mom and he didn't want her worrying.

Besides, when Aleta Bravo started to worry, she might get his dad involved. And if his dad got involved, steps would be taken. The two of them might end up boarding a helicopter and tracking him down in the middle of the Gulf.

No joke. It could happen. His parents had money and

they had connections and when they tracked you down, you got found.

So now and then, he had no choice but to call his mom back, both to keep her from worrying *and* to keep from getting rescued whether he needed it or not.

She was still talking, all cheerful and loving—and way too determined. "I only ask because I have several terrific women I want you to meet this time. Do you, by any chance, happen to remember my dear friend Billie Toutsell?"

He did, vaguely. Not that it mattered if he knew the woman or not. He knew what she had.

Daughters.

At least one, probably two or three.

His mom continued, "Billie and I go way back. And I've met both of her girls. Brilliant, well brought up, beautiful women. Cybil and LouJo. It so happens both girls will be in town for Thanksgiving week…" *In town* meant in San Antonio, where his mom and dad and brothers and sisters still lived. "And I've been thinking it would be nice to invite both of them out to the ranch over the holiday weekend, maybe Friday or Saturday. What do you think?" Before he could tell her—again—that he didn't want to be set up with any of her friends' daughters, she went right on. "Maybe Billie and her girls would even like to come for Thanksgiving dinner and our reaffirmation of vows."

After forty years of marriage, his parents were reaffirming their wedding vows, which was great. They'd had some troubles in the past few years, even separated for a while. He supposed it made sense that they would want to celebrate making it through a tough time, coming out on the other side still married and happy to be together.

But did his mother have to invite him *and* every available single woman in south Texas to the big event?

What made him so damn special? His mother had six other sons and two daughters and they'd all been allowed to find their own wives and husbands. In fact, as of now, he was the only one who had yet to settle down. That, somehow, seemed to have triggered a burning need in her to help him find the woman for him.

Hadn't she done enough? She'd already introduced him to both of his former fiancées. Rachel, whom he'd loved with all his heart, had been killed eight years ago, run down by a drunk driver while crossing the street. He'd thought he would never get over losing her.

But then, three years later, he'd met Wanda at a family party, over the Christmas holidays. His mother and Wanda's mother were friends. He shouldn't have gotten involved with Wanda. But he had. And it had not ended well.

Evidently his mom thought the third time would be the charm. "Oh, Travis. I'm so glad you'll be there."

"Wouldn't miss it," he muttered. "But, Mom, listen. I really don't need any help finding a girlfriend."

"Well, of course you don't, but opportunity is everything. And you're always off on some oil rig somewhere. How many women are you going to meet on an oil rig?"

"Mom, I—"

She didn't even let him finish his sentence. "It's been years. You have to move on. You know that." She spoke gently.

"I *have* moved on."

She sighed. And then she said briskly, "Well, it never hurts to meet new people. And, you know, I've recently been acting as a docent—twice a month at the Alamo. It just so happens that I met a lovely young woman there, also a docent, Ashley McFadden. I know you and Ashley would hit it off so well. She's perfect. Great personality. So smart. So funny."

Travis winced and sent a desperate glance around the lounge. He could a use a little help about now. He needed someone to rescue him from his own mom.

But rescue was not forthcoming. He was alone with a wide, dark flat-screen TV, a row of snack and drink machines, random sofas and chairs and a matched pair of ping-pong tables. Across the room, a couple of roughnecks were Wii bowling on the other TV. Neither of them even glanced his way.

Faintly all around him, he could hear pounding and mechanical noises and the mostly incomprehensible babbling from the PA system, sounds that were part of life on the *Deepwater Venture,* a semi-submersible oil platform fifty-seven miles off the coast of Texas.

His mother chattered on, naming off more charming young women she knew, more of the still single daughters of her endless list of women friends. He was starting to think he would just have to back out of the Thanksgiving visit, to tell her he wasn't going to be able to make it home after all.

Sorry, Mom. Something big has come up, something really big. I just can't be there....

But then he heard swearing. And the swift pounding of heavy boots on the stairs. The sounds were coming closer, descending on him from the deck above.

He knew the voice: Sam Jaworski, the rig manager in charge of the drilling department—aka the tool pusher. Sam was one of eight women on the rig. The safety officer was also a woman. And the rest worked in food service or housekeeping.

Sam, in coveralls, safety glasses and a hard hat, stomped into the lounge at full volume. She was on a roll with nonstop, semi-dirty, surprisingly imaginative language.

His mother was *still* talking. "So you see, I have found several fun, smart, attractive girls you'll get a chance to meet."

Sam sent him a quick acknowledging glance. He raised a hand in greeting. She gave the roughnecks a wave and then clomped over to the coffee machine. She poured herself a cup. There was a patch sewn on the right butt cheek of her coveralls. It read I Ain't Yo' Mama. She had to stop swearing to take a big swig of coffee.

But as soon as she swallowed, she was at it again. "And then dunk his sorry, skinny ass in a burnin' barrel of bubbling black crude…"

Travis grinned for the first time since he'd picked up the phone to call his mom. Sam's swearing was always more enthusiastic than obscene. And it never failed to make him smile.

And then he said, without even stopping to consider the possible consequences, "Mom, I already have a girl." He held back a chuckle. *Well, sort of a girl.*

Sam took off her hard hat and safety glasses, turned toward him and propped a hip against the counter. She slurped up a big sip of coffee—and swore some more.

On the other end of the line, his mom let out a delighted trill of laughter. "Travis, how wonderful. Why didn't you say so?"

"Well, Mom, you haven't exactly let me get a word in edgewise."

"Oh, honey." She was instantly regretful. "I'm sorry. I was just so glad to hear from you. And I wanted to…

Well, it doesn't matter now. Forgive me for being a poor listener?"

"You know I do."

She asked eagerly, "What's her name? Do I know her?"

More choice expletives from Sam. He turned to the wall, cupped his hand around the mouthpiece of the phone, and told his mother, "Samantha, Mom. Samantha Jaworski—and no, you don't."

His mother made a thoughtful sound. "But you've mentioned her often, haven't you, over the years?"

"Yeah, Mom. I've mentioned her." He'd known Sam for more than a decade now.

"And she's nice, isn't she? You two have been friends for a long time, as I recall."

"Yeah, we have. And she's…she's lovely." He slanted a glance at Sam as she sniffed and rubbed her nose with the back of her grease-smeared hand. "Very delicate."

Sam stood six feet tall and she was stronger than most men. She had to be, to get where she'd gotten in the oil business. Most tool pushers were older than she was. And male.

On a rig, the buck stopped at the tool pusher. Sam was on the drilling-contractor payroll. She did everything from making sure work schedules were met to setting up machines and equipment. She prepared production reports. She recommended hirings and firings and decided who was ready for promotion. She supervised and she coordinated. She trained workers in their duties and in safety procedures. She requisitioned materials and supplies. And if it came right down to it, she could haul and connect pipe with the best of them.

On this job, Travis had had the pleasure of working closely with her. He was the company man, paid to represent the interests of the oil company South Texas Oil Industries. Some pushers didn't get along with the company man. They didn't like being answerable to the exploration and operation end of the business. Sam didn't have that problem. She not only had her men's respect, but she also worked well with others.

She was an amazing woman, Sam Jaworski. But delicate?

Not in the least.

"I get it now," his mother said. "I've been chattering away and the whole time you've been trying to tell me that you're bringing her to Thanksgiving, to the reaffirmation of our vows."

Crap. He should have seen that coming. Suddenly, his little private joke took on scary ramifications. "Uh, well…"

"Honey, I understand how it's been for you." She didn't, not really. But he knew she meant well. She kept on, "You've been…hurt and let down before. I can see where you might be afraid to let it get serious with Samantha. But that's all right. Just ask her to come with you. Just take that step."

"Well, I…" He stalled some more, grasping for the right words, the magic words that would get his mother off his back about this once and for all. Those words didn't come. "Mom, really, I don't think that's a good idea."

"Why not?"

"I just don't, okay?"

His mom finally gave it up. "All right, if you don't want to invite her, if your relationship hasn't gotten to that point yet, well, all right." She sighed. And then she brightened and teased, "At least Cybil and LouJo and Ashley will be happy to know they still have a chance."

Trapped. His gut churned and his pulse pounded. And then he heard himself say, "As a matter of fact, Sam and I are engaged."

It just kind of popped out. He blinked at the wall. Had he really said that?

His mother cried out in joy. "Travis, how wonderful! I can't believe you didn't tell me until now."

Had Sam heard him say that? He sent the tall, broad-shouldered woman in the grease-streaked coveralls another furtive glance. Uh-uh. She'd turned back to the sink to wash her hands. As he faced the wall once more, he heard her rip a paper towel off the roll.

He looked again. Clomp, clomp, clomp. Coffee mug in hand, she sauntered over to the nearer TV and grabbed the remote. The screen came alive and she started channel surfing.

Meanwhile, on the other end of the line, his mother was on the case. "And that settles it. You must bring her with you. I won't take no for an answer, not now."

He stared at Sam's I Ain't Yo' Mama backside, at her short brown hair, creased tight to her skull from the hard hat's inner band, at her big steel-toed boots. Had he lost his mind? There was no win in lying to his mom—especially not about being engaged. "Uh, well…"

"Please, Travis, invite her. I'm so happy for you. And you know we're all going to want to meet her."

"Mom, I—"

"Please." Her voice was so gentle. And hopeful. And maybe even somewhat sad—as though she knew that in the end, he was going to disappoint her, that Sam would not be coming with him, no matter what his mother said to encourage him to bring her.

Now he felt like a complete jerk. For lying about

Sam. For disappointing his mom. For everything. "Look, Mom. I'll…check with Sam, okay?"

Dear God in heaven. Where had *that* come from? Bad, bad idea.

"Oh, Travis." His mom was suddenly sounding happy again. "That's wonderful. We'll be expecting both of you, then."

What the hell? "Uh, no. Wait, really. You can't start expecting anything. I said I would *ask* her."

"And I just know she'll say yes. Two weeks from today, as planned. Love you. Bye now."

"Mom. I mean it. Don't… Wait! I…" But it was no good. She'd already hung up.

He took the phone away from his ear and gave it a dirty look. Then he started to call her back—but stopped in mid-dial.

Why ask for more trouble? Hadn't he gotten himself plenty already?

Grumbling under his breath, he snagged the phone back onto the wall mount, yanked out a chair at the table a few feet away and dropped into it.

Sam had been waiting for Travis to finish on the phone. She watched as the two roughnecks wrapped up their bowling game and went back up the stairs.

Good. She didn't need anyone listening in.

She heard Travis hang up, and then the sound of a chair scraping the floor as he pulled it out from the table. She switched off the TV and turned to him. "That roustabout Jimmy Betts? Born without a brain. A walking safety hazard. Give that boy a length of pipe and someone is bound to get whacked in the frickin' head."

He seemed distracted, slumped in the chair, a frown

on his handsome face. But after a second or two, he said, "He'll learn. They all do—or they don't last."

Sam let a snort do for a reply to that. And then she tossed down the remote and went to join him. She plunked her coffee on the table, swung a chair around and straddled it backward. Stacking her arms on the chair back, she leaned her chin on them. She studied him. He stared back at her, but his brown eyes still had a faraway look in them.

"Your mama, huh?" she finally asked. "Driving you crazy again?"

He grunted. "That's right."

"She still trying to find you the new love of your life?"

He grunted a second time and looked at her kind of strangely. She got the message. He wasn't in the mood to talk about his mother and her plans to get him hogtied and branded.

Sam could read Travis pretty well. After all, they'd been friends since way back when he was nineteen and she was eighteen. Back then, Travis had worked on the oil well at her dad's South Dakota ranch.

So, all right. Not talking about his mother was fine with her. She had something else on her mind anyway.

Sam indulged in a glum look around the lounge. It was a large room. But the low ceiling, the absence of windows and the fluorescent lighting gave the space a sort of subterranean glow. It made Travis look tired, turned his tanned skin kind of pasty. She didn't even want to think about how it made *her* look.

Travis's dark brows drew together. "Got something on your mind, Sam?"

Oh, yes, she did. "You have no idea how frickin' tired

I am of being on this rig. And I could seriously use a tall cold one about now, you know?"

They grunted in unison then. There was no liquor allowed on the rig.

Most rig workers had the usual two-weeks-on, two-weeks-off rotation. Not the pusher. Sam had been on the rig for over a month now, working twelve-hour shifts seven days a week. A week more and she would be back on land at last. She could not wait. And the rock docs—the engineers—were saying that the four-month drilling process was within days of completion. Her job on the *Deepwater Venture* was ending anyway. She wouldn't be signing on to another rig to start all over again.

"Travis, I've been thinking…"

He waited, watching her.

She sat straighter and swept both arms wide, a gesture meant to include not only the lounge, but every inch of the semi-submersible rig, from the operating deck and the cranes and derrick soaring above it, to the ballasted, watertight pontoons below the ocean's surface that held the giant platform afloat. "I used to love the challenge, you know? Doing a man's job and doing it right. Earning and keeping the men's respect—in spite of being female, even though I was younger than half of them. But lately, well, I'm thinking it's time to change it up a little. I'm thirty years old. It's a time when a person can start to wonder about things."

He tipped his head to the side, frowning. "What things?"

"Things like getting back to the real world, like living on solid ground full-time, like…I don't know, letting my hair grow, for cryin' out loud, getting a job where I don't end up covered in drilling mud and grease at least once a shift. Sitting in an employee lounge that has actual windows—windows that look out on something other than water and more water."

He made a low noise. Was it a doubtful kind of sound? What? He didn't think she could make it in a desk job?

She scowled at him and raked her fingers back through her sweaty, chopped-off hair. "And you can just stop looking at me like that, Travis Bravo. Yeah, I know what working in an office is going to mean. I get that I'm going to have to clean up my language and maybe even learn to wear a damn dress now and then. And I'm ready for that."

He kept on looking at her. Studying her, really. What the hell was he thinking?

She threw out both arms again, glanced left and then right—and then directly at him again. *"What?"* she demanded.

He swung his boots up onto the molded plastic chair next to his. Way too casually, he suggested, "So, Sam. Want to come to my parents' wedding?"

Okay, now she was totally lost. "Your parents' *wedding?* Didn't that already happen? Y'know like, oh, a hundred years ago? Travis, I have no idea what you're talking about."

One corner of his mouth quirked up. "Well, okay. Technically, it's a reaffirmation of their wedding vows. It's happening out at Bravo Ridge." He'd spoken of Bravo Ridge often. It was his family's ranch near San Antonio. "It'll be on Thanksgiving Day."

She sat back and folded her arms across her middle. She'd always wondered about his family, the high-class, powerful San Antonio Bravos. It would be interesting to meet them all, to match the real, flesh-and-blood people to the faces in the pictures Travis had shown her over the years.

Then again, maybe not. "I don't think so...."

"Come on. Why not?"

"Well, to be honest, from everything you've said about your family, I don't think I'd fit in with them."

"Sure you will."

"I don't *even* have the clothes for something like that, let alone the manners. And I don't have any fancy pedigree, either. I'd probably embarrass you."

"You could never embarrass me. You're the best. And what do you mean, pedigree? It's America. We're all equal, remember? And if you're nervous about your clothes, I'll deal with that."

She looked at him sideways. "How, exactly are *you* going deal with *my* clothes?"

"I'll buy you some new ones."

"No way. I buy my own stuff. But even if I maxed out my credit cards getting a whole new wardrobe, well, I still wouldn't know which frickin' fork to use."

He swung his feet to the floor and canted toward her in the chair. "So we'll get you a coach. A few days in Houston beforehand should do it."

"Um. Travis, I'm not really understanding what exactly you're up to here."

"I just said. You'll have time. A whole week to get ready after you're back on land, plenty of time to buy the clothes and work with the coach."

"The coach," she repeated blankly.

"Yeah, the coach. Someone who's an expert on all that stuff—on the clothes, the makeup, the...use of the silverware, whatever. By the time you meet my mom, you'll be more than ready."

"More than ready for...?"

"Everything." He smiled. It wasn't a very sincere smile.

She rubbed her temples with the tips of her fingers. Really, he was making her head spin. "Travis, cut the crap. What *exactly* are you trying to talk me into?"

He glanced away, and then back. "Before I get too specific, I just want to know you'll keep an open mind about the whole thing, okay?"

"Yeah, well. Before I can keep an open mind, I need to know what I'm supposed to be keeping an open mind about."

He hoisted his feet back up on the chair again. "It's like this. I want you to help me get my mom off my back."

She followed. Kind of. "You mean about all the, er, *suitable* young women, right?"

He nodded. "I need you to be my date—for a week, including Thanksgiving."

"You think if you bring a date, your mom will stop trying to fix you up?"

He pulled a face and scratched the back of his head. "Well, yeah. For a while. If my date was…more than just a date."

"What do you mean, more than just a frickin' date?"

"Okay, it's like this. I want you to pretend that you're my fiancée."

Travis didn't find the look on Sam's face the least bit encouraging.

She swore. Colorfully. And then she jumped up from the chair, strode around the table to him—and slapped him upside the back of the head.

He shoved her hand away. "Ouch! Knock it off."

She gave a disgusted snort. "Have you lost your mind?"

He put up both hands to back her off. "Look. It just… slipped out when I was talking to her, okay?"

"It? What?"

"She was all over me, pressuring me, going down the list of all the women she wants me to meet. And then you came down from the deck and I, well, all of a sudden, I was saying I already had a girl. I said *you* were my girl and we were engaged."

Sam did more swearing. And then she returned to her chair, grabbed the back of it, spun it around and sat down in it front ways that time. "What *have* you been smoking?"

"Not a thing. You know that. And can you just think it over? Please? Don't say no without giving it some serious consideration. You get the coach and the clothes to help you change up your life. And I have a few strings I can pull, too, for you. To make sure you get the job you want."

She had her arms folded good and tight across her middle by then. "There's just one teensy problem."

"What?"

"It's a big wonkin' lie."

"I know that, but it can't be helped."

"Sure, it can. Call your mom back. Tell her you lied and I'm not your girl after all. And when you want a girl, you'll find her yourself."

"Sam, come on…"

She pressed her lips together, blew out a breath—and flipped him the bird.

But he refused to give up. The more he thought about it, the more this looked like a solution to his problem.

A temporary solution, yeah. But still. Even temporary was better than no solution at all.

"Look," he said. "You do this for me, I figure it's good for up to a year of peace and quiet on my mother's part."

"Why don't you just *talk* to your mother? Tell her how you feel, tell her you want her to back off and mind her own business."

"You think I haven't? It doesn't matter what I say, she thinks she's doing the right thing for me. She thinks it's for my own good. And when my mother thinks what she's doing is for the good of one of her children, there's no stopping her. There's no getting her to see the light and admit that she's got it all wrong."

"But making up some big old lie is not the answer. It's…just not you. You're a straight-ahead guy. No frills and no fancy footwork. I've always liked that about you."

He laid it right out for her. "Sam, I'm desperate. I need a break from this garbage. I need to be able to go home for once without having a bunch of sweet-faced Texas debutantes in their best party dresses lined up waiting to meet me. I need to be able to call my mom without being beat over the head with all the women she wants to introduce me to."

"Maybe if you just gave it a chance with one of them, you'd find out that—"

"Stop. Don't go there. You know I'm not up for that. I *had* the love of my life. She died. And I already tried it with the woman who could never take her place."

"But it's been years and years since you lost Rachel. And just because it didn't work out with Wanda doesn't mean there isn't someone else out there who's right for you."

He gave her a really dirty look, and then he glanced away. "You're starting to sound like my mother. I don't need that."

"Travis, I only—"

He turned to meet her eyes again. "Help me out, Sam. Help me out and I'll help *you* out. Win-win. You'll see. You can have the new life you've been dreaming of. All you have to do to get it is a little favor for a friend."

Chapter Two

A week and a day later, Sam entered the lobby of Houston's Four Seasons Hotel.

She wore a gray pantsuit with a white blouse and black flats. Not exactly glamorous. But hey. At least it was something other than coveralls, steel-toed boots and a hard hat.

Unfortunately, her hair was being really annoying that day. It was only an inch long, for cripes' sake. But still, it insisted on curling every which way.

Her makeup? She wore none—and not because she hadn't tried. Three times, she'd applied blush, lip gloss and mascara. She'd picked those up the day before at Walmart in an effort to look more pulled-together for this big adventure she probably shouldn't have let herself be talked into in the first place. Each time she put the makeup on, she'd had to scrub it right off again. It just didn't look right on her. So in the end, she decided to go without.

The Four Seasons was about the fanciest hotel in Houston. She'd expected old-fashioned elegance. But the lobby was modern. The furniture had clean, trendy lines. The carpets were in black-and-white geometric patterns. There was also bright color—in the modern art on the walls, in the purple pillows, all plump and inviting on the tan and off-white sofas.

And where the hell was Travis, anyway? He'd promised he would be here waiting for her.

She tried not to gape like the oversize hayseed she knew herself to be. She told herself it was all in her mind that the bellmen and concierge clerks were staring at her and wondering what she was doing there. What did a concierge clerk care if she was as big as a horse and every bit as muscular? So what if she looked more manly than most of the guys in the place? She had as much right to be there as anyone else.

And she did have her pride. Chin up, her black leather tote hooked on a shoulder, she sauntered past the check-in desk and chose a sofa thick with bright pillows beneath a giant circular chandelier dripping with about a hundred thousand crystals.

When she reached the sofa, she turned and lowered herself into it with care. She kept her knees together, her black flats planted on the thick carpet, neatly, side-by-side. Easing the tote off her shoulder, she put it at her feet. And then, sitting very still and very straight, she folded her hands in her lap and she waited.

She tried not to squirm, tried to keep her face calm and composed. The minutes crawled by.

Travis, you SOB, where are you?

He'd better get there damn soon or she wouldn't be waiting when he finally did arrive. She pressed her lips together, swallowed, felt the nervous sweat beginning to seep through the underarms of her new shirt.

Wasn't there some old saying about how a person should beware of all situations that require new clothes?

Uh, yeah. Exactly.

Travis, unless you show up right this minute, I am going to get up and walk out of here. And then, the next time I see you, I will beat the ever lovin' crap out of you....

"Sam. Great. There you are...."

So. He was there. At last.

Sam let out the breath she hadn't realized she was holding. Turning to look over her shoulder, she watched him striding toward her, wearing really nice black jeans and a sport jacket, looking like he owned the place. With him was a short, skinny man in a striped shirt with a big white collar, linen pants and suspenders. The man's thick, wavy blond hair was bigger than he was. Sam could have picked him up with one hand, tucked him under her arm and carried him several city blocks without even breathing hard.

She snatched up her tote and rose to meet them.

"Lookin' good," said Travis. He grabbed her in a quick hug. When he let her go, he turned to the tiny, bird-boned guy with the big hair. "Jonathan, Sam. Sam, Jonathan."

The little guy gave her the once-over through eyes as small and bright and birdlike as the rest of him. "Hello, Samantha. I can see we've got our work cut out for us."

Her coach. Of course. Pretentious frickin' twit. She started to say something to put him in his place, but then changed her mind. He might be pretentious, but then again, he was also right. No point in beating up the messenger. She had a lot to learn if she wanted a different kind of life. "Yeah," she said drily. "I hope you're up to the job."

Travis said, "I found him on the internet. And I'm betting he's the best."

Jonathan tossed his big hair. "No time to waste, is there? Shall we go up?"

The suite was spectacular. All in relaxing colors—dusty greens and creamy tans and warm golds, with a great view of downtown Houston. Two bedrooms. One for her, one for her coach.

Travis had his town house in the city.

She stood at the window and looked out at the skyline and worried about how much this had to be costing him.

He came to stand with her. "Great view, huh?"

"Yeah. Where's Jonathan?" she asked the question low, out of the corner of her mouth.

"He's in his room, getting settled."

She decided to go ahead and ask him about the expense. "This all looks…really pricey, Travis."

"That's right." He sounded so pleased with himself. "Didn't I promise you a crash course in how the other half lives?"

"I'm just saying it's enough that you hired me my own personal coach. That had to cost plenty. And then the clothes. That'll be plenty more. You really didn't need to spring for a suite at the Four Seasons."

He put an arm around her shoulder, gave it a reassuring squeeze. "Only the best for my favorite fiancée."

She eased out from under his hold. "You're blowing me off."

"No, I'm not."

"It just, you know, seems like it's kind of overkill.

Way too frickin' expensive overkill. I mean, I know you have your investments and all, but I hate to see you waste your hard-earned money."

"Stop worrying—and anyway, I didn't raid my portfolio for this." He leaned in closer and lowered his voice to a soft growl. "Did I ever tell you about my giant trust fund?"

"You did, but you always said—"

"—that I would never touch it. And I haven't. Not once. Until now."

She turned to him, met his kind dark eyes. "You broke into your trust fund for *this?*"

He gave her an easy smile. "About time, I was thinking—and no, I didn't *break* into it. It's mine, after all, just sitting there, waiting for me, the prodigal son, to finally take advantage of what being a Bravo has always offered me."

She smiled too, then. "The prodigal son. I never thought of you that way. And I thought a prodigal was a wild-living big spender."

"I was thinking more in the sense of the son who left home."

"Well, you are that."

"And my mom only wants me to come home."

"And get married to a nice Texas debutante…"

"Lucky for me, I have you to save me from that."

She had the strangest desire to lay her hand along the side of his smooth, freshly shaved cheek. But that seemed uncalled-for. They weren't pretending to be engaged *yet,* after all. "Yeah, well," she said vaguely. "We'll see…."

"Ahem." It was Jonathan. He stood over by the sitting area, holding a laptop against his narrow chest. He set the laptop on the gleaming glass surface of the coffee table and then clapped his skinny hands together. "All right, then. Let's begin." He sat down on the sofa and patted the cushion next to him. "Samantha, come and sit by me." She sent Travis a what-have-you-gotten-me-into glance and then went over and sat next to Jonathan, who signaled to Travis with a dramatic flourish. "You, too. Have a seat." Travis claimed a wing chair across the coffee table.

Sam was realizing that she found her new coach kind of amusing. She liked his take-charge attitude and self-assurance. He might be little, but every sentence, every gesture, was delivered on a grand scale. "So, Jonathan, what's your last name?"

He turned slowly to look up at her, one pencil-thin eyebrow raised. "Just Jonathan, darling."

Oh, wow. Now she was his darling. She chuckled. "Well, all right."

Travis got up and went to grab an apple from the basket on the granite wet bar. "I flew Jonathan in from L.A. And before I did, I checked out his references. He comes highly recommended." He bit a big, crunchy hunk out of the apple.

Jonathan almost smiled—or at least the corners of his tiny mouth lifted a fraction. "I have my own cable show," he said proudly. *"Jeer-worthy to Cheer-worthy."* He opened the laptop and fiddled with the keyboard for a moment. His picture appeared on the screen. He sat in a plush leather chair in a red-walled room, his hair bigger and wavier than it was in person. A bookcase behind him was filled with gold-tooled leather volumes and accented with what seemed to be valuable antiques. "My website," he said. She'd already figured that out, of course, from the ornate gold header at the top of the page. "JustJonathan.com."

"Uh. Real nice," she said.

"Thank you, darling." He clicked the mouse. A really sad-looking redhead appeared on the screen. Ruddy skin, frizzy hair, a face as round as a dinner plate. "Amanda Richly. Before." *Click.* "And after," he said proudly.

The second image was the same redhead. But the same redhead, transformed. Now her hair was thick and wavy and completely unfrizzed, her skin pink and perfect, her blue eyes framed by long, lush red-brown lashes. She was no longer sad. In fact, her happy smile brought out the cute dimples in her cheeks.

"Wow. Way to go, Jonathan." Sam elbowed him in his itty-bitty ribs.

He almost fell over sideways. But not quite. "Please don't hurt me, darling," he said drily. She laughed. And then he preened, "Trust me. I know what I'm doing."

"I can see that." She shared a nod with Travis, who remained by the wet bar, polishing off his apple.

Jonathan clicked through several more transformations. Each one was amazing. Sam was impressed and she told Jonathan so.

Finally, he snapped the laptop shut and frowned at her. "If we are to work together, I need to be able to be perfectly frank."

"Go for it." She braced herself for the bad news.

"You're a disaster, my sweet." He caught her hands, turned them over, gave a small gasp of pure distress. "Look at these. What have you been doing with them, scraping barnacles off a ship's hull?"

"Close," she confessed.

He shook his head. "Never mind. Don't tell me. I don't need specifics." He turned her hands over again, set them on her knees, and patted the backs of them.

Next, scowling, he touched her hair. And then he caught her face between his soft, warm palms. "We must get you to the spa immediately," he announced. "You will need *everything.* It's going to take a while. And the peels, the scrubs, the masks and the mud wraps, the hair, nails and makeup are only the beginning. There will be shopping. Intensive, goal-centered shopping. I will go with you, of course, give you guidance, save you from yourself should you try and buy another unfortunate pantsuit."

She winced and looked down at the pantsuit in question. "Unfortunate? I bought it yesterday. I know it's not great. But I thought it was better than just unfortunate."

He wiggled a finger at her. "Remember. Absolute honesty."

"Yeah. All right. Hit me with it."

He caught the fabric of her sleeve, fingered it and shuddered. "You must learn to buy clothing made from natural fibers, my love. It not only looks so much better, but it also lets the skin breathe and doesn't trap odors."

"Odors," she echoed weakly, way too aware of the lingering dampness beneath her arms.

"I noticed you had just that big black bag."

She shrugged. "Well, I only brought a couple of changes of underwear and some pj's. I thought we would be buying the rest."

"Very good. Excellent. Out with the old and all things polyester. And in with the new. By the time I'm through with you, you won't be afraid of five-inch Manolo Blahniks, or a little color."

She wasn't a complete idiot. She knew who Manolo Blahnik was. She'd watched a few episodes of *Sex and the City* back in the day. "Uh, Jonathan. Maybe you didn't notice. I don't wear high heels because I'm already taller than just about everyone else."

"Yes, you are. And your height is spectacular."

Travis folded his big frame back into the wing chair. He was grinning. "Yep. Absolutely spectacular."

She blinked at him. "Uh. It is?"

Jonathan patted her arm. "You also have excellent bone structure. Fabulous cheekbones."

Her sagging spirits lifted. She pressed her fingers to the cheekbones in question. "Well, that's good."

"And I can see you are in prime physical condition. We can use that."

"Er…we can?"

"Oh, yes. Gone are the days when a pretty woman had to be tiny and delicate. It's okay at last to be a woman of substance. Muscles, wide shoulders, strong calves and hard thighs are the height of fashion now."

Maybe it wasn't as bad as she'd thought. She dared to grin.

Jonathan frowned, shook his head and then smoothed his acres of hair carefully back into place. "Don't become overconfident, my love. You've got a lot to learn. And a limited amount of time to do it in."

At Jonathan's request, Travis got up to go a few minutes later.

"You will not see Samantha until Saturday evening," her coach announced in what Samantha considered a very grim tone. "For the final test."

"Test?" Sam piped up weakly.

"Don't ask." Jonathan remained deadly serious. "Not yet. We are only beginning. And there's a long way to go before we're ready to discuss the final test."

Travis gave her a hug at the door. That was the second time he'd hugged her that day—first, in the lobby, now here, as he was leaving. As a rule, she and Travis didn't hug much. Especially the past few months when they'd been working on the rig together. Hugs would not be professional.

But now, with his strong arms around her, she realized how much she enjoyed getting the chance to lean on him. He was a couple of inches taller than she was, and even broader in the shoulders and deeper in the chest. It felt good to hug him. She knew she could hug him hard and never hurt him. For a girl of her size and strength, that was a rare thing.

He took her by the shoulders and held her away from him so he could meet her eyes. "You going to be okay?"

She nodded and forced a smile for him. "Go on. I'll be fine." She stepped back from the comforting circle of his hold. He opened the door and went through it.

Instantly she wanted to reach out and grab him back. She'd always found his presence reassuring—and she could really use some reassurance about now. She took a step out into the hallway and watched him stride confidently toward the elevators.

It was kind of funny, really. She risked her life just about daily on the job. An oil rig, after all, was a pretty dangerous place. But she'd never been as scared as she was right then, in that hotel suite, watching Travis walk away from her. The very idea of having to learn to get her girly on freaked her the hell out. It would be easier if Travis could stay.

"Shut the door, Samantha." Jonathan's voice was almost tender.

She stepped back into the room and did what he told her to. And then she leaned her forehead against that door and thought about what a good friend Travis had been to her over the years.

At the end of the first year of their friendship, just before she turned nineteen, he'd helped her get her start in the oil business. He'd spoken up for her when she tried for her first job as a roustabout on a land rig. They didn't want to hire her because she was a woman and what woman could hold up under the grueling physical labor that would be required of her?

Thanks to Travis, she got that job, as what they called a "worm," the lowest of the low in the rig pecking order. She got that job and she kept up with the men. She did it all. She hauled pipe and dug trenches, cleaned up mud and oil and whatever else got all over the equipment. She cleaned threads, scraped and painted the various rig components. She worked her ass off and she never shirked.

That first job was where she'd met a certain rough-neck, Zachary Gunn. She'd fallen in love with Zach—fallen in love for the first and only time in her life. And when Zach turned out to be a rotten, no-good bigmouth jerk who told everyone what he'd done with her and that she'd been really bad at it, Travis was there.

Travis beat the ever-lovin' you-know-what out of that sorry SOB. And then kicked him off the rig.

As a rule, Sam fought her own battles. But that one time, it meant more than she could ever say to know that Travis Bravo had her back.

"Time to get started," said Jonathan. "Tell me you're ready."

Sam straightened her spine and turned to face her coach. "I'm ready. Let's go."

Chapter Three

That first day was really bad.

Before they did anything, Jonathan took a bunch of pictures of her from different angles, pictures of her standing, pictures of her sitting. Pictures from the front, the back, the side. Full-length pictures and also close-up ones.

She knew what those pictures were: the "before" pictures. She knew they were awful.

And she sincerely hoped that the "afters," days from now, would be a whole lot better.

Once Jonathan decided he had enough ugly shots of her, he had her sign a paper giving him permission to use the pictures on his website. And then he took her to the hotel spa.

It was a nice place. Sam loved that it was simple, not froufrou or frilly in the least. It was soothing just to be there.

Until the torture started.

Jonathan said her skin needed all the help it could get. There was deep-tissue cleaning and a chemical peel. There was hot mud wrapped all around her in steaming wet towels. There was waxing—of her legs and under her arms. The bikini wax was the worst.

She'd rather take a bath in drilling mud than get that done again.

Jonathan laughed when she told him that. "You'll get waxed, darling. And regularly. A woman should be sleek. Smooth. Excess body hair is not the least bit feminine."

She grunted. "Gee, Jonathan. Thanks a bunch for sharing."

There was massage. That wasn't so bad.

But after that, there was the manicure and the pedicure. Those went on forever and involved soaking and exfoliating and scrubbing at every callous and rough spot, of which there were many.

Hours later, when they were finished with her for the day, her face was lobster-red from the peel and they'd given her booties and white gloves. She had to slather on this gooey ointment before bed nightly, they had told her at the spa, both on her hands and her feet, and then wear the gloves and booties to bed every night for the whole week.

She was starving by the time she got back to the suite. She wanted a burger and fries and a strawberry shake. Or at least a big slab of meatloaf and a mountain of mashed potatoes with a healthy side of mushy canned green beans. On the rig, the kitchen was open round-the-clock and you could get yourself a huge pile of hot food—heavy on the starches and fats and red meat—any time you got the least bit hungry.

Not here, though. Jonathan ordered room service for them.

When it came, she wanted to break down and cry. All day being waxed and plucked and pummeled in the spa. And for dinner, she got an itsy-bitsy mound of barely cooked broccoli, three tiny red potatoes. And grilled salmon.

Actually, it was delicious. But it wasn't enough to keep a fly alive.

She begged for more. Jonathan refused to let her even have one more dinky red potato. He said she wasn't getting enough exercise to eat the way she was apparently accustomed to eating.

It was too much. She yelled at him. "Jonathan, I would be frickin' happy to exercise. I'll go down to the gym right this minute and bench-press my butt off if you will only swear on your life that there'll be a blood-rare T-bone and a baked potato slathered in butter and sour cream waiting for me when I get back up here to this frickin' tasteful, so-classy suite."

He only shook his head. He was a slave driver, that Jonathan.

After the piddly-ass meal, they had grammar lessons. He made her take a vow that she would never use the word *frickin'* again in this lifetime. And then he tutored her on how to eat at a table set with endless pieces of unrecognizable silverware.

It was actually pretty simple, once he explained that you started with the outermost fork or knife or spoon and worked your way in. And if in doubt, you waited to pick up the next tong or cracker or pointy lobster-picking thing until you were able to subtly observe what your host or hostess did with it.

"Subt-ly," Jonathan repeated, making a big deal

of both syllables. "And by 'subtly,' I mean a sideways glance in the direction of the hostess in question. No open-mouthed ogling. One must learn, darling, to accomplish one's goal in such a way as not to telegraph one's ignorance to the table at large."

"Gotcha," she answered, feeling vaguely resentful. Yeah, okay. She did have a lot to learn, but she'd never been the kind to stare with her mouth open.

He sighed in a way that indicated she caused him endless emotional pain. "*Gotcha.* Another word you would do well to remove from your vocabulary."

"Jonathan, you keep on like this, I won't have any *frick*—er, darn words left."

"But, darling, you will learn new ones. I will see to that—and as concerns your elbows…"

"Yeah, what about 'em?" She pushed back her sleeve. "They've been creamed and scrubbed and buffed just about down to the bone."

"Yes, they do *look* much better."

"Thanks, but that's not what I was getting at."

"It doesn't matter what *you're* getting at. You're the student. You're here to watch, listen and learn. And as to elbows, they are under no circumstances to be allowed on the surface of the table while one is still indulging in the meal. Understood?"

"Yeah, I knew that." Not that she'd ever cared all that much where she put her elbows while she was eating. But still. Everybody knew they weren't supposed to be on the table, even if most people didn't give a damn either way.

"However." There was a definite gleam in Jonathan's beady little eyes. "*After* the meal, while one lingers, chatting, enjoying the heady conversation that so often swirls around the table when one is in good company…

then, and only then, is it considered acceptable to delicately brace one, or even both elbows on the tablecloth."

She couldn't help grinning. "Delicately, huh?"

"Yes, well. We'll have to work on that."

After the lessons on which piece of silverware to use when, they moved on to her clothing. He said they would try some preliminary shopping tomorrow. He wanted her to think about what colors would work on her—bright, vivid jewel colors, he said. "And some neutrals. But. No. Gray. Ever." He made each word a sentence. And then he elaborated. "Gray does nothing for your coloring, Samantha. Less than nothing. Gray makes you look embalmed."

"Gee. Good to know."

"Sarcasm is not appreciated."

"I'll keep that in mind, Jonathan—if you will."

There was more lecturing on the subject of natural fibers. She would wear cotton, silk, linen and wool. And *only* cotton, silk, linen and wool. "And no frills. We'll go for simplicity with you. And some drama. But nothing fluffy or ruffled. Nothing too…precious. Because, darling, you are not the precious type."

Of course, he had examples to show her on his laptop. She thought he was absolutely right in his judgment of what should work well for her clothing-wise, so she didn't give him too much of a hard time during the wardrobe lesson. She listened and did her best to absorb what he taught her.

At nine-thirty that evening, she was allowed a cup of tea and an orange. He admonished her to hold her teacup just so, to sip without slurping—and never to chew with her mouth open.

Somehow, he inspired the brat in her. She longed to open her mouth good and wide and stick out her tongue at him *before* swallowing the section of orange she'd been so cautiously, *delicately* munching.

But she didn't. She kept her mouth shut and she swallowed the orange and she sipped without slurping at her unsweetened tea.

He gave her a book to read when he sent her to bed: *Miss Manners' Guide to the Turn-of-the-Millennium.* She turned the pages with white-gloved fingers because both of her hands were greased up and encased in the special gloves they'd given her at the spa.

She even laughed now and then. Miss Manners was funny. And most of her advice made sense really.

Once you got past the strange realization that the way Miss Manners used words was almost identical to the way Jonathan talked.

The next day was worse.

It was the shopping. She hated it.

She'd really thought she had a pretty good idea of the clothing rules Jonathan had drilled into her the evening before. But it wasn't the same, being out there in some fancy, expensive department store, trying to choose something vivid in color with nice, simple lines—in cotton, linen, silk or wool—when there were racks and racks packed with skirts and blouses and dresses and every other damn thing you ever might consider wanting to wear.

It made her feel sick to her stomach. Suddenly she was longing to be back on the rig, wearing her boots and coveralls, slathered in drilling mud, hitting the deck as Jimmy Betts swung a length of pipe in her direction.

Plus she was starving. *Frickin'* starving, as a matter of fact—and no, she didn't say the forbidden word out loud.

But boy, was she tempted to.

She needed a decent meal and she needed to *not* have to shop anymore.

But Jonathan was relentless. He wouldn't let her go back to the hotel.

At noon, he took her to some prissy, ferny downtown lunch place. And he ordered her a salad and an iced tea with lemon. She wanted to kill him. She truly did. Just snap his tiny twig of a neck between her two big hands.

But then she reminded herself that she was going to do this. She was sticking out this ridiculous crash course in being a suitable pretend fiancée for Aleta Bravo's precious prodigal son. She *needed* this, and she knew it. She wanted a chance at a new life.

And if being waxed and peeled and plucked and starved half to death, if having to shop all day and all night until she finally managed to find something simple and bright in a natural fabric—if getting *trained* in how to sip tea and sit down at a table with rich people...

If all that had to be done for her to get a fresh start, well, fine. She would do it. She would not give up.

She was made of tougher stuff than that.

So she ate her salad, slowly. Calmly. In small bites, chewing with her mouth shut. She sipped her iced tea.

And then they shopped some more.

It didn't get easier.

In the end, after hours and hours of lurking twenty feet away, watching her *subtly* out of the corner of his eye, Jonathan came to her rescue. He started choosing things for her to try on.

Loaded down with shopping bags, they got back to the hotel at six-thirty. Sam now had five new dresses, six pairs of incredibly expensive shoes, four sweaters, three shirts, two pairs of designer jeans…and more. Much more.

Jonathan had chosen everything. His taste was just disgustingly great. Even with her chopped-off hair and no makeup and her face still red from yesterday's peel— she wasn't getting the hair or the makeup until near the end of her training, he had told her—she could see the difference the right clothes made.

At the hotel, he ordered quail for dinner—two of them each. Two tiny plump birds with a side of slivered carrots, which were drizzled in some heavenly sauce. She wanted to fall on those dinky birds and shove them, whole, into her wide-open mouth. She wanted to devour them, itty-bitty bones and all.

But she waited, hands and napkin in her lap, for his instructions.

He surprised her. "One eats quail with one's hands," Jonathan said. "Some foods are simply too small, or too bony, to be eaten any other way. In fact, the bones themselves are quite delicate and flavorful. Eat them, too, if you wish. But please, crunch in a quiet manner. And eat slowly, as always, savoring the tastes and textures, avoiding any unfortunate displays of grease or bits of meat on the lips and chin."

Then, as she chewed the heavenly little things with her mouth closed and tried not to listen to her stomach rumbling, he told her that there would be more shopping. And she would get better at it.

She didn't tell him he was frickin' crazy, but she thought it.

After the meal, there were more lessons. In polite conversation. In how to sit in a chair properly, for cripes' sake.

By the time she finally had her bedtime snack—an

actual glass of milk and one slice of lightly buttered toast—she only longed to escape to her own room.

Alone, she took a shower and brushed her teeth, greased up her hands and feet and put on the booties and the gloves. She climbed into bed and started to reach for the Miss Manners book.

But then she just couldn't. It was bad enough listening to Jonathan all day. She didn't need more of the same in her nighttime reading.

She tossed the book to the nightstand.

It was a big book and it slid off and hit the plush bedroom carpet with a definite *smack*. She didn't even bother to get out of bed and pick it up. Instead she grabbed the TV remote and pointed it at the television—but no. Forget TV. Forget everything.

She threw the remote down to the carpet, too. And she gathered her knees up with her greased, white-gloved hands and she put her head down on them.

And for the first time in eleven years, since way back when that rotten jerk Zachary Gunn broke her heart and she swore off men forever, she burst into tears.

She was so miserable right then that she didn't even have enough pride left to stop being a baby and suck it up. Great, fat, sloppy tears poured down her face and she let them.

Her nose ran. She didn't care. She let it happen, only controlling the flood in the sense that she tried her damnedest not to make a single sound. She gulped back her sobs because apparently she did have some pride left after all.

And she didn't want Jonathan to know how frickin' stupid and awkward and foolish she felt. She could do a man's job in a man's world—and do it better than most guys. She'd reached the top of the food chain on an offshore rig at an age when most men would have been proud to simply be holding their own as roughnecks. But when it came to being a woman, well, that was turning out to be a whole lot harder than it looked.

She cried and cried, really letting go, feeling very, very sorry for herself, biting her lip to keep from snorting and sniffling.

And then her cell rang.

She decided not to answer it. She kept on crying. In three rings, the call went to voicemail and again she was alone with her tears and her misery.

Then the room phone rang. She tried to wait it out, but the minute it stopped ringing, it only started again.

And she knew that if she didn't pick it up, Jonathan would be tapping on her door, asking her what was the matter, hadn't she noticed her phone was ringing?

Oh, she could just hear him now. *When one's phone rings, Samantha, it is customary to answer it.*

If she let it get to that, she would have to reply and he would hear her clogged, teary voice and know that he had gotten to her, big-time.

No way was she letting him know that. She'd held her own against some burly, badass roughnecks in her time. How could she let bird-boned, big-haired Jonathan get the better of her?

She grabbed the phone. *"What?"* she demanded in a soggy, broken whisper.

"Sam?" It was Travis. "Sam, what's going on? You didn't answer your cell. And I called the room twice."

"Yeah, I noticed." A sob got away from her, followed by a watery hiccup.

"Sam, are you all right?"

She clutched the phone harder, feeling ridiculous and needy and weak and hopeless and sad. "I'm, uh…" She put her hand over the phone, swiped at her eyes and then groped for a tissue with her white-gloved hand.

"Sam, talk to me. Please. What's the matter with you?" He sounded so worried, so...scared even. For her.

He was worried for *her*.

That meant a lot.

And then he said, "Sam, I'm coming over there. I'm coming over there now."

"No!" The word escaped her trembling mouth on a sob. "You can't. Uh-uh." She ripped a tissue from the tasteful beige box on the nightstand. "You know you can't. You can't even see me. Not until my final test."

"Forget the test," he said and really seemed to mean it. "It doesn't matter. None of it matters if you've had enough. It's not a big deal. We can call the whole thing off right now."

Call the whole thing off. He wouldn't mind or be mad at her if they called the whole thing off.

She could, she realized. She could do that. Call an end to this torture, give it up. There was no law that said she had to stick it out.

She could give it up and head straight for her private hideaway in San Diego. Walk on the beach, soak up some rays.

And then sign up for a new job on a different rig, go back to the challenging and profitable life she had made for herself.

"What about—" another sob escaped her "—your mother?"

"I'll find some other way to get her off my back. Don't worry about that. Just say the word, Sam. And you're off the hook. I mean that. Sam? Did you hear me? Sam? Are you there?" Travis seemed really worried that she might have hung up on him.

But she hadn't. She was sniffling. And thinking…

And coming to realize how very much she wanted this, how seriously invested she was in seeing the whole thing through.

"Damn it, Sam. Say something."

And she did. "No, I don't want that. I don't want to give it up. I want to…get through this. I want to make good at it because it does matter. It matters a lot. And that's why you can't come over here. Because Jonathan wants it that way. And that's fine with me. I am doing exactly what Just frickin' Jonathan tells me to do."

"Uh. You are?"

"Yeah. I am—and don't you dare tell him I said the word *frickin'*. Got that?"

"Absolutely. I won't. Whatever you say. But—"

"I *can* do this. I *will* do this. I am sticking with this program and I am going to get some serious girly going or I will die trying." She blew her nose, good and hard. By then, well, it didn't seem to matter all that much that Travis would figure out she'd been crying.

"Sam."

She sniffed, shamelessly that time. And it felt kind of good, really. It was kind of a relief. To let go. To cry and not care that someone might know it. "What?"

"Are you…crying?" He asked the question in a kind of awed disbelief.

"So what if I am, huh?" She grabbed another tissue and scrubbed her soggy cheeks. "So what if I am?"

"But you *never* cry."

"Well, I'm crying now. Or I was." She ripped out yet more tissue. "But at this point, I've moved on to mopping up the mess."

"So, uh, what's happened?" He sounded totally flummoxed.

She tried to explain. "Nothing. Everything. This is even harder than I thought it would be."

"It is, huh?" His voice was gentle. Understanding. "Listen. I meant what I said. If you want to back out—"

"Uh-uh. No way. I'm not giving up. I'm going through with it, no matter what."

"If you're sure that's what you want…"

"I am sure, yes. So stop asking me." She settled back against the pillows, gave one last sniffle. "I guess I kind of expected to be bad at this. I just didn't expect to care so much."

"Who says you're bad at it?" He seemed honestly puzzled.

"*I* say. And I ought to know—oh, and Jonathan, too. He thinks I suck the big one. He looks at me in that pained, superior way of his…."

"Wait. Jonathan told you that you suck?"

"He didn't have to tell me. It's written all over his snooty, pointy little face. As far as he's concerned, I can't do anything right."

"But that's not what he said to me."

She snuggled back into the pillows. "Huh? Said to you when?"

"When he called me a few minutes ago to let me know how you were getting along. He said you were making great progress and he was really impressed with you, that he hadn't realized at the beginning how much potential you actually had."

Now she sat up straighter. "He didn't. You're lyin', trying to make me feel better."

"God's truth, Sam."

She gave a very unladylike snort—the kind of snort she wouldn't have thought twice about making just a few days before. "And you think it would kill him to say that to *me?*"

Travis snorted right back. "Come on, you know how you are. The madder you get, the harder you work. Maybe he's figured that out about you."

She fiddled with the phone cord, twisting it around her gloved index finger. "Well, then why are you telling me he said nice things about me? Maybe I'll get lazy now I know he's only pretending to look down on me."

"Not a chance. You haven't got a lazy bone in your body—and it was pretty clear to me you needed encouragement."

She pulled her finger free of the coil of cord, feeling better about everything, feeling ready to face tomorrow. Feeling she could even handle the awful, disgusting shopping that would happen the day after that. "You're a good man, Travis Bravo. Thanks."

"You need me, you call me."

She made a soft sound low in her throat. "I think I can make it now."

"I'm here. Just remember."

He said goodbye a few minutes later. She hung up the phone thinking that she was a lucky person to have a friend like Travis.

Turning off the light and pulling up the covers, she lay on her back in the dark with a smile on her face. Jonathan had said he was impressed with her. Travis had been there to talk her down when she needed it.

She knew now she could make it. In only a few days, she *would* be ready.

She would go with Travis to San Antonio and play his bride-to-be for his family. Yes, it was a big lie and she didn't believe in lies.

But no one was going to be hurt by the deception.

She was just giving Travis's mom an excuse to take a break from her never-ending matchmaking, giving Travis a break, too. For a while, anyway, he wouldn't have women thrown at him constantly when he wasn't interested in anything like that.

He'd loved Rachel Selkirk, loved her deeply and completely, the way only a good, true-hearted man can love his woman. And he didn't want to go there again, didn't want to take the chance of being hurt like that again. Just like Sam didn't want to be hurt.

Sam folded her hands on top of the covers and stared up at the dark ceiling above and thought about how, maybe, after she got through the week with the Bravos, after she found her new job, she just might consider maybe going on a date again. She might consider giving love and romance and all that stuff another chance.

The thing with Zach had been so long ago. Maybe it was time she let it go, got her girly on in more ways than just her clothes and learning to sip tea without slurping.

Hey, a woman needed love in her life.

And Sam Jaworski knew now that she was just like most other women. A little taller and a lot stronger maybe. With a different kind of job history than most women had.

But with the same hungers in her lonely heart.

She closed her eyes and drifted off to sleep.

And dreamed of Travis.

It was a hazy, indistinct sort of dream. When she woke up the next morning, she didn't remember much about it. Except that she and Travis were together.

And in the dream, she'd started to feel sad because she knew it was all a lie and it wasn't going to last.

Because the honest truth was, she never wanted it to end.

Chapter Four

She got through the next day without once wishing she could wring Jonathan's neck.

Even though he pushed her constantly to do better, to try harder, even though he remained as snooty and superior as ever, well, she was okay with that. If Travis hadn't told her what her coach really thought about her, she never would have guessed that Jonathan believed she was doing well.

But Travis *had* told her, and his telling her had boosted her confidence enough that she threw herself into her training with new enthusiasm. She worked even harder than before.

And that second shopping trip on Thursday?

It wasn't easy, but it was better. She discovered she was getting the hang of what to look for, getting an eye for spotting the finds in an endless sea of different fabrics, colors and styles.

They went back to the hotel that day with more shopping bags than the time before. Jonathan couldn't help smiling at how well she'd done.

And she laughed. "I know you're proud of me, Jonathan. I can see it on your face."

"Ahem. Well. Don't get too confident. We have a lot more to do."

She nodded. "I know. And I'm ready for whatever you can throw at me."

His eyelids drooped lazily over those sharp dark eyes, a look of pure satisfaction. "Perhaps you would enjoy a T-bone steak, rare, and a large baked potato this evening as a reward for work well done?"

She clapped her de-callused hands. "Oh, Jonathan. You have no idea."

"An hour in the gym first," he ordered gruffly.

She was only too pleased to pull on the clingy, sexy workout clothes they'd bought that day and head down to the hotel gym. She kicked butt on the treadmill and then pumped iron for all she was worth.

And at six-thirty that evening, she was treated to the most beautiful slab of beef she'd ever seen. She wanted to saw off a huge, juicy hunk and shove it in her mouth, to chew without worrying about keeping her lips together, to let the juice run down her chin.

But she didn't. She put her napkin in her lap and she picked up her fork and knife and took her time about it. She cut each small bite smoothly and neatly—no sawing. She chewed slowly and thoroughly. She even managed to make polite conversation while she ate.

Jonathan didn't once have to reprimand her.

And it was….kind of fun really. Kind of graceful and satisfying. Eating slowly with care wasn't half-bad after all.

The next day, Friday, they "worked" her wardrobe. Jonathan showed her how to mix and match the various pieces, to make several outfits out of a skirt, skinny pants, a sweater and various accessories.

They also "did" packing. He produced a gorgeous set of designer luggage and showed her how to pack for various types of excursions—from a weekend in the country to five days in Manhattan to a tropical getaway and an Alaskan cruise. She laughed at that. At the idea of Sam Jaworski packing up her designer duds and heading for the Big Apple or Jamaica or the land of the midnight sun. She also practiced packing for the week with the Bravo family.

That day, they went out for lunch and for dinner. It was important to use her new skills in the real world, Jonathan said.

And the next day, all of a sudden, it was Saturday. The last day of her training, the day of her final test.

Jonathan told her what the test would be: That night at seven, Travis would arrive to take her out for the evening.

She worked her butt off in the morning, reviewing with Jonathan. It was something of a test in itself, to prove how much she remembered of all that he'd taught her, how much she could apply with seeming effortlessness.

Over lunch at Quattro, the gorgeous Italian place in the hotel, Jonathan actually praised her outright. He said she was amazing him. He said that he was proud of her.

She went back upstairs floating on a cloud of success and good feelings.

Then came the afternoon in the spa.

It wasn't as bad as the first time. She didn't have to get another peel and she didn't need waxing.

Still, there was the endless sitting as she had the manicure and the pedicure, the hair color and cut. She worked with the makeup consultant for a couple of hours, learning what products she needed, learning how to apply them.

It all took too long and she would just as soon have been down in the gym bench-pressing triple her weight, working up a good, healthy sweat.

But when it was done, well, she looked in the mirror and saw her dream self staring back at her, as tall and strong as she'd ever been—and yet, so much more. Even her too-short hair looked terrific, with highlights and lowlights, the gamine-style cut bringing out her cheekbones, kind of showing off the nice oval shape of her face. And the makeup was perfect. It enhanced her best features and minimized her flaws.

She returned to the suite, where Jonathan called her amazing for the second time that day.

By then it was almost six. Time to put on the beautifully fitted knee-length stretch satin dress with its skinny straps and built-in bra. A big rhinestone cuff and four-inch Dolce & Gabbana black lace pumps completed the outfit. She grabbed her small satin bag and the cute velvet shrug to keep her shoulders warm outside in the cool November darkness.

And she was ready.

When she came out of her room, Jonathan actually applauded.

She laughed and spun in a circle. "Pretty good, huh?"

He got out his camera and took a whole bunch of pictures. Sam almost felt nostalgic. Was it only Monday that they'd started together? Had she come so far in such a very short time?

It appeared that she had.

The firm tap on the suite's door came at seven on the dot.

She went to answer.

The look on Travis's face when she opened the door…oh, it was priceless. He actually gaped.

And then he said, his voice barely a croak, "Sam? My God. Sam."

She laughed in delight. "Oh, Travis…" And she threw her arms around him. He stiffened at first—because she seemed so different, like a stranger?

She wasn't sure. She started to feel kind of awkward, that she had maybe scared him by jumping all over him.

But then he relaxed. His arms came around her. He hugged her good and tight and he whispered, "You are drop-dead gorgeous, you know that?" He pressed his cheek to hers. "And you smell so good…."

She could have stood there, holding him tight like that forever. She liked it, so much, the glorious feel of his big, hard body pressed against hers. In his arms right then she felt so…feminine. Not soft, exactly. She was too buff for that.

But smooth. Definitely. And curvy. And very much a woman in every single way.

Reluctantly, she stepped back from him. They stared at each other, both of them grinning.

And Jonathan said, "Come along, you two. We'll have a toast." He'd ordered champagne. It was waiting, on ice, in a silver bucket. The bellman had already popped the cork.

Travis filled a crystal flute for each of them and then offered the first toast. "To you, Sam. I knew you could do it. And you have. You're incredible. I always knew you were good-looking. I just didn't realize how beautiful you really are."

She basked in his admiration and approval, thinking that the week of torture and starvation and grueling hard work had been worth it.

And then Jonathan said, "Sam, I wish you all the success and continued admiration you so richly deserve. When you get back here to the suite from your night out with Travis, I will be gone."

She felt teary-eyed suddenly. "Oh, no. So soon?"

He nodded his big head of beautifully highlighted hair. "Because, darling, my work here is done. I hardly expected what a triumph you would make of our time together. But you, my love, have come so far, so fast. I swear to you, my head is spinning. I will leave you my numbers. Do call now and then and tell me how you're doing."

"Oh, Jonathan. Yes, I will. And thank you. Thank you so much."

He waved a hand. "The pleasure was all mine. Check my website in a few days."

She groaned. "That's right. The awful 'before' pictures."

"Ah, yes. But also the ones I took this evening. I think any woman would be proud to look as you do right now."

She hugged Jonathan before she and Travis left him. He seemed so tiny and fragile in her arms. She whispered more thank-yous. And she promised to call.

They had dinner at Restaurant Cinq in a gorgeous hotel and art gallery called La Colombe d'Or. The building itself had once been the mansion of an oil baron.

To start, there was Petrossian caviar with homemade blinis. Sam had never in her life had caviar before. She found she liked the salty, rich taste.

Then came the toasted goat cheese, roasted beet and mixed greens salad, the three-chili rubbed pork tenderloin with Granny Smith applesauce and roasted corn relish.

Sam remembered to eat slowly, to enjoy every bite.

And even better than the wonderful food and great service was the handsome, dark-haired guy in the beautiful charcoal wool jacket and checked silk shirt across the snowy white tablecloth from her.

He looked at her so…appreciatively. As though he couldn't get enough of the very sight of her.

Okay, yeah. She knew this thing between them was just for now, just for tonight and the next week with his family. She knew they were only pretending, that it wasn't, in the strictest sense, real.

But so what? She didn't care. She was set on loving every minute of it. It was a new beginning for her. The start of a different kind of life.

Which, come to think of it, made it mostly real, after all. Yes, she was only going to be his fiancée for a week. But the woman she was tonight, in the black camisole dress with the lacy high heels and the sparkly rhinestone cuff—she actually *was* that woman now. She had re-created herself in the past week, with Jonathan's help.

Her new self was no lie.

They talked easily, comfortably together, as always. As comfortably as they did when they'd meet for beers at some wood-paneled neighborhood sports bar right there in Houston.

But Restaurant Cinq was hardly a neighborhood bar.

And the way she felt right now, looking at him across the table, the glow of candlelight shining in his eyes?

Well, it wasn't the same as when they went out for a beer. Not the same at all.

They spoke of his family. Of his brothers and sisters, their wives and husbands and also their kids. About how much his dad had changed in the past couple of years.

"He used to be a real hardass, my father," Travis said.

She took a slow, thoughtful sip of her wine. "I remember. You always used to roll your eyes a lot when you talked about him. You said your grandfather, James, was a tough guy, real mean. That he drove all his other sons away. Only your dad refused to go. He stuck it out."

Travis nodded. "And inherited everything when Grandpa died. Because no one chases Davis Bravo away or denies him what's his by birthright." He leaned closer. "Your eyes…"

She blinked and then gave a nervous chuckle. "Uh, yeah. I have two."

"No, I'm serious, Sam. Your eyes are amazing." At his praise, she felt a warm glow all through her. And he wasn't finished. "The way they tip up at the corners— and the color. Just a gorgeous blue. So bright. Are you wearing contacts, is that it?"

"Nope. But I did get some help from the excellent cosmetician at the hotel." She sat back in her chair. "You know, I could really get used to all this flattery."

"Uh-uh." He frowned. "It's not flattery, it's…" He glanced away. He seemed almost embarrassed. "I'm having a little trouble getting used to the new you." And then he looked at her again and grinned. "But I'm dealing. I'm working with it. And the view from my side of the table is spectacular."

She sat forward, too. "Thank you. I mean that—and now back to your dad. You were saying he's changed...."

"Yeah. He's...more patient than he used to be. Not so overbearing. Not so sure he's got all the answers before anyone even asks the question. More willing to admit that he's not always right. He's mellowed, I guess you could say. And that makes him a lot easier to get along with."

"I think I'm going to like him."

"I think you will, too."

"And your mother?"

He shrugged. "Other than the relentless matchmaking, she's a great person. Always there for her kids. All nine of us. She was born a Randall, which is a big name in San Antonio, and she's involved in all the upscale social stuff. Charity work, the country club. But even with all that, she's pretty down-to-earth. Not a snob, not in any way."

"Good. Because I *have* been thinking, Travis."

Twin lines formed between his dark brows. "You sound way too serious." His fine mouth flattened out. "You're backing out of the whole thing, right?"

"No."

His expression relaxed. "Whew."

She set down her fork. "But I don't want to pretend I'm someone I'm not."

His dark eyes grew darker. "Did I ask you to be someone else?"

"No. No, you didn't. But I..." She put her hands to her cheeks—and was surprised all over again at how soft and smooth her skin felt. Not really like her cheeks and hands at all. "I just mean that beyond the basic lie we agreed on, beyond my pretending to be your fiancée, and also beyond the new clothes and the new look and everything Jonathan taught me about how to…behave in social situations—beyond all that, I still want to be the same Sam Jaworski I was before I walked into the Four Seasons Hotel last Monday morning."

"That works for me. It's not a problem."

"Let me finish." She put her hands in her lap, laced her fingers together. Because Jonathan had taught her not to rest her elbows on the table until she was done with the meal. "I want my own history," she said. "I want my crazy dad who loves me and raised me after my mom left us, my dad who's retired now, riding around the USA in his Winnebago Adventurer with his new girlfriend, Keisha, who just happens to be four years younger than I am. I want to be the girl who came from a run-down ranch in South Dakota, the one who's just spent five weeks straight on the *Deepwater Venture* and is planning to look for a new job on land now. I want to be the girl who's had you for a friend ever since she was a lonely, oversize eighteen-year-old hayseed."

"Sam." He reached across the table. And when Travis reached out, she couldn't help but respond. She gave him her hand.

Instantly, something deep inside her went all soft and mushy. He wrapped his fingers around hers and the feel of his skin touching hers was so perfect, so comfortable and yet thrilling at the same time, so absolutely right.

He said, "You were no hayseed."

She allowed herself a hint of a smile. "Oh, yeah, I was. And I'm proud of who I was—of who I really am. We don't need to go into all that's happened in the past week, into my big makeover. We can just tell them we've known each other for years and suddenly, since we've been working on the *Deepwater Venture* together, we realized that it had been…" She hesitated over the scary word. And then made herself say it. "...love all along."

"That sounds good to me."

"You proposed a couple of weeks ago, the day before you talked to your mom and agreed that you'd ask me to the ranch for Thanksgiving."

"Okay, that'll work." He rubbed his thumb across the back of her hand. Her skin seemed to heat beneath that simple brush of a touch. "Did I say something to make you think I wanted you to pretend to be someone else?"

"No, you didn't." It seemed dangerous, somehow, to sit here with him like this, their gazes locked together, holding hands across the table. Gently, she eased her fingers free of his. She picked up her wine again, sipped, set the glass down, each movement smooth and deliberate. Jonathan had said that a fine meal in good company should never be rushed. "I just wanted to be sure we understood each other, that we're on the same page about how it's going to be."

He hadn't moved since she pulled her hand from his. He was watching her, his gaze shadowed and yet so intent. "We're in agreement, Sam," he said at last. "You can stop worrying."

After dinner, they went upstairs to visit the Colombe d'Or art gallery. Sam knew zip about art and recognized none of the artists' names or the paintings on display. Still, it was fun to walk around the beautifully decorated rooms and admire the bright pictures, her hand tucked companionably in the crook of Travis's arm.

Outside, the parking attendant had Travis's Cadillac waiting. He held her door open for her, and she slipped into the plush embrace of the soft leather seat without a stumble in her four-inch heels, without letting her tight skirt ride higher than mid-thigh.

"Thank you," she said as the attendant closed the door. Travis pulled away from curb. She turned to him. "What next?"

He sent her a quick glance, and then turned his gaze to the street ahead. "Depends on what you're up for. We can go to a party. Or walk around downtown. Or go see a movie..."

"Whose party?"

"Oh, just the CFO of STOI." South Texas Oil Industries. It was the company Travis worked for. She knew he got invited to a lot of fancy parties, partly because he was well-liked by the people he worked for. And partly because he was one of the San Antonio Bravos. She was quiet, considering. After a moment or two, he sent her another glance. "Sam?" He said her name softly.

A shiver went through her, to hear him say her name so low and intimately—and also because she was actually considering choosing the party over the safer activities of a movie or a walk downtown. To hold her own among the management people, the white-collar types. That would be something. As a rule, oil workers and upper management lived in separate worlds. If they went to the party, it would be a true test of all that Jonathan had taught her.

"No pressure," Travis reminded her. "Wherever you want to go..." He eased the car to the curb again and parked, but left the engine running.

She frowned at him. "Why are we stopping?"

He reached across and captured her left hand. "Whatever you decide, I think you need to start getting used to this." And before she could ask him what he was talking about, he slid a gorgeous square diamond onto her ring finger. She blinked down at it, all bright and sparkly in the lights from the dashboard. "A perfect fit," he said, and his white teeth flashed with his smile.

The party was in River Oaks, one of Houston's most exclusive neighborhoods. And the CFO's house was like some English castle, all of stone, with tall, many-paned, brightly lit windows. A wide, curving drive led up to the entrance and every light and chandelier in the place was ablaze in the darkness.

An attendant opened her door for her. And Travis came around and took her hand, tucking it comfortably into the crook of his arm, just like in the art gallery at Colombe d'Or. She looked down at her smooth, beautifully manicured fingers wrapped around his strong forearm, resting on the fine wool of his jacket. The big square diamond twinkled at her and she had a sense of such complete unreality.

Like Cinderella in the fairy tale, entering the ballroom already on the arm of her prince, wearing the magic dress created with a wave of her fairy godmother's wand and a healthy dose of bibbity-bobbity-boo. A modern Cinderella, though, one whose fairy godmother wasn't a plump, sweet gray-haired lady, but a skinny guy with big hair and a whole bunch of attitude.

It was a beautiful evening. She met the CFO and his wife and a lot of other people who worked for Travis's company. A few of them even knew who she was, being something of a legend, a tool pusher who was not only young for the job, but a woman, as well.

They all accepted her, treated her as one of them. Evidently, if you knew how to handle yourself and could carry on a decent casual conversation—if you looked the part of a woman that Travis Bravo might marry—

well, no one asked questions. Why should they? Appearances, in the end, counted for a whole frickin' lot.

She smiled to herself as she thought the forbidden word.

Travis leaned close to her. "What are you smiling about?"

She turned and looked right at him. "I was just thinking that I'm having a terrific time."

Midnight came. She and Travis were in the walnut-paneled library, sipping champagne. The ornate clock on the mantel chimed the hour. Sam smiled again as the chimes rang out. Nothing happened. She didn't look down to see her little black dress turning into a pair of greasy coveralls. Her black lace shoes did not suddenly become muddy steel-toed boots. She wasn't Cinderella after all.

Uh-uh. Her transformation was going to be a permanent one.

It was two-thirty a.m. when they got back to the Four Seasons. Travis had his suitcases already packed and in the Cadillac. In the morning, they would be driving up to San Antonio straight from the hotel.

He grabbed his overnight bag from the trunk and passed the keys to the valet. They went up to the suite.

Travis had his card key out when they got to the door. He stuck it in the slot and pushed the door open.

Sam went in ahead of him. She eased the shrug from her shoulders, dropping it and her bag to a chair.

With Jonathan gone, the suite seemed strangely empty. She wandered through the sitting room and into the bedroom where he had stayed.

Travis followed her. He tossed his bag onto a chair. "Strange, huh? The covers on the bed turned back, chocolates on the pillow and not a sign that Jonathan was ever here."

She sat on the edge of the bed and braced her hands on the bedspread to either side of her. "I was just thinking the same thing." But then, wasn't that how it went with a fairy godmother? They were gone in a sparkle of fairy dust as soon as their work was done.

And speaking of sparkles...

She glanced down at her left hand. The engagement diamond glittered in the light from the bedside lamp.

Travis said, "You were incredible tonight."

She felt suddenly shy and couldn't quite bring herself to lift her head and meet his eyes. "You think I passed my test?"

"With flying colors—and remember when Steve took me aside, just before we left?"

"I remember." Steve Daily was the CFO of STOI and their host at the party.

"He asked me where I'd been hiding you."

"In plain sight." She looked up then and laughed. "Wearing coveralls, safety glasses and a hard hat, on the *Deepwater Venture*."

He held her gaze. All night, he'd been doing that. He would look at her and she would stare back at him and somehow, neither of them seemed to want to look away. "I think it's going to be a piece of cake, getting you that job you're hoping for."

"Oh, I hope so."

"As soon as the week in San Antonio is over, you'll need to polish up your résumé."

As soon as the week's over...

She didn't want to think about it being over. Why should she? It hadn't even started yet.

But then she reminded herself not to get carried away

with this fantasy of being Travis's true love. The love part wasn't real.

She had to remember that.

The possibility of a new life in a new job...that was the goal here.

"I'm flying to my place in San Diego afterward," she said. "I'll get to work the minute I get there, get that résumé all ready."

He kept on staring at her, his eyes so dark and soft. "Good. I'll be putting out the feelers. You might have to take a serious pay cut to start, maybe pick up a few online classes to get up to speed...."

Actually, she'd been thinking of going back to school. Maybe full-time, to get a degree. But a starter position and some online classes were an option, too. "You know I can do it. Whatever I need to do." She reached down, slid off one lace shoe and then the other. It felt good to be out of them. She wiggled her toes in the thick bedroom carpet.

He said, "Oh, yeah. I know you can."

"And I have a good chunk of money saved, plus what my dad put aside for me when he sold the ranch, so I'll be fine."

"I know you will." He held down his hand to her.

She took it without really stopping to think that touching him, right now, when it was just the two of them alone in the room where he would spend the night, well, maybe that wasn't such a smart idea. She'd been getting lost in way too many fantasies about him lately, getting so she thought of him as much more than her good old buddy Travis.

Much, much more.

His fingers touched hers.

Warmth spread through her from the point of contact.

He gave a gentle tug.

She rose and he reached out and wrapped his free arm around her.

It was like a dream, a magical dream that she wished she wouldn't have to wake up from. He held her gaze, his eyes so soft, full of admiration. And maybe something more, something hot and hopeful and deliciously dangerous.

And then he moved in that crucial fraction closer.

Excitement crackled through her as understanding dawned.

Travis was going to kiss her—and not just on the cheek or the forehead, the way he did now and then. Not some brotherly little peck, the usual friends-only kiss.

Uh-uh. She could see it in his eyes.

For the very first time, he was going to kiss her the way a man kisses a woman he desires.

Chapter Five

Travis knew he shouldn't kiss her. There was no reason to kiss her right now, no one to put on a show for. There was only the two of them.

Alone in his room.

It was a really bad idea to kiss her right now.

But he didn't give a damn if it was a bad idea. He *wanted* to kiss her. He burned for it.

The whole evening had been the strangest thing. An exercise in shifting realities.

Being out with Sam, who was like family to him. Sam, for whom he felt frank affection and definite protectiveness.

Sam, who was the same Sam he'd always known. And yet…not the same at all.

Suddenly she was not only big and strong and smart and capable, a loyal friend with a hell of a mouth on her.

Now she was…very much a woman. All woman. In-your-face, sexy-as-all-get-out woman. Six feet of knock-your-socks-off gorgeous. With those iridescent blue eyes of hers that tilted so temptingly at the corners, that body that was strong and broad-shouldered and muscular as ever, but sleek and smooth and dangerously exciting, too.

And the scent of her...

He nuzzled her velvety cheek, breathed her in. She didn't smell like a tool pusher anymore.

She smelled of exotic flowers, of a tropical night, of spice and sweetness.

He couldn't stop himself. He didn't want to stop himself.

He touched his lips to hers.

Her mouth trembled slightly, and then went so soft and willing. Instantly, he was aching to go further, to guide her down to the bed, to lower those skinny black straps on that curve-hugging, eye-popping little black dress. He wanted to kiss her all over. And then, after that, to roll her under him and bury himself in her hot, strong sweetness, until she wrapped those long, hard, smooth legs around him and cried out his name as she came.

No.

He wasn't going to do any such thing.

He'd already taken serious advantage of her when he talked her into posing as his bride-to-be. It was enough—too much. He had no right to try to get her in bed. That would be flat-out wrong. She deserved better than that.

He gently clasped her silky shoulders. She made a small, way-too-feminine sound of regret as he put her away from him.

Her eyes were full of light—and questions. She lifted

a smooth hand, touched her lips where he had kissed her and she whispered his name on a sigh. "Travis…"

He caressed her short, silky hair, brushed it fondly with the backs of his fingers, thinking how he wanted to take her mouth again.

Promising himself he would do no such thing.

He said, "It's late. We should get an early start tomorrow."

She lowered her fingers from her lips. "You're right." And then she bent and scooped up those lacy black shoes. "Good night."

He just stood there, staring, trying to deny how much he wanted to pull her close to him again.

A smile tugged at one corner of that beautiful mouth of hers and she whispered, "If you want me to go, you'll have to move out of the way."

He blinked as he realized he was blocking her path to the door. "Uh. Yeah. Right. Sorry." He stepped aside.

And then he couldn't resist turning to watch her leave. The black dress clung to every tight, perfect curve as she walked away from him, her hips swaying just enough to make him ache for what he was missing, those sexy black shoes of hers dangling from the fingers of her long, strong right hand.

How easy it would be to go after her, to grab her free hand, to haul her back to him, wrap his arms around her, kiss her again and again and again.

But he didn't.

Somehow, he kept his head.

She turned when she reached the doorway to the sitting room. "See you tomorrow." She quietly shut the door behind her.

He sank to the edge of the bed, wondering what he had gotten himself into.

Thinking he should call the whole thing off.

And knowing he would do no such thing.

In the morning, he was up at seven. He showered, dressed, packed up his overnight bag and was ready to go at seven-thirty. The drive to Bravo Ridge, outside San Antonio, would take more than three hours. He wanted to be on the way.

But he hesitated at the door to the sitting room, his hand on the doorknob, feeling edgy and way too aware of that brief, amazing kiss the night before. It annoyed the hell out of him, to be all nervous and unsure—about Sam, of all people.

Would she be up yet? Would he have to knock on the door to her room and tell her to get moving, they needed to head out?

And then how long would he have to wait for her to be dressed and ready? The Sam he'd always known could be ready for anything in five minutes flat. She didn't need all that time for deciding what to wear and fiddling with her hair and putting on makeup, the way most women did.

But because she wasn't exactly the Sam he'd always known anymore, he had no way to gauge how long it would take her to pull herself together so they could get on the road.

He pulled open the door.

And there she was, sitting on the sofa by the picture window, downtown Houston spread out behind her, all dressed and ready to go. And she looked terrific, in sexy skinny jeans and a soft, clingy blue-green sweater that showed off all those dangerous curves he'd somehow never realized she had until last night.

Her suitcases were waiting by the door.

She rose to her feet. "Morning." And there were two places set at the table in the corner. He could smell bacon. "I ordered breakfast. Hope that's okay."

"Uh. Great." He felt guilty, for doubting her, for assuming that because she was gorgeous now, she'd be lazing in bed. She might look so good she messed with his head, but inside, she was still Sam. He needed to remember that.

They sat down to eat. He looked at her across the table from him, so fresh and pretty in the morning light, and he thought about Rachel, for some unknown reason. Rachel, with her long black hair and deep brown eyes, sitting across from him in another hotel room, years and years ago. Rachel, drinking coffee, nibbling toast, the future—*their* future—bright and full of promise, spread out ahead of them.

They'd been so happy, he and Rachel. They'd had no clue that death was going to snatch her away from him. That she would be gone from him forever within a few short weeks of that beautiful getaway engagement trip to Mexico.

He couldn't take that kind of loss again. He needed to remember that.

Sam was looking at him sideways. "Something wrong?"

He shook his head. "Not a thing." He polished off his scrambled eggs.

A bellman appeared with a cart as they finished the meal. Sam had called for him to carry her bags down.

The car was waiting, out at the front entrance. Sam had asked for it, too. The bellman loaded their bags in. Travis tipped him and the valet.

They got in, buckled up and were on their way.

* * *

Travis didn't say much during the ride to San Antonio.

Sam took her cue from him. She stared out the window at the highway ahead of them and she thought about last night, about the magic of the evening they'd spent together.

About that one sweet, too-short kiss they had shared.

She'd gone back to her room and gone right to sleep. And in the morning, when she woke up, she'd lain there for a minute or two, wondering if that kiss had been a dream after all.

But she knew that it wasn't. Travis really had kissed her. And she truly believed he'd wanted to kiss her some more.

She wished that he had.

They stopped for a soda and a restroom break midway. She offered to drive.

He said no, he was doing fine.

They set off again. Once or twice, she tried to get some conversation going. She remarked on the weather. She asked him a couple of questions about his brothers.

Each time, he replied by using as few words as possible. Clearly, he didn't want to talk.

So, fine. She had an iPod and her trusty Miss Manners book, which reminded her of Jonathan and made her smile. She read and she listened to music.

When at last they neared San Antonio, Travis turned the Cadillac north toward the Hill Country on a road called Farm to Market. Sam started to feel a certain restlessness about then.

They couldn't be far from the family ranch now. Soon she would meet his mother and his father, his brother Luke, who ran the ranch. And Luke's wife, Mercy, and their two children. And any other of his sisters and brothers who had shown up for Sunday dinner.

It was a thing with the Bravos, Travis had told her: Sunday-afternoon dinner at the ranch. They didn't all show up every time, but they all had an open invitation. And because it was the Sunday before a very special Thanksgiving when Davis and Aleta would renew their vows, Sam had a feeling there might be a lot of Bravos there that day.

She put the book down, put her iPod away.

"How you holding up?" he asked.

When she turned to meet his eyes he was smiling. "A little nervous, I guess," she admitted.

"You look terrific and my family will love you."

It was exactly the right thing for him to say. She forgave him for being Mr. Strong and Surly through most of the ride. "Thanks. I needed that."

"There might be a lot of them," he warned.

"I was thinking that there probably would be."

"But the good news is they're great people. I think you'll enjoy yourself."

She nodded and turned her gaze back to the road.

But now, all of a sudden, he wanted to talk. "Sam."

She kept her eyes focused front. "Yeah?"

"About last night…"

Her throat felt tight. "Yeah?"

"I think it was a good thing that I kissed you." What was he getting at? She wasn't sure she wanted to know. He added, "I mean, we're supposed to be engaged, right?"

"Right." Out the windshield, the land was gently rolling now, dotted with limestone outcroppings. There were oak trees and cattle grazing in the dry winter grass of wide pastures. Cottony clouds dotted the sky.

He said, "It would be odd, to pretend to be engaged without even having kissed, don't you think?"

She did glance at him then. He was staring straight ahead. A muscle twitched in his jaw. And she almost smiled, feeling a certain fondness for him, and sympathy, too, as he tried to get her talking on a not-so-easy subject. At the same time, she felt a prickle of annoyance. He'd shut her out for most of the ride—and now, when they were almost there, he suddenly decided they just *had* to rehash last night.

"Odd?" She frowned and turned to watch the rolling land go by out her side window. "Yeah, I guess it would be, to be engaged without ever sharing a kiss. But we're not really engaged, so what does it matter?"

"Sam…" He waited until she met his eyes before he looked at the road ahead again. "My mom has got to believe we're for real, you know?"

She stared at his profile, at his nicely chiseled jaw and manly blade of a nose. "How could I forget? Didn't I just spend a week and a big ol' pile of your money whipping myself into shape so I can pull the wool over your poor, trusting mama's loving eyes?"

He gave her another quick glance—one that almost made her laugh. He kind of reminded her of Jimmy Betts after she reamed him a new one for almost knocking one of the rock docs off the rig with a length of pipe.

"You're pissed at me." His voice was flat.

She almost denied it, but come on. They might be about to tell a whopping lie to his mom and the rest of his family, but right now it was just the two of them. The least she could do was keep it honest between them. "Duh. Yeah. I'm a little ticked off at you. You've hardly said a word to me all morning. And now, all of a sudden, you want to go into detail about how great it is that you kissed me. Not because you *wanted* to kiss me, but because we're about to fake being engaged and we need all the practice we can get to make it look real."

Without warning, he swung the Caddy to the shoulder and braked to a squealing stop. The guy in the pickup behind them leaned on the horn as he swung past them and went on by.

Sam pressed her lips together and stared out the windshield as the pickup vanished around the next turn.

"Sam. Damn it, Sam." He said a few more choice words. And then he was quiet. And then finally, "Come on. I'm sorry, okay?" He did sound like he meant it.

And she felt sorry, too, but she still couldn't make herself look at him.

He turned off the engine, undid his seat belt and shifted in the seat, leaning across the leather console. She was way too aware of him, especially now that he'd moved closer. He rested his elbow on the back of her seat, his forearm against her headrest. And then she felt his touch at her temple, so lightly. And then gone. "What *is* this?" he asked, his voice low and teasing—and puzzled, too. "You and me fighting? We never fight."

She undid her own seat belt. He backed off an inch or two so she could slide the shoulder harness out of the way. And then she turned to him. He leaned close again. His handsome face was only inches from hers. She could smell his aftershave. She'd always liked his aftershave. It had a clean, fresh scent.

"We never kissed, either." She glanced down at those tempting lips of his—and then back up into his eyes. "Until last night. First time for everything, I guess."

He touched her hair, the same way he had done the night before, brushing the backs of his fingers against the short strands. And he spoke so softly, "I liked kissing you. I liked it a lot."

She held his eyes. "Don't say it."

He frowned. "What?"

"That you liked it *too much*."

He chuckled then. "You know me way too well."

"Yeah, I do. So from now on, don't feed me any bull. I can see it coming a mile away."

"You *sure* you're still up for this?"

She gave him a patient look. "What did I tell you the other night when you called me at the Four Seasons and caught me bawling my eyes out?"

He grunted. "That you *were* sure and I should stop asking you if you wanted to back out."

She leaned into him sideways and nudged him with her shoulder. "So what about you? Is it possible that *you're* the one who wants to back out?"

"Hell, no."

"You're not feeling guilty for trying to pull a number on your mom?"

"Sure, I feel guilty, but I want her off my case for a while. If you're still on, we're going for it." He started to retreat back behind the wheel.

She just couldn't leave it at that. She caught his arm. "Maybe you should kiss me again, before we go. I mean, how many engaged people do you know who've kissed only once?"

He stiffened, but only for a second. And then he took up the challenge and leaned close once more. "I guess I deserved that." His lips were an inch from hers. She felt his warm breath across her mouth.

"You know you did," she whispered back, loving the shiver of excitement that stirred just under the surface of her skin.

His glance slanted down, toward her mouth. Her lips seemed to tingle in anticipation.

Yeah, okay. Maybe she was playing with a big ol' ball of fire. And that wasn't smart. But there was a certain feeling of power she had now, knowing that Travis found her attractive, knowing that he wanted to kiss her, even if he felt that he shouldn't.

There really were definite benefits to being all feminine and womanly. Benefits she'd never understood before. It felt *good* to be womanly, to look in a man's eyes and see that he wanted her.

She thought of Zach Gunn then, of her one measly attempt to find what other women had—a little romance in her life, for cryin' out loud. Had Zach ever even once looked at her the way Travis was looking at her now?

She couldn't remember.

And truthfully, at this point, she didn't even care.

Travis said her name then. "Sam…" So soft and gentle, and with something like wonderment, too.

She had to resist the longing to lean in that fraction more and make the kiss happen. Because she wanted *him* to do it. She wanted him to make that choice.

And finally, he did.

He closed the tiny distance between them and his mouth touched hers—gently, at first. Kind of soft and careful, a kiss with a question in it.

But then she sighed in delight.

And that must have been the answer he was waiting for.

Because he slanted his mouth the other way and reached to pull her even closer, easing his big hand around the back of her neck, sliding his fingers up into her hair.

The kiss deepened. It seemed to happen so naturally,

so simply. His lips pressed hers more firmly. And she let her mouth relax.

And then she felt his tongue—who knew *that* would feel so good? But it did. It felt amazing, rough and wet and tender, teasing at her lower lip, slipping inside….

More cars passed, close enough that the Cadillac rocked a bit. She hardly noticed. She did think, vaguely, that they should probably get going, that it wasn't safe to be parked on the narrow shoulder of the road, kissing.

And kissing some more.

He caressed the back of her neck with his warm, slightly rough hand. And her skin seemed to tingle all over, as if his touch somehow set off a chain of happy fireworks under her skin. As if her body recognized these sensations he brought to life in her.

Recognized them. And wanted more.

Another shiver of pleasure went through her. She let out a low, excited sound.

And he moved his hand to cradle her cheek. His tongue stroked hers. His finger grazed her earlobe. And then his thumb was there, too. He caught her earlobe, rubbed it gently. The small, circular strokes thrilled her. Combined with the way his tongue was moving, so wet and hot and intimate, claiming the secret inner flesh of her mouth…

It was dizzying. Disorienting. Like looking down from an enormous height—say from the top of the derrick on the *Deepwater Venture*—looking down and considering letting go, sailing off into the sky, soaring over the blue sea so far below, forgetting that you didn't have wings, that you couldn't fly and the fall would kill you.

And that was too much.

A small, frantic sound escaped her. She slid her hands up between them, pressed at his shoulders.

Instantly he released her.

She opened her eyes, blinked at him, felt the world come bouncing back into focus again.

"Had enough?" he asked gruffly. His lips were red from kissing her and his eyes…they were darker than ever. She saw the heat in them. And some confusion. And anger—that she had goaded him into the kiss? Probably.

But why the confusion?

She wanted to ask him, but somehow, right then, she didn't dare. He seemed…almost a stranger to her at that moment. A stranger, and way too male.

She knew her lips must be at least as red as his. And her heart was pounding harder than it should have been. That scary, disoriented feeling hadn't completely faded.

"Yeah," she admitted. "I've had enough." And then her pride kicked in. "For now."

He almost smiled. "You always were too honest for your own good."

A certain sadness came over her. Strange. Her emotions were all wonky. She'd gone from turned-on to scared to sad, all in the course of maybe sixty seconds.

Gentling her voice, she reminded him, "You're honest, too, Travis. At least most of the time. It's one of the things I like best about you."

"So, then." He retreated to his seat and snapped his seat belt back on. The key was still in the ignition. He gave it a turn. The Caddy's engine purred to life. "You ready to go and tell lies to my mother?"

She put on her own seat belt. "As ready as I'll ever be."

Chapter Six

Ten minutes after they left that spot on the side of the road, Travis turned the car onto a long private driveway fenced to either side. Horses grazed in the wide pastures beyond both fences.

The driveway curved and revealed a sweeping turn-around in front of an imposing white house with thick pillars marching proudly along the facade. Wide steps led up between two central pillars to a long veranda. The front yard had been beautifully landscaped. Sam could see gardens in the side yards and even caught a glimpse of more gardens in the back.

"Impressive," she said.

Travis sent her a look. "The house is modeled after the Governor's Mansion. My grandpa James believed in living large." He stopped the car near the front steps. A guy in jeans and a cowboy hat came jogging toward them along another driveway that led around to the side.

Travis rolled down his window. "Hey, Paco."

"Travis, good to see you again."

Travis pushed open his door and got out, leaving the engine running. He came around and pulled open Sam's door, offering her his hand. She took it, telling herself to ignore the thrill that quivered through her, just from laying her fingers in his.

As she got out, Paco slid behind the wheel.

Travis said, "Paco, this is Sam, my fiancée."

Paco leaned across the seat to tip his hat at her. She smiled at him and nodded. "Hi, Paco."

"I'll have your suitcases brought in," he said to Travis.

"'Preciate it." Travis shut Sam's door and Paco drove the car away.

They turned together for the stone steps that led up to the veranda.

Right then, the big carved front doors swung open. A slim, good-looking older woman in soft linen pants and a white sweater emerged. She had sleek auburn hair and wore a welcoming smile. Beside her was a tall, imposing man with thick silver hair. Even if Sam hadn't seen pictures of them, she would have known who they were: Travis's mom and dad, Aleta and Davis. Travis had his father's broad shoulders and proud bearing. And his mother's smile.

"Travis! You're here!" Aleta called, real joy in her voice. She rushed down the stairs, her husband keeping pace at her side. When she reached Sam and Travis, she grabbed her son in a hug. "Oh, I can't tell you— I'm so glad you've come to us. It's been way too long." And then, breathless, she let him go and turned to Sam. "Samantha?"

Sam liked her on sight. She might be rich, from a

big-time San Antonio family, but Aleta was no snob. There was something so honestly warm and welcoming about her. "Aleta, great to meet you at last."

Travis's mom grabbed both her hands and gazed up at her all misty-eyed. "Oh, I'm so happy to meet you." She pulled Sam close. They hugged. It was a little awkward, but not too bad. Travis's mom was maybe five-seven, tall enough that Sam didn't dwarf her like she did some women. When Aleta stepped back, she shook her head, laughing, "I promised myself I wasn't going to fall all over you."

Davis offered a hand to Sam. She took it. He set his other hand on top of hers, enclosing it. "Wonderful to meet you, Samantha." He had cool green eyes. Watchful eyes. But he seemed sincere enough in his greeting.

Sam smiled and nodded.

And finally, they went up the wide steps and in through the big doors.

There were more Bravos inside—a whole bunch of them, as Sam had pretty much expected. Travis made the introductions, which seemed to go on forever, there were so many of them to meet.

Eventually, though, everyone settled down. Some of them wandered away from the big front living room into other areas of the giant house. It was not yet noon, and dinner wouldn't be for a few hours yet.

Sam had just finished chatting with Luke's wife, Mercy, about the drive from Houston, and the beauty of the Hill Country when Aleta spoke from directly behind her. "Feeling overwhelmed by Bravos?"

Sam turned and smiled down at Travis's mom. "Maybe a little bit."

Aleta grabbed her hand. "Come on. Paco's carried

your things up to your room. I'll take you there. You can have a few minutes to settle in and catch your breath."

Sam looked around for Travis, but one of his brothers must have dragged him off to another room.

"This way," said Aleta, and pulled her toward the foyer and the wide curving staircase.

Sam followed. She was slightly on edge about being alone with Travis's mom for the first time, a tad worried she might mess up and put her foot in it somehow.

Then again, Aleta was only being thoughtful. And a break about now wouldn't be half bad. There really were a whole lot of Bravos. It was kind of stressful, trying to keep the names matched with the right faces. Time to rest and clear her mind before dinner would help a lot.

Aleta led her to the third door on the left along the wide second floor hallway. "Here we are." She gestured for Sam to go in ahead of her.

"It's lovely, thank you," Sam said, "lovely" being one of those general-purpose polite words she'd picked up from Jonathan. In this case, it was the right word. The room *was* lovely, painted a sunny yellow, with carved white wood trim and white curtains. The cherry furniture was old and beautiful and her suitcases were waiting at the foot of the four-poster bed, which had old-time acorn finials. There was even a bay window that gave a nice view of the side gardens and provided a small sitting area.

The door stood open on the room's private bath. Another door, also open, led to the next room over. That room had blue walls and the furniture was heavier and darker than the pieces in Sam's room.

Aleta hovered near the door to the hall. She gestured toward the blue room. "That's Travis's room, through there."

"Ah," said Sam, for lack of anything better.

"Not his room from childhood. We never lived here at the ranch when the children were growing up. We would come, the same as now, for weekends and holidays. The kids took whatever rooms were convenient at the time."

"Yes, I know. Travis said you lived in town when he was small."

"Davis and I still keep a suite here. But it's really Luke and Mercy's house these days." Aleta waved a slim hand in the direction of the open door to the blue room. "I wasn't sure. Separate rooms. A shared room. Travis was not…forthcoming."

"This is perfect. Really."

"Good, then." Aleta folded her hands together. "Excellent." Sam thought she would go, but then she sucked in a careful breath. "I wonder if we might talk a little, before I leave you to yourself…."

Alarm bells went off in Sam's head. "Uh. Well, sure."

"Wonderful." Aleta shut the door to the upstairs hall.

Sam reminded herself that she *liked* this woman. And that she and Travis had agreed she would just be herself. Her *new* self, yes, but still, she had no deep secrets that Aleta might trip her up with—plus, there was no reason Travis's mom should even *want* to trip her up. "Well, um. Have a seat." There were two small upholstered chairs in the window nook. Aleta took one. Sam sat in the other.

"Travis has mentioned you often, over the years…"

"Ah. Well, he's always been good to me, looked out for me, I guess you could say. Ever since I was a lonely kid living with my dad on our family ranch not far from Sioux Falls."

"He always spoke of you fondly."

"He's…a good guy."

Aleta smiled. "Yes, he is."

"He helped me get my first job. And we've always stayed friends. And then, on this most recent project, we ended up working closely together."

"I'm glad that you know each other well. It gives you a good foundation to build on."

"Yeah. I…think you're right about that."

"You said you were raised by your father?"

"I was, yes."

"And your mother?"

The old wound throbbed a little, a scar long-healed but still sensitive if you poked at it. "My mom left us when I was three. She didn't much care for ranch life."

Real sympathy shone in Aleta's clear blue eyes. "You've never seen her since?"

"I have, yes. I used to visit her, now and then, in Minneapolis, where she worked as a secretary. But that was in those first few years after she left. When I was nine, she married her boss. He isn't a bad guy, but he's kind of shy, I guess you could say. I never had much in common with him. They had two daughters eventually—twins. I didn't ever fit in there. It just got easier for everyone if I stayed at the ranch with my dad."

"Easier? But you're her *child*."

Sam could see where Travis got his tender, protective streak. "The truth is, we never got along, my mom and me. I made it more than clear that I didn't want to be with her, even for a visit. I was pretty young, but still, I knew how I felt even then. I took my dad's side when she left."

"And why wouldn't you take your father's side?" Aleta asked sharply. "I'm sure you felt abandoned. I'm sure you…" She cut herself off. Pressing her lips together, she lowered her head for a moment. When she spoke again, her voice was calm. "I apologize for jumping to conclusions."

Sam grinned. "Hey, jump away. I *did* feel abandoned. And I hated her for it."

Aleta frowned. "And do you still hate her?"

Sam shrugged. "Not so much anymore. I'm older. I can see her side of it, too, now. We...keep in touch. Maybe a phone call at Christmas or my birthday. But we're not close. I don't think we ever will be."

Aleta reached across the space between them to clasp Sam's hand. Her touch was light. And reassuring, too. "I'm glad that you don't hate your mom. Hatred doesn't do anyone any good—and I'm so pleased to see you and Travis together. I've been worried about him, and driving him crazy, I know. Trying to get him to start dating again. To find someone special."

"You've been matchmaking." Sam shook a finger. She hadn't expected to feel so instantly comfortable with Travis's mom. But she did—comfortable enough right off the bat to give her a hard time. She leaned closer to the older woman, lowered her voice to a confidential whisper. "Travis told me everything."

Aleta laughed and confessed, "I *have* been matchmaking. I admit it." She grew serious again. "You do know about Rachel—and Wanda?"

"Yeah, I know. My dad still owned the ranch and I was working on a land rig, coming home for weekends, when Travis and Rachel got engaged. Travis brought her to meet us. It was a Saturday. She stayed for dinner. I really liked her."

Aleta made a sad little sound in her throat. "She was a lovely girl. You know he met her through me? Wanda, too."

"Uh-huh." Sam had met Wanda once, too. And she'd liked her well enough. Not as much as Rachel, but she'd seemed like a nice person. At least at the time.

Aleta gazed out the window. "I thought it would kill him when Rachel died. I was sure he'd never try again. But he did. With Wanda. And then I felt so guilty, the way *that* turned out. I wanted to make up for steering him wrong."

"Aleta, not your fault."

Travis's mom straightened her shoulders, refolded her hands on her linen-covered knees. "You're right, of course. And as it turns out, my efforts to find him someone new weren't required because there was you."

They both heard the hall door open in the room next door. "Sam?" Travis appeared in the open doorway between the rooms and spotted them. He leaned against the doorframe. "Okay, what are you two up to?" He was teasing, but there was a note of real suspicion in the question.

His mother rose. "Talking about you, of course." She went to him, kissed his cheek and patted his arm. "I was just seeing that Samantha was comfortable in her room."

Sam stood up, too. "And I am. Very."

"So, then. I'll leave you two alone." Aleta crossed to the door and paused before she went out. "Dinner at two."

"We'll be there," Sam promised.

Aleta shut the door behind her.

Travis waited until they both heard her footsteps moving toward the stairs before he said, "Mercy told me she saw Mom dragging you up here."

"She didn't have to drag me. Really. I like her. A lot."

He came toward her, looking much too manly and handsome in jeans and a sweater the color of dark red wine. "She's a charmer, all right. People jump through hoops for her. She's got that sincerity thing going *and* she has all the right connections."

"I think she *is* sincere."

Travis shook his head. "You've fallen for her. Just like everyone does."

"Fallen?"

He moved a step closer, lowered his voice. "I mean she's charmed you. And you trust her." The light from the windows slanted in on them, bringing out glints of gold in his dark brown hair. "You'll end up telling her everything, wrecking my brilliant plan to get her to let me find my own damn girlfriends."

"I do trust her, but I promise I won't mess up the plan."

He was doing that thing again, holding her gaze. Not letting go. She felt the now-familiar shiver, warm and delicious, as it moved through her body. "Travis?"

"Hmm?"

"You're looking at me *that* way again."

"What way is that?"

"You know, like you're going to kiss me."

He lifted a hand, brushed the back of his fingers along the side of her neck. Such a simple touch, to feel so good. To make her burn. "Would that be so bad if I kissed you?"

"No, I don't think so. Not bad at all…" She sounded breathless. Because she was.

He stroked her temple, touched her hair. "This…with us?"

"Yeah?" Definitely. Breathless.

"I swear I had no clue. I never thought of you this way."

She didn't know what to say to that. She knew he'd never seen her as a woman—not really, not until last night. And it hadn't bothered her before. She'd accepted that they were friends and nothing more. Somehow, though, it did kind of bother her now. She ached for her old self, for the woman she'd always been, the one no one seemed to see. It hadn't been all that great being the invisible woman. But she had learned to live that way, become accustomed to it.

Twin lines formed between his brows. "Okay, that's a lie."

She frowned, too. "What's a lie?"

"I did think about maybe asking you out at first."

"You did?" She wasn't sure she believed him.

"Yeah, but your dad said he'd kill me if I laid a hand on you."

Sam swore under her breath. "I never knew—and he's more talk than action, you have to know that."

Travis shook his head. "He loves you. And he thought he was doing right by you. And I like your dad. I wanted him to like me. So I kept my hands off. And you and me, we became friends. I guess I got used to things being that way, to seeing you as a pal and not as a woman."

Her throat clutched. If she spoke, she knew her voice would break. So she simply gave him a soft smile and a slow nod.

"Sam…" The way he said her name told her everything. She read his intent.

And she read him right. He cradled her face. And he kissed her.

Their third kiss.

It was as good—no, better—than the two that had

come before it. They stood in the yellow room, sunlight pouring in on them, and they kissed.

Her mouth knew his now.

And welcomed it.

He gathered her close, so tenderly. He cradled her against him. She drank in the taste of his mouth, gloried in the hardness of his body pressing all along hers.

She knew him. She knew that what had happened with Rachel had damaged him, deep down. And then all the awfulness with Wanda had only made him more certain that love wasn't for him. He probably wouldn't be changing his mind about that.

Not even for her, not even though he trusted her and cared for her and treasured her as a friend.

If she let this go where it seemed to be going, if she took advantage of that doorway between their two rooms, she would have to go into it with her eyes wide open. She would have to accept that she was one Cinderella who would get to keep the glass slippers, but would most likely have to let her prince go.

And what about their friendship? Even she, with her limited experience in the male-female arena, knew that bringing sex into a friendship—even a really solid friendship—could blow it all to hell.

He lifted his mouth from hers, took her shoulders and spoke with tender gruffness. "I could stand here kissing you forever. Or at least, until dinnertime."

She put on a teasing grin. "You're so easy."

He touched her cheek. He seemed to really like that—touching her. Which was fine. She liked it, too. He said, "But we should go back downstairs."

"Right."

He took her hand. "Come on."

She leaned closer, breathed in the scent of his aftershave, and kissed him again, a quick kiss that time. "You go on. I'll be down in a few minutes. I want to unpack."

Travis went to the game room and played pool with his brother Jericho and Jericho's wife, Marnie. They seemed real happy together, Jericho and Marnie. They were easy and content with each other.

And yet, they had that spark between them, too. Travis had always kind of thought that Jericho would never settle down. He'd been the family rebel, the complete bad boy, and he always said he liked his women tall and curvy and gone in the morning.

Marnie was short and slim, with a certain toughness about her, not what Travis would have thought of as Jericho's type. But they'd been married within weeks of their first meeting. And it had turned out to be a great match.

Travis won the game with Marnie. And then Jericho won the second game. Donovan, who was married to Travis's sister Abilene, rolled up in his wheelchair to take on the winner. Donovan was good. But Jericho was better.

By the time Jericho won that game, it had been over an hour since Travis left Sam upstairs. He started to wonder. Had she come downstairs yet?

Was she okay? Nervous about being surrounded by his relatives? Hanging back in her room to get away from all of them?

But she hadn't seemed anxious about his family. She'd breezed through the endless introductions, so cool and easy. She really knew how to handle herself around a crowd now.

And then she'd gone upstairs and gotten cozy with his mother.

The new Sam was pretty much a revelation, all the way around.

He thought of her room upstairs, of the door that connected it with his, of how much he liked kissing her, how he'd like to share a whole lot more than just kisses with her.

Then he told himself not to think about that.

Thinking, after all, too often led to doing. He'd always looked after Sam. And having sex with her wouldn't be looking after her. There were about a thousand reasons they shouldn't go there. And then there was the heat between them—the heat that made all those reasons too damn easy to forget.

He glanced at his watch.

A half an hour until dinner. Where was she?

He turned for the door to the long hallway that led to the front of the house.

And there she was. She'd changed into a slim skirt and a different sweater.

Their eyes met. Wham. Like a big bolt of lightning, searing him where he stood.

He realized there was no way he would last the coming week without holding her naked in his arms.

Jericho said, "Hey, Sam. Want to play?"

She smiled at his brother. "Eight ball?"

"That's the game."

"Sure." She went to the table, expertly racked the balls and then chose her cue from the ones on the wall while Jericho broke.

Travis sat back down. Jericho sank four balls and missed the next shot. Sam took over. He watched her play as he'd done so many times in the years he'd known her.

She won that game and then took on Matt, second born and CFO of the family company, BravoCorp. Sam ran the table that game. Poor Matt didn't have a chance.

She was something, all right.

But it wasn't her skill at pool Travis was admiring.

Uh-uh. It was the way the sweater showed off her breasts and the skirt hugged her body. It was the flexing muscles in her calves when she bent to sink a shot.

Matt's wife, Corrine, challenged Sam next.

Travis's sister Abilene sat down next to him. She leaned close. "It's good to see you in love again after all these years." Abilene chuckled. "You can't take your eyes off her."

He wanted to tell his sister to mind her own business, but how smart would that be? She and the others were *supposed* to think he was in love with Sam, that he couldn't help staring at her. He answered as a man in love would answer. "She's the best thing that ever happened to me."

"And you've known her for years…"

"Yeah, funny how that happened. We've both been on the same job for several months now. Working closely together."

"Working together. I know how that can be." Abilene shifted her glance to her husband, who sat in his wheelchair on the far side of the pool table. Donovan seemed to sense his wife had glanced his way. He turned to meet her eyes. They shared a slow smile.

Travis felt some relief, to have his sister's knowing eyes on her husband, instead of on him. "How's that dream house you two are building coming along?"

"It's finished," Abilene said. "We moved in six months ago. I love it."

"Good."

She turned to him again. "And you are out of touch, my dear brother. You know that, right?"

"Guilty as charged."

"I'm hoping Samantha will make you come home more often. I'm planning to talk to her about that."

"You're as bad as Mom."

"Not quite. But give me a couple of decades, I will be."

"You're scaring me, Abilene."

"Just don't be a stranger."

Right then Kira, Matt and Corrine's older daughter, stuck her head in the door. "Grandma says it's time for dinner." Kira was—what?—nine now? She'd always had a bossy streak. Apparently, that hadn't changed. "Everyone has to come and sit down."

Corrine said, "Tell Grandma we'll be there soon, sweetie." She banked a shot and sank another solid.

"Mom. Now."

Corrine sent her daughter a quick smile and took another shot. Two more solids dropped into pockets.

Kira pulled a face. "Well, hurry up, please," she huffed, and marched off the way she had come.

Corrine laughed. "My daughter is destined to rule the world."

Matt winked at his wife. "It could happen. After all, she's as beautiful as her mother and almost as smart."

"You're a smooth talker, Matt Bravo." In quick succession, Corrine dropped the rest of the solids and then the eight ball.

Sam applauded. "Oh, you are *good*."

Corrine grinned. "I'll give you a rematch if you'll

come visit me at Armadillo Rose. That's the bar I own in San Antonio. We're closed tonight and Monday. But Tuesday would be good."

"We'll all come," said Marnie. "Make it Bravo family night."

"It's a date. I'll expect you." Corrine hung up her cue.

"What do you say, Travis?" Sam sent him a questioning glance.

"Sure," he said. "Sounds great."

Corrine added, "And Sam, another thing. Friday is Black Friday. And that means shopping. We meet up in town at 4:00 a.m. It's the first year we're all going together—all the women in the family. We want you to come, too."

Shopping—and at 4:00 a.m., no less. Travis had a feeling that wouldn't be Sam's idea of a good time.

But she put on a big smile anyway, and said, "I would love that."

When they went in to dinner, Travis held out Sam's chair for her, taking total advantage of the moment to bend close and breathe in the faint scent of that tempting perfume she wore. "Having a good time?"

She sent him a look that flirted and challenged. "A *great* time."

"I'm glad." He took his own seat, smoothed his linen napkin on his lap.

They'd had the salad and the girls from the kitchen were serving the prime rib when his dad started the toasts.

The first was to having the whole family together. Everyone raised their glasses. Even the two oldest kids, Kira and Ginny, picked up their glasses of milk and held them high. Four-year-old Ginny was his brother Gabe's stepdaughter.

"To our whole family." Kira echoed her grandfather.

"Our whole family, yeah!" Ginny chimed in.

Luke's son, Lucas, shouted, "Yeah!" and sucked on his sippy cup.

Travis was starting to feel a little sentimental, sitting there at the long table with its embroidered white cloth. He loved his big family, and he was happy for all of them, that each of his brothers and sisters had found someone they wanted to spend the rest of their lives with. That his parents had worked out their problems and still held the seats of honor at either end of the table, that they were still giving each other tender glances, so proud of their children, so pleased with their grandchildren.

The next toast was for Abilene and Donovan. Abilene was expecting their first child in May. Donovan caught his wife's hand as they all raised their glasses again.

And he brought it to his lips. "You changed my life," he said. "Thank you."

Abilene's eyes were definitely misty. "You're welcome."

"You're a complete sentimentalist." Donovan's voice was husky.

And she answered, grinning through her tears, "You bet I am. A big bowl of emotional mush…"

Everybody laughed, though Travis didn't think the rest of them got the joke any more than he did. It was clearly a private thing, between Abilene and her husband.

Travis watched them together, thinking how they had it all. Just like his other sister Zoe and his half sister, Elena. Zoe and her husband, Dax, had a happy toddler. And Elena and Rogan had a big, handsome baby boy.

And then there were his brothers. All six of them.

Each had found the woman for him and then been man enough to work through whatever crap got in the way of a good life with the right partner. They were brave men, his brothers. They'd fought to claim their happiness.

Travis realized he admired them.

Maybe he needed to take a lesson from them—and from his sisters. And his mom and his dad, too.

Maybe it was time to let the pain of losing Rachel go. To accept that he'd made a big mistake with Wanda. And move on. To stop turning away from the possibilities life offered for fear of what might happen if he dared to take another chance.

He turned to catch Sam's eye. She gave him a glowing smile that had his heart beating crazy-hard inside his chest.

And when he reached for her hand, she gave it. Willingly. Without a second's hesitation.

She amazed him. She could hold her own with the toughest roughneck around. And then, inside of a single week, with a little coaching from an expert, she'd turned out to be one hell of a gorgeous, tempting, sexy woman, as well. Every time he looked at her now, he didn't want to look away.

He wove his fingers with hers as his dad raised his glass again. "And now, to Samantha and Travis. Samantha, we are so glad to welcome you as part of the family. Travis, congratulations. My son, you are one very lucky man."

Chapter Seven

At a little after midnight, Sam stood at the bay window in the yellow bedroom. She could see the waxing moon, riding high in the dark sky above the softly rounded overlapping hills.

It had been a great day and an even better evening. Travis had stayed close to her after dinner. He'd been frankly affectionate, taking her hand in his, laying his arm casually and possessively across her shoulders when they all sat together in the living room for after-dinner coffee. And then later, in the game room, when the two of them played checkers, he took any slightest excuse to catch her eye, to share an intimate glance with her.

He also touched her knee under the table. And he brushed her leg with his. He acted like he couldn't keep his hands off her, like he didn't want to let her out of his sight.

She'd basked in his attention. And she didn't really

care if he was faking it for the sake of the family. She was having the best time of her life and she'd decided to just go with it. To love every minute and not worry about what would happen when the week was over. The end seemed a long way away. After all, it was just midnight, barely the beginning of the second day.

She heard the hallway door open in his room. Because she'd left the adjoining door standing wide in invitation, it took only a glance over her shoulder to see the light go on when he flicked the switch in there.

"Sam?"

"In here." She turned again to the window and the crescent moon swinging from a star out there in the night. The soft sound of his footsteps approaching thrilled her.

He came and stood behind her. And he did just what she'd hoped he might do. He stepped close and his big arms came around her. She settled back against his solid strength with a sigh. He nuzzled her hair. She tipped her head to the side, anticipating the touch of his mouth against her neck.

And then his lips were there, so soft and warm. "What are you doing, alone here in the dark?" His breath fanned her skin as he spoke.

"Watching the moon." She turned in his embrace, slid her hands up his hard chest. "Waiting for you."

He kissed her. There, at the window in the soft darkness, with only the muted light from the other room and the faint glow provided by the moon.

When he pulled back, his eyes shone in the dimness. "It's funny…"

Something had changed in him. She felt it, *knew* it. She touched his lower lip, so soft compared to the rest of him. "Tell me."

"I roped you into coming here, into pretending we're in love."

"Uh-uh, you didn't rope me into anything. I came because you offered me the way to make some changes in my life. And also because you're my friend and I'll do just about anything to back up a friend."

He framed her face in his two hands. "Even something pretty stupid?"

She gave a low chuckle. "Yeah. For a friend like you, I'll even do stupid."

He traced her brows with a touch that lingered. "I want you to know..."

"What?"

"I think I've been played by my own game."

"Played?"

"I think I...needed for this to be fake. At first. Otherwise, I couldn't make myself take the leap. Take the chance." He shook his head. "Am I making any damn sense at all?"

She held his gaze. "You are making perfect sense."

He brushed her cheek with his thumb. "So...if this, with us, turned into something real..." Her heart expanded inside her chest. And the darkened yellow room suddenly seemed a magic and wondrous place, filled with light. He asked, "Could you maybe be into it?"

She didn't play coy. Coy wasn't her style. "I could. Yeah. No maybe about it."

He sucked in a slow breath, said her name so softly. "Sam."

She commanded, "Kiss me again."

He didn't need to be told twice. He took her mouth, his tongue delving in. She kissed him back, stoking the fire. And she pressed her body against him, drinking in the groan it brought from deep in his throat, feeling the hard ridge beneath his fly, the proof that he really did want her. Her breasts tingled and down below she felt so soft and hot, a melting kind of heat…

When that burning kiss ended, he said, "I don't want to push you…" His voice was low and rough.

She gave a husky laugh. "Oh, yeah, you do."

His mouth quirked up at one corner. "All right. I do." Then he grew serious. "I know you've been hurt, Sam."

She held his gaze. "We both have."

"And this is pretty sudden."

"Sudden? We've been friends for twelve years."

"You know what I mean." He looked at her so intently. As though he could see into her heart and liked what he saw.

She confessed, "Yeah, I do know." Joy. She felt such joy. It filled her like a golden light, bright as the sun. She laid her hands on his chest again. She could feel his heartbeat. And the diamond he'd given her caught a random ray of light from the other room and glittered in the darkness.

Somehow, the sight of that sparkling stone brought the doubts creeping in, turning the golden glow of her joy a little gray around the edges..

This magic between us started with a great, big lie….

And they were *still* lying to his family.

He must have seen the shadows in her eyes. "What? Tell me."

She touched the side of his face. "I was thinking that maybe we need to stop lying to your family."

He didn't hesitate. "Fine. We'll tell them in the morning."

She winced. "You're so brave. And all of a sudden, I'm a total coward."

"It's your call."

She wrinkled her nose at him. "You always say that."

His eyes shone. "Because it is—and you can look at this way…."

"I'm listening. Give me an excuse *not* to tell them. And make it a good one."

"All right. How about this? Tonight the lie is starting to become the truth."

She did like the sound of that. "Not bad." She turned in his embrace, taking his arms, wrapping them around her again, resting back against him, absolutely loving how easy it was becoming for her—to touch him. To *be* touched by him.

His lips brushed her hair. "I'm just saying we could wait awhile. See where this goes. Now it's not about my family anymore. It's about us. You and me."

"Us," she echoed, loving the sound of that simple little word. She gazed out at the moon. Really, he did have a point. They weren't lying to his family anymore—or they weren't *completely* lying. Not if they were really together now.

A lie is a lie, said a reproachful voice in the back of her mind.

Sam shut her eyes with a sigh.

Travis whispered in her ear, "Do me a favor."

She sighed again. "Anything. You know that."

"Don't overthink it. Decide tomorrow."

He was right. About everything. They would bust themselves to his family. Or they wouldn't.

It would work out between them—or it wouldn't.

That was the beauty of falling for Travis. She trusted him so completely. He wasn't Zachary Gunn. Travis was the right man to take a chance on.

This, for them, tonight, was the real beginning.

You didn't ask how it would end when you were only at the beginning.

You had to be willing. Truly willing. She saw that now. Willing to give yourself, willing to let the right man hold your heart in his hands.

Willing to open yourself.

Yeah, she might get hurt. Her heart could end up bruised and battered. But a heart, after all, was for loving.

And loving was about what you gave, not what you got back.

He took her shoulders, turned her to face him again. And he kissed her.

Everything made sense then, when his mouth touched hers. She put away her doubts and kissed him back. She drank in the taste of him, reveled in the feel of him.

A few moments later, he whispered in a prayerful voice, "I want to be with you, Sam. All night long."

"I want that, too." She touched his hair, at his temples, loving the warmth of the silky strands against her fingertips, loving that he saw her—*really* saw her—as a woman now.

"But I don't want to rush you," he said, so tenderly. "And I've got nothing. No condoms."

She gave him a slow smile. "We could probably manage to find some of those tomorrow...."

"Tomorrow." He made a low sound, almost a groan. "You're right. We need to wait." But his eyes said he didn't want to let her go. And he didn't let her go. He gathered her close again, kissed her some more.

Long, endless arousing kisses.

His hands caressed her back, moving lower, cupping

the twin curves of her bottom, bringing her tightly into him. So she could have no doubt of her effect on him.

Sam loved every touch, every brush of his lips against her own, every stroke of that hot, hungry tongue of his. She didn't want to stop any more than he did.

But she knew that they had to.

And so did he.

With a low, bleak-sounding moan, he took her by the arms and put her away from him. His dark eyes blazed down at her. "Good night. I mean that." He released her and stepped back. And then he turned sharply on his heel and started for the open door to his room.

Sam realized then, as he walked away from her, that she couldn't do it—she couldn't let him go.

In an instant, she'd kicked off her shoes, whipped her sweater over her head and reached behind her to unclasp her bra. "Travis." She dropped the bra to the floor.

He turned. Saw her standing there, naked from the waist up. His eyes flashed molten. He said something dark and intimate. She couldn't make out the word. But she took his meaning. "Sam, come on. Don't do this to me."

"You could…stay here with me tonight," she said softly, feeling suddenly shy and way too vulnerable. "We could…be together in every way but that one."

He said her name again, raggedly, "Sam…" It was a plea.

"Well, I mean…" It was hard to keep holding those burning eyes of his. But she did it, somehow. She didn't look away. "If that's all right with you. If that's…something you would feel comfortable with."

"Comfortable." He growled the word. And then he

came back to her in three long strides. "You have no clue what you do to me, do you?"

She felt a smile tremble across her lips. "Oh, I think I do. I think…you do the same thing to me."

He took her shoulders. "I can't believe this is happening."

"I know exactly what you mean."

"You are so beautiful. You always were. Why didn't I see it before? How could I have been so blind?"

"Stop talking, Travis. Stop talking and kiss me."

He obeyed. He kissed her, so deeply, as his hands strayed, skimming the tops of her shoulders—and downward. He cupped her breasts.

It felt wonderful. Perfect. Just right.

She started walking, guiding him backward, toward the waiting turned-back bed. They fell across it, kissing and kissing, pulling at each other's clothing, rolling, so she was on top. And then he was on top.

There were clothes flying everywhere. His shoes hit the bedside rug, one thud. And then another. His sweater landed on the lamp, his socks…

Who knew where his socks went?

They were gone. And so were his jeans.

And his silk boxers, too.

She rolled again, to gain the top position. And she loved the way he felt, pressed so close, skin to skin. At last.

He whispered her name as she kissed him.

She touched him, running her hungry hands over his broad, hard chest, tracing the sexy trail of hair that ran down the center of him, over his flat belly, and lower, all the way to where the hair grew thick between his lean hips. Then she encircled him.

He was so hard. She stroked him, still kissing him.

He groaned his pleasure into her open mouth. She had no shame with him, no shyness, even though she'd only known one other man, one single time, before him.

Her skirt was off and then so were the little panties that matched the hot-pink bra she'd dropped on the floor by the windows.

And then he touched her. In her most secret place. She opened for him.

And after that, well, she lost track of the world. Of time. Of everything.

There was only his caress, his magical, tender fingers making her body feel weightless and yet heavy and lazy at the same time. Making her rock her hips up to him, making her beg him not to stop.

Never, ever to stop.

There were no barriers. She felt utterly safe—and yet in danger, too. A tempting sort of danger, the kind that couldn't be denied.

He urged her onward, into the expanding hot light of her own pleasure, until she felt herself hitting the peak. Oh, it was wonderful. The waves of completion rippled outward, from her center to the top of her head, the tips of her fingers, down all the way to her toes.

Until there was nothing but his touch. And her body. And the slow, delicious fade into sweet satisfaction.

A little later, she took him to the same place he had taken her.

And then at last, side-by-side under the covers, cuddled up close, they whispered together.

They talked about their work on the *Deepwater Venture*.

She told him that yes, she was still sure that she wanted to try for a land job now. "This may sound crazy, but I'm thinking of going back to school. I mean, more than just a few classes. I have enough money put away to go for two years, straight through. With the on-line classes I've taken, I've almost got my bachelor's degree already. I'm thinking I might like to become an accountant."

He blinked. "That's a long way from being a tool pusher, Sam."

"I know, but that's okay. It's *good*. I'm pretty damn smart, you know?"

"I do know."

"And I want to try something completely different."

"You want to get out of the oil business?"

"Could be." She rolled to her stomach, braced up on her elbows. "But then, the oil business needs accountants, too, right?"

"Good point." He slipped a tender hand around her nape, pulled her close and kissed her.

When she lifted her mouth from his, she asked, "You think it's a bad idea?"

He brushed the side of his finger along the length of her arm. "I didn't say that. You just surprised me, that's all."

She took his lips again, a quick, hard kiss. "The more I think about the college thing, about *really* changing things up, the more I like it."

"I see." Then he asked, "Will you spend Christmas with your dad?"

With a happy sigh, she turned on her side, settling her head on the strong bulge of his shoulder, resting her hand lightly over his heart. It was a revelation, just to lie like this, together. Naked and warm under the covers.

He nuzzled her hair. "I asked you a question."

"Who knows?" She turned her head into his body, pressed her lips to the curve where his shoulder met his broad torso. Then she snuggled back down again. "My dad likes to keep all his options open the past few years, since he sold the ranch. He and Keisha lead a footloose kind of life."

He traced a heart at her temple—at least it felt like a heart. "Maybe we could come here, spend Christmas at Bravo Ridge."

She kidded, "Next you'll be asking me what I'm doing New Year's."

"You know, I just might." He brushed her hair back from her forehead. "Ted and Keisha can come, too."

"Right. Park the Winnebago out in front. So classy. Your mom and dad will love that."

He traced the outer curve of her ear. She loved the way he touched her, so casually—and yet so intimately. He said, "It's a big ranch. Plenty of room for a Winnebago."

It seemed to her he was pushing kind of hard on the Christmas thing. She teased, "I thought you said you didn't want to rush me…."

He caught her chin with a gentle hand and held her gaze. "I lied."

She scolded, "You know, you've been doing way too much of that lately."

"You're right. I'll have to watch it." He smiled. And then he kissed her.

After that, they didn't need words. They let their bodies do the talking. It was a very satisfying "conversation," even if they did have to stop short of letting go completely.

And it wasn't until much later, as he slept in her arms, that she started thinking again—or maybe over-thinking. Whatever you called it, well, she couldn't help but reconsider the issue she'd blown off when he first brought it up.

He'd said he didn't want to rush her.

And then, well, he did kind of seem to be doing just that—no, not with the lovemaking. She had made the choice on that. And she wasn't sorry. Not in the least. She was thirty years old. About time she spent a beautiful night with her own personal Prince Charming.

But really, he *had* done a head-spinning about-face that night. In the space of a few hours, he'd changed from a guy who wanted nothing to do with love—to someone who looked at her as though he couldn't wait to spend the rest of his life at her side. A guy who wanted to invite her dad and his twenty-six-year-old girlfriend to the family ranch for Christmas.

True, the change was a dream come true for her.

Still, something about it didn't seem right.

Sam scowled into the darkness. Then again, maybe *she* was the one with the problem. He offered her exactly what she'd been longing for....

And she ended up wide awake in the middle of the night, holding him close to her—and worrying that there must be something wrong with him.

Chapter Eight

In the morning, Sam's worrisome doubts disappeared.

Maybe it was waking up to find the thin almost-winter sun peeking through the drawn curtains—and Travis smiling at her.

She pretended to grumble. "What are you grinning about?"

He lifted up on an elbow, the gorgeous muscles in his arms and chest flexing as he moved. "I had a great time last night." His hair looked slightly blenderized and his eyes were low and lazy.

"Me, too." She thought about the things they'd done last night. Then she thought how they would probably do those things again tonight—and more, if they managed to get their hands on a box of condoms. Such thoughts made a fluttery weakness down in the center of her, made her want to pull him close to her, keep him there, in her bed, all day long and into the night again.

"You should see your face," he said. "Your eyes are making promises. And your mouth is driving me wild." He bent close—and bit her chin. It was a tender bite, more of a gentle scrape of his teeth against her skin, really. It didn't hurt.

But it did make that weakness in her center turn liquid. "Oh, Travis…"

"I love it when you say my name that way—like I make you weak in the knees."

"You do," she whispered. "In the knees. Everywhere…"

He eased a hand beneath the covers. His rough, tender fingers danced across her skin.

She moaned and let her eyes drift shut.

Several minutes passed before she opened them again. By then, she was breathless and limp. And very much satisfied.

It seemed only fair to make sure he was satisfied, too.

Somehow, they were still in bed at five of nine. She insisted that they shower separately. It was the only way to guarantee that they wouldn't get distracted and end up staying in their rooms for half the day.

She was dressed and finishing her light makeup, brushing on the final touch of mascara, when she saw him in the mirror, standing in the bathroom doorway. He looked so good, freshly shaved and wearing khakis and a dark blue sweater with the sleeves pushed halfway up his corded forearms.

He watched her with a definite gleam in his eyes. "Seeing you with your clothes on just makes me want to take them off you again."

She paused with the mascara wand a few inches from

her face. "Forget that. Your family will think we're a couple of sex fiends."

"So what? Happily engaged couples tend to be sex-obsessed."

"But we're not engaged. Not really." She went back to stroking on the mascara.

"But are we sex-obsessed?"

She decided not to answer that one.

He arched an eyebrow. "So, have you decided to tell them all that you're not my fiancée after all?"

She stuck the wand in the base, screwed it shut. "I met them only yesterday." She blew out a breath through puffed cheeks and admitted, "I just don't want to do that at this point. I can't believe I'm such a frickin' coward."

He made a chiding sound with that clever tongue of his. "Did you just say frickin'?"

She canted her chin high. "Hey, I may know how to dress and put on makeup and use the right fork now, but underneath, I'm as crude and unrefined as I ever was."

"And I'm really happy about that." He seemed to mean it.

And it mattered to her that he hadn't forgotten the Sam he'd always known. Still, she warned, "Well, just remember, I can take you down if you get out of line."

He grunted. "Doubt it."

She dropped the mascara back in her makeup bag. "Want to try me?"

In the mirror, his eyes flashed with sudden, wonderful heat. "Tonight. In bed."

"Bawkbawkbawk."

He came away from the door. In the mirror, she watched him approach. Was it just her, or was it suddenly hotter in there? His gentle hands clasped her shoulders. She shut her eyes, drew in a slow, steadying breath. He asked, "Who're you calling chicken, huh?" It was a threat. A really tempting one.

"Chicken?" She put on a puzzled frown. "Did I say that?"

He bent, kissed her neck, drawing on the skin a little. Not enough to leave a mark, but enough to send a shiver running under her skin. He caught her eyes again in the mirror. "Take it back?"

She turned to face him. "I guess, for now, I'll have to, won't I?"

He grinned. Slowly. "You will if you plan to make an appearance downstairs anytime soon."

As far as Travis was concerned, they could have stayed upstairs in their rooms all week. He could have called a pharmacy and had the condoms they needed delivered. He could have asked to have their meals left at the door.

Him and Sam. Who knew?

It was a question he'd been asking a lot lately—ever since he'd seen this new, exciting side of her. She was a revelation.

In the past six or seven years, he'd slowly come to realize that she was probably the best friend he had. His best friend. And now this. Every hour he was with her, he was happier with himself and the world.

He wanted to keep her safe. And at his side. If he could do both of those things, well, he'd be one lucky guy. The higher-ups at STOI were constantly offering him opportunities to work full-time on shore. He could step up to rig superintendent, with a number of company men on different rigs reporting to him. In fact, a promotion was available to him in the next couple of months if he wanted it.

So he could come home most nights. And she was making a change, too, giving up work on offshore rigs. He was glad about that. The work was too dangerous.

Accounting. Now, there was a job where you couldn't get hurt. He approved of that for her.

Well, except that getting her degree would mean she'd be putting in long hours in class and studying. And didn't accountants work sixty-to-seventy-hour weeks?

All that time. Away from him…

Anything might happen to her. The most innocent activities—something so simple as walking across the street—could spell disaster. He knew that too well.

They would have to talk about it, about what was the best choice for her, for *them*.

He took her hand, kissed the back of it. "You just *have* to go downstairs, huh?"

She eased her fingers from his hold and looked at him sternly. But her beautiful eyes were shining. "You recently spent a big pile of money improving my manners, and now you want me to be rude?"

He tried to look pitiful. "It's rude to stay here with me?"

"It's rude to go visit people and then not spend any time with them—which I don't need to tell you because you have a mama who loves you and brought you up right."

He had to admit he agreed with her. So they went downstairs.

When they entered the big, farm-style kitchen, his mom and dad were the only ones there. The older couple sat at the table, sipping coffee.

His dad said slyly, "We were wondering if you two would ever get up."

"Don't listen to Davis," his mom instructed. "You two are on vacation. Stay in bed every day till noon if it suits you."

Travis bent over her and kissed her cheek. "Thanks, Mom. We just might."

She reached back and patted the side of his face. "It does my heart good to see you so happy, honey."

"I am," he said. Sam was watching them. He met her eyes. Zap. Just sharing a look with her got him hot.

Davis got up. "How about my famous sourdough pancakes, maybe some bacon and scrambled eggs?"

Sam said, "Davis, I think you read my mind."

"Where is everybody?" Travis went to the counter to get the coffeepot and a couple of mugs for him and Sam.

Davis was already at the stove. "Elena and Rogan went out to the stables with Mercy and Luke." Bravo Ridge was a working horse ranch. Luke bred quarter horses, both for work and for show. "They took the kids." The kids, Travis assumed, would be Elena and Rogan's baby, Michael, and also Mercy and Luke's two, Lucas and little Serena. The rest of his brothers and sisters and their families had gone on home because they all lived nearby. Elena and Rogan, though, made their home in the Dallas area, and had driven down to the ranch for the week.

Some of the Bravo family relationships were…interesting, to say the least.

Elena and Mercy were very close. Mainly because Elena was not only his dad's illegitimate daughter, but she was also Mercy's sister, though not by blood. Mercy had been adopted at the age of twelve by Elena's mom, Luz, and Luz's husband, Javier.

In fact, until just a few years ago, everyone except

Luz had believed that Javier Cabrera was Elena's natural father. When the truth came out, there had been big trouble in both families. That was when Travis's dad and mom had separated. Luz and Javier had lived apart, too.

But everyone seemed to have worked through the old garbage now. They all got along.

"We're all invited to Abilene and Donovan's for dinner tonight," said his mom.

Sam grinned. "I'll get to see their new Hill Country dream house."

His mom, always big on touching, reached over and patted Sam's hand. "Yes, you will. It's a beautiful place not far from Fredericksburg."

Travis set Sam's coffee in front of her. She sent him a smoldering glance. "Thanks." He considered plunking his mug and the coffeepot down on the table, grabbing her, tossing her over his shoulder and heading for the stairs.

But then he had another idea. He put his own mug down in the place beside hers. "Abilene and Donovan's isn't all that far from the cabin…."

His dad had turned the burners on under the cast-iron griddle. He cracked an egg into a striped bowl. "That's right." He asked Sam, "Travis tell you about the cabin?"

"He did, yeah." Her gaze and Travis's met again. She wore a fond, knowing smile. It was good, he was thinking, to be with a woman who knew his history, who had heard all his stories of growing up a Bravo. She not only understood him better because of all that she knew about him, but she also had a common ground with his mom and dad and the rest of the family. She turned to Davis again. "He's always said it was beautiful there, that your whole family used to go there camping when he was growing up. Sounded like heaven to me."

His dad cracked another egg and agreed, "It's a beautiful spot." He picked up a wire whisk and started beating the eggs with it. "The cabin was pretty much a shack in the old days, when we all used to camp there. A few years back, we had it renovated. Now it's not only picturesque, but it has all of the comforts of home."

At his mother's nod, Travis refilled her coffee. He carried the pot back to the counter and suggested casually, "Maybe I'll take Sam to the cabin today, show her around."

Sam glanced at him sharply. And then she rolled her eyes—but quickly, so neither his mom nor his dad would catch her doing it. She'd guessed what he was up to. Which was maybe the drawback of being with someone who knew him so well.

So what? A few slow, deep kisses and she'd be glad he'd carried her off to the family cabin.

They could get condoms in Fredericksburg. And the cabin was cozy and private, with a nice, big comfortable bed in the bedroom.

His mom beamed. "What a lovely idea."

After breakfast, they toured the stables. Sam was raised on a ranch. She'd been riding since she was barely able to walk. She was brimming with praise for Luke's horses and the first-class operation he ran.

Luke asked if they wanted to ride, to get out and see more of Bravo Ridge. Sam said she'd love that. Travis started to get his hopes up. He could just picture it—the two of them, riding out alone, finding some private place in a stand of trees to hobble the horses and share a few kisses.

He was thinking they could spread a saddle blanket on the ground. Yeah, there was a nip in the air, but they could warm each other up real fast.

His big plans quickly crashed and burned. Elena and Rogan decided to go with them. Mercy said she'd watch the kids.

So it was the four of them.

It turned out to be a good time. Elena and Sam seemed to hit it off, which wasn't all that surprising. Sam got along with everyone in his family. For Travis, it was an opportunity to get to know his half sister and her husband a little better. Rogan and Elena had met a year and a half ago, when Rogan came to San Antonio to buy out Javier Cabrera's construction business.

Rogan was a big, good-looking guy with a winning smile, of Irish descent. Travis found he approved of the way that Rogan looked at Elena, a world of love and admiration in his green eyes.

They were back at the ranch by one. Mercy had lunch ready. So they didn't get away until two. They were expected at Abilene's by six.

That gave them four hours to themselves. Travis planned that they'd spend the majority of it naked in the cabin, rolling around on that nice, big bed.

But they had to stop in Fredericksburg to get the condoms. He pulled in at the Walgreens off Main and told Sam he'd be right back.

She made one of those snorty noises she used to make all the time, before the big makeover and her transformation into the sexiest woman on planet Earth. "Forget that. It's not like I'm some sweet little Texas rose. I'm not the least embarrassed to be seen buying my own contraception."

He gave her a long-suffering look. "I was more thinking of making it quick. You know, so we can be alone?"

"It won't take any longer if I come in."

"Sam, I'll only be a minute."

"You mean *we'll* only be a minute because I'm coming in."

There'd never been any arguing with Sam once she
made up her mind about something. She'd already
leaned on her door and swung her long, strong legs out.

They went in together.

And then, once she got to the condom display, well
of course she insisted on acting just like a woman: She
had to read every damn label. The only thing she was
sure about was that he needed a large.

Which, he had to admit, was gratifying.

She was intrigued by the textured ones—for greater
stimulation. And she kind of thought the ones with different fruity flavors would be fun. Did he want the
"extra sensitive"? Would that give him a better experience?

A couple of other shoppers rolled their carts by while
Sam rattled on about the various benefits and drawbacks
of each and every option. Travis could have been embarrassed, but he wasn't. And the other shoppers seemed
more amused by her candor than anything else.

And really, Sam was damn cute. He liked her frank-
ness. And she'd always had a great sense of humor.

They bought six different kinds because she couldn't
come to a clear decision about which of those six was
going to be the best choice. Forty-five full minutes after
he pulled into the parking lot, they were finally pulling
out again.

The ride to the cabin was a pretty one, even in late
November, with the rolling fields either mowed or dry.
It was only a few miles from Fredericksburg.

They turned onto a dusty dirt road for the last half mile. And then, finally, the land opened up and there was the rustic old cabin in the middle of a wide, rolling field that in the spring and early summer was vivid green and thick with wildflowers.

Sam put her hand on his arm. "Stop the car."

"What the...?"

"Travis, come on. Stop. Now."

He put his foot on the brake and eased the Cadillac to the flattened grass at the narrow shoulder. "What?"

"Look. In front of the cabin. Somebody's already there."

He craned closer to the windshield. "What the...?" At the end of the porch, he saw two motorcycles parked side-by-side, shiny chrome gleaming in the winter sunlight.

Sam was grinning. "Looks like a pair of really nice choppers to me..."

Choppers. Custom motorcycles. His brother Jericho built choppers. And Jericho's wife, Marnie, worked with him at his motorcycle shop, San Antonio Choppers.

And hadn't Marnie and Jericho mentioned how much they loved riding their bikes in the Hill Country, and that they often visited the cabin?

Sam gave a low laugh. "Marnie and Jericho, that's my guess. What *do* you think they're doing in there?"

"Maybe we should go find out," he answered in a growl.

She chuckled. A maddening sound. "The blinds are drawn. I really get the feeling they're not going to appreciate being disturbed."

Travis couldn't believe it. Jericho had beaten him to the cabin. He grumbled, "We might have gotten here first if we hadn't had to spend an hour choosing condoms."

"It wasn't *quite* an hour," she teased. "And I really did have fun picking them out."

"Yeah." He slumped in the seat and scowled out the windshield. "I noticed."

She leaned across the console, hooked her cool, smooth hand around the back of his neck and dragged him closer to her. He was forced to meet those amazing, tip-tilted iridescent blue eyes. "Don't be bitter," she coaxed. "I personally hope they're having a terrific time in there." And then she kissed him.

And he forgot to be annoyed. How could he be aggravated when she kissed him like that? Like he was the only man in the whole world.

Like she could go on kissing him for hours and never get tired of it. He breathed in the scent of her perfume and kissed her back.

But eventually, with a reluctance to match his own, she did pull away. "Let's go back to Fredericksburg for a while, until it's time to go to Abilene's."

Fredericksburg. Great. The town had been founded by German settlers back in the mid-1800s. There were restaurants, a main street lined with shops and museums, a historic district, peach orchards and brew pubs.

He grumbled, "Now you want to go play tourist."

"Sure, why not?" She leaned close again. He got another heady whiff of her perfume. And she whispered in his ear. "Travis…"

"What?" He kissed her cheek. He couldn't stop himself.

"Don't be grumpy."

"I'm not."

"Yes, you are, which means you're lying again. And you said you were going to stop lying, remember?"

He turned his head so he could brush her lips once more with his. He couldn't get enough of the feel of that mouth of hers. "Lying *and* grumpy. That's pretty bad."

She was smiling at him. "That's right. You're no fun when you're grumpy."

"I'm disappointed, that's all."

"Yeah, and you're also a grown man, not some spoiled little boy."

"Am I getting lectured?"

"Yes, you are. I'm flattered and happy that you want to be with me, but it's just not happening right now. You might as well accept that. We can still enjoy ourselves, even if it doesn't involve the use of a single one of those condoms I spent all that time picking out."

He knew she was right. He'd been acting like a sulky kid. "Yes, ma'am."

"Don't make me hurt you. Say it like you mean it."

He returned her smile. "Yes, *ma'am.*"

And then she reached down and put her hand on his knee. She used her strong fingers, massaging a little. He stifled a groan. She said, "Or you know what? We could stay right here. I've never used a condom in a car before…"

He knew that she hadn't. Before this, with them, she'd only been with one other guy. That SOB, Zach Gunn. And that was only one time.

He was seriously tempted. Enough so that his pants were getting way too tight.

But no. Just because she was so open and willing and sweet about everything didn't mean he had a right to sulk until she offered to do him in the car because the cabin was taken.

It was their first all-the-way time they were talking about. It should be in a bed. Not in his Caddy on the side of the road.

"Or," she whispered, her clever fingers trailing up the inside of his thigh, making him ache to haul her close, "we could get a room in Fredericksburg…."

He put his hand over hers. "Uh-uh." He gently peeled her fingers off his thigh and brought them to his lips.

Her eyes were soft as a summer sky. "Changed your mind, huh?"

"It's not going to kill me to wait until tonight."

"Coulda fooled me." She laughed.

He kissed the back of her hand, and then gently returned it to her lap. "So. Fredericksburg."

"Sounds like fun."

And it *was* fun.

They strolled along Main Street hand-in-hand, visiting half the shops there. At the Fredericksburg General Store, she bought a Betty Boop Christmas ornament and a souvenir billed hat that said "Happiness Is Drinking German Beer."

They stopped in at a bakery for coffee. He watched her gorgeous face across the two-seater corner table from him and thought how just being with her was the greatest. How he could really see himself spending his life with her.

And that kind of scared him. Enough that she noticed.

"Travis? You okay?"

"Fine." He picked up his coffee cup, took a slow sip. "Why?"

"You kind of slipped away there all of a sudden."

He had the craziest urge right then to take her hand—

the one with his ring already on it—and tell her he wanted to make it official. To make it real between them in every way. He wanted to marry her.

Right away, as soon as they could get a license.

Before…

What?

Before I lose her. The words echoed in his head.

But that made no sense.

Sam was just as into this thing between them as he was. There was no reason to think he was going to lose her.

And how could he lose her, anyway? She was Sam. His best friend. A guy didn't just suddenly lose his best friend.

Unless something happens to her. Like something happened to Rachel…

Rachel.

When the accident happened, the wedding was only a week away. The day before, Rachel's grandmother, in Dallas, had taken a fall. So her mom and dad had driven up there to make sure the old woman got the care she needed.

Because Rachel's parents couldn't be reached and he was the fiancé, he'd been called in to identify her.

Rachel, so pale and still on that cold steel table. Not Rachel anymore, not really.

Because Rachel was gone. Lost to him. Forever and ever. He couldn't get his mind around that.

Never to see her again. Never to hear her laugh.

Never to call her his wife.

He hadn't cried. There were no tears in him. There was nothing in him. A certain numbness. A will for revenge.

But there would be no revenge. The drunk bastard

who'd hit her was dead, too. He'd wrapped his sports car around a light pole a few minutes after he'd run her down.

Powerless. He'd felt powerless. Rachel was gone forever. He hadn't been there to save her and there was nothing he could do to make it right. His gut twisted.

And then he chucked his cookies. Right there in the morgue. He'd thrown up all over his own damn boots....

"Travis?" Sam's voice came to him. Her face swam into view.

What the hell did he think he was doing, anyway?

Wasn't it only yesterday morning that he'd sat across from Sam in the suite at the Four Seasons and told himself he would never leave himself open for that kind of pain again?

"Travis? Travis, are you okay?" Sam leaned toward him across the table. There was a world of worry in those blue eyes of hers.

He blinked, shook his head. "Fine. Really. Didn't I already say that?"

"You don't look so good." She reached out.

He caught her hand. Her capable, soft, strong hand.

And everything changed. Just from the touch of her hand.

All at once, he was...okay. Truly okay. His crazy, irrational fears receded.

There was just him. And Sam. In this cute little bakery. Sharing the afternoon before heading to his sister's for a family dinner.

"Sorry," he said. And he leaned across the table.

She still had questions in her eyes. But she met him halfway, shared the kiss he offered, a quick, innocent kiss, given that they were sitting in a public place. "But are you—?"

He didn't let her finish. "I mean it. It's nothing."

She freed her hand from his and sank back to her chair. "So how come I don't believe you?"

"Sam." He waited for her to meet his gaze. "I was just daydreaming, that's all."

"You didn't look like you were daydreaming." She kept her voice low, for his ears alone. "You looked like you saw a ghost."

A ghost. Well, in a way, he had. But he wasn't seeing a ghost now. He saw only Sam. Everything would be all right. He was ready for this. Ready at last. "No ghost. I promise you."

She opened her mouth to say something—and then she changed her mind. Instead, she picked up her coffee cup, sipped from it, set it carefully down. And then she turned her head to stare out the window.

He just sat there. He knew her so well. She wasn't the kind to push and prod at a man. All he had to do was wait.

It worked. After a minute, she turned to him again. "I would…" She seemed to fumble for the right words. "You know I'm here, right? Anything you say to me, I can take it."

"I know." He said it firmly but gently. "But there's nothing."

She glanced away again, but only for a second. Then she resolutely faced him once more. She sucked in a slow breath and she made herself smile. "Well, okay, then. If you say so."

Chapter Nine

Other than the strange and unsettling incident in the bakery, Sam had a great time that afternoon and evening. She and Travis toured the Pioneer Museum before heading for Abilene's house.

The house was southeast of Fredericksburg on a beautiful piece of land, with a clear creek running in the back and a view of craggy limestone peaks from the kitchen windows. It had a giant great room at its heart and an extra kitchen outside for use in the warmer months of the year. It was on two levels, with an elevator as well as a staircase, so that Donovan could get around with ease in his wheelchair.

By six-fifteen, everyone in the family was there—except for Jericho and Marnie. They rolled up on their choppers at six-thirty, looking windblown and slightly flushed and way too pleased with themselves.

The family was gathered in the great room then, filling the vaulted space with lively conversation and the occasional burst of shared laughter. They sipped cold drinks and munched finger-food appetizers. All the kids who were old enough to walk were either playing with Abilene's two rescue kittens or following her three mutt dogs around, trying to pet them.

Travis leaned close to Sam when Jericho and his wife came in. "They look happy."

She whispered back, "Well, who doesn't enjoy a nice, long...ride?"

He laughed and put an arm around her, drawing her close to brush a kiss at her temple. Aleta happened to be sitting in her line of sight. Travis's mom saw their interaction, including the quick, affectionate kiss. And she beamed in motherly satisfaction.

Sam realized she no longer felt guilty for pretending to be engaged. There really was nothing to feel that guilty about anymore. She and Travis were...what?

The word came to her: *serious.*

Yeah. They were serious about each other, about this longtime friendship of theirs that had bloomed overnight into something so much more. Something so sweet and real. And hot.

Sam was glad it pleased Aleta to see them together. His mom seemed to believe that all Travis had ever needed was to let go of the past and find a good woman to make his life complete.

Maybe that was true. Sam didn't mind at all thinking of herself as the good woman his mama had been hoping he'd find. The only thing that nagged at her was the question of whether he'd really let the past go—or if maybe there was something else that was eating at him. She needed to talk to him about that.

But somehow, so far, she hadn't found a way to *get* him to talk about it. Which was weird in itself.

She and Travis had always been able to talk about everything. He knew all her secrets.

And she was the one he came to when he needed to talk. She knew how much he'd suffered when he lost Rachel. And how rotten he'd felt when Wanda took off with another guy, how he'd blamed himself. Because he was still in love with Rachel—or at least, with the memory of Rachel. And Wanda had known.

But today, in the bakery, he'd lied right to her face. She'd seen the stricken look in his eyes. Yet he'd insisted that there was nothing wrong. She should probably have kept after him, not given up until he busted to the truth.

Then again, well, everything was changing between them now. They were creating a whole new kind of relationship. Maybe she needed to be patient with him, give him time to get used to being more than just friends, time to open up to her the way he always had before.

His warm fingers closed over hers. Everyone was going in to eat. Holding hands, side-by-side, they followed the crowd to the dining room.

Travis couldn't wait to get Sam back to their rooms at Bravo Ridge.

But they stayed at Abilene's until midnight after all. They played Texas Hold'em with Abilene, Donovan, Jericho and Marnie. It was fun, really. And he knew Sam was having a great time.

When he finally eased the Cadillac into the six-car garage down the curving path at the side of the ranch house, all was quiet. Luke and Mercy, Elena and Rogan, and their kids had returned earlier. So had his parents.

He and Sam went in the front door and tiptoed up the stairs together. The second he got her inside his room, he pushed the door shut and turned the privacy lock. He tipped up her chin and found her mouth in the darkness.

"Wait here," he whispered against her sweet, parted lips.

She made a low, questioning sound, but she didn't say anything.

He left her to turn on a lamp. And before he went to her again, he detoured through the open door to her room. He engaged the privacy lock on the hall door in there.

He was back at her side in seconds. "Alone at last," he whispered.

She laughed and shook the Walgreens bag she'd carried in from the car. "With plenty of condoms."

"All is right with the world." He took her free hand and pulled her over to the side of the turned-down bed.

And then he took her in his arms.

The Walgreens bag dropped to the rug as she kissed him. Within maybe sixty seconds, her clothes and his clothes were in a pile at their feet.

They had to stop kissing to dig through all the clothing and retrieve the bag.

"Got it." She held it up with a triumphant smile.

He grabbed her wrist, pulled her to her feet—and back into his arms. He couldn't get enough of the silky, strong feel of her body, of her full, firm breasts and her shapely wide shoulders. He stroked her back, tracing the bumps of her spine. And then he slipped a hand between them, drinking in her gasp of excitement as he dipped a finger into the wet heat of her.

She was so ready. And so was he.

He needed to be inside her, joined with her. But he tried to remember that there had been only one other time for her, all those years ago, and that that one time hadn't been good. He forced himself to take it slow, using his thumb to tease the swollen heart of her pleasure, dipping his fingers inside.

She moved against his touch, moaning, and he felt her inner muscles relaxing, felt the greater wetness. He eased another finger in. She sighed in pleasure. He knew she was right at the edge.

But she didn't allow him to take her over. Instead, she pushed him onto the bed and followed him down. The Walgreens bag crackled as it ended up under him. Her mouth still fused to his, she gave a tug and freed it.

And then she broke the scorching kiss. She was pulling away from him.

He tried to catch her, to take her lips again and resume the kiss, to regain the deep and intimate touch. But she was quicker.

Laughing and breathless, her face and upper chest flushed with excited color, she sat back against the pillows. Gathering her gorgeous, muscular legs up, crossing them yoga-style, she opened the bag. "Hmm, what do we have here?"

"You," he said darkly, still flat on his back, his desire for her way too evident. "You're driving me crazy. You know that, right?" With her legs crossed like that, he could see everything, all sweet and pink and so temptingly wet for him. And it wasn't only that. It was the sheer animal beauty of her, the strength and power in every sleek, smooth inch.

She reminded him of the women in the science fiction novels he couldn't get enough of as a kid—warrior women, tall and commanding, who lived in strange jungles on faraway planets, who dressed in leather pelts and hammered silver and hunted fantastical creatures using only a shield and spear. Women who didn't need men—or thought they didn't.

Until the right spaceship captain dropped out of the sky.

"I think…this one." She pulled a shiny red box from the bag and dropped the bag onto the nightstand.

As if he cared which one she chose. He grabbed her ankle. "Come back here."

"Patience, patience." She reached down, peeled his fingers free, brought them to her lips—and sucked his index finger into her mouth. He almost lost it right there. And then she rubbed her tongue around it. He gritted his teeth, closed his eyes and looked away. Finally, she let his finger go. And she teased, "A well isn't drilled in a day."

He groaned and turned to look at her again. It made him ache to look, but it was a glorious kind of pain. "Don't talk about drilling," he pleaded. "It just isn't fair."

"Whoever told you it was going to be fair?" She opened the box and removed a wrapped pouch. Then, taking her sweet, agonizing time about it, she shut the box and set it on the nightstand with the bag. "Hmm." She neatly tore the wrapper off the pouch.

And then, just like that, her bright, bold confidence vanished. Holding the naked-looking circle of lubricated latex, she bit her lip and sighed. He saw the shy and tender woman within, the one she'd spent years trying to hide from the tough, able men who worked in the oil business.

His heart turned to mush.

That time when he reached to touch her, it was to soothe her. He clasped her knee, lightly, gently. "Hey. Okay?"

She confessed, her head tipped down, "I'm a little… nervous, I guess."

He sat up then, scooted around beside her, and laid an arm across her velvety-smooth shoulders. Drawing her close to him, he guided her head down against his chest. "We don't have to do this right now."

She gave a sad little chuckle. "That's not what you've been saying all afternoon."

He smoothed her hair, rubbed her shoulder. "I'm sorry. I know I was an ass this afternoon."

Of course she had to jump to his defense. "No, you weren't."

"I was." He kissed the crown of her head, loving the clean, silky feel of her hair against his mouth, enjoying her fresh scent. "I do want you. So bad. It's like a revelation to me, you know? You and me. Together. After all these years."

"Yeah, I get that. I know what you mean. It's the same for me."

"But, Sam, I can wait until you're ready. Until you're…comfortable."

"I *am* comfortable. It's only…" She lifted her head and they gazed at each other. She admitted in a small voice, "It was pretty bad, that one time with Zach."

Zach Gunn. The bastard. He said intently, "The guy was a major jerk."

"I took the wrapper off this thing—" she still had the condom in her hand "—and it all came back. How rough he was. How much it hurt. How I tried to be…I don't know, brave. Tough. To act like I knew what I was doing. And it only got worse. It only hurt more. But I stuck it out. And then afterward, he went and told everyone how bad I was in bed. He said I might be female, but I sure wasn't a real woman. No wonder I was stronger than half the guys on the rig."

Listening to her now, seeing the old pain haunt her eyes, he wished he could get that SOB alone again, rearrange his face a second time. "You *are* a woman. *All* woman."

A wobbly smile came and went. "Oh, Travis…"

"And I would never do you that way. I couldn't stand to hurt you. And what happens between us, that's only between us."

"I know."

He gave her a coaxing smile. "Though if I *did* talk about you—which I never would—it would only be about how amazing and beautiful you are. How I can't get enough of you. How you drive me stark raving out of my mind and I sincerely hope you will continue to do so for a long, long time to come."

Hesitantly, she lifted her free hand. Her fingers brushed the side of his face, so lightly, before she withdrew them. "But the things that have happened to us in the past…they can be powerful. They can still have a grip on us. If we let them, they can destroy our happiness. They can ruin what we have now. You know?" Her eyes searched his.

And he realized she wasn't talking about only herself. She meant those bad moments he'd had in the bakery in the afternoon. "The past is not going to ruin what we have, Sam." He spoke slowly. Deliberately. "I won't let it. *We* won't let it."

She sucked in a trembling breath. "You sound so sure."

"Because I *am* sure."

"Well." She smiled again, a much brighter smile. "That's good. That's really good." She held up the condom. Gulped. And then her gaze dropped to his lap. She touched him—a shy touch, quickly withdrawn. "Looks like I kind of…ruined the mood."

But the brief caress was all it took. He felt the warm ache of arousal and began to grow hard again. "Not a problem," he told her gruffly. "I'm easy when it comes to you."

"Oh, yeah. I like that about you. I like it a lot." She reached out again and her cool, smooth fingers closed around him.

Now he was the one gulping. He stifled a moan.

She asked, "Is it all right if I…?"

He did moan then. "Anything. Everything…"

She stroked him, long slow strokes. And then she shifted her legs around, folding them under her. She lowered her mouth and she took him inside.

Her soft, slick wetness surrounded him. She drew on him, rhythmically.

He wove his fingers in her hair, guiding her a little, wishing he could last forever. But within a few too-brief minutes, he was way too close to letting go.

He took her shoulders. "I can't…no more…"

With a sigh, she sat back on her folded knees. Her lips were shiny and red. So kissable. And the flush was back on her high cheekbones.

He pulled her toward him again, covered her mouth with his own. They shared one of those kisses that lit up the night.

Finally, she whispered, her lips moving against his, "Is it okay if I…put it on you?"

"Yeah. It's okay. It's more than okay." He brushed

his mouth back and forth on hers as he spoke. He pulled away enough that they could share a smile.

Then they drew apart.

With care, she positioned the condom and rolled it down into place. "There." She sat back on her folded knees again and slanted him a look. "So…maybe if I kind of let you take over from here?"

"Whatever you want, Sam. I mean that."

"Okay." She stretched out beside him on her back and shut her eyes. "Go ahead, then." Her voice had a barely-discernable tremor.

For a moment, he just sat there, staring at her long, strong body, at her soft lips and closed eyes. He wanted to make it good for her. He wanted to wipe out the only memory she had of what might happen between a man and a woman.

He wanted to be the only man she thought of when she thought of this.

He made the first touch feather-light. With a finger, he traced her brows. A small sound escaped her—of anticipation or anxiety? He couldn't tell which.

"You're so beautiful, Sam…." He traced the bridge of her nose, the curve of her forehead, the tender indentation at each temple, the high crests of her cheekbones.

And then he bent close. He kissed the places he had already touched.

By the time he settled his lips onto hers, she was smiling a little. She opened to welcome him.

He drew that kiss out forever. It lasted even longer than some of the other endless kisses they had shared. With his lips and his tongue, he urged her to forget whatever fears she had, to be easy inside herself.

To let bad memories go.

As he kissed her, he touched her, slowly and thoroughly, the way he had the night before.

He cradled her breasts, teasing the nipples until she lifted toward him and moaned her excitement. Only then did he take the caress lower. He rubbed her flat belly. He ran his hands down the twin curves of her hips.

And he stroked her thighs.

In time, she began to move her hips, inviting him. She whispered breathless encouragements against his lips. "Yes. Like that. Oh, yes…" And then she eased her legs apart, the signal he was waiting for, her body's assurance that she wanted more.

He was only too happy to give her more. He touched her intimately, parting her.

She was wet and open. She spoke against his mouth. "Oh, Travis. Please…" She rocked her hips into his touch. He caressed her more deeply.

And then he eased one leg between her thighs. She gasped—and moved her sleek thighs even wider apart. He settled himself between them, carefully, doing his best to distribute his weight so he didn't crush her beneath him.

No, she wasn't the kind of woman he could easily crush. But still, he didn't want her to feel smothered or hemmed in or overpowered. Not in any way.

Only then did he lift his mouth from hers. Her eyelids fluttered open. She looked at him, her gaze glazed and hungry.

"Touch me," he whispered. "You set the pace."

She didn't hesitate. She reached down between them and took him gently in her hand. She guided him home.

He braced up on his elbows to get more control. And in an agony of slowness, he pressed in.

Little by little, he entered her. Pushing in a fraction, holding still, watching her flushed face for any sign that she didn't welcome him, that he might be hurting her.

But she only lifted toward him. She wrapped her arms around him, whispered, "Yes, it's good. More..."

At last, he filled her. Her body stretched and gave around him. They were together in the most complete way.

She rocked her hips up to him.

He held still, letting her take him, do what she would with him, letting her set her own pace. It was pure torture, to hold back so she could lead the way.

Pure torture, but in a really good way.

She lifted up, took his mouth again, plunged her hot, wet tongue inside.

He knew then. She was okay with this. More than okay.

Her sweet, strong body called to him. He couldn't help but answer. He rocked his hips toward her. She rose to meet him.

And after that, he was lost in sweet, consuming heat. He let go and let it happen.

The world spun away and it was only him and Sam and this miracle of pleasure that burned so hot and bright between them. There was only her kiss and the magical scent of her, the feel of her beneath him, rocking him hard and fast, holding on so tight as they rose to touch the stars.

Sam was a happy woman.

Truly happy.

Yeah, okay. Part of it was the sex. After she got past her own fears and awkwardness, it had been terrific. Better than she'd ever dreamed it might be. But also, well, she believed Travis when he said he wouldn't let the past ruin what they'd found together. The nagging worry that something wasn't right with him receded.

She could just enjoy being with him.

And she did. They spent Tuesday at the ranch. Tuesday night, they went to Armadillo Rose, the San Antonio bar owned by Matt's wife, Corrine. Davis and Aleta had volunteered to stay behind and watch the children. The three younger couples—Elena and Rogan, Mercy and Luke, and Sam and Travis—rode into San Antonio in Rogan's SUV.

Armadillo Rose, which had been owned by Corrine's mother before her, was a funky, fun place with loud music and cute bartenders in skimpy tops and cowboy boots.

Corrine had pitchers of margaritas brought to their table, and Asher, Travis's oldest brother, and his wife, Tessa, joined them. A few minutes later, Matt showed up. And then Marnie and Jericho, too.

They played pool. Corrine even took a break to take on Sam. Sam won that time, two out of three.

It was a family party in more ways than one. Not only were five of the seven Bravo brothers there, but Marnie and Tessa—like Elena and Mercy—were sisters. Before Marnie married Jericho and Tessa said "I do" to Ash, their last name had been Jones.

Marnie told funny stories of growing up in the wild, woolly Jones clan in a tiny town in the California Sierras. She and Tessa had a crazy old grandpa named Oggie and a stepmother they adored. Tessa said that their dad had been a wild man until he settled down with their kind and loving stepmother. They also had two much younger half brothers who, Marnie announced, were

born to carry on the Jones tradition of generally raising holy hell.

Sam could so relate. She ended up telling a few stories about her dad, who had a real thing for fireworks.
She even revealed his nickname, Ted the Torch. Every
Fourth of July, he insisted on buying every bottle rocket
and firecracker he could get his hands on. Twice he'd
been cited and had to pay whopping fines for setting
off fireworks where fireworks weren't allowed.

The five couples and Matt stayed to close up the
place. It was raining as Rogan drove them home, a misty
kind of rain. Sam and Travis sat in the rear seat. She
rested her head on his shoulder and watched the jeweled
drops speckle the windshield up in front and thought
that she had never in her life felt so…accepted.

Not only was Travis as gone on her as she was on
him, but she also adored his family. His brothers were
the greatest. And his sisters and sisters-in-law, well,
Sam liked them all. They were good people. It seemed
like a hundred years ago that she had worried they
might look down on her.

A little while later, alone in their rooms, Travis
showed her again how good it could be when a woman
found the right man.

Wednesday morning, Irina, Caleb's wife, called. She
invited Travis and Sam to dinner that night. Because
they were going to San Antonio in the evening anyway,
she and Travis decided to spend the day in town, just
the two of them.

They toured the Alamo in the morning.

Travis told her that his mom sometimes worked as
a tour guide there. And that before he said he was engaged to Sam, Aleta had been planning to set him up
with another tour guide named Ashley.

Sam couldn't resist teasing him. "Maybe we should ask if Ashley's giving the tour today...."

He put an arm around her and pulled her close. "Don't even think about it." He kissed her then, a quick, possessive kiss that made her breath catch in her throat. It was a revelation to her. How just being with him made every moment so full, so exciting. He spoke again in a low growl. "Keep looking at me like that and I won't be responsible for my behavior."

"That was my plan." She leaned her head on his shoulder. It didn't get any better than this. To be with him in the truest way, held close in the warm circle of his arm.

Their tour guide, as it turned out, was a tall, slim, balding man named Otis. He spoke eloquently of the history of the Alamo, explaining that it had been built as Mission San Antonio del Valero, one of five missions along San Antonio's Mission Trail. Otis went on to tell the old story with feeling, all about how, in 1836, 189 Texan soldiers bravely defended the fort for thirteen days before finally being massacred by six thousand of Santa Anna's troops.

After the Alamo, they had lunch at a great Mexican restaurant and bakery in Market Square. When they'd finished the meal and the waiter had cleared off their plates, Travis took her left hand across the table.

He rubbed his thumb across the big diamond on the ring he'd bought her. "It looks good on you. Really good."

She squeezed his hand. "I love it. I do. And I have to be careful."

He tipped his head to the side, frowning. "Be careful of what?"

"Well, I mean, lately, I could almost forget that this

isn't really my engagement ring, that we're not really engaged."

He brought her hand to his mouth, brushed his lips across her fingers. The touch of his mouth on her skin made her think of their nights together, made her wish for a thousand more of them. "It feels real to me, too." He lowered her fingers to the table again, put his other hand over hers, covering the bright diamond, enclosing her hand in both of his. "I want us to *make* it real."

Her heart stuttered in her chest, and then began racing. "Um, Travis?"

"Yeah?" His eyes gleamed.

"Did you just ask me to marry you?"

Chapter Ten

Instead of answering her question, he said, "Wait, I should be on my knees, right?" Which, she realized, *was* the answer to her question.

She gripped his hand, embarrassed. Thrilled. Blown away. "Oh, no, really? Right here in the restaurant?"

"Absolutely." He was off his chair and on one knee before she could stop him.

A guy at a nearby table remarked, "Now, that's the way you do it."

Somebody else applauded.

Travis still held her hand in both of his. And he said with feeling, "Sam, it's you. You're the one for me. Say yes."

She looked down into his eyes. And she thought how this was exactly what she'd dreamed of, what she'd longed for, in her secret heart—even when she hadn't dared to admit that a life with Travis was what she wanted more than anything.

At the same time, an unwelcome voice in the back of her mind whispered, *Whoa, slow down. This is happening way too fast.*

Sam closed her mind to that voice, to her doubts. She had everything now. She *was* the woman she'd always believed she had no chance of ever being. And Travis wanted her for his wife.

He wanted her for real, not just because his mom wouldn't get off his back.

He was offering her what she'd always yearned for. No frickin' way she was turning him down.

"Sam." He looked up at her with such hopeful tenderness. "Help me out here. Give me an answer. The right answer. Say yes. Please."

She knew half the restaurant was listening in now. Even the waiters had stopped to watch.

The annoying voice echoed in her head again. *He knows you won't put the brakes on. Not here. In a public place. He knows you could never embarrass him that way....*

No.

That wasn't true.

It was only the voice of her doubts, the voice of her insecurities, the voice of the lonely girl she used to be. She wasn't letting that voice stop her from grabbing her happiness with both hands.

"Sam?" Did he sound worried now?

She couldn't stand that. "Yes!" She laughed—in nervousness and in joy. "Yes, of course. You know that. Yes."

He swept to his feet, pulling her with him, and gathered her into his arms. Everyone in the restaurant seemed to be clapping. "You had me worried there for a minute," he whispered.

"Sorry. You kind of caught me by surprise."

"It's okay. I forgive you because you gave me the answer I was looking for. Kiss me, Sam."

She didn't hesitate that time. She kissed him with all the love and longing she'd been holding in her heart.

Just for him.

For way too long.

At Caleb's house that evening they held hands underneath the table.

Irina beamed at them. "Love. It makes the world go round and round." Her gaze strayed to Caleb and they shared an intimate glance.

Who knew? Sam found herself thinking. What had started out as a lie had ended up becoming the truth. The beautiful, amazing, absolute truth.

Engaged to Travis. If someone had told her two weeks ago that Travis would take a knee in the middle of a restaurant and propose to her for real, she would have laughed and said, "No way. Never. Not a chance."

So much for all her old assumptions.

She had conquered her worst fears—that she wasn't quite good enough, wasn't woman enough, didn't have enough class. And as a result, she had won her prince.

And speaking of princes...

Sam met a real one that night. His name was Rule.

Prince Rule Bravo DeCalibretti. He was a cousin to the Bravos, the second-born son of one of Davis's long-lost brothers. Born in Montedoro, a tiny principality on the Mediterranean, His Highness was visiting America for the second time. Rule said he enjoyed getting to know his father's country a little. Rule was tall and dark and handsome, as all princes should be. He was staying with Gabe and Mary Bravo and would be coming out to Bravo Ridge tomorrow to celebrate Thanksgiving—that most American of holidays—with the San Antonio branch of the family.

And Rule wasn't the only royalty there that night. Irina was a princess. Seriously. Or she would have been, if things had been different. There was actually a book about Irina's life. A big, fat one, with lots of glossy pictures. Sam thumbed through it, thoroughly amazed. Irina didn't seem the least unhappy that she would never be a queen. She was the picture of contentment living in San Antonio with the husband she adored and their gorgeous little daughter.

Sam and Travis left Caleb's at a little after eleven. They were back at the ranch before midnight.

Holding hands, they climbed the stairs to the rooms they shared. He took her in his arms the minute they shut the door behind them.

"I wanted to tell them all tonight," he whispered. "That we're together. That you're really mine."

"But they wouldn't have understood." She brushed a butterfly-light kiss across his mouth. "Because they all think we were already engaged."

He claimed another kiss, a longer, deeper one. And as he kissed her, he took hold of her sweater and eased it up over her ribcage. She raised her arms. They broke the kiss long enough for him to pull the sweater over her head. He reclaimed her mouth and he turned her, continuing the kiss, and waltzed her backward to the bed. They fell across it together.

He lifted away enough to add, "And if I told them that I asked you to marry me today and you said yes, then I would have had to explain everything…."

She touched his cheek, already scratchy from a day's

worth of beard. "It'll make a good story, one of these days."

He smiled. "Something to tell our kids, when they think we're old and boring."

"Our kids…" She considered that possibility. "I never thought…you and me. Kids." She nudged off her shoes, heard them plunk to the bedside rug.

"Well, think about it now," he said gruffly, sitting up to get rid of his own sweater. "Because it's going to happen."

"And I'm so glad." She pushed him back down and leaned over him, laying her hand on his chest, which was so wonderfully broad and deep and heavy with muscle.

Another kiss. She caressed him, running the backs of her fingers along the side of his neck. Then she pushed away and sat up.

He caught her arm. "Where do you think you're going?"

She gave a lazy shrug. "Well, I *was* going to help you with your boots…."

"Ah." He let her go, lay back and folded his hands behind his head. "In that case, okay." He held up a boot.

Shaking her head, she slid off the bed, braced her feet on the rug, took the heel in one hand and the toe in the other and pulled. The boot slid off easily. She took the other one off, too, and his socks as well, while she was at it. Then she stretched out beside him again.

Idly, he traced the line of her hair where it curled against her temple. And then he let his finger glide lower, around the line of her jaw, down the jut of her chin, the length of her throat. He lingered for a moment or two at her collarbones, tracing one and then the other. He laid his warm palm against her upper chest. It felt so good there, so right.

Finally, he skimmed the top of her low-cut satin bra, making her sigh.

With his gaze, he followed the slow progress of that skimming finger. "With you here, I really feel I'm... coming home at last, you know?" His voice was touched with roughness and desire. He glanced up again and their eyes met.

She scanned his face. It was a good face, the kind of face she would never tire of looking at. "I'm glad, Travis. So glad..."

A slight frown creased his brow. "What would you think about moving here?"

The question surprised her. She rose up on an elbow. "South Texas Oil has something for you here, in San Antonio?"

"Not STOI. BravoCorp."

BravoCorp. The family business. Davis was president and chairman of the board. Caleb was the top sales rep, Gabe the company attorney, Matt CFO and Ash CEO. BravoCorp invested in any number of different projects. Once they'd been mostly in land development, but with the economic downturn, they'd diversified. Now, they had various investments they managed all over the country, in Spain and in South America. Also, for as long as she'd known Travis, they'd put a good chunk of their capital into oil.

She took a not-so-wild guess. "They still want you to take over the family oil interests?" He'd mentioned in the past that he could always have a place in the family business. He'd just never wanted that before.

He rubbed her shoulder, caressed the length of her arm. "My dad brought it up yesterday. And Gabe mentioned the idea again tonight. I would be vice president in charge of petroleum exploration and development."

"Whoa. Way impressive."

"The money would be really good, a big salary, great benefits and a strong bonus structure." He named an eye-popping figure.

"Wow."

He was watching her closely. "Say it," he grumbled.

"Oh, come on. You know what I'm thinking."

"So come out with it."

"Well, you've always said you wanted to make your own way."

"I see things differently now. We're getting married. We want to have kids, so coming home to stay, being near the family, it suddenly has a big appeal."

"I can understand that." She also experienced a certain…wariness. That feeling she'd had in the restaurant, when he proposed, that they were moving awfully fast, talking about changing everything up when she'd barely gotten used to the astonishing fact that they were together and they both wanted to stay that way.

It wasn't that changing things was bad. She'd been making some changes herself after all. It was only… well, he surprised her. All of a sudden, he was talking about going to work with his family when he'd never been the least willing to consider such a thing before.

He touched the flare of her hip. She shivered a little in anticipation of the other places he might touch. Her apprehensions faded as desire bloomed.

And then he said, "We could get our own place here, in San Antonio. A really nice place in a great neighborhood. Since you're not taking another job offshore anyway, you could just take a hiatus for a while."

Her misgiving came creeping back. "A hiatus? From?"

"Work."

She just didn't get it. "But, Travis, I want to work."

"I put that wrong. Because you *would* be working. It's a full-time job, to be a mother. To raise a family."

"Well, yes, I can see that. I get that. But I told you, I want to get my degree, get a new job…"

"But there's no hurry to do that. It's not like with kids."

"What do you mean?"

"You're thirty years old, Sam."

"Well, yeah. And I—"

"Sam." He didn't wait for her to finish. "We need to get on with having those kids we've been talking about. You know that we do. And you need to be…safe, most of all."

What did he mean by that? "Safe from what, exactly?"

He wasn't looking at her.

She touched his face. And then she had to wait several seconds before he turned her way and she could see his eyes. "Safe?"

He didn't answer right way. But then, gruffly, he confessed, "I wouldn't make it. I couldn't do that again. If something happened to you…"

"Travis." She laid her palm against his beard-scratchy cheek, held it there, a touch meant to comfort, to reassure. "What happened to Rachel, you know that was a one-in-a-million thing. One of those things that could happen to anyone. Not something you could have protected her against."

"Not true. If I had been there, it might have been different."

"What? You were going to stick by her side every minute of every day?"

"Don't exaggerate."

"I'm not. It's just, well, life itself is frickin' hazardous. No one gets out alive."

He glared at her. "You know what I mean, Sam." And then he softened his tone. "We just have to be more careful, you know?"

She really, really did not like this. "You're not making sense. Are you telling me I'm not supposed to walk across the street by myself?"

His eyes were so dark, so determined. "I can protect you. I *will* protect you."

"Travis, that's just not realistic. Some things you can't protect another person against."

"You can't know that. You can never know that. There's always something a man can do so that the bad stuff can be prevented."

She could see that she needed to try a different tack with this. "Look at it this way."

"What way?" He didn't look the least receptive.

She refused to give up. "I've done a very dangerous job for over a decade. And see?" She gestured down the length of her body. "All in one piece, in perfect health."

He still wasn't buying. "You're purposely misunderstanding me."

"No." She searched his face. "I'm not. Honestly, I'm not."

"I want us to get married right away." He spoke so intently. Heatedly. "I want to buy a house. And I want to have kids."

She realized she had to say it right out loud. "Look, you're...moving awfully fast, don't you think? Maybe too fast?"

There. She had said it. Spoken her concern out loud. And she instantly saw that it had done her no good.

He refused to understand. "Fast?" He growled the word. And then he sat up and swung his feet to the floor.

"Travis…" She tried to catch his arm. He only shrugged off her touch as he stood. "Travis, come on…"

He ignored her plea and moved on silent feet to the window. He stared out on the dark side yard, his broad, bare back set against her. "What do you mean fast? I thought we were both agreed about what we wanted, about how it would be."

"Well, I just…" She tried to frame an answer, to explain how his beautiful proposal that afternoon had happened so quickly, given that they'd been lovers for only a couple of days—quickly, and also like something of a manipulation, made right out in public like that, where putting him off would have shamed him.

But she didn't want to go there if she didn't have to. Because it *had* been a great moment. And she *did* want to marry him, to have children with him. It was a wonder and a miracle to her, that she'd finally found what for so long had been only a distant dream to her.

But her frustration was mounting. "You know, the least you can do is look at me when I'm talking to you."

Slowly, he turned and faced her again. "We finally found each other. *Really* found each other. This is our chance. Why can't you see that?" His eyes were shadowed, but he spoke with such passion. Somehow, that gave her hope. They did want the same things. He just wanted everything right now. She was more cautious. She just didn't see why they needed to rush.

Lowering her feet to the rug, she rose to her height. "Oh, Travis, please." She went to him. He watched her approach, his jaw set, his eyes flaring to anger again. She halted a foot away from him. Somehow, it didn't seem safe to get closer. "I know it's our chance. I agree with you. I'm so happy that we're together now."

"Right," he spoke with a clear edge of sarcasm. "So happy you refuse to let me take care of you."

She kept her head high, her voice low and even. "But you can't just ask me to give up all my dreams. To suddenly, overnight, be someone I'm not."

"Someone you're not." He repeated her words, heavy on the irony. "So what you're really telling me is that you don't want to marry me?"

"I never said that. Of course I want to marry you."

"You don't want to have kids, then."

"Yes. Yes, I do. I love you and want to marry you and have kids with you. I also want to go back to college and finish getting my degree—and then find a job that works for me. It's the twenty-first century, Travis. I don't see why I can't do all those things."

"I didn't say you couldn't. I said there had to be priorities."

She took a slow, careful breath. "And your priorities are?"

"I told you. I want to move ahead with our plans. I want to have a baby right away. Maybe your going to college and getting started on that new career will have to take a back seat for a while."

"What you mean is that you want to move ahead with *your* plans and *my* plans will have to wait."

"Marriage and children," he said flatly. "That's my plan. You told me a minute ago that you wanted that, too."

"I do."

He made a low, angry sound. Raising a hand, his bicep flexing powerfully, he raked his fingers back through his hair in a gesture that spoke all too clearly of his exasperation with her.

They'd reached an impasse. She got that. She hadn't spent all her working life dealing with men and finding ways to break through stalemates not to recognize a deadlock when she saw one.

Someone had to give. She very much doubted that that someone would be Travis.

At work, she always tried to figure out the deeper problem in a situation like this, to get down to what was holding the other guy back from working with her and moving forward, and also to admit to whatever her own issues were. Sometimes the root problem would be something as simple as the need to be right.

A man hated to be wrong—well, so did a woman. But for a man, especially, being right seemed keyed into the drive to survive. Men had a basic need to protect others—women and children most of all. And to protect others they had to make the right decisions. They often held on to bad decisions because they couldn't stand to face the simple fact that they'd been wrong in a judgment call, that they hadn't been effective protectors.

Protection.

What had he said a few minutes ago? *I can protect you. I will protect you....*

Yeah, that was the key here. He wanted to protect her. He wanted to make sure that what had happened to Rachel could never happen to her. He *needed* to believe that he *could* protect her against accidents of fate—even though what he needed to believe just wasn't true.

"What?" he demanded. "Why are you looking at me like that?"

Where to even begin? "Travis, I..." He waited, glaring. She made herself continue. "I think that we need to…talk about Rachel."

His face was set against her. "What for? This has nothing to do with Rachel."

"I think it does—or at least, it has to do with what happened to Rachel. And what that did to *you*." She held out her hand. With some reluctance, he took it. "Come on." She pulled him back toward the bed. He went— dragging his feet a little, yeah. But he went. She sat on the edge of the mattress and pulled him down beside her.

He sat with the same lack of enthusiasm he'd shown for giving her his hand. "Okay," he grumbled. "Say it, whatever it is."

She twined her fingers with his. "It wasn't your fault that Rachel died."

"I know that." He shook his head. "I'm not a child, Sam." He spoke more in reproach than in anger. She decided to take that as a good sign.

"Well, all right." She bumped her shoulder against his, squeezed his fingers. "Just checkin'." She slanted him a glance and saw he was looking at her.

His gaze had turned softer. "Sam…" His voice was softer, too. "It's like some miracle, you and me. I never thought I would be willing, you know, to…go there again. To take a chance on losing everything all over again."

"I know. I do remember how much you loved Rachel."

"I couldn't…make it work, with Wanda."

"I know."

His eyes had changed again. They were far away now. "I thought I could. But she just…wasn't Rachel. I would look at her and wonder how I got there with her. I realized too late that she wasn't the one for me. I wanted to prove to myself I was over Rachel. So I asked Wanda to marry me—and then I never really gave her a chance. I drove her away, into that other guy's open arms."

Sam made a low noise in her throat. But she didn't speak. This was, after all, for him to say.

And then he was looking at her again, really *seeing* her. "But with you...it's so good with you. Partly because we were friends for all those years first, I think. You really changed things up during that week with Jonathan. And I finally saw you as a woman. All woman. But you're still Sam, still the same person I've always known. I don't think of Rachel—or of anyone else—when I look at you. I just see...you. You're *all* that I see." He pulled his hand from hers—but only to wrap those gentle fingers around the back of her neck and pull her close for a slow, tender kiss.

When they came up for air, she whispered, "I feel the same about you. Oh, Travis. You're everything to me. I want us to work this out, to find a way that we both get what we want. We can't...do that if you're pushing too hard, if you're trying to make me into someone I'm not."

He pressed his forehead to hers. "I get that. I do."

"You can't...protect me absolutely. There is no such thing as absolute safety. We're *not* safe in life. The best we can do is try to be a little bit wise, and a little bit careful. And brave. We need to be brave."

He rubbed his cheek against hers, his beard stubble creating a slight, lovely friction. "Yes, ma'am."

Had she actually gotten through to him? She did hope so. "So you'll stop...pushing me?"

He cradled her face in his hands. "I just want us to be married."

"Okay. I get that. I want to be married to you, too. But I also plan to go ahead with my education, to get my degree and—"

"You said that. I get it."

Did he? She wasn't sure. She wanted to find a way to pin him down about it.

But another thing she'd learned through all the years of doing a man's job—you didn't beat an issue to death with a man. You could lose whatever ground you might have gained if you kept after him too long. Sometimes you just had to table the discussion and come back to go at it again another day.

It was a process she'd never particularly enjoyed.

"Sam?" He nuzzled her ear, nipped at her earlobe.

Down below, she felt that wonderful, warm weakness. "Yeah?"

"Marry me."

A low laugh escaped her. "Wait a minute, didn't I already say that I would?"

"I mean let's set the date. Let's go for it."

She gulped—and started to feel railroaded again.

But then she stopped herself. It wasn't the wedding that she had a problem with. It wasn't being Travis's wife. She *wanted* to be his wife, she truly did. "You… have a date in mind?"

"December. The third Saturday, I think."

"Uh. December. As in next month? A few weeks away…?"

"That's it," he said softly. Why did that seem like much too soon? She wasn't even sure yet that they had an understanding, that he wouldn't be pressuring her constantly to stay home, to get pregnant ASAP, to give up college and her plans for a new career. He took her chin, guided it around so she looked in his eyes. "I was thinking we could get married here, at Bravo Ridge."

"Here?" she echoed weakly, still trying to get her mind around the enormity of the step they would be taking.

He nodded. "My mom would be thrilled to help in any way she could. She'll make sure the wedding is exactly the way you want it. We could invite the families—yours and mine. And any friends you want to be there and even some of the guys we've worked with over the years, if you want."

She was scared to death. Which probably proved that Travis wasn't the only one with emotional issues here.

Oh, yeah. Definitely. Setting the date was freaking her out.

And yet, well...

What he suggested sounded pretty much perfect. It did. Just the kind of wedding she would want if she was going to have one. Small and comfortable. The family. And a few good friends.

Strange. To think of herself as a bride. But kind of nice, too.

Still, she hesitated to say yes. It didn't feel right to her. And she couldn't decide whether it didn't feel right because he was pushing her again—or if the problem actually was hers.

She'd been on her own for so long, answerable to no one but herself. Being married—even to Travis, even if he backed off on his sudden campaign to make her into his happy little homemaker—well, it was pretty frickin' huge. It really was.

Getting married would change her life even more completely than she'd been planning on changing it.

Was she ready for that?

He spoke again. "You talked about Rachel…."

"Yeah?"

"Well, one thing I always wished I'd done differently…"

"Yeah?"

"I just wish we'd been married, you know, Rachel and me? If it had to happen, if I had to lose her, I wish we had been married first. I wish, just for a day or two, she might have been my wife." He shut his eyes. Made a low, pained sound deep in his throat. "God, I can't believe I said that." He shook his head. "I mean, she died. What the hell did it really matter, whether I ever called her my wife?"

Tenderly, she told him, "It mattered to you, Travis. It mattered a lot."

He blew out a breath and muttered, "Now you'll think I'm a complete wuss."

"Uh-uh. No, I don't think that. Never. I think you're brave and good and…true at heart. That's what I think, Travis Bravo. That's what I *know*."

"Then say yes, Sam," he whispered. "Say yes to you and me."

And when he put it that way, well, her heart melted. When he put it that way, what else could she say but, "Yeah, all right."

He took both her hands in his and he sat back from her a little. His eyes were bright as stars. "Say that again."

She swallowed down the lump in her throat and she said it right out loud. "Let's get married, Travis. Let's do this thing. Let's do it here, at Bravo Ridge. On the third Saturday in December."

Chapter Eleven

Travis kissed her. For a long time.

And then he said, "Tomorrow at dinner we'll tell them all that we've set the date."

"Oh, Travis…" She shook her head.

His gaze grew wary. She saw worry there, that she would find some way to put him off. "Why not?"

"Tomorrow your mom and dad reaffirm their vows."

"So?"

"Well, it should be *their* day, don't you think? I'd rather talk to your mom about it on Friday—and Mercy, too. I mean, it's her house. Shouldn't we ask her if she's up for having our wedding here?"

"There's no need to ask her. She'll be fine with it."

"I just think it's the right thing to do, you know? To talk to your mom and Mercy first."

He looked at her for a long time. Finally, he said, "I have to ask…."

"What?"

"Are you stalling me?"

"No, I'm not. I promise I'm not." She was proud of how open and sincere she sounded. Even though maybe she *was* stalling. Just a little.

But he seemed to believe her. Slowly, he nodded. "All right. But first thing Friday morning, we'll—no. Wait a minute. Friday's the big shopping thing, right? You, Mom, Elena and Mercy will be out of here before dawn."

Black Friday. She'd totally forgotten. "Well, yeah. But we won't be out shopping forever."

"Trust me. I know how Black Friday goes. It will last until three or four in the afternoon. At least."

"So then, we'll talk to your mom and Mercy as soon as we get back."

He held her gaze. "Friday afternoon, then. When you get back here to the ranch…"

"Absolutely."

"I'm holding you to that."

"Travis, come on. I won't let you down."

"Say that again."

"I won't…" Her words trailed off as he laid the pad of a finger against her lips.

"On second thought," he said softly, "don't tell me. Show me."

Davis and Aleta reaffirmed their marriage vows at one in the afternoon on Thanksgiving Day in the big living room there at the ranch, surrounded by their children. And their children's children.

Sam, who never let anyone see her cry, found herself kind of misty-eyed over the whole thing. Davis was handsome and imposing as always, in a fine gray-striped suit, silver-gray silk shirt and blue tie. Aleta looked like a bride again, in a cream-colored silk shirt-dress that flattered her slim figure.

When they shared the kiss that reaffirmed their life-long commitment to each other, Sam wasn't the only with tears in her eyes.

Later, they all sat down at the long table in the dining room to share Thanksgiving dinner.

Aleta said, kind of shyly, "I have written a special grace, just for this special day."

Davis, looking pretty choked up, cleared his throat and said somberly, "Let's bow our heads."

Everyone did, even the little ones.

And Aleta's gentle voice filled the high-ceilinged room. "We thank you, Lord, for this day, for this fine meal laid before us, for all of us, together. For the ties that bind us, the ties that hold us, heart to heart. We are ever grateful for your understanding. And for your patience as we slowly come to learn and accept our own failings—and then overcome them. As we find what really matters in this life—the love we share. The love we give. The love we always find waiting, strong and abiding, when we are so very sure there is no hope. On this day made for thankfulness, we are grateful beyond measure. Thank you. Amen."

"Amen!" crowed little Lucas. "Amen, amen, amen!"

Smiling, lifting their heads again, everyone said it, "Amen."

That night, as soon as they were alone in their rooms, Travis pulled Sam close. "I talked to Mom about the wedding."

The muscles between her shoulder blades jerked

tight, but she was careful to keep her voice neutral. "When was that?"

"I got her alone for a few minutes just now. And I talked to Mercy, too."

"I wondered where you'd gone off to." She eased free of his embrace and went to the windows.

"Sam…" He came to her, put his hands on her shoulders. Warmth spiraled down inside her. She was a total sucker for his lightest touch. He spoke softly, coaxingly. "I told Mom I knew I was out of line to ask her now, that I'd promised you we'd wait until tomorrow so that today could be all about her and dad."

"And she said…?"

"She said what a wonderful woman you are."

Sam made a humphing sound and kept her back to him. "Yeah, right. What else was she going to say?"

"You have to know she was thrilled. Why wouldn't she be? This is what she's been waiting for. The last of her kids, finally making the leap. She said she was so happy for us. And that she'd be glad to help in any way she could. And she meant it. And Mercy told me she was honored that we wanted to have the wedding here. It's getting to be a family tradition. Mercy and Luke got married here, at the ranch. And so did Elena and Rogan."

Sam shook her head and kept her gaze on the distant, silvery moon. "We had an agreement."

"Sam." He turned her to face him. "You're right. I should have waited, like we agreed. I'm sorry, okay?" He looked at her so hopefully. "Forgive me?"

She wanted to stay annoyed at him.

Which was kind of petty, the more she thought about it—petty, and also dishonest. Because she *had* been stalling, even though she kept telling him that she wasn't.

She started thinking about how far they'd come. Friends. To lovers. To so much more.

So okay. She was scared. Of her own insecurities. Of the past that hadn't really let him go.

But holding a grudge because he hadn't kept to the letter of some minor agreement would do neither of them any good.

She went into his waiting arms and rested her head in the crook of his shoulder. "You're forgiven."

"Good." His deep voice rumbled under her ear. He stroked her hair.

It would be all right, she told herself. They would make it work, together, create a good life, the two of them.

She sighed and snuggled closer.

He lifted her chin for a kiss.

The next morning, long before dawn, taking care not to wake her sleeping fiancé, Sam eased back the blankets, slipped her feet to the rug and tiptoed from bed.

She met Mercy, Elena and Aleta downstairs. They drove into San Antonio, to Tessa's house, where the rest of the women of the family were gathered.

In two vehicles, they caravanned to North Star Mall. And they shopped without a single break until well past noon.

It was Sam's very first Black Friday experience. She bought presents for everyone on her Christmas list—which had grown considerably since she'd come to San Antonio. The stores were crowded. It was a total zoo.

Before Jonathan, she never would have lasted an hour

in the hordes of eager, mostly women shoppers. She would have run screaming for the parking lot.

She made a mental note to call Jonathan and thank him. She even bought him a rhinestone-studded set of suspenders at Saks Fifth Avenue and had them gift-wrapped in festive green and red. He would probably hate them. They weren't tasteful in the least.

But she didn't care. She knew that even if he looked down his fashion-forward nose at them, he would love that she had gone out and found them just for him.

At lunch, the talk was all about how Sam and Travis had set the date. Everyone said they'd be there, at the ranch, for the ceremony and the family party after.

They shopped some more.

Sam took a break around two. She wandered out of Dillard's, her arms full of packages, and dropped gratefully onto a sofa in a sitting area next to a Christmas tree. Aleta emerged from the same store a couple of minutes later. Sam called her over and scooted down enough to make a place for her.

They sat together, listening to the endless loop of piped-in Christmas music, watching a couple of toddlers chase each other around the tree, laughing, stumbling, falling—and then picking themselves right up and chasing each other some more.

Aleta was smiling. "Every year I tell myself I really don't need to put myself through the Black Friday experience again. And then every year when Zoe or Mercy or Tessa or Corrine insists I come with them, well, I just can't say no. And this is the first year we've all gone together. I have to say, it's been great."

Sam tipped her head back and took in the giant gold bell tied with a ginormous red bow suspended above their heads. "I have loved every minute of it," she said, and meant it. "Even though I have to tell you. My feet are killing me."

"Oh, honey…" Aleta put her hand over Sam's. "You have no idea." *Honey*. It was what Travis's mom called her own children. And her daughters-in-law. Sam got the total warm-and-fuzzies at that moment. She felt accepted. Loved, even. Aleta really was an amazing person. She had a truly generous heart. She leaned a little closer to Sam. "And speaking of shopping, we must find you your wedding dress soon. There's not a lot of time to waste."

Sam laughed, though deep inside apprehension stirred. "Blame Travis. He wants to get married and get married now."

"And you don't?"

Sam met Aleta's clear blue eyes. "I admit I wanted to wait awhile. It's all happening so fast with us."

The faint lines between Aleta's brows deepened. "But you've known each other for so long."

Sam glanced away. "True."

Aleta squeezed her hand. "And you seem so happy together."

"We are. It's just…oh, I don't know…."

"Did you want a big wedding? So many girls do. If you do, we can—"

Sam groaned. "Oh, please God. No."

"You just feel…rushed?"

"A little. I…" Sam let her voice trail off. She knew she never should have started this conversation.

There was just too much that Travis's sweet mom didn't know for Aleta to be able to understand Sam's doubts and concerns. Maybe someday, Sam would tell Aleta everything. About the Sam she had been, the Sam she'd suddenly become with the help of Travis's trust

fund and her own personal fairy godmother. About the
fake engagement that had magically become real. About
Travis and his need to make her his wife, now, immediately, the way he hadn't done with Rachel. But today,
at the mall, in the middle of the Black Friday shop-a-
thon? Uh-uh. Not the right time.

Plus, well, it seemed disloyal to Travis, to tell
Aleta that they'd pretended to be engaged because she
wouldn't stop throwing women at him. She needed Travis's go-ahead to get into that.

And was any of it information Aleta actually needed?
No. What mattered to her was that Sam and Travis were
together, that her prodigal son had come home at last.

Aleta made a worried sound. "It's a big step, getting
married. And it's not unheard-of for a bride to have
some misgivings. But if you really feel it's too soon…"

"No." She put on a bright smile. "I want to marry
Travis. So much. I honestly do."

"But honey, you said you feel rushed."

"Only a little."

"You're sure?"

"I am positive." She said it so firmly that she almost
believed it. "This wedding—at the ranch, with you and
the whole family there—it's just the kind of wedding
I've always dreamed of."

"You can talk to me. I want you to know that. Any
time you need a sounding board, or just someone to listen."

"Thanks, Aleta. I'll remember that."

Aleta shifted beside her, bending to pull her packages closer at her feet. "Will you invite your mother to
your wedding?"

"I was thinking I would, yeah. And my stepfather. And
my wicked half sisters, too." Not that they would come.

Aleta was chuckling. "Oh, your sisters are wicked, are they?"

"Not really. But..."

"What? Tell me."

Sam sighed. "They are a couple of snobby little twits."

"Twits, huh?"

"Well, they're a lot younger than me. And we never really got along. They're twins, did I mention that?"

"You did, yes. That first day you arrived."

"Dina and Mila. They're fifteen now. I haven't seen them in a couple of years." The last time had not been fun. The two had whispered about her behind their tiny little hands and giggled every time she entered a room where they happened to be.

"I'm glad you're inviting them," Aleta said. "And your father...?"

"Well, I've been meaning to warn you about him."

Aleta faked a look of alarm. "I need a warning?"

"He's a crusty old guy. And his girlfriend, Keisha, is younger than I am. They live in a Winnebago. So the Winnebago would be coming to the wedding, too."

"The Winnebago is welcome."

"Well, I'm just saying. My family is a little odd."

"If they're *your* family, they're *our* family."

Sam shook her head. "I think you should wait until you meet them to make that call."

Sam phoned her mom the next morning.

"Samantha, how wonderful," Jennifer Early Jaworski Carlson said when she heard the news. "Of course I will be there. And Walt and your sisters would love to come, too."

"Uh. Well, great, Mom." Sam felt slightly shell-

shocked. She'd never for a second expected her mom
to say yes. Let alone announce she was bringing Walt
and the Terrible Twins. "Have you got a pencil?"

"Right here." Her mom repeated the date that Sam
had already mentioned.

"That's it." Sam gave her the address and phone number of the ranch. "And Mercy—that's Travis's sister-in-
law—has said you're welcome to stay here, at Bravo
Ridge, if that works for you."

"How kind of her. I'll talk to Walt. See if he wants
to drive down, or if we'll fly—and I'll call within the
next couple of days and let you know if we'll be taking
your fiancé's sister-in-law up on her thoughtful invitation."

"Well, okay. Great. Terrific, then."

"*You're* getting married," said her mother wonderingly. As if she'd never in million years thought *that*
would happen. Sam tried not to feel defensive. But her
mom had a habit of giving her grief about how she
needed to dress up now then, how it wouldn't hurt to
be just a little bit feminine. How a man appreciated a
woman who *acted* like a woman. Around her mother
and her mother's family, Sam had always felt like a
freak—and an oversize one at that. "What about your
dress? I'll help you with that. Come on up to Minneapolis and I'll take you shopping."

"Thanks, Mom, but I've got it handled."

"You're *certain?*" Her mom's complete lack of faith
in Sam's ability to choose her own wedding dress was
not the least flattering—even if, until Jonathan, her
mom would have been right.

"I'm positive. I'll find my own dress." Sam made a
few more polite noises and said goodbye as fast as she
could after that.

Travis, fresh from the shower, wearing only a pair of snug faded jeans and looking like an invitation to sin, appeared in the door to the blue bedroom. "Your mom?" At her nod, he grinned. "You should see your face."

She blinked and shook her head. "They're coming to the wedding. All four of them."

"Good for them."

"Hah. Easy for you to say. Wait until you meet them. They're everything I've ever told you they were. And more—or should I say *less?* They're all so tiny and disgustingly cute." Her mom was five-one and so very dainty. The twins took after her. Walt was taller, but not by a whole lot.

"Bring 'em on." Travis entered the room and came toward her in long purposeful strides. When he reached the bed where she sat, he dropped down beside her. He laid his hand on her thigh.

It felt good there. Too good. She gave him a rueful glance and warned, "Your mom and Mercy and Elena and I are going shopping in half an hour."

His warm fingers stayed right where they were. "You shopped all day yesterday."

"That was Black Friday."

"So? Shopping is shopping."

"Spoken like a man."

He leaned close enough to nibble on her ear. "A man starved for his woman's undivided attention."

She picked up that tempting hand of his and put it down on *his* thigh. "I'm sorry. I have to go. Yesterday we bought mostly Christmas presents. Today we're doing wedding stuff. Mainly we'll be looking for my wedding dress. And we're visiting a florist and bakery to talk flowers and cake."

He put his hand back on her leg and bent close a second time to nuzzle her neck. "I can be fast when I need to be. This won't take long at all."

The warmth of his breath, the damp scent of his hair, still wet from the shower, the just-shaved feel of his cheek against hers…they all conspired to make her weaken. And yearn. She really couldn't get enough of him. "I still have to, um, call my dad…"

"Like I said. I'll make this quick." He went right to work, sliding his hand up into the cove of her thighs, cupping her over her jeans.

Sighing in surrender, she eased her thighs apart. "Not *too* quick."

He unzipped her zipper, undid the snap. "Quick, but not too quick. Coming right up."

"Oh, Travis…" She let him guide her back across the bed.

And for a little while, she forgot all about her mom and her stepdad and the Terrible Twins, about the wedding that was going to be upon them in a few too-short weeks. She forgot her fears and her doubts and her insecurities.

There was just the two of them, her and Travis, alone, making beautiful, perfect, just-right love.

Twenty minutes later, she called her dad.

Ted Jaworski's response was laughter. Sam's dad was six-foot-ten and barrel-chested. He had arms like tree trunks. And when he laughed it could make the floor shake. "Travis?" He sucked in a breath and laughed some more. "You're marryin' *Travis?*"

Sam gritted her teeth. "Yeah, Dad. And you and Keisha are invited."

"That rich boy take advantage of my little girl?"

Sam loved her dad, but he could really annoy her without half trying. "Travis is not a boy. And I am not the least bit little."

Ted gave another of those ground-shaking laughs. "You know what I told him when he first showed up and started sniffin' around you."

"Oh, come on, Dad. Travis is not some hound dog. He never *sniffed* around me. Never."

"Maybe you didn't think so. But a father notices that kind of thing—and anyway, you haven't let me tell you what I told him."

As if she wanted to know. "Dad—"

"I said, 'Travis Bravo, you lay a hand on my little girl and I'll take it off with a hacksaw.'" Ted laughed some more.

She waited for him to wind down a little before remarking, "You know, Dad, I could have gone my whole life without knowing that."

"I don't believe it. You and Travis. Gettin' hitched. What do you know?"

"That's right. Travis and I are getting married. The question is, are you and Keisha coming?"

"We wouldn't miss it, baby girl. It's out at that big Bravo spread down there in Texas, right?"

"That's right."

"Lots of open land. And in Texas, they don't have all that many stupid laws against fireworks...."

"Dad. Listen. I mean it. No."

"Did I ask you a question? I don't think I asked you any question."

"No fireworks, Dad. Do you hear me?"

If he did hear, he refused to admit it. "We're comin'," he announced. "With bells on. You count on it, baby. I'll be there to give my little girl away."

* * *

Sam found her dress that day. It was snow-white satin, with a halter top that bared most of her back. She also chose the flowers she wanted in her bouquet, in blue and purple, with touches of white. She and Aleta agreed her colors were purple and blue, with silver and white for accents.

"Perfect for a holiday wedding," Aleta declared.

Sam's head was spinning by the time they got to the bakery. There were as many options when it came to a cake as there were for wedding dresses and bridal bouquets. She met with the bakery's wedding consultant and couldn't decide.

Which was fine, as it turned out, because Travis was supposed to get input on the cake. The cake lady suggested that Sam and her groom return to the bakery on Monday and make their choice.

Monday. The make-believe week of playing Travis's bride was supposed to be over Sunday. Travis had planned to return to Houston. Sam had a plane ticket for San Diego.

But then make-believe had somehow become reality.

She turned numbly to Aleta, who sat beside her. "We're supposed to leave Sunday...."

Aleta gave her a fond smile. "It's all workable, don't worry." She told the cake lady, "We'll call you early in the week and get everything settled."

"It's simple," Travis said that night when they were alone in their rooms. "I'll stay an extra day. I'll go to Houston on Tuesday. Worst case, I'll need up to a couple of weeks to wrap things up with STOI."

They were sitting on the bed together. She dropped

back across the mattress, face up. "So you're doing it? Going to work for BravoCorp?"

He stretched out on his side next to her. "Yeah. Is that okay with you?"

"Of course." She stared past him, at the milk-glass ceiling fixture mounted on a plaster medallion above. "If it's what you really want."

"It is." He sounded absolutely certain.

She could use a little more of that, of certainty—not about Travis. She had no doubt that he was the one for her. But about everything else, she wasn't so sure. All day, as she shopped for her wedding dress and chose her bouquet and listened to the cake lady go on about ganache and fondant and raspberry fillings, she'd felt kind of wispy and fragile, two words she'd never before even considered in connection with herself. She asked in a voice that sounded distant to her own ears, "So we'll be looking for a house in San Antonio?"

He touched her shoulder. "Sam, are you okay?"

She turned her head toward him, gave him a smile that only wobbled a little. "So much is happening. I'm a little dazed, I guess. I've still got my ticket to San Diego for Sunday."

Sunday, when it was all supposed to have been over. When her sweet fantasy of loving Travis—of having him want to spend his life with her—would be only a memory. When her magic carriage turned into a pumpkin and her ball gown into rags.

Except now, it wasn't going to be over. Now, she really was Travis's true love.

And they were getting married in two and a half weeks.

"Cancel it," he said.

She blinked, refocused on his dear face. The plane

ticket. They were talking about her flight to California. "Guess I'll have to." She folded her hands on her stomach.

He rested his hand on hers. "You can stay here for as long as you and Mom need to do all the wedding stuff. Then you can fly to Houston, stay with me at the town house. We should be back here by a week before the wedding, I'm hoping. As soon as we get here, we can start looking for a house."

She thought of her place in San Diego, her own private retreat from the world. Would he ask her to give that up? He just might. She had to be ready for that.

The wispy, fragile feelings faded. She was instantly stronger, more like her old self.

No. Not a chance.

She wouldn't give up her San Diego apartment. No way. "I want to keep my condo in San Diego."

He bent close, kissed her. "No problem." He said it easily, without the least hesitation.

Well, good. That wouldn't be an issue, then. And the more she thought about San Diego, the more she wished she could steal a little time there—to get her bearings. To decompress. "In fact, maybe I'll fly to California while you're in Houston. I can spend a couple of days packing up the things I want to bring with me to our new house here." Yeah, it was a great idea. She could catch her breath there for a day or two, get a break from the big rush to the altar.

His eyes held hers.

And she knew then. Absolutely.

He was going to try to stop her from going to her place. And she wasn't allowing that. She couldn't allow that.

And that meant they were going to end up arguing.

He said, "Every night you're not in my bed is one night too many away from you."

Oh, yeah. She knew what he would say next. He was going to tell her that he wanted her to come straight to Houston, that he wanted her with him, not off on the beach in California.

Sam braced herself to make a stand.

Chapter Twelve

And then Travis said, "But sure. Fly to San Diego. Pack up what you want to bring. Ship it here and store it, or have it shipped once we get our house."

She gulped. She couldn't believe it. She'd been ready for a fight. And there wasn't going to be one—not about this anyway. "Uh. Sure. All right. I'll do that."

His eyes were gleaming. He seemed so happy, making plans—for their future. "And I thought we could save the honeymoon until after the holidays. Then maybe we'll go someplace in January or February, someplace tropical, with blue lagoons and palm trees...."

That did sound kind of nice. But where was the catch?

Wait a minute.

Maybe there was no catch. Maybe she ought to stop looking for problems where there really weren't any.

"I would like that," she said, meaning it. And then, well, why hold back? They needed to revisit the issue of her career plans. Now was as good a time as any. "I'm thinking I can take online courses over the winter. And in the spring, I'll see about getting into the college of business at UT San Antonio for the fall semester."

He bent close again. "Still determined to get that degree and become an accountant, huh?"

She looked at him levelly, though her heart had kicked into overdrive as her adrenaline was suddenly surging. "Yes, I am. Any objections?"

"Hell, no. You've got a dream and you have a right to make it real."

She tried not to stare openmouthed as the surge faded off, leaving her feeling slightly hollow and more than a little ashamed of jumping to yet another conclusion.

She reached up, touched his beloved face, dared to ask, "What about how I need to get pregnant and stay home where you can protect me?"

He gave her a wry grin. "Well, I thought about that. And I decided you were right. About all of it. I hate that I can't protect you from anything that might ever happen to you. But that's how it is. What I *can* do is everything in my power to see that you're happy. I want you to have what you want—everything you want."

She searched his face, hardly able to believe that he had come so far on this big issue—so far and so fast. She should probably quit while she was ahead. But then she heard herself asking, "And a baby...?"

He kissed her nose. "I rethought that a little, too. I was thinking, if we could start trying in, say, a year? That would give us some time just for us."

"Oh, Travis..." She wrapped her hand around the

back of his neck and brought him closer to her. "A year would be workable. I could go for a year."

He looked pretty pleased with himself. "See? I can take a hint."

"You can. And you did. You amaze me sometimes."

"Good. A man needs to be amazing. At least now and then."

She laughed and then she kissed him. And then she whispered, "Time for us. We need that."

"Yeah, we do." He kissed her cheek, her nose again, the other cheek.

She bit her lower lip, as the enormity of it all flooded over her again. "And even given that we're waiting a year before we start trying, well…a baby. And a college degree. And a new career. It's a lot."

"I would help." He kissed the space between her brows. "And with me working for BravoCorp, the money will be no issue. We can hire quality childcare to give you a break, and someone dependable to cook and clean."

"When you put it like that, it all seems possible."

"It *is* possible, Sam. With you and me, together, there's nothing we can't do."

Monday, as planned, they went to the bakery and chose a dark chocolate cake with chocolate ganache and mocha buttercream filling. The icing would be white buttercream with pearled borders. Real orchids, purple ones, would cover the top layer and cascade down over the two lower tiers.

Tuesday morning early, she drove him to the airport and he caught a flight to Houston. He left his Cadillac for her to use.

Travis called that night. They talked for hours. And

when they finally said goodbye, the silence that followed left her yearning and empty and longing to call him all over again, just to hear his voice.

That made her feel weak and needy, which were two things Sam Jaworski was not and had never been. Until now.

He wasn't all that far away and they'd be back together soon.

Still, she missed him. So much.

It was scary, really. To feel that way. To ache all over just for a certain man's tender touch. For the sound of his voice, the brush of his lips against hers.

She'd spent a lot of her life wishing she might feel just this way. And now that she did, well, it was magic.

And it was awful, too. Fearsome and huge and more than she'd bargained for.

She slept in the bed in the blue room where they'd spent most of their nights during Thanksgiving week. It made her feel closer to him.

He called Wednesday night, too. He said it looked like he would be back in San Antonio by the middle of the following week. STOI was sorry to see him go. They'd even offered a nice promotion and a generous raise and benefits package if he would stay on. He'd thanked them and turned them down. And since the *Deepwater Venture* project had wrapped up, he was at an ending point anyway. It wasn't all that complicated to wind things down.

He asked how all the wedding preparations were going.

Sam laughed. "Your mother's a marvel."

"So I'm guessing that means it's going well?"

"Better than well. There's really nothing for me to do."

A silence on the line, then, "You okay with that?"

She laughed. "Are you kidding? I'm thrilled with that."

"Well, if you feel like she's taking over…"

"No way. Your mom's not like that."

He grunted, a disbelieving sound. "Come on, she does have a bossy side. You know she does."

"Not with me. With me, she's…" Her throat locked up and her eyes got misty. Sheesh. She was getting to be a frickin' emotional disaster lately, she truly was.

"Sam? Still there?"

She made herself answer around the lump in her throat. "Right here."

"You all right? You seem kind of—"

"I'm great." She said it with feeling—maybe more feeling than necessary. "And I love your mom. She's the best. Don't you say a word against her or you'll be answering to me."

"Whoa. Next you'll be saying how you can take me."

"Yeah, well." She put on her best macho bluster. "You know I can."

He chuckled then. It was a very sexy sound. "Anytime. I'll be looking forward to it."

"You're so easy."

"Only for you."

She suggested, "And listen, on the night before the wedding?"

"What about it?"

Her cheeks felt too warm. She knew she was blushing, which was silly. "I was thinking we could sleep in separate rooms. You know, be a little bit traditional. Is that dumb, do you think?"

"However you want it, Sam. That's how it'll be."

"Well, I want that, for you not to see me on our wedding day until I walk down the aisle to you. I don't know why I want it exactly. But I do."

"You got it."

They talked some more, about the wedding, about the house they would be looking for, about how soon they would be together again.

After she hung up, she had that too-familiar burning need. To call him back. To hear his voice...

Really. What she *needed* was to get a grip.

Her mom called on Thursday. Yes, she and Walt and the twins would *love* to stay at the ranch for the wedding. "We don't mind roughing it a bit for your big day."

Sam laughed. "Well, don't worry, Mom. You won't have to rough it at all. The ranch house is more of a mansion really. It's surrounded by beautiful gardens. There's a big pool with a fountain and wading pool and spa. And there are tennis courts..."

"Oh. Well." Her mom sounded stunned. "All right, then. It sounds very nice. We'll arrive on Friday morning, stay over for the wedding Saturday afternoon. And return home Sunday afternoon."

"I'll tell Mercy. She'll be pleased."

"And honestly. I should do *something,* Samantha. I want to help out. After all, I *am* the mother of the bride."

"Mom. It's fine. You don't have to. It's a very small wedding and Aleta—Travis's mom—she's taking care of everything."

There was a silence, followed by a small, pitiful sniffling sound.

Oh, no. "Mom? Mom, are you crying?"

Her mother sobbed outright. "I never thought you would get married. Not to a man anyway. I never even thought you *liked* men...."

Terrific. A sexual orientation talk with the mother

she hardly knew. Not. Going. To. Happen. "Mom. Come on, Mom, don't cry…"

"I'm sorry. I'm so sorry…" There was more sobbing. The sobs had that scary sound. The sound that said she was never going to stop.

"Mom. Hey. It's okay. There's nothing to be sorry about."

"We never did get along. I never…understood you." Her mother hiccupped and then sobbed again. "Hold on, I need a tissue…."

"Mom. Really. We don't need to…" She heard a delicate, distant honking sound. Her mother blowing her nose.

And then she was back on the line again. "You're so…big, Samantha." A tight sob. Another honk at the tissue. "You're just like your father. Big and strong and loud and overbearing. You always make me feel so small. So…insignificant."

"Uh, well. Gee, thanks."

Her mother let out a small, sad little wail. "Oh, now I've gone and put my foot in it. Now you'll hate me even more than ever."

"Mom, I don't hate you."

"You do. You know you do. You always did. Your father turned you against me on the day you were born…."

"Mom, come on. Don't go there. Please?"

Her mom went right on as though Sam hadn't spoken. "And we never bonded and now you're getting married and you don't want me to be involved in any part of it."

"Mom, hold on. I invited you, didn't I?"

"I'm sure you felt you had to."

Okay. Too true for comfort. "Look, um…" Good frickin' gravy. What to say next? "You really want to be involved?"

"Oh, didn't I just *say* that? See, that's another thing. You never listen to me when I speak. Just like your—"

"Mom, I'm going to hook you up with Aleta, okay?"

"A-Aleta?" Sniffle. Honk. "Your fiancé's mother?"

Please don't hate me for this, Aleta. "Yeah, Travis's mom. She will call you. Today. She'll…get with you."

"G-get with me?"

"Yeah, you know, consult with you. Get your input and assistance on what has to be done. I know she'll be so happy to have help." *Oh, I am a stone liar and I am going straight to hell.*

"She will?"

"Of course." Like there was anything left to do. Like there was anything her mom could do anyway up there in Minneapolis. "And to…get to know you. She's real big on family, Aleta is."

"She is?"

"Yeah. Real big." Well, at least that part was true. "Are you going to be home for a while?"

"I…well, yes. I'm at home. The twins are at school. Walt is at the office. I'm just thinking of what to put together for dinner."

"All right. I'll have Aleta call you."

"But when?"

"Right away."

"In a few minutes?"

"Aleta's not here right now. But as soon as I see her and give her your number. Within the next couple of hours."

"Oh, Samantha. I don't want to butt in."

Oh, yes, you do. "It's fine, Mom. It's good. She'll call. Within the hour."

"All—all right. All right, Samantha. I…well, I love you, you know?"

"I love you, too, Mom," Sam said because that's what you say when your mom says she loves you. And then, finally, she managed to say goodbye.

The minute she hung up, she knew she should call her mom right back and bust to the truth that Aleta didn't need anyone's help, that everything was pretty much done and her mom should just come to the wedding and leave it at that.

But if she called her mom back, there would be more crying.

Sam couldn't stand that. She felt like crying herself half the time lately. She just might crack if she had to listen to one more of her mother's sad little sobs.

Yeah, it was wrong to drag Aleta into this. But then again, if anyone could make the situation better, it would be Aleta.

Unfortunately, Aleta and Davis had gone back to their own house in a ritzy San Antonio neighborhood the day before. It was bad enough to ask this of Travis's mom. She couldn't do it over the phone.

She called Aleta, but only to make sure she was home.

Travis's mom answered on the first ring. Sam wanted to burst into tears then, just at the warm sound of Aleta's voice.

She held it together. "Hey, it's Sam. I was wondering if I could come by now for a few minutes?"

Aleta said, "Of course."

A half an hour later, Sam was sitting next to Travis's mom on a sofa in the sun room of Aleta's beautiful Olmos Park house, a delicate china cup filled with coffee in her hands and a plate of sugared pecan cookies on the low table in front of them.

Sam groaned. "I don't even know how to ask you this."

Aleta sipped from her china cup. "Anything. I hope you know that."

Sam set her cup and saucer down before she dropped them. She wanted to lean on Travis's mom, just put her head on the smaller woman's slender shoulder. "I've done a bad, bad thing."

Aleta set her cup and saucer next to Sam's. And then she did exactly what Sam had longed for her to do. She put an arm around Sam and drew her closer. "Tell me. We'll fix it. Together."

Sam let her shoulders slump. "It's my mother. There's no fixing my mother…."

"Oh, no. She's not able to come to the wedding after all?"

"No, it's not that. She's coming. But she's hurt because I didn't include her in the planning part. She wants to help. And I…I'm so sorry, Aleta. I didn't know what to do, so I told her you might have something she could do and I would have you call her."

Aleta smiled. A *real* smile. "Perfect."

Sam hung her head and made a low sound of pure misery. "You say that now, but wait until you talk to her. She will drive you insane. And it's not like you even need her help."

"But, honey, *she* needs to help, to be involved. You can see that, can't you?"

Sam grunted. Even if it was unfeminine. "Yeah. I suppose so."

"And it's great. Because this way she and I will get to know each other a little. And she'll be a part of the wedding. And she'll feel better about everything."

"You make it sound so…simple and clear."

"But it's not—not to you, and probably not to your mom. I understand that. My mother is gone now. But she and I…we had our issues, believe me. It's the first love, between a mother and her child. Sometimes it's a very painful love."

"Oh, Aleta. She said that I hate her. I *don't*."

"I know. You told me. That first day you and Travis arrived at the ranch, remember?"

"I just… I never really thought that she even cared. But I guess she did."

Aleta touched Sam's hair, a light, fond touch—there and then gone. "That's important. For you to know that."

"So why doesn't it make me feel any better? I just feel…confused." And about a lot more than just her mother, if the truth were told.

"Big changes are stressful. Even good changes. It will be fine. You'll see."

Sam took Aleta's soft, beautifully manicured hand. "Thank you. Thank you from the bottom of my heart."

"You are more than welcome. And you are not to worry. Your mom and I will get together and talk and she'll choose the things she wants to do. Maybe the dinner menu—or any of the wedding weekend meals. There will be several. We haven't firmed those up yet. What does she enjoy doing?"

"Um, knitting. Sewing. Scrapbooking. Baking. She loves to make those novelty cakes. Cakes shaped like guitars, a bunch of cupcakes arranged to look like a bear or a giraffe or a giant flower…." She'd made Sam an oil derrick birthday cake once, with chocolate syrup for crude oil. That had been the weekend when the twins snickered every time she got near them.

Aleta squeezed her shoulder. "See? There are lots of possibilities for her to choose from. This is wonderful."

"Oh, Aleta. You say that now…."

"I say it because it's true. She loves you and she wants to help and that's what matters."

"You're right. You're absolutely right."

Aleta picked up the plate of cookies. "Now have a cookie and let me have your mother's number. I'll give her a call."

Aleta really was a wonder. She got Sam's mom working on some special surprise. Evidently, her mom was pleased with whatever it was she had in the works. She called Sam later that night and said what a sweet woman Aleta was and how she and Walt and the twins were really looking forward to their Texas visit, to meeting Travis and his family and being there for Samantha's special day.

Disaster averted, thanks to Aleta.

Friday, Aleta came out to the ranch and they discussed the wedding dinner.

After two hours of talking about menus and place cards and centerpieces, Sam crossed her eyes and pretended to fall against the couch cushions in a dead faint. "Any more wedding talk and I swear it will be the end of me."

Aleta laughed. "Well, that's fine because we're good to go. I have what I need from you and you don't have to hear the word *wedding* for at least the next week."

"Hah. Can I get that in writing?"

Aleta sent her sly glance. "Well, there may be an occasional *mention* of flowers or table arrangements…"

"See? I knew you didn't really mean it." Sam sat up straight. "But if we are pretty much on top of things, I was planning to take a few days at my place in San Diego before I meet Travis in Houston…."

"Well, then, go."

"You're sure?"

"I'm adamant. Go."

The next morning, Sam flew to San Diego International.

She was at her beach condo by noon—well, okay, her *near*-the-beach condo. From her living room window, if she squinted, it was just possible to see a tiny slice of the blue Pacific between a pair of luxury high-rises.

The beach wasn't far away, however. She could get there on foot from her front door. That afternoon she walked barefoot along the shore for over two hours. Then she went back to the condo and started packing. Travis called at seven. They talked until ten.

The next day, she walked for three hours and had the rest of her packing done by dark. She poured a glass of wine and went out onto her tiny balcony—and wished she was in Houston, with Travis at the town house.

She'd had some vague idea that being at her place, on her own, by the beach, would clear away the wispy, wimpy feelings, make her more like herself again.

But it didn't. Not really. Being alone only made her ache all the harder for Travis, made her feel itchy and uncomfortable in her own skin.

When he called an hour later, she told him she would be there, with him, the next day.

He met her at the airport, by the baggage carousel. She ran to his arms and kissed him until she felt like her lips might fall off. It was a serious get-a-room kiss. And when they finally stepped apart, both gasping for air, he grabbed her suitcase in one hand and her arm in the other and hustled her out to where he had a limo waiting.

They went straight to his place, where they fell into bed together and didn't get up until dinnertime.

The next day was Tuesday. He went off for his last day at STOI. His town house was stacked with boxes. He'd been working hard, getting himself packed for the move to San Antonio.

She spent the day filling more boxes with his things. And she spent the night in his arms.

They flew back to San Antonio the next day and headed for the ranch, where they would be staying until they got their own place. Thursday, they started looking for a house—which they found on Friday. They made an offer that afternoon.

By Monday, after a couple of counteroffers, they signed the contract. They would be moving in the first week in January.

When they left the Realtor's office, Travis kissed her and headed off to BravoCorp for his first day in the family business. Sam watched him walk away from her and wished she had a job to go to.

She went back to the ranch and got on the internet and signed up for three online accounting classes that would start in the second week of January. That should keep her busy—or it would when January finally rolled around.

Getting that edgy-under-the-skin feeling, she wrapped the presents she'd bought on Black Friday. Once the wrapping was done, she carried all the ones for the Bravos down to put under the giant tree that Mercy and Aleta had put up in the living room. On one of the lower branches, she also hung the Betty Boop ornament she'd bought that day in Fredericksburg.

Mercy gave her some priority-mail boxes and she put the presents that had to be mailed in those, and addressed them. Most were for her mom and her mom's family. There was also one for Ted and one for Keisha. She sent that to the P.O. box they kept in Tucson. And finally, there were the suspenders for Jonathan. She slipped a note in the box, inviting him to the wedding.

No, she didn't really expect him to come. But still. It seemed only right that he should be there if he could make it.

Mercy, a large animal vet, was going through nearby Kerrville on her way to treat some farmer's sick goat. She took Sam's packages to mail.

After Mercy left, Sam put on jeans and some old work boots she'd brought back from her condo and went out to the stables. Once she convinced Luke that she really wanted to pitch in, he put her to work mucking out stalls. Just like old times, back on the ranch in South Dakota. She broke a nail in the process.

Jonathan would not have approved.

For the rest of the week, she spent a few hours in the stables every day. Luke seemed happy to have her help and she got along with the hands just fine. It was better—*she* was better—when she kept busy.

That last week before the wedding, which seemed to drag by in some respects, was gone in an instant.

Her dad and Keisha arrived Thursday evening. They rolled up in the Winnebago at a little before dinnertime. She'd been watching for them and ran out to greet them.

Her dad emerged, wearing Wranglers, rawhide boots, a straw cowboy hat and a plaid Western shirt, his belly hanging over his belt buckle, his laugh booming out. "There's my baby girl…"

"Dad!" She ran to him. Still laughing, he enfolded her in his beefy arms. He smelled of the cheap cigarettes he wouldn't stop smoking and his laughter seemed to shake the world.

When he stopped squeezing the breath out of her, he took her arms and held her away from him. "Will you look at you?" He let out a long, piercing wolf whistle. "Hotter'n a firecracker. It's a whole new Sam."

She smiled up at him. "Dad, glad you could make it."

Travis was right behind her. "Ted, how you been?"

Her dad reached for Travis's hand. "Been messin' with my baby, have you? Didn't I warn you about that?"

Travis laughed. He'd always liked her dad and had never been the least put off by the loud laugh and booming voice—let alone the towering size. "What can I say? Guilty. And really, really happy about it."

"Well, as long as you're marryin' her, I guess I'll have to let you live."

Sam caught sight of Keisha then. Her dad's girlfriend was just stepping down from the motor home. As usual, she had her red hair in tight cornrows. She wore a long, baggy dress with a bulky gray sweater that looked like she'd stolen it from some absentminded professor, suede elbow patches and all.

Keisha smiled wide, showing the cute gap between her two front teeth. "Sam! Hey! Wow! Look at you! You are lookin' *good!*" Somehow, everything Keisha said sounded like it had an exclamation point after it. She was the most enthusiastic person Sam had ever known.

"Hey, Keisha. Thanks. It's good to see you." Even with the baggy dress and sweater, Sam could see that Keisha's belly was bigger than Ted's. She went and gave Keisha a hug, felt the bulge of the younger woman's stomach pressing into hers.

Yep. Definitely. Her dad's girlfriend was pregnant.

Her dad was laughing again. "Surprise! You're getting a little brother or sister, baby girl. Me and Keisha are expecting the first week in March."

"I *know* he's brought fireworks," Sam said between clenched teeth later that night, when she and Travis were alone.

Travis sat next to her on the bed checking his investments on his laptop. "You know your dad. One of a kind."

She elbowed him in the ribs. Hard. "When he sets them off in the middle of the night and then burns down the stables sneaking a smoke, you won't be so thrilled with his rugged individualism—and what was he thinking? He's almost sixty. He smokes too much. They live in a frickin' motor home. And, true, Keisha's about the nicest, happiest person on the planet, but she's never seemed much like the motherly type."

"She's a good woman. She'll manage. And maybe they're planning on settling down."

"Yeah. Right. When porcupines get Visa cards."

Travis laughed and put his laptop on the night table. Then he hauled her close and kissed her until she almost forgot that her dad and his girlfriend would soon be giving her another half sibling young enough to be her own child.

When he lifted his mouth from hers, she gained several IQ points and remembered all the things that were bothering her. "And tomorrow, my mother and *her* family are coming."

He took both her wrists and pinned them to the bed beside her head. "It's terrific that they're coming."

"The twins will be following me from room to room, snickering behind their hands."

"No, they won't."

"Yes, they will. Secretly, they've always believed I was really a man."

"But I'll be there. To attest to your womanhood with a wide, happy and very satisfied grin on my face."

"Don't you dare."

"Sam. Relax, will you? You're way too tense about everything."

"I am. It's true. I'm a nervous wreck. Me. Sam Jaworski. Who could arm wrestle half the roughnecks on the *Deepwater Venture* and win two out of three. What's happening to me?"

He bent close, nipped her earlobe. "You're getting married."

"Yeah. Whoever thought *that* would happen? Not my family, that's for sure."

He grazed her chin with his teeth. "Let me take your mind off your problems...." He kissed her breast right through her silk shirt and lacy bra.

She moaned and tried to pull free of his grip. "Let go of my wrists, will you?"

"Not until you promise you won't say another word all night about your dad or your mom or anyone in your family." He kissed her other breast.

For a long time.

Finally, sighing, she whispered, "My family? What family?"

"That's the spirit."

But he still didn't let go of her wrists. Not for several minutes. Not until she was enthusiastically begging him for more.

The Carlsons arrived at ten-thirty the next morning.

At her first sight of the new Sam, Dina said, "Huh? Puh-lease. No way."

Mila didn't say anything that Sam could hear. But she did whisper something behind her hand.

Their mother burst into tears. "Oh, Samantha. You're beautiful. Oh, Samantha. I never knew...."

Walt, looking slightly befuddled as always behind the heavy black frames of his glasses, said, "Ahem, well. Samantha. What a nice surprise." Sam wasn't sure if he meant the changes in her—or that she'd finally found someone willing to marry her.

Sam introduced them to Travis. He said how happy he was to meet them at last. He actually seemed to mean it. He shook Walt's hand, kissed her mother on the cheek and gave each of the Terrible Twins a warm and welcoming smile. Really, he was a prince in the truest sense of the word.

Her mother, so tiny and delicate in a pink suit and ruffled lilac-colored blouse, stared up at him, wet-eyed. "Well, I am so pleased to meet you, too, Travis. I can't tell you *how* pleased..."

Paco and one of the other hands were there, ready to help.

Travis said, "Paco and Bobby will take your bags inside."

"Oh!" Her mother gave him a trembling smile of over-the-top gratitude. "Thank you so much, Travis. Yes."

And then Ted appeared, smoking a cigarette, bearing down on them from the driveway that led to the garage and the space beside it where he had parked the Winnebago. Keisha waddled along in his wake.

Sam's mother watched them approach, a look of absolute horror on her fine-boned face. "I see your father has already arrived," she said weakly. "And he still hasn't stopped smoking." Was she going to faint, right there in the driveway? She'd damn well better not.

"That's right," Travis said cheerfully, as if everyone's mother got the vapors like some anemic heroine from a Victorian novel—as if everyone's dad had a pregnant girlfriend less than half his age. "He and Keisha got here yesterday."

"Ah. Yes," Jennifer said feebly. "Keisha. Of course."

The twins snickered and whispered to each other as their mother kind of sagged against Walt, who put his arm around her and pushed his glasses back up the bridge of his nose.

Ted descended on them. He dropped his cigarette and stomped it with his big boot. "Well, if it isn't Jennifer and Walt and their two gorgeous girls."

Keisha was right behind him, her hand under her belly to stop it from bouncing as she hurried to keep up with Ted's giant strides. "Hello! I'm Keisha! So amazing to meet you at last!"

Inside, Sam introduced her mom and Walt and the twins to Aleta and Davis.

Travis's parents were great. They shook hands and smiled sincerely and said all the right things. Then Sam led the Carlsons up to their rooms.

The twins went straight into their room and shut the door. Which was fine with Sam. Great, actually.

She wasn't so lucky when it came to her mom.

Jennifer wanted to talk. She shooed Walt from the room and took Sam's big hand in her tiny little pink one. "Samantha, sit with me." There were a pair of ladder-back chairs by the window. Her mom led her over there and they sat. Sam couldn't help recalling how Aleta had done more or less the same thing, that first day Sam arrived at the ranch with Travis. But somehow, when Aleta did it, Sam had felt flattered and only too happy to chat. With her mom, she dreaded what might happen next. "Now," said Jennifer. "Tell me everything."

Everything. Right. "Gee, Mom. That would take a while."

It was, of course, totally the wrong thing to say. Her mom's pretty face crumpled and her eyes filled with tears. "I only...I just thought we might...touch base a little. Is that so much to ask?"

It wasn't. Sam knew it wasn't. "Of course not. What did you want to know?"

Her mother pressed her lips together, put on a smile and tried again. "Well, I mean, look at you. You're *gorgeous*."

"Thanks, Mom."

"How...well, I always knew you had good bones. That you could be attractive if you'd only try. And now you're...I have no words. I'm just stunned."

"It's a long story."

"And I would love to hear every detail."

Sam had to admit that her mom was being kind of sweet really. That she was only trying to be appreciative and supportive. So Sam gave her an abridged version of the makeover, leaving out the part about how it had all started because Travis needed a fake fiancée. Sam said that she had wanted to make a change and getting professional help seemed like the best way.

When she was done, her mom clapped her little hands. "Oh, that is wonderful, Samantha. I'm so proud of you." Jennifer. Proud of her. That was a first.

Sam basked in the moment. "Well, thanks, Mom."

"And let me guess the rest. Your old friend Travis

took one look at the new you and realized how blind he'd been."

"Pretty much, yeah."

"And now, here you are, getting married to your own personal prince charming."

That made her smile. "He is a prince, isn't he?"

"I know you must be so happy at last, to be in love with a wonderful man and to know that he loves you back."

"I am happy. Very much so." *Not that I wasn't before.*

"And if you had only listened to me, this could have happened years ago."

Bam. The sucker punch. As always. Sam kept her cool, even though her stomach had tied itself in about a hundred little knots. "Well, I didn't listen to you. And it didn't happen until now. And I'm more than happy with the way things have turned out."

Her mother shook her pretty blond head. "Oh, Samantha. Always so proud."

"I'm only saying that it all worked out. Can we leave it at that?"

"Of course," said her mother. She meant, *of course not.* "I just…well, I don't have to tell you. I mean, what can your father be *thinking?*"

It was pretty much what Sam had said to Travis the night before. But somehow, when her mom said it, it sounded snotty and mean-spirited. "Leave it alone, Mom."

"Yes, well. I suppose I should."

"Please."

"It's a terrible embarrassment. In front of Travis's lovely family."

"The Bravos don't seem to mind. They seem to think

Dad's kind of fun. And everybody likes Keisha. I mean, what's not to like?"

"But is he going to *marry* her?"

Sam realized that on top of her stomach hurting, she was getting a headache. "I don't know, Mom. I figure that's none of my business."

Her mother visibly flinched. "What was that? One of those barely veiled criticisms of yours?"

You ought to know, Mom, Sam thought but somehow managed not to say. Barely veiled criticisms were her mother's weapon of choice. Sam got up. "I don't want to fight with you, Mom. I just don't."

Her mother rose, too. "You're right," she said stiffly. "I don't want to fight either. I only want for us to get along."

The day before the wedding continued. Endlessly.

There was lunch in the sun room, where her mother and father actively ignored each other—her father talking too loud and too much, her mother saying little, but making small, outraged, impatient sounds and constantly pinching up her small pink lips. The twins, their sleek blond heads pressed close together, snickered constantly. Walt looked befuddled and Keisha occasionally said something harmless and sweet with the usual exclamation point after it.

The Bravos—Davis and Aleta, Mercy and Luke and Travis, too—took it all in stride. Sam knew they weren't bothered in the least by her dysfunctional family. They made easy conversation and filled in the hostile silences with new, interesting and yet uncontroversial topics of discussion. Little Lucas was his usual adorable self and baby Serena lived up to her name, sitting quietly with her toys around her, beaming up at anyone who stopped and spoke to her.

Sam's headache got worse. She wondered how she had gotten here, in this big, beautiful house, with Travis's wonderful family and her totally messed up one. She thought of the *Deepwater Venture*—of all the rigs she'd worked on. And she saw herself, tall and capable and spattered with grease and drilling mud, striding confidently across the drilling platform, secure in her idea of herself and her place in the world.

She didn't feel so secure now. She felt like she didn't have a clue who she really was. She had no idea where she was going.

Or if she would ever get there.

Did other brides feel this way? For all their sakes—and the sake of their poor grooms—she hoped not.

The other Bravos started arriving around four. Dinner that night was sort of a rehearsal dinner, just minus the rehearsal.

They all came, each of Travis's brothers and sisters, and their wives and husbands and kids, too. Dinner went nicely, Sam thought. With so many people there, her hulking, loud dad and passive-aggressive mom kind of disappeared in the crowd. She started to believe she just might make it through the weekend after all.

After dinner, Travis's brothers kidnapped him. All the men—Walt and Sam's dad included—drove away in various vehicles to meet up at some agreed-upon location for an impromptu bachelor party.

Sam and the other women stood on the porch, laughing and waving, as the men drove away.

When he came back, Travis would sleep alone in the blue room that night. And Sam would stay in the yellow room, with the door shut between them. She'd really wanted it that way when she asked him if they could sleep separately on the last night before the wedding.

But somehow, as the evening went on and Sam visited with her soon-to-be sisters-in-law and Aleta and Keisha, and tried to be nice to her mom and the Terrible Twins, she found herself wishing that when he came home, he would go straight to the door between their rooms, push it open and climb into bed with her. There was something about his solid presence in the bed that eased her fears and calmed her anxieties.

With Travis's strong arms around her, she knew who she was again. Her doubts about whether she was cut out to be his wife—to be *anyone's* wife—seemed meaningless and easy to ignore.

It was midnight when she climbed the stairs to the yellow room. She shut the door to the hall and also the one to the blue room. Then she stood at the windows for a long time and stared at the new sliver of moon out there in the wide Texas sky and wondered what was wrong with her.

She didn't like her mother much and she wanted to bitch-slap both of her half sisters. Her dad drove her nuts.

But her birth family wasn't what this weekend was about. This weekend was about her and Travis. Travis, whom she loved.

Travis, who was just right for her, who made her body glow with pleasure and who warmed her once-lonely heart.

She was the luckiest woman in the world.

So why was she longing to run away from her own wedding?

Chapter Thirteen

Travis accepted another Jack Black on the rocks and joined in the drinking song Ted had started.

As bachelor parties went, it was a tame one, held in one of the wood-paneled rooms at his father's club. Tame was fine with Travis. There was some loud music—when Ted wasn't calling for it to be shut off so he could lead them in another raunchy song. The liquor flowed freely and there were even some good-looking women there. Not that any of his brothers, his brothers-in-law or his father seemed to care. A couple of his brothers had been players back in the day. But now, they were all like him. One-woman men.

Even Ted, who sure knew the lyrics to a lot of dirty ditties, wasn't the least interested in the bachelor party babes. True-blue to Keisha, who certainly deserved a good man. Walt, too, apparently, had no interest in a little bachelor party fooling around. He stayed well away from the women. Because he was too shy to try anything or because Jennifer was the only woman for him, Travis couldn't have said.

It was kind of fun really. Kicking back with the other men of the family, drinking a little more than he probably should have, listening to rock and roll and Christmas music and singing along with Ted.

Or it would have been fun, if Travis could only shake the scary feeling that he was going to lose Sam. The same as he'd lost Rachel. The same as he'd driven Wanda away.

Every night the past week or so, he would wake up at three or four in the morning and just lie there, watching Sam sleeping, thinking how he'd never felt the way he felt for her—not even with Rachel—and wondering what tricks God and fate and blind misfortune might have up their sleeves for him this time.

Yeah. All right. He had a problem. And he knew it. And he was working with it. He knew he had…issues, as a woman would put it. As Sam herself had put it a few weeks ago.

He knew that Sam was right when she said it wasn't his fault that Rachel had been run down by some out-of-it drunk driver. Sam was right when she said that he couldn't protect her from every single bad thing that might ever happen to her.

And as soon as he'd given some serious thought to those things that Sam had said, he'd taken steps to get past his own irrational terror of losing her.

He'd made himself back off on all the plans he had that hemmed her in. He'd agreed to put off trying to have a baby. He'd made it clear to her that he would support her in getting her degree and her start in accounting. He saw that it was only right, for her to have the life she wanted.

He *wanted* her to have the life she wanted.

Everything seemed good between them. Everything seemed right.

Except that sometimes, when he looked in her unforgettable blue eyes, he saw panic.

Sometimes he was sure he was losing her, even though he'd done everything he could think of to keep from driving her away.

He wanted the damn party to be over. He wanted to go back to the ranch and to Sam. Yeah, all right. They'd agreed to spend the night before their wedding in separate rooms.

Too bad about that. He wanted to shove open the door that separated them—to break it down, if he had to. He wanted to take her in his arms and never let her go. He wanted to tell her that she was everything to him and it was going to be all right.

But the bachelor party wasn't over. And he was the groom, so he had an obligation stay to the end.

Plus, well, what if his fears were all in his own mind?

Hey, it was possible. Because he had issues, deep-seated fears. And if the whole point was not to hem her in or freak her out, well, what could she feel but hemmed in and freaked out if he burst in on her in the middle of the night just to make sure she wasn't planning on running away from their wedding?

At some point, he had trust in her. Trust in what they had together. A man couldn't make a woman stay with him.

He could only be the best man he could be for her.

And let fate and God and blind misfortune do what they would.

Ted started another song. Travis raised his glass and joined in.

The party lasted until after three. Then he rode back to the ranch with his dad, Luke, Ted and Walt—Rogan went with Caleb; he and Elena and baby Michael were staying at Caleb and Irina's for the weekend.

The five men took their boots off before tiptoeing up the stairs.

Travis entered the blue room as silently as he could. The bed was empty and the door to the yellow room was closed. Just as he and Sam had agreed it would be.

He set his boots by the bed and went on stocking feet to that shut door. He didn't open it.

But he did stand there for a very long time, wanting to open it, *aching* to open it. And telling himself that wouldn't be right.

Sam woke at six on her wedding day.

She sat straight up in bed and stared at the door to Travis's room.

Shut.

She wanted to leap to her feet and race to that door, to throw it open, and run to him, to climb into bed with him and hold him and whisper…everything.

All her fears. Her doubts. Her scary, nonsensical desire to throw on some clothes, tiptoe down the stairs, sneak out the front door and down the wide steps and take off along the driveway to the road.

To run and keep running.

To never look back.

Until she knew who she was again.

Until she could return to him secure in the knowledge that she was good enough. Ready enough.

Woman enough.

She didn't, though—didn't go to him, didn't run away. She was not only riddled with doubt, but she was also a coward. Which was why she lay back down and closed her eyes and drifted off into a fitful, unhappy sleep until eight, when Mercy came to get her.

Sam put on some jeans and a cotton shirt and followed Luke's wife down the back stairs and out the back door where a limo was waiting, Aleta and Sam's mom, Keisha and the Terrible Twins already inside. The limo rolled along the single-car pebbled driveway that circled the house and then down the wider driveway to the road. Keisha said what a great day it was for a wedding. Aleta and Mercy agreed. Sam's mom was subdued. Dina and Mila were downright civil. They giggled about how cool it was, to be chauffeured in a limo.

Not once did they snicker behind their hands.

Sam realized she was glad they were there.

The limo took them to Gabe and Mary Bravo's ranch, where Travis's sisters and his other sisters-in-law were waiting. And not only all the Bravo women.

There was a surprise guest. He emerged from behind Mary's Christmas tree a moment after Sam walked in the front door. He wore forest-green trousers and a festive red shirt—and the rhinestone suspenders she'd sent him when she mailed him the card inviting him to the wedding.

Sam did not burst into tears at the sight of him. But almost. "Oh, Jonathan. I didn't think you'd come!"

"Darling, I wouldn't have missed this for the world. I called Travis when I got your invitation. He had Mary get in touch. She graciously offered me accommodations here."

Sam hugged him, hard. "Oh, I'm so glad to see you."

"Don't crush me, my love. You simply don't know your own strength." He wiggled from her grasp and smoothed his big hair.

Mary announced that breakfast was served. They all filed into the large, comfortable dining room and sat down to eat.

The food was really good, but Sam was too nervous to eat much. Jonathan, seated on her right, leaned close to her and told her not to pick at her meal. He said she needed food in her stomach.

In spite of the tension that tugged at the muscles between her shoulder blades and tied her belly in knots, she laughed. "I never thought the day would come when you would tell me to eat *more*."

"That is exactly what I'm telling you," he replied. "There is nothing as unattractive as a weak and peckish bride."

She wrinkled her nose at him. "Peckish?"

"Irritable from lack of proper nourishment," he elaborated in the snooty tone of voice she'd come to love.

So she did what he told her to do and ate some more. There was something so comforting about having him there. She could almost relax a little. After all, like Travis, he knew who she really was. He'd been there with her when she made all the changes that had led her to this day when she would become Travis's wife.

Travis's wife. It seemed so huge and impossible. Panic clawed at her again.

She ordered it to be gone.

After the meal, the stylists, cosmeticians and nail techs arrived. Mary played an endless stream of holiday music and everyone got manicures and pedicures. And hair and makeup, too.

Travis's sister, Zoe, was a semiprofessional photographer. She took a lot of pictures that morning. She would photograph the wedding party, too.

Jonathan, in his element, supervised the general beautifying. He advised the twins on nail colors. "Not that one, my sweet. It looks like dried blood—type O, I'm sure. This is your sister's wedding, but she's not marrying the Lord of the Night. Let's go for something a tad less…vampiric, shall we?" He also suggested that Sam's mom wear her hair in soft waves around her face rather than the tighter curls she usually went for. Both the twins and her mom did what he told them to.

There was just something about Jonathan. He knew how to bring out the best in a woman, and women, no matter their age, sensed that. They tended to trust his judgment without question.

A light lunch was provided at noon.

And then it was back in the limo to return to Bravo Ridge.

By one-thirty, a half hour before the simple wedding ceremony, Sam was dressed in her bridal finery and pacing the floor of the yellow room. She was beyond nervous by then, and more panicked than ever, so lost in her own anxiousness that she almost didn't hear the light tap on the door to the hallway.

But then the tap came again.

She called, "Come in."

Her mother, in a pretty lavender mother-of-the-bride dress, slipped through the door. She carried a large rectangular box in one hand and a bag in the other. Both the box and the bag were of shiny cobalt-blue foil, and both were tied with ribbons in white, silver and various shades of purple.

Sam got the picture. It was time for whatever special surprise Aleta and her mom had cooked up between them so that Jennifer would feel she'd contributed to the wedding.

Her mom sighed. "You are a vision."

Sam felt the knot of tension in her stomach loosen a little. Okay, she and her mom had never enjoyed that close of a relationship. And Jennifer could drive her crazy with her constant advice on how to be more feminine, with her passive-aggressive remarks that made Sam want to shout at her to cut the crap and man up.

Still, Jennifer did care. It was so obvious from the hopeful, yearning look on her still-pretty face, from the way her little hands shook just a bit, ruffling the ribbons on the blue foil bag.

Sam gave her a big smile—a real smile. "Thanks, Mom."

Jennifer swiped away a tear with the back of the hand that held the beribboned bag. "Come…let me show you." She turned for the bed and sat on the edge of it, setting the box to the side and holding the bag so carefully in her lap. Sam went and sat down beside her. Her mom handed her the bag.

Sam fiddled with the ribbons. It took forever to get them untied. But her mom didn't try to interfere the way she usually would. She sat there, her hands in her lap, until the ribbons were all undone. Sam sent her a questioning look then. But Jennifer only smiled.

So Sam reached in and took out a blue velvet box. She opened the lid to find a bracelet sparkling with alternating clear and purple gemstones.

"It was *my* mother's," said Jennifer. "Diamonds and amethysts." Amethyst was Sam's birthstone. And she'd been named after her mother's mother. "Your grandmother Samantha's birthstone was amethyst, too—here. Let me put it on you." Solemnly, her mother lifted the bracelet from the box. Speechless, Sam held up her arm and her mother hooked the little heart-shaped platinum clasp at her wrist.

The diamonds sparkled at her, bright as the one in the ring Travis had give her. Sam spoke in a voice that was thick with emotion. "It's so pretty."

"I wanted you to have it. As they say, 'Something old.'"

"Oh, Mom…" Sam reached for her mother.

"Samantha…" Her mother hugged her back.

It was a great moment. One to remember and treasure. Just her and her mom, with all the tough years and the bad feelings put aside. The knots of tension within her seemed to loosen just a little. And the panic, at least right then, had subsided to a vague shiver of unease.

There was more in the bag, something borrowed— her mother's diamond earrings. And a blue garter. Sam donned the earrings, eased the garter up under her dress to mid-thigh.

And then her mom gave her the box.

Sam opened it with the same slow care she'd used to untie the ribbons on the bag. Inside, was a large blue book.

Samantha and Travis…

"Aw, Mom. A scrapbook…"

"It's not finished yet. The last third is empty. That will have the wedding pictures, and the honeymoon, too, and I'll do more work on the cover, once I get the pictures of both of you…"

Sam turned the pages. She touched the lock of her own baby hair, the tiny pink sock and the little yellow bib.

There were lots of pictures of her growing up. Pictures of the Sam she always used to see when she looked in a mirror—the Sam some people mistook for a boy. There were pictures of her in her mom's arms. And with her dad at the ranch. Riding Old Jay, her favorite gelding, and sitting in the back of her dad's pickup in a plaid shirt with the sleeve's torn off. There was even a picture of that awful birthday weekend not all that long ago, and of the cake her mom had made to look like an oil rig, the twins in the background, sticking out their tongues.

Her mother put her arm around her. "You were always such a very capable child. So…self-sufficient."

She leaned into her mother's embrace. "Yeah, I was that."

She moved on to Travis's section of the book, saw his baby pictures, a blue sock, and a bib that was yellow, like hers. His brothers and sisters were in some of the pictures. She turned the pages and watched her love grow into manhood, saw him in his graduation cap and gown, in a tux, holding out an orchid corsage, and in a hard hat and coveralls on the rig at her dad's ranch.

"Aleta sent me everything for Travis's section," said her mom. "She really is one of the kindest, most generous women I've ever met…."

Sam looked in her mother's eyes. "We can all learn a lot from her." She said the words and then tensed, sure her mom would take it wrong.

But her mom only nodded. "Yes, Samantha. Yes, we can."

They sat there, for a few more minutes, just the two of them. Sam started at the beginning of the scrapbook again, looked at every memento, every snapshot, one more time. Then, with loving care, she put it back in the blue box and folded the tissue paper smoothly around it.

"I want to show Travis," she said.

"Of course. You can send it back to me later, along with the pictures and any keepsakes from the wedding and after."

The wedding and after...

After, when she and Travis would be married. Together. Bonded for life before the whole world.

Was that what scared her, what made the panic rise? She knew then, with certainty, that it was not.

Her mom told her again that she was a beautiful bride. "I wish you all the happiness your two hearts can hold," she said. "I wish you more patience than I ever had, more wisdom. And I'm so glad that you and Travis are longtime friends and well-suited. Sadly, your father and I weren't suited at all. But you will do better, I know it in my heart."

So strange and wonderful that her own mom, who'd never in her whole life seemed to understand her, should suddenly be saying just the right things.

Sam said it again, "Thanks, Mom."

And then Jennifer was rising. "I love you," she said. "I wasn't always there when I should have been. And I didn't always love you as you needed loving. I know that. But I did love you. I *do* love you, Samantha. And I always will."

"I love you, too, Mom."

Jennifer went on tiptoe and Sam bent down so that her mom could kiss her cheek. It seemed to Sam a kiss of blessing, a kiss of acknowledgment and acceptance. At last.

Her mother slipped out the way she had come.

Sam stood there, by the bed, unmoving, until there was another tap at the door.

It was Mercy. She looked terrific in midnight blue. "Oh, you look beautiful."

Sam mustered a smile. "Thanks."

"Want some help with your veil?"

Sam went to the vanity set, took the short layers of organza banded with rhinestones and pearls off the edge of the mirror and handed it to Luke's wife. She pulled out the padded stool and sat.

Mercy pinned the veil in place and Sam took the hem and guided it over her forehead, smoothing the ends so it just covered her face. "Perfect," Mercy said.

Sam sat for a moment, gazing at her own reflection in the mirror, thinking about her mom and her dad, about Keisha and Walt. About the Terrible Twins and all the Bravos, every one.

And about Travis, most of all.

Then she pushed back the stool and rose again. She took her bouquet of orchids and white roses from the stand on the tall dresser.

"Ready?" Mercy asked in a hushed, excited tone. At Sam's slow nod, she added, "Your dad's waiting at the top of the stairs." And then she was gone.

Sam's heart started racing and her hands, around the base of the bouquet, felt suddenly clammy. Her feet in her gorgeous rhinestone-accented wedding shoes seemed nailed to the floor.

But somehow, she did it, she lifted one foot and then the other and within ten steps, she was at the door. She pulled it open.

And even with her heart going spooked-rabbit fast, pounding a furious drum roll in her ears, she could still hear the wedding march, floating up from the living room downstairs. And there was her dad in his best black wool suit, standing at the top of the staircase.

He saw her and offered his arm.

Her pulse rat-tat-tatting in her ears, she went to him and hooked her arm in his.

He said, "There's my beautiful, big, strong baby girl."

And she loved him so much right then. He smelled of cigarettes and the moth balls he stored that old rarely worn suit in and she realized he was one of the dearest, truest men in the world.

Almost as dear and true as Travis.

He turned, taking her with him, starting down the stairs.

It was like a dream, only not a dream. A real-life sort of dream. She floated down the stairs on the arm of her father. The carved double doors to the living room stood wide.

They went through, and began the walk up the blue velvet aisle between the rows of white rented folding chairs. Her family and Travis's family rose and turned to watch her progress.

Travis waited at the other end.

In his eyes, she saw so much love.

And worry, too.

For her. For the doubts she saw he knew that she had.

He knew because he knew *her*. He accepted her completely.

As she was now. As she had been. As she would be in the future as the years fled by—so fast. Too fast.

Oh, she could see it all. And it was good. It was right.

She was the Sam she had always been. Strong and tall and able to stand toe-to-toe with any man. She hadn't lost herself after all.

She was exactly who she'd always been.

And yet, because of Travis, because of what they were together, she was also so much more.

It wasn't anything to be afraid of, these changes that

seemed to deny who she was. Because they didn't deny her, not really. They only made her *more.*

She reached his side. The nice minister Aleta had found started to speak.

But Travis put up his hand. The minister fell silent. Sam gave her dad her bouquet to hold for her and her dad stepped away.

Travis took her fingers, guided her to face him. He took her veil and lifted it, smoothing it back over the crown of her head and down. Now nothing stood between them, not even that transparent film of bridal white.

He took her hand again—and then the other hand, too. And his eyes were on her, holding her gaze. He whispered, "Are you sure? Are you absolutely sure? Because I know I pushed you to get married too fast. And if it's just too soon for you, we can call it off right now. It's all right. I'll understand. I can wait, Sam. I see that now. Until you're sure, no matter how long it takes, I'll wait."

An hour before, she might have nodded. She might have told him she couldn't do it, she needed more time.

But something had happened—in those precious moments with her mother, and at the sight of her father. And also, well, just because there is a time in a woman's life when she has to push her deepest fears aside.

She has to say, yes. Absolutely. I will. I love you. I will join my life with yours. And we will make something better and stronger together than either of us could ever be on our own.

This was that time. And Travis was the man. The right man for her.

She told him, "Yes, Travis. I'm sure. I love you. I want to marry you. I want to marry you right now."

He let out a slow breath. "You mean it. You really mean it."

"I mean it." And she kissed him, even though they weren't even married yet, even though the minister hadn't been allowed to say a single word.

No one in the white chairs so much as moved or made a sound—not that Sam cared much what the family did. For her, it was all about Travis. All about the kiss.

When the kiss ended, he said slowly and clearly, "I love you, Sam Jaworski."

"And I love you, Travis Bravo."

They turned together to the waiting, slightly baffled-looking minister. "Go for it," Travis told him.

A wave of laughter rose from the family behind them. More than one of them applauded.

And then the minister began, "Dearly beloved, we are gathered here together..."

Sam said her vows out loud and proud and sure.

Travis's voice was lower, softer, but no less certain. He had the ring ready. He slid it onto her finger, snug against the engagement diamond he'd given her before they knew it would all end up being for real.

And when the minister said, "You may kiss the bride," Travis pulled her close and settled his mouth on hers so tenderly, in a kiss that promised everything— his strong hands and his good heart. All the years of their lives.

And his love, most of all.

It wasn't until they turned back to face the family that she noticed her dad had disappeared. Mercy stood in his place holding out her bouquet.

Sam reached to take it.

And out the arched front windows, the fireworks

began with a bottle rocket shooting toward the wide Texas sky.

Sam growled low in her throat. "He'd better not burn anything down, or I swear I will kill him."

Travis only laughed and pulled her close for another tender kiss.

* * * * *

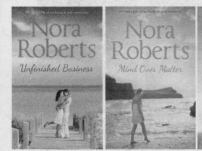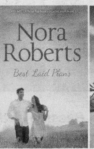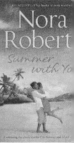

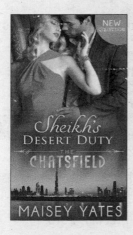

MILLS & BOON®
By Request

RELIVE THE ROMANCE WITH THE BEST OF THE BEST

A sneak peek at next month's titles...

In stores from 17th April 2015:

- **Forbidden Seductions** – Anne Mather, India Grey and Kimberly Lang

- **Mistress to the Magnate** – Michelle Celmer, Jennifer Lewis and Leanne Banks

In stores from 1st May 2015:

- **Untamed Bachelors** – Anne Oliver, Kathryn Ross and Susan Stephens

- **In the Royal's Bed** – Marion Lennox